Hearts of Pride and Passion . . .

"Give me the dagger, child," Conn said softly.

A wave of heat and pain washed over Gelina. She blinked to clear her vision. Conn crept closer. The dagger shook violently in her hands. "The only way you'll get your dagger is in your heart if you don't leave me be," she said.

"You're no match for me right now. And I've no desire to hurt you."

"I'd rather be skewered by your sword than by those men you're going to give me to. The weapons they'd use on me would be far more terrible than any you bear."

Conn closed his eyes briefly. "I spoke in anger and haste, lass. 'Twas an idle threat to wring the truth from you."

Her laugh cracked into a sob. "More lies. They flow so well from lips as smooth as yours. Even now you try to disarm me with eyes so blue and kind. All a lie. A vicious, hurtful lie."

Without lowering his gaze, Conn laid his sword aside. He spread his arms in surrender. "My heart, milady. My heart for your dagger. As proof of my pledge. . . ."

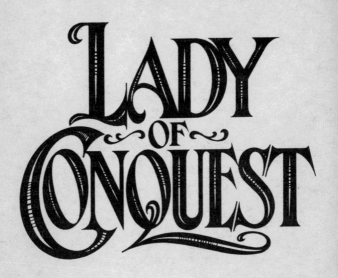

LADY OF CONQUEST

TERESA MEDEIROS

BERKLEY BOOKS, NEW YORK

LADY OF CONQUEST

A Berkley Book/published by arrangement with
the author

PRINTING HISTORY
Berkley edition/August 1989

ISBN: 0-425-11686-7

A BERKLEY BOOK ® TM 757,375
Berkley Books are published by The Berkley Publishing Group,
200 Madison Avenue, New York, N.Y. 10016.
The name ''BERKLEY'' and the ''B'' logo
are trademarks belonging to Berkley Publishing Corporation.

PRINTED IN THE UNITED STATES OF AMERICA.

10 9 8 7 6 5 4 3 2 1

For Michael, who holds the dark at bay,
and for Drayton and Linda, my parents,
who read
all the first chapters of all the books I wrote
when I was twelve

Author's Note

More than a thousand years before Sir Thomas Malory immortalized the legend of King Arthur and his Camelot, a kingdom arose from the mists of Ireland—a kingdom founded on honor, chivalry, and the dreams of one man.

In A.D. 123, Conn of the Hundred Battles defeated his rival, Cathair Mor, and united all of Ireland under one high king. Conn's skills as a mighty warrior preceded his reputation as statesman and king. But once established on the throne at Tara, he devoted himself to fostering a legion of warriors known as the Fianna, who ushered in a glorious age of valiant deeds.

For the first time in Ireland's history, men knelt before their king to take oaths of chivalry, capturing the hearts and minds of the Irish people for centuries to come. Masters of love and battle, Conn and his Fianna are still celebrated today in poetry, legend, song, and in the romance of *Lady of Conquest*, the tale of a mighty king and the young girl who would test his every belief with her love. . . .

LADY
OF
CONQUEST

Prologue

Kevin Ó hArtagain stepped into the cave with sword drawn in shaking hands. Shame wedded with fear as he remembered the oath he had taken before his king. No matter what odds he faced, his weapon must never shake in his hands. If his comrades in arms could see him now, they would scoff in disbelief at his trembling limbs. They had witnessed him savage both men and beast in battle with teeth bared and a growl on his lips. Looming over most opponents, he was not a man many would care to confront in darkness.

And here he stood in the shadowed corridor of this cave, his scalp tingling as sweat poured between his braids in icy rivulets. Fear cavorted in his eyes; the shadows thrown by his torch danced on the walls.

He continued, scuttling sideways like a crippled crab to keep the wall at his back. An oversized torch at the rear of the cave sprang into light with the pop of a small explosion. He tossed down his own torch, leapt to the center of the corridor and crouched behind a stalagmite that reached to the ceiling. The riotous light revealed what lay in wait for him. His hand slid in the slime that coated the stalagmite. The black void in the pit of his stomach grew, threatening to obliterate him with its terror.

The specter stalked him with stealthy grace, throwing nightmarish shadows against the stony walls. An executioner's black hood masked its features. Green eyes glittered deep within the recesses of the hood like an illusion, briefly seen and quickly doubted. The massive sword in the gloved hand of the hellish apparition gestured toward the stalagmite Kevin crouched behind, in grim invitation. Kevin closed his eyes and thought of the four men who had come here before him. Four dead warriors tossed out to rot like foul vegetables in the mossy woods.

Anger began to build, displacing the paralyzing fear. It started in his smallest toe and crept upward like a stabilizing vine. It gave his limbs the braces they needed to slowly rise, step out from his mock shelter and turn to meet the demon. A daring smile twisted his lips. Sword clutched in both hands, he advanced and parried the first vicious swing of the weapon wielded by his foe.

The voluminous black cloak surrounding the monster danced with a life of its own upon each swing; Kevin was dwarfed. The dexterity he had worn like a badge of honor served only to prolong the ordeal into a slow motion nightmare in the flickering recesses of the cavern. The creature cut at him, each stab tearing smooth flesh and exposing muscle, tissue, and an ever-increasing torrent of blood.

The torch at the back of the cave flickered as Kevin Ó hArtagain, a warrior of the king, went down under a quick thrust of the sword, which pierced his sternum and lodged a blazing fire in his chest. With his final grip he grasped the fine steel from which it was wrought. Holding it tightly enough to slice into the fingers of his right hand, he read the inscription carved into the hilt of burnished gold—*Vengeance*.

The sword was snatched from his weakening grip. The last image imprinted on his dying brain was of the thing in front of him retreating with peculiar grace—and falling apart at its abdomen. The last sound he heard was a young girl's maniacal laughter echoing throughout the chilly cavern; his eyes fixed at an angle in front of him in a death stare.

❖

PART ONE

A LOVE SONG
He is a heart,
An acorn from the oakwood.
He is young.
A kiss for him!

—Author unknown
7th or 8th century

❖

Chapter One

❖

It was a gray day, as bleak and still as the faces that filled the great hall. Clouds hung low in the late afternoon sky, thick with the promise of rain; tension hung low in the air, promising no release. Mer-Nod frowned, deepening the lines that creased his brow as he contemplated the unnatural pall that had fallen over the court on this dreary day.

Gone were the voices raised in argument. Gone the laughter, the music, the poets' tales. A thick layer of apprehension had been laid upon the tongues of the people, muffling hundreds of voices to a low murmur. The poets sat at Mer-Nod's feet, honoring him as chief poet even in their silence. The harps stood untouched, propped against the fine-grained yew walls like forgotten toys. Cupbearers milled through the hall, filling goblets with ale and ears with the rumors they had heard. With his head thrown back and eyes closed in muttered prayer to Morigu, a juggler sat cross-legged on the floor, nine golden apples cradled in his lap.

Mer-Nod pushed back the long dark hair that fell over his shoulder. Soft gray wings framed his face, lessening the severity of his hawklike nose and penetrating dark eyes. A full bottom lip belied the solemnity of a jutting jaw covered by a day's growth of dark beard. With one foot propped in the chair, he stared over the crowd.

A fine edge of anticipation cut the air, as sharp as the gleaming blades that hung in the scabbards of the men who stood out from any vantage point in the hall. Their sun-darkened faces were etched with the fine lines only the wind can engrave. Tight, sleeveless jerkins exposed not an ounce of excess fat on their hard, muscled bodies.

The fighting men mingled in the great hall, some absently flirting with the young girls, others speaking in hushed tones with the farmers and shepherds. When they crossed the hall, they were greeted with pats on the back and words of encouragement as the crowds parted to let them through. They were the Fianna, the protectors and adored of Erin. Battling and hunting, they roamed the island, making love and making legend each roving hour of the day. And they were dying now, one by one, their mutilated bodies left to putrefy in the dank woods.

Mer-Nod sighed and closed his eyes, knowing no one would dare speak to him in such a state. They would assume he was composing. How he longed to oblige them! His hand itched for a quill. What a tale of victory he would wring from Kevin's defeat of the monster! Already he was planning the metrics for the piece, his long fingers drumming a rhythm on the oaken arm of his chair.

The murmur at the door rose to a buzz and people stumbled over one another in an excited flurry, clearing a path for the king who was joining their vigil. Faces stiff with worry cracked into heartening smiles, not daring to show their fear to the man who made his way through their midst.

His stride was long and sure. Replacing his ceremonial robe was a short tunic similar to the one worn by his soldiers. At exactly six feet, he met the lowest standard for entry into the Fianna. His body was muscular, with leonine grace coiled in each movement. A few silver threads sprang obstinately from his dark mane of curly hair.

His face arrested the eye's attention. Dark blue eyes surrounded by a thick, black fringe of lashes peered out from behind the lock of hair that threatened to hide them. His nose was straight, not thin enough to be called aquiline. A dark beard covered his jawline, surrounding full lips. It was a mouth that could be stretched into a boyish smile to dazzle his courtiers; it was a mouth that could tighten to a fine line when leading his men into battle.

He was not a man to hide his emotions and if pushed against the wall, his blue eyes would darken, gleaming like unfathomable gems. They called him Conn of the Hundred Battles, and he had swept through the Isle of Erin like wildfire in a dry forest, uniting and conquering until he was ruler of all.

Mer-Nod allowed a rare smile to cross his lips. Conn's path

to the throne was marked by clasped hands, pats on the back, and an occasional kiss for an infant thrust into his face.

Conn winked at Mer-Nod as he neared the judge's chair. "Perish the gloom, poet. I'll waive your taxes for a genuine smile."

He stood before the throne and raised his arms to the people. An immediate hush fell over the hall. A baby's cry cut shrilly through the silence.

All eyes turned to Conn as he spoke. "Runners approach from the north. They should arrive within the hour. They bring us the news we seek." The voices rose, then fell silent again as he stepped off the narrow dais and paced before the throne. "I see many frightened faces." He turned to look accusingly at the crowd, then resumed his pacing. "We have been presented a great challenge . . . a dragon with a craving for our spirits. It seeks to maim and destroy not only our men, but our wills as well." Conn faced the crowd, hands resting lightly on hips. "The question is—are we going to let it succeed?"

A woman near the front nervously bit her lip. Two soldiers stared each other down from the floor below the king.

A nasal voice carried over the crowd, breaking the silent spell. "And the answer is . . ."

All eyes, including Conn's, turned upward. High on the wall was a narrow platform, and perched on that platform was a midget grasping a trapeze hooked to the ceiling. An audible gasp rose from the crowd as the small man sailed smoothly from his perch, knees hooked around the trapeze bar. Upside down, his head barely missed the heads of the taller men of the Fianna.

He finished his sentence with an awful grimace, ". . . not while I live."

The tension was broken, and laughter rang through the hall. A wide smile spread across Conn's face as he strode to a lower place in the center of the crowd. On the midget's next pass, Conn grabbed the trapeze and swung the acrobat around to face him.

"What in the name of Behl do you think you're doing, Nimbus?" he hissed.

Lacking a hat of his own in such a precarious position, the jester swept off the hat of the man nearest him. "Sire, what a delightful surprise!"

The crowd guffawed as Conn twirled the trapeze with agonizing slowness.

"I surrender!" Nimbus yelled. "These loyal subjects of yers may revolt if I dump the thick bean pottage I had for me lunch on their heads." Several men and women scurried to remove themselves from that vile threat.

"The only thing revolting around here is you," Conn rejoined, pulling the midget by his ears until they faced each other again.

Nimbus leaned close to Conn's ear and whispered, "I feared ye were losing their attention, sire. I sought only to help."

Conn whispered back, "I guess 'tis better than swinging in on a noose like you did last time. You almost gave me apoplexy." Without warning he shoved the trapeze away from his body to send Nimbus squealing through the air.

Conn called to the crowd, "Though it galls me to confess it, the jester speaks the truth. Our spirit triumphs."

He neatly sidestepped Nimbus's grab at his nose as the trapeze sailed by again. Cheers of support rose from the floor.

A man marked as a butcher by his rumpled, bloody apron raised his voice and goblet. "We have civilized this country!" The cheers swelled to a roar.

A handsome, brown-eyed soldier added his voice. "Are we not the people who have driven Eoghan Mogh, the enemy of Erin, south to a land as black and barren as his soul?" The jugglers began to toss their golden apples into the air one by one.

"And are not the Romans afraid to set foot on our shores for fear we'll send them weeping back to their goddesses of war?" proclaimed a rawboned farm woman.

Two of the poets began to tell in unison a tale of Macha Mong Ruad, Red Hugh's flame-haired Amazon daughter. The room was transformed, eyes shining with hope. Goblets were raised across the hall in toasts to Kevin's prowess, Conn's generosity, and the dreams of a new land founded on honor and chivalry.

Conn waited until the trapeze's momentum died, then plucked the tiny man from it and rested him gently on his feet. They walked to the throne together, Nimbus pausing once to yank on the braid of a sullen blond soldier, whose eyes followed him with a narrowed stare as he rubbed his stinging pate.

"What was the purpose in that?" asked Conn as he sat on the throne.

"Don't like Ó Caflin. Shifty eyes."

"If you're such an astute judge of character, tell me the nature of the creature we have sent Kevin to dispatch?" Conn asked, stroking his beard.

Nimbus perched on the arm of the throne and stroked his smooth chin in perfect imitation. Dodging Conn's absent-minded swat, he said, "The creature is simply a man, not a monster or a giant."

"A man who could slay four of the Fianna? I scoff, Nimbus."

"And"—Nimbus continued as if never interrupted—"I think this man is allied with Eoghan Mogh, sent to antagonize ye and distract us all."

Mer-Nod, who had been listening as he walked over to lean against the wall, said, "Eoghan Mogh has been banished to the south, running like a child to his fosterers. He'll not trouble us for a long while."

Conn chuckled derisively. "Some say he builds a kingdom in the south and plans a great strike against Tara. In the state I left him in last, I doubt if he could find the gold to raise a tent."

Nimbus slid off the throne and began to pluck slyly at Mer-Nod's feathered mantle.

Conn closed his eyes and leaned back in the throne. "Tell me a tale, Mer-Nod. I am weary and long to hear of glory."

Mer-Nod opened his mouth to speak and felt the rhythmic tugging behind him. He turned on Nimbus, dark eyes flashing, as the midget reappeared with a handful of red and gold feathers.

"May the gods curse you, you runt. Unhand my cloak!"

Conn laughed as Mer-Nod, who prided himself on his dignified demeanor, began to chase a gleeful Nimbus around the throne.

A trumpet blast from outside the rampart halted Mer-Nod's murderous attempt as well as all other activity in the hall. Conn's hands tightened into unrelenting fists. Nimbus walked around to stand at his feet while Mer-Nod resumed his posture against the wall, composing his face into indifference with effort. Golden apples fell to the floor, as a juggler's eyes fixed on the door. The poets halted in mid-sentence, their stories aborted in mid-battle. Children darting here and there were stilled by the grasping hands of their mothers.

Conn rose as the massive double doors swung open. A protective veil lowered itself over his eyes. Like a sunny field smothered by a great thundercloud, his face closed to an unreadable mask.

Standing in the doorway were a man and woman, covered with sweat and grime. They were runners, legendary athletes who could circle the Isle of Erin in a single day.

The woman stepped out of the doorway for a long moment and as she reappeared, the cause of their delay became wrenchingly clear. She led a roan into the gathering. On its speckled back, Kevin took his last ride. A muffled sob burst from the crowd and a young girl slid to the floor in a dead faint.

Kevin's body was draped over the horse's back, blood caked thick in his red hair. The rusty stains stood in startling contrast to his death pallor. His head was twisted to one side; his eyes stared blindly into the crowd as the horse was led to the center of the hall. Those closest shuddered and stepped back, wondering what was last beheld by those terrified orbs. The ragged edges of a wound gaped in his back where a sword had exited his heart. More than one of the Fianna thought they heard Kevin's excited laughter echoing in the corridors of their memories. A soldier watching the grim procession drained his ale in a single swig, his hands trembling for the first time.

Only the sound of weeping accompanied Conn as he moved off the dais, enthralled by the sight before him. His eyes were chips of blue ice. As he reached the horse, he stretched out his hands and cradled the head of his dead friend. Leaning down as if to whisper something, Conn made a noise that started as a growl in the deepest part of his throat. The hairs on the back of Nimbus's neck stood erect as a fierce battle cry was wrung from Conn's grief.

The hall sprang into fevered activity. Men from the Fianna surrounded Conn, bloody and black oaths pouring from tight-ened lips. He turned to the nearest soldier and whispered something that colored the man's face ashen. The man darted to the door, Nimbus fast on his heels.

Raising his hands over his head, Conn silenced the hall. "I am going to kill the bastard myself." His lips twisted in a bitter

grimace. "Sean Ó Finn has gone to prepare my mount.
Mer-Nod will act as regent until my return."

The silence of the hall exploded in an uproar. Loud protests,
blended with shouts of encouragement, climbed to deafening
bedlam.

Mer-Nod left his position along the wall and strode toward
Conn, fighting to make himself heard over the cacophony of
voices. "Conn, that's insane! We can't afford to lose you!"

Eyes gleaming, Conn replied, "You won't lose me. When I
return to Tara, I will bear the head of the monster that slew
Kevin. Be it man or beast, it will die at my hands."

Sean Ó Finn returned. Eyes averted, he told Conn, "Your
mount is prepared. There are supplies for five days."

Nimbus also reappeared, struggling with a sword as long as
his body.

Conn took the sword and raised it in the air. His voice rang
through the hall. "For Kevin, for the Fianna, for Erin, the
creature shall die!"

Sheathing the sword, he ran through the door and leapt upon
the back of the huge Arabian stallion that awaited him. Kicking
the horse into full gallop, he thundered through the gates of the
rampart.

Nimbus stood unnoticed in the flurry of the crowd. One small
grubby hand went up to rub his throbbing temples.

The bleak sky began its surrender to an even bleaker darkness
as Conn galloped away from the fortress. Wispy clouds scuttled
across the horizon, blown by nervous bursts of cool wind.
Lacking the warmth of sunshine, the day's dampness had failed
to wear off and only became more pronounced as the light faded
in the east. The leaves on the trees trembled in anticipation of
the darkness to come. The eerie purple glow of twilight suffused
the landscape, transforming the green fields into darkened
velvet. The only sounds that cut through the deepening twilight
were the steady hoofbeats of Conn's horse and the lonely cry of
a tern in the distance. As Conn left the path and descended into
a sodden field, a light drizzle began to fall. The last light of dusk
now vanished, he slowed his horse to a walk and entered a forest
thick with tangled vines and clinging bracken.

He pulled his cloak tight around him as his mount picked its
way through the undergrowth. Fury was running circles in his

mind. He felt the chill in the air as if someone else was cold and it was his duty to wrap that mortal up warmly. Kevin's lifeless form was imprinted on his brain by a burning brand. Bright-eyed, quick-tempered Kevin, broken and bleeding. His body would be shrouded, carried to his clan by the Fianna as a grim reminder of the oath they had taken when Kevin was sent to join their ranks: "We swear to accept Kevin's death or maiming without seeking satisfaction or vengeance, except that which his brother warriors will reap." The blackness of rage bubbled through Conn's veins. As he left the forest for a meadow, he urged the Arabian into a gallop.

Rain was falling, and the moon had begun its descent when he slipped off the horse in a clearing. The apple in his knapsack found its way into the horse's mouth, and Conn smiled for the first time since leaving the fortress. Silent Thunder had sailed far over the ocean in a crowded cargo hold to become his battle steed. He ran his hands over the satiny blackness of the horse's haunches. Not one marking marred the starkness of its beauty. He looped the reins around a bush and left the beast to graze.

Shaking the rain from his hair, he foraged through the forest until he had gathered enough branches and greenery to shelter both himself and a fire from the steady downpour. He warmed his hands over the flames and absently wished that Nimbus were there to ease the silence. Memories of other forests gathered around him; the heat of other fires warmed his hands. The spirits of the five dead surrounded him, laughing and boasting, planning battles for the morrow. For a fleeting instant his nose caught the aroma of fresh venison roasting over an open pit.

He stood, cursing himself for his fancies. The forest seemed to stir around him, and he sat again, wondering if sleep would be difficult or just impossible. His tense fingers smeared cheese across a thick chunk of bread. The fires of his anger burned too deeply to leave room for fear. He would unmask this hooded slayer and put him to a merciless death. Wrapping himself in his cloak, he settled down to sleep. At this time on the morrow he would reach the cavern. He must be ready. He sank into an abyss of sleep mercifully devoid of dreams.

Conn and Silent Thunder were already traveling north when the sun rose the next morning. The day dawned with a warm southerly breeze that played over his features as if to smooth away the lines of tension creasing his forehead. Larks and martins sang into a sky that was the delicate blue of the inside of a robin's egg. An occasional cloud, as white and fleecy as the underbelly of a newly birthed lamb, floated across its serene canvas. As he moved north, the terrain grew hillier and the rolling emerald sward gave way to rocks and loose shrubs beneath the horse's hooves.

The sun sank in an orange ball of glory behind the western horizon, so different from the past day's muted departure. He had reached the drumlins. The foothills were steep but lay between the mountains and the plains that surrounded the misty hill of Tara.

Darkness shrouded the landscape. He lit a torch to guide their steps. Treacherous stones lay waiting to send a horse into a fatal misstep. Conn's eyes could faintly discern shadowed indentations in the cliffs that he knew to be small caves. According to his calculations, the larger cavern he sought must be less than a league away. A trickle of sweat eased its way down the back of his neck.

He halted Silent Thunder and sat, eyes closed, deep in thought. A young lad, desperate to join the Fianna, had made this same journey to conquer the creature who had already sent three of the Fianna to gory deaths. He had been the only one to return. His hysterical tale of a cloaked giant who had at the last moment removed the sword's point from his fear-constricted throat and released him had traveled quickly to Conn. Just as the beast intended, he thought bitterly.

Eyes still closed, he called to mind the face of each man who had died in that cavern. Five fierce warriors gone, leaving him to avenge their blood.

Opening his eyes and kicking Silent Thunder into a canter, he once again let out the battle cry that had so chilled Nimbus. It reverberated through the drumlins with a roaring echo. He knew that if someone or something lay in wait for him, he was giving it enough warning to bait the trap. The wind fanned the torch clutched in his left hand to a glowing beacon as he guided the horse, using only his knees.

Directly in front of him at two hundred paces lay an opening in the cliff, huge and beckoning. An eerie green glow suffused the ground and air. Conn slowed the horse to a walk, every muscle a hard cord of tension.

He called out hoarsely, "Bastard, when you see my torch, the next sight you see will be the fires of the underworld!"

He drew back his arm and tossed the torch into the mouth of the cave. He turned the horse and made his way alongside the cliff. His cloak fell unheeded to the ground. When he could no longer see the green glow over his shoulder, he slid off the horse and blew softly into its nose. Pulling out his massive sword, he continued up the cliff face on foot, placing each step so as not to jar the loose rocks. Pausing only once to glance behind him, he climbed until he was at the top of the drumlin that housed the cavern.

Sheathing his sword, he dropped to his knees and ran his hands over the rocky surface. He heard no sound from below. Near the apex of the hill he found what he sought. His knees, scraped raw through the cloth of his breeches, were abruptly cushioned in soft grass. His fingers dug into it, finding the contours of a makeshift trap door fashioned from a piece of wood covered with soil and grass. He leaned back on his heels, lips twisted in an unpleasant smile. From this vantage point a lone rider could be spotted leaving the plains before he ever entered the hills surrounding the cavern. He became more convinced that he was dealing with an intelligent creature, perhaps a giant.

He loosened his sword in its scabbard. Lifting up the trap door a fraction of an inch, he saw a faint glow from the cavern below. His eyes darkened to midnight blue as he heaved aside the door and dropped a heel-stinging distance, landing as silently as a great cat on unrelenting stone.

He found himself crouching at the rear of a large hollow room. The only sound that cracked the silence was the rhythmic drip of water from the dangling stalactites. At his back was a sheer rock wall. To his right was a barely discernible passageway that led deeper into the bowels of the cavern. Inside the main entrance two rows of torches had been placed along the wall, emitting the ghastly glow he had seen from outside. And between himself and that entrance stood his enemy, still facing the night, ignorant of the intruder in his domain.

The babbling boy who had returned from this place had not lied. A huge, black cloak covered the ghoul from head to toe, a span that nearly doubled Conn's own height. A faint demarcation at the back of a cowl drew the line between head and body.

Conn's eyes were caught and held by the shining sword wielded in the creature's hands.

All he need do to end this confrontation was rush forward without warning and ram his sword between the creature's ribs. But the same code of honor that had refused to send more than one man to defeat a single creature stopped him. He pulled his blade, allowing the red hot center of his rage to return until the golden hilt he clutched seemed to glow with the heat of it.

He stepped forward. "Turn around, evil spawn, and meet the fires of the underworld I promised you!" His voice rose from a whisper to a roar.

The creature turned so quickly that it swayed, nearly losing some precarious claim on balance. With the torches shining behind it, Conn saw that the cloak was not opaque but was almost sheer. He blinked, convinced there was something amiss beneath it.

But there was no time to dwell on the thought. As the creature regained its balance, it swung on Conn with a two-handed blow from the sword that slammed into his shoulder and almost sent him to his knees. He growled, parrying the next blow easily. His fury culminated in a strength that rushed through his body like pure energy. Thrusting through the midst of the dark cloak, his sword felt no contact with flesh but he struck again, trying to estimate where the giant's heart would lie.

Still struggling to regain its balance, the creature swung again, aiming for a severing blow to Conn's neck. He leapt aside as the blade whistled past his throat and matched the giant's swing with a lunge of his own. The swords clashed again, the bitter clang of metal against metal echoing through the cavern. Conn fought like a man possessed.

He made a clever feint only to be surprised by the giant's lightning quick riposte. The enemy blade sliced his left forearm, drawing blood. The pain eluded him but he could feel the blood soaking into the sleeve of his tunic. He retreated against the wall as the creature advanced, each step bringing the shining blade closer to his face. Conn's swings blurred as he attacked again and again, not allowing the creature to do anything but parry his thrusts. The extra effort it took to aim at the chest so high above his head rendered his arms aching and leaden. The wall at his back became a trap, a tomb.

The giant leaned forward and for the first time Conn saw the glint of green eyes beneath the hood. Wielding the sword like a massive hammer, the creature struck a blow to Conn's ear that sent his head reeling. He fought to hold onto his sword as bells rang around him. The creature moved in for the death blow.

Conn summoned his last ounce of strength and plunged his blade directly in front of him. Expecting to penetrate the giant's kneecap or thigh, he started as he felt the solid connection of the sword sinking deep into flesh. The creature swayed and Conn took the opportunity to thrust the sword upward, high above his head where he again felt contact with flesh and bone. The smell of blood like the smell of fear assailed his nostrils.

In a macabre dance the giant reeled, cape tangling around its legs. Conn sank to his knees and watched in amazement as the creature fell in two pieces. A high-pitched scream was drowned out by the clatter of the sword as it crashed to the ground, sending up an echo that reverberated through the cavern and Conn's aching head.

Too dumbfounded and exhausted to move, Conn watched as the bottom half of the giant crawled out from under the voluminous cloak and fled into the night, leaving only a profuse trail of blood to mark its path. Eyes wide, Conn crawled toward what was left. The cloak shrouded the inert lump it had become.

He reached the cloak and touched a corner of it. Warm blood drenched it, sticky to his fingertips. He slowly drew it toward him and leaned over to find himself staring into the face of a young boy.

Chapter Two

❖

A ghastly pallor descended on the boy's face. Conn could see the faint rise and fall of his chest beneath the cloak. His stunned fingers brushed the translucent skin stretched taut over high cheekbones, desperate to determine the youth's age but failing. Conn's thumb traced the shadowed circles beneath his eyes. A low moan escaped his parted lips.

Conn stripped back the thin material and rolled the boy over his knee to examine his wound. His sword had pierced the back of one bony shoulder between spine and arm, missing the heart by a hand's length. Blood flowed freely from the wound. Conn's mind, still bearing the brunt of shock, acted separately from his hands as they tore off strips of material from the cloak to staunch the steady stream of blood.

This was no giant of a warrior who lay limp in his arms. The boy was one of two people acting together with a flow of motion so well defined that none of the Fianna had been able to discern their separate parts. If they had, they hadn't lived to tell the tale. Conn wiped the sweat from his brow; his aching fingers tightened the makeshift bandage. He wanted the lad alive. Sitting back on his heels, he felt the slow trickle of blood oozing from the deep slash in his own arm. He reached out and picked up the sword lying less than a foot away, marveling at its workmanship. A nagging bell of familiarity tolled in his mind. Engraved in the hilt was a word whose large, uneven letters did not match the fine craftsmanship of the rubies encrusted beside it.

"Vengeance," he whispered.

The boy drew a shuddering breath. It was inconceivable that he had wielded this sword so well. The weight of the hammered silver sent shooting pains down Conn's exhausted arms. He ran his hand over the boy's arm. It was a lean arm—smooth, taut, and strangely muscular when compared to the sculpted cheeks and the shoulder blades that jutted out at sharp angles above his wound.

Spurred into action, Conn took the remainder of the cloak and wrapped up the sword before tying it around his belt. There was no predicting if the bottom half of the creature would live long enough to procure help from some unknown source. His first successful sword thrust should have descended deeply into the gut of the person supporting the boy.

He picked the boy up, carrying him like a baby. His head drooped against Conn's shoulder; his short-cropped hair brushed Conn's beard and Conn breathed deeply of a scent as fresh as the pure spring waters bubbling deep within the cavern. A searing flash of anger shot through him as his fingers sank into the familiar beaten leather of garments identical to his. Five leather belts hung around the youth's waist, each marked with the clansname of a man now resting beneath his ancestral cairn. As Conn moved toward the mouth of the cave, his hands cut deeply into the boy's shoulders and legs. The boy nuzzled his face into Conn's tunic. A ragged moan escaped his throat. Conn loosened his grip.

He made his way down the narrow path where Silent Thunder waited, untethered. He heaved the boy onto the horse's back and climbed into place behind him. The top of the boy's head brushed Conn's chin as he slumped against his chest, surprising Conn with his height.

The pale moon sank behind the horizon as Conn guided Silent Thunder south to a forest of towering trees. A lush carpet of pine needles muffled their steps. They wended their way through the trees until they passed a gurgling stream, swollen by the summer rains and cradled by thick moss. The boy's moans grew more frequent at the jolting motion of the horse.

Conn pulled him off the horse and settled him into the mossy bank, his tense fingers checking the bandages for fresh blood. The boy breathed a gentle sigh as Conn lowered his head against a clump of earth. Sooty lashes fluttered against the smattering of freckles on the boy's cheeks, then lay still. Conn's thumb traced the Gaelic purity of the boy's face. The smooth chin held not even the hint of stubble. The lad was young, younger than the boys who came to the Fianna with their hearts full of dreams.

Younger than Kevin had been when he had knelt before Conn to swear his fealty. The boy turned his face toward Conn's hand; his mouth moved against Conn's calloused palm. Conn jerked his hand away. However young the boy was, he was old enough to murder.

With canteen in hand, Conn moved a few feet along the brook until he found a wide ledge. He leaned out to scoop up some of the cool, tempting water.

A sense beyond hearing or sight jerked his head around. He rolled to the side, hearing the dagger whistle past his shoulder. He reached out a powerful arm but caught only air. The boy sailed past him and went tumbling head first into the rushing stream. Conn leapt into the chill water. His hands fumbled beneath the surface, closing on the boy's jerkin and drawing him upward. Conn's dagger glinted wet and lethal in the boy's clenched fist. Conn caught his wrist and gave it a vicious twist, sending the dagger flying out of his grasp to the muddy bank. Ragged nails raked Conn's wounded arm, igniting a white hot anger.

Conn clamped his lips together and shoved him under the water. He drew him out sputtering and spitting, then shoved him under again as a balled fist caught the underside of his chin. Again he dragged the boy thrashing and cursing from the churning water. It slowly penetrated Conn's fury that the hands clinging to his neck did so in desperation, their deadly intent forgotten.

He shoved the boy away from him like a rag doll. Too weak to stand, the boy sank to his knees and disappeared under the water. Conn dragged himself out of the stream and staggered across the clearing.

He looked back to find the stream's surface broken only by white-tipped froth. He hesitated, not wanting to care if the demon's whelp with the pretty face sank back to the hole he had come from. Water rushed over the pocket where the boy had disappeared.

With a vicious curse Conn plunged into the stream. His hands swept beneath the water and caught in the boy's hair. He hauled him out of the stream and dragged him across the slimy bank. With a heaving cough the limp body came to life and wrapped itself around Conn's ankles. The boy's teeth sank into Conn's calf as they rolled away from the stream. Conn's curses blended with his. Pinning the boy beneath him with his knees spread on his shoulders, Conn drew back his hand and slapped him hard.

Conn jerked in a breath. The boy's jerkin had fallen open. The linen shirt clung to the hills and valleys of the heaving chest between Conn's thighs like a second skin. He cursed softly, staring at breasts that were small but well-shaped and undeniably feminine. The volatile child subdued beneath him was a girl, not a lad. The Fiannic oath promising gentleness to all women echoed through his mind, eliciting both anger and shame.

His body relaxed as he felt the girl's muscles yield. Her face dissolved in a paroxysm of grief and the tears flowed, tracing a grimy path between her eyes and ears. Conn gently wiped her cheek with the back of his hand, wondering how he could have been so blind as to mistake her for a boy. He moved off her and gathered her up in his arms. Her body slumped as he stroked her short-cropped hair.

Her voice was muffled into his shoulder as she spoke three hoarse words. "Where is he?"

Conn spoke softly even as his hands tightened their grip. "If you speak of the one who was with you, he's dead."

He stared into an eastern horizon fraught with the light of dawn and knew his words to be true if his blow had struck as deeply as his sword had reverberated in his hands. Her body stiffened again, and his eyes fell on the dagger lying in the mud a few feet away.

"Please let me go," she said, lifting her head from his shoulder but avoiding his gaze.

"Why?" Conn asked. "So you can ambush me up the trail a few leagues from here?" He shook his head. "No, thank you. I've seen you wield sharp objects and I've no desire to see it again."

"I want to bury him. I never had the chance to bury my father and mother." A single tear slid down her cheek but her words were tinged with icy calm.

He jerked her around to face him but she still refused to meet his eyes. "Just who by the blood of the gods were your mother and father? Who was evil enough to spawn your murdering soul?" He baited her, seeking truth between the cracks he sensed in her tenuous reserve. When his question met only silence, he asked, "How old are you? And who was this man?"

A tremor ran through her. "I am a thousand years old. What concern of it is yours?"

Conn's gaze traced the insolent curve of a cheek pure enough to belong to a druid priestess and almost believed her. His hand tightened on her wrist, pressing into the tender flesh. The skin around her lips blanched but she did not flinch. His eyes narrowed.

His grip changed subtly. His hand slid up her arm and over the wet, cracked leather of the jerkin. His palm cradled the damp skin that fluttered over the pounding pulse in her throat. His fingertips grazed the tiny hairs at the back of her neck and she could not hide her shiver.

"Are you a woman or a child?" he asked in a voice that was not unkind.

Stony silence met his question.

His finger traced the curve of her cheek. "Your flesh is curiously unlined for one so ancient."

She turned her face away from him and stared into the forest. Conn cursed as his patience evaporated in a wave of anger and exasperation. His hands caught in the worn collar of the jerkin. He snatched her up like a puppet, the heat of his anger in the face of her pale indifference spreading uninvited to his loins.

"'Tis clear you're old enough to murder my men and steal their clothes. If neither your face nor your lips will tell me your age, perhaps I shall examine what lies beneath Conor Ó Murchada's jerkin for my answers."

She hung unmoving in his grasp, her eyes still averted. Her helplessness disarmed him. He lowered her. He touched his fingers to the bandage beneath her jerkin; they reappeared stained with pale pink water.

"You're bleeding again. Are you trying to kill yourself?"

She raised arrogant eyes to meet the dark blue of his. "No, Conn. I'm trying to kill you." A smile twisted her lips.

Conn stared mesmerized at the glittering, emerald eyes—the bitter, wounded eyes of a woman set deep in the face of a child. The nagging bell of familiarity tolled again. His gaze never leaving hers, he went to the horse and took a length of rope from the knapsack. She offered him no resistance as he bound her hands.

"You know who I am," he said. "When you decide to tell

me who you are, I will unbind you. In the meantime, I would like you to think carefully about what's going to happen to you when we reach my fortress.''

The girl's face was impassive. Her chin tilted in cold defiance as she stared mutely into his glittering blue eyes.

''You will go on trial for the murders of five men—Conor Ó Murchada, Ryan Ó Brosnahan, Brian MacRuairc, Kyle MacRuairc, who had the misfortune of belonging to the same clan, and Kevin Ó hArtagain. You should be familiar with the names.'' He gestured to her waist where the leather belts hung, condemning her without a word. ''If I can keep the MacRuaircs from cutting out your heart before the trial, the public court will determine your guilt. If they decide you are guilty, I will pass sentence.''

He knelt beside her, taking her chin in his unyielding hand. ''I shall then let you choose between two just punishments. I will either turn you over to the clans of the men you killed''— his eyes searched her face for any sign of emotion—''or I will have you beheaded.'' She flinched imperceptibly, the only indication she had heard his words.

Without another word he bound her feet and threw his cloak over her. The sun floated over the horizon as exhaustion forced both of them to sleep. Conn's sleep was light, his mind tuned for any sound.

The afternoon sun had dried his garments when he awoke. Shaking off the grogginess of slumber, he hugged his knees and watched the girl sleep. With her face peaceful in repose, she looked five years younger than any guess of her age Conn might have made. Stubby, dark eyelashes fanned on her freckled cheeks, shielding him from the woman's hatred he would find in her eyes when she awoke. An unexpected twinge of yearning tightened his throat as she yawned softly and snuggled deeper into his cloak. He wished for an instant that he were a different kind of man.

He shook his head in disbelief at the thought of this innocent and the ice-hearted killer in the cavern sharing the same lithe body. An unnatural flush, which did not seem to claim the sun as its precursor, had risen on her face. He reached out a hand and gently touched her cheek. The smooth skin felt hot to his callused fingers. Her eyes fluttered open to meet his, then shut again as if displeased at the sight.

"Water?" she croaked.

"I was fetching you some water when you tried to send me down the creek with my own dagger in my back."

Conn rose. He returned with a canteen full of the sparkling water and squatted beside her. Putting an arm around her shoulders, he lifted her and touched the wet rim of the canteen to her lips. She leaned against him and drank deeply. Conn took a corner of his jacket and gently wiped away the drops of water that escaped her thirsty lips. Her bound hands were clenched into fists between them. She hid her tremble with a cough but not before Conn could see that sleep had robbed her of anger, but not fear. He drank, the cool water soothing his parched throat.

"We must travel. Your wound is festering. It needs to be seen by one of my physicians," he said.

"Wouldn't it be more convenient if I died on the journey there?" the girl said caustically, her eyes glazed.

Conn shook his head. "Too many unanswered questions. If you are so determined to die, I insist you wait until I at least have learned your name." He pulled a piece of meat from his knapsack. "Here. You need to eat." He unbound her and put the thin strip of meat in her hand.

"I cannot eat this. Only kings and high poets can eat steak." He saw no trace of sarcasm in her face, only confusion.

"Are you not hungry, nameless one?"

She bit reluctantly into the meat. A look of greedy pleasure transformed her face into that of a child's. Conn hid a smile as she stuffed the meat into her mouth with ravenous hands.

He stood and began to pace, hands locked behind his back. "As I see it, if you will tell me who this man was, it might not be necessary to tell everyone at the fortress exactly who you are. You said your father was dead. So was this man your brother or your cousin?"

The girl shook her head without slowing her eating.

Conn ignored her and continued. "You are very young. It seems to me that this man of yours ensured that all of the blood in this grim affair would be on your hands, not his."

Her eyes narrowed to dangerous slits as she downed the last bite with an audible swallow.

"This man used you and made a fool of you, teaching you to fight some twisted battle that should have been his."

The girl reached to her waist for a sword that was not there. "He was never like that. He loved me!"

Her eyes fell as she realized her error. She rubbed a grubby hand through her auburn hair until it stood up in nervous spikes.

Conn turned on his heel. "Was he your lover then?"

She stared at him for a long moment. "He was."

Conn paced away from her. "He must have been a fine lover, indeed. Fine enough to commit murder for."

She lifted her chin. "The finest. Finer than any of the Fianna ever dreamed of being."

Conn raised an eyebrow. "And what prompted you and your charming lover to murder my men?"

"Not murder. Justice."

The ghost of a smile hovered around Conn's lips. He crossed the clearing in two strides and knelt in front of her. She shrank back but refused to lower her gaze.

"You're lying," he said. "A man wants a woman in his bed, not a dirty, little cave urchin. If he was your lover, he'd been living in a cave far too long. It addled his wits."

She crossed her arms. "Believe what you like. You will anyway. You always did."

Conn rubbed the back of his neck to keep from smacking her. He exhaled a slow breath. "Dearest child," he said, pronouncing each word with infinite patience, "I am not asking for the truth. I am commanding it."

She blinked wide eyes. "Now that puts a new slant on things, doesn't it?" Conn stood as she climbed unsteadily to her feet. She swept off an imaginary hat and bowed until her forehead touched her knees. "Grant me a thousand pardons, Conn. I must confess. The man was . . . ,"—a teasing sigh; a sly glance from beneath downswept lashes—". . . my lover."

"Nonsense. You've probably never kissed a man with anything but the tip of your sword. He had to have been a cousin or a broth—"

Before Conn could finish, she pressed her lips to his in a kiss as childish as it was affecting. His hands moved to her waist to push her away but stayed of their own volition, resting lightly against the linen shirt. He could have counted every rib without opening his eyes.

He took a step backward. "Good," he said briskly. "Then you shall be well prepared for the attentions of the MacRuairc clan should they decide not to end your life. Since you choose to flaunt your murderous liaison with this man, 'tis fitting you should spend the rest of your life tied to a farmer's bedstead at the mercy of his sons and all their kinsfolk.''

Her face paled. Conn stared coldly into her stricken eyes, ignoring a pang of guilt. "You offer much to protect this man, whatever he was to you, but I fear my tastes don't run to lying murderesses who fancy it justice to leave behind a trail of grieving widows and orphans."

She plopped to the ground. Her fingers tore up a hunk of moss. Her voice was hoarse. "There is no justice for orphans in this world. The sooner they learn that, the better off they will be."

Conn dropped his cloak around her shoulders. "And for those who made them orphans?"

She gave him a half smile that would have been devastating if not overshadowed by the blind hatred in her sparkling eyes. "You tell me, sire."

Conn crossed the clearing and threw the knapsack over Silent Thunder's back. He tightened the straps with a jerk. "If I give you my oath not to question you further about the man, will you give me a name to call you?"

"Gelina."

The whisper came from right behind him. He was halfway turned when the rock came down on the back of his head with a dull thud. Before he hit the ground, the girl had stripped him of his sheath and dagger and was gone.

Gelina stumbled over a rock and slammed into a tree. Pain exploded in her shoulder. She bent double, concentrating all of her effort on not crying out. She leaned against the tree until she could breathe again. Her eyes combed the forest. She listened but heard only the whisper of needle against needle high among the swaying pines. She found the sinking sun and darted to the left, leaping and dodging branches like a startled doe. The muffled crunch of her bare feet against the pine needles profaned the sacred silence of the forest. She prayed silently for some merciful druid goddess with a gentle hand to take pity on her and hide her from the monster-king.

She ran until the ache in her shoulder deepened to unrelenting pain. The sun dove toward the earth, brushing her forehead with fingers dipped in flame and dappling the forest in shadow. She stumbled and fell again. She crouched on her hands and knees, her head hanging between her shoulders. Her nails dug into the cool soil. She scrambled to her feet.

She burst into a shadowy glade and found not a goddess but an irate god, his powerful, dark form thrown into silhouette by the last slanting rays of the sun. She dropped to her knees and threw her arms over her head. He roared her name. The warning came too late.

Conn was a foot away with sword in hand when she whipped the dagger from its sheath and brandished it in front of her with both hands. Conn stopped. He slowly squatted, turning his blade flat to make a larger shield.

"Give me the dagger, child," he said softly.

A wave of heat and pain washed over Gelina. She blinked to clear her vision. Conn crept closer. The dagger shook violently in her hands. "The only way you'll get your dagger is in your heart if you don't leave me be," she said.

"You're no match for me right now. And I've no desire to hurt you."

"I'd rather be skewered by your sword than by those men you're going to give me to. The weapons they'd use on me would be far more terrible than any you bear."

Conn closed his eyes briefly. "I spoke in anger and haste, lass. 'Twas an idle threat to wring the truth from you."

Her laugh cracked into a sob. "More lies. They flow so well from lips as smooth as yours. Even now you try to disarm me with eyes so blue and kind. All a lie. A vicious, hurtful lie."

Without lowering his gaze, Conn laid his sword aside. He spread his arms in surrender. "My heart, milady. My heart for your dagger. As proof of my pledge."

Gelina hurled the dagger. It was a crooked throw, and Conn didn't have to duck for it to miss him by a hand's length. She spun around to flee, tripped on a tangled root, and went sprawling on her stomach.

His arm circled her waist before she could scream. The setting sun burnished the blade in his hand to orange fire. Gelina closed her eyes, oddly thankful that his ruse of halfhearted kindness was over and the monster hiding behind his kind, blue eyes was revealed. She waited for the kiss of his blade on her throat.

The dagger caught in her shirt and jerkin, ripping them asunder and baring her shoulder to the flirting caress of the setting sun. He cut away the bandage from her shoulder. His curse was short and descriptive. His weight vanished. She lay with her cheek pressed to the cool earth, hiccuping softly, until he gently lifted her. He wrapped his shirt around her. She slumped against his bare chest like a cloth doll and closed her eyes.

Conn frowned as the blistering tirade he had planned to deliver fled his mind. After a short, puzzled silence, he asked, "And where were you fleeing in such haste, milady?"

"To bury my"—she came to a dead halt, gave a puzzled frown, then smiled brightly—"lover. Yes, I was going to bury my lover." This brought forth a rippling wave of mirth that deepened to a shuddering cough. Conn cradled her thin body to his until she lay spent and shivering in his arms. "Forgive me, sire. I fear I'm more of a mind to be cuddled than cursed. Don't fret. It'll pass or I will. 'Twill save you the expense of executing me."

Conn took her chin between his fingers. "You wouldn't dare die. I won't allow it."

"Ever arrogant," she said with a faint smile. She reached up and touched the softness of his beard with the tips of her fingers. "I thought kissing you would be like kissing a bear."

He caught her hand in his. "It was the first time you'd kissed anyone, was it not?"

She nodded. "And the last, I fear." Her eyes widened. "I wasn't supposed to tell you that, was I? I cannot keep my lies or truths straight in my pounding head. 'Tis unchivalrous of you to question me. Cease, I command it." She closed her eyes and wiggled imperious fingers.

His brogue was soft, almost musical. "Milady, if I had believed you were as versed in all of your alleged lover's arts as you are in murder and thievery, I would have been hard pressed to resist your sweet offer."

"Sweet," she croaked. The shallow rise of her chest barely stirred Conn's shirt.

"Sweet," he said. He was leaning forward to kiss her parted lips before he realized what he was doing. He quickly shifted his kiss to the tip of her nose, afraid to stop touching the fey child for fear she would slip away.

Her chest did not rise for a long moment. Conn touched his cheek to her lips, praying for a whisper of breath. Gelina began to shake with something deeper than the chill of her fever.

"Sweet," she murmured without opening her eyes. She sniffed twice and realized with disgust that she was going to cry. She buried her face in the damp hairs of Conn's arm. "Couldn't you just cut off my head and finish it? Rodney would be so disappointed in me. You've been kind, and I've kissed you instead of killing you properly."

"Not for lack of trying," Conn said quietly. He watched a pink-tipped cloud puff its way toward the sunset. "Rodney? 'Tis an unusual forename for a lad born on the Isle of Erin. 'Tis a name from Britain across the sea, is it not?" He stroked Gelina's dry, hot brow. "Indeed, I've met only one lad in all of Erin with that name. His father journeyed much on the sea and delighted in naming his children names he encountered during his travels. I believe he had a daughter, too—a flame-haired imp with the sweetest smile."

Conn tilted her chin with one finger. He searched her drawn face, his eyes shadowed. Gelina flinched as a shooting pain traveled up the back of her neck.

"Rodney Ó Monaghan? Was that your brother's name?"

She nodded wearily.

Conn said softly, "Then you must be . . ."

He hesitated, and she finished for him in a voice that was barely a whisper, "Gelina Ó Monaghan, daughter of Rory Ó Monaghan and Deirdre."

Conn touched her smooth cheek in wonder. "I used to pick you up and toss you in the air until you squealed. You were a beautiful little thing. Why, you can't be more than sixteen now."

"Fifteen." Gelina looked with blind entreaty into the dark blue eyes that had haunted her for so long. "I don't want to talk. I hurt."

The flush in her drawn cheeks had deepened. Conn could feel the heat radiating from her body. He whistled softly. Silent Thunder trotted into the glade.

Gelina put her arms around Conn's neck, and he lifted her to the horse. He mounted behind her and pulled his cloak around them both. His arm circled her waist with more gentleness than he intended. He urged the stallion into a walk.

Gelina leaned back, surrendering to the seductive comfort of his broad chest. She felt a bizarre sensation of safety unlike anything she had felt in too long to remember. Her trembling slowly eased although her memory of what had caused it did not. Her gaze fell on Conn's hands wrapped tight around the reins. A jagged scar crossed two of his knuckles. She bit her lip and the trembling started anew. Conn gently rested his chin on her head until he felt her relax against him. Sinking into a stuporlike sleep, she began to dream.

She stood high on a scaffold in the courtyard of a towering fortress. A noose of braided hemp lay around her neck, making her collarbone itch. She flinched as a rotten potato spattered across her face. Blue eyes glittered beneath the executioner's hood. Scattered throughout the crowd, skeletons with hunks of rotting flesh hanging from their bones leered and pointed at her with accusing fingers.

The scaffold grew hotter; flames reached for her. The executioner stretched out his black-gloved hand and pulled the mechanism that dropped the trapdoor out of the bottom of the scaffold. She hung there, unable to breathe and unable to die. As her body swung around, she faced the executioner. He removed his hood with a flourish and she stared into her brother's black eyes and heard again the bone-chilling laugh she had heard the night they had ambushed the first warrior of the Fianna. She fought to scream in the unbearable heat, unable to wring any sound from beneath the constricting bond of the noose.

Gelina opened her eyes to find Conn standing over her with a dagger. She choked on the bile rising in her throat and choked on the scream denied her in the dream.

As if still dreaming, she heard Conn's soft brogue. "Gelina, I must lance your wound and clean it. I want you to drink this."

She sputtered as a bitter amber liquid was poured down her throat. A warmth that was more pleasant burned a fiery path down to the pit of her stomach. At first she was only aware of gentle hands rolling her over and probing her shoulder; then a searing agony began there and traveled the length of her body, erupting like a volcano into a scream that echoed over the plains.

The next day she awoke only once. She opened her eyes to find bright stars shining in the ebony sky above her. Violent trembling wracked her aching body. The night breeze rushed over her like a frosted north wind. She looked at the stranger lying beside her.

He cupped her neck with his hand and felt her uncontrollable shaking. She rested her cheek against his palm, rubbing against his skin in a primitive search for warmth. With an abrupt motion he tucked his cloak around her and threw himself on his back with arms crossed. His eyes searched the night sky. He glanced at her. She was still watching him with naked bewilderment, unable to understand what she had done to displease him. The tenseness left his body in a sigh. She saw nothing but kindness in the blue depths of his bloodshot eyes. He lifted the cloak. Stretching out so his body covered the length of hers, he drew her into his arms, seeking to warm her sweat-dampened body with his own heat. She felt his cool lips brush the tangled hair at her temple. Gelina laid her cheek against his chest and slept again.

Chapter Three

❖

Nimbus sat with legs folded and back resting against the wooden wall outside the hall. Curled up beside him was a black and white dog with its head tucked underneath its front paws. The jester stuffed a cooked gamehen into his mouth, ignoring the trail of grease that dripped from his chin to his burlap breeches. He chewed voraciously, his jaws seeking to dispel the tension his mind could not.

Five days and still silence from the north. The atmosphere inside the castle was dour enough to make waiting for Kevin's unfortunate return seem like a carnival in contrast. There were no antics from Nimbus to lighten the mood. He had spent the morning crouched under a table in the kitchen, hidden from the cook by a stained tablecloth, suffering through her long-winded diatribe on the king's foolishness until he could grab the chicken in his hands.

He relished the fowl all the more, knowing how the rotund cook would shriek when she discovered her newly baked bird had flown the coop. A single drumstick remained from the feast when he heard the sound of hoofbeats approaching the fortress. The dog beside him raised its head and peered at him with crossed eyes.

Five hefty horses trotted into the courtyard, more suited to the fields than the long journey their sweat-sheened coats spoke of. The men astride them mopped their florid brows, also appearing more suited to the farmyard than the courtyard.

"Idiot, has the king returned?"

Nimbus struggled not to look offended at their use of a common term for jester although he could not prevent a quick upward roll of his eyes. "No sign of him yet. Ye can stable yer horses yonder." He pointed, rising to his feet.

They guided the horses away, one of the younger men pausing to call over his shoulder, "We're the MacRuaircs. We've come to see that justice is done."

The graying man next to him stretched out an arm and cuffed him smartly on his ear. "No need to explain to him. He be daft. Stunted. He don't understand."

Nimbus flipped an obscene finger at their backs, chicken leg hanging forgotten in his hand. The dog gently relieved him of his burden and sidled around the corner. Nimbus shot him a disgusted look, too offended to give chase.

People assumed that a stunted growth included a stunted mind. Nimbus was fond of explaining to Conn that although his height barely reached four feet, three of those feet were occupied by his brain. With a ribald dig to his ribs and a leer at any passing maid, he would then elaborate on the source of those other twelve inches. A smile appeared on Nimbus's face as he thought of Conn's laughter, then faded as rapidly as it had come.

He was again distracted by hoofbeats as a handsome white horse cantered into the courtyard. The tall, blond soldier who dismounted drew a sigh of disgust from Nimbus. Barron Ó Caflin had ridden out often in the last few days, spurring his mount north only to return a few hours later with sweat on his brow and a smirk on his thin lips.

Tying his horse to a post, he tossed out, "Any word yet?" in Nimbus's direction.

The midget crossed his arms and leaned against the wall.

"Ah, kind sir, ye honor me with speech! What be the grand occasion?" He blinked innocent cocoa-colored eyes.

"The grand occasion is going to be your burial if you don't form a civil tongue in your mouth," Barron replied, leaning toward him with a menacing scowl.

"Go pick on someone yer own size, Barron . . . like a roach."

Barron reached down and grabbed him by the collar, lifting his feet off the ground. "I asked a simple question, even for a simpleton to answer."

"I've a question for you, Ó Caflin."

Barron dumped Nimbus to the ground at the sound of the commanding voice behind him and turned to face Mer-Nod, whose stern visage was twisted in a sarcastic smile.

Barron bowed, giving the chief poet the respect he was due. He swept off his cap with a flourish and said, "And for you, sir, no question is too difficult."

Nimbus sneered as he climbed to his feet, brushing dirt from the seat of his breeches.

Mer-Nod did not mince words. "Each day you ride north over the plains, then turn and veer south, cutting a wide swath around the fortress. Just what is your business?"

The smile plastered on Barron's face faded and his skin paled. "Who told you that?"

Mer-Nod allowed his enigmatic smile to spread. "Do not forget my ancestor, Cesard the magician. He deigns to whisper cryptic secrets in my ear."

Barron struggled to regain his composure. His eyes lingered on the poet as if expecting to see an apparition hovering about his ear lobe. With studied nonchalance, he uncorked the canteen at his waist and took a large swig, wiping his mouth with the back of his hand. The fine red lines in his eyes seemed to spread spontaneously.

He shrugged. "I enjoy the ride. This inactivity while we await our king's return is galling to me." He backed toward the door. "Always a pleasure to converse with you, Mer-Nod."

As Mer-Nod glanced at Nimbus, Barron swallowed and continued, "And you, too, Nimbus, of course." His shoulder slammed into the doorframe as he whirled around and disappeared into the hall.

Nimbus emitted a guttural growl. "Never thought the likes of

ye would come to me rescue. Just where did ye garner that little
gem of information?''

Mer-Nod scowled mockingly. "What? You have no faith in
my powers of intuition?''

"None.''

"At least you are blunt, Nimbus. A childhood friend of Ó
Caflin's followed him one evening after Conn left.''

Nimbus scratched his head. "What do ye think he plans?''

"He bears close scrutiny because I do not know. Keep an eye
on him, Nimbus. See if you can underhear his conversations.''
Mer-Nod walked slowly back into the fortress.

"'Tis overhear, ye oaf!'' Nimbus called after him. He
muttered to himself, "Never did like Ó Caflin. Shifty eyes.''

The hours passed, interminably shifting into another day.
The air hung hot and heavy both inside and outside the fortress.
The heat made a fire unendurable; the ashes in the fireplace
grew cold. Farm work ground to a halt as families came one by
one to join the vigil inside the great hall. Many slept, seeking to
dull their worry in an unsound rest marred by muttering and
tossing. The silence was broken only by the click of a dog's
nails resounding off the hard wooden floors. The futures of the
men of the Fianna, who had pledged their allegiance to Conn
until death, hung in the air by a palpable thread, easily snipped
and impossible to repair.

The soldiers who were present had formed a circle in the
corner, heads bowed. Some of them offered prayers to the
gods—Agron, cu Roi mac Dairi, and Behl. Others simply sat,
eyes closed and minds blank. Only one of them prayed for
Conn's death, his golden head bowed in mock prayer and
concern.

Sean Ó Finn felt his despair deepen as the sun rose high,
marking the return of another noonday. Only he bore the burden
of the words Conn had whispered to him the day he had
departed to slay the monster. "Seven days, Sean. If I do not
return in seven days, declare me dead and choose a king. Do it
quickly or Eoghan Mogh will descend on this fortress within a
fortnight.''

An iron band stiffened around Sean's heart on the noon of
this sixth day. His most fervent prayer had shifted, and his mind
was unable to form the words that they be spared the sight of
Conn's mutilated body. So he simply sat in the gloom of

silence, watching motes of dust sparkling in the sun's shining rays.

Sean's eyes found the throne and began to sting. Nimbus sat there with his head lowered onto his arms, his posture one of abject misery. The hall had lost its air of expectancy. Hopelessness reigned. Even the court jester had succumbed.

Nimbus's head flew up as a horn sounded a single golden note. Nobody stirred. Eyes met in disbelief, unsure of the reliability of their senses. A second note sounded, shrill and tense with vibrato. The hall exploded into action. Men and women fought to reach the door, bodies slamming into one another. Sleepers were rudely awakened by boots crunching over their hands and hasty kicks aimed at their backsides. The mass of bodies hit the narrow doorway, which nearly stopped the flow. Curses flew as those in the back began to shove. Nimbus crawled on hands and knees through the legs of the crowd until he emerged from the door, blinking in the bright sunlight.

Shielding his eyes, he stared up at the corner tower to see Mer-Nod conversing with the watchman. As the hall emptied into the courtyard, all eyes turned to the tower.

Mer-Nod lifted his arms in a plea for silence. "A rider approaches from the north. The steed is Conn's."

A single uproarious cheer rose from the crowd. Embraces were shared by strangers. Hats flew into the air, their owners not caring if they returned. The court musicians found their harps, flutes, drums, and mandolins and began to play a rollicking, if somewhat disjointed, tune. A rotund farmer stood, hat clutched in hands, silent tears coursing down his cheeks. Two young lovers shared a passionate kiss, their parents too excited to chastise them. Paying no heed to anyone else, Nimbus did three somersaults in quick succession, his twisting muscles expressing his joy in a way he could never verbalize.

As the wooden gates swung inward, the men of the Fianna gathered in the forefront to flank the entrance. The rider could now be seen in the distance as he slowed his horse to a walk to cover the final steps of his journey. The carriage of his head was unmistakable.

As Silent Thunder carried Conn into the courtyard, cheers arose from all sides and arms waved in jubilant salute. Buttercups and rhododendrons were strewn in his path. Conn smiled

widely and lifted his hand in a simple gesture of recognition
from what appeared to be a limp bundle in front of him on the
horse. As he raised his arm to salute, the cloth fell back to reveal
emerald eyes set deep in an ashen face.

Chapter Four

❖

Gelina peered over the top of Conn's arm in awe at the emotion
she sensed in the huge crowd. Adoration, respect, joy, and now
amazement played across the blur of faces that bobbed in her
vision. She felt overwhelmed in the presence of such an
overflow of emotions. The world had revolved around she and
her brother for so long that she felt herself fading in the presence
of so many. She leaned against Conn, pressing her back into his
chest and fought against terror as faceless hands brushed them.

Gasps of amazement traveled the length of the crowd as her
face was revealed. Cries rose into the afternoon sky.

"Who is it?"

"Where is the monster?"

"Has he killed it?"

"We want its bloody head!" This voice came from the corner
where the MacRuaircs had set up camp.

"'Tis a child!"

"Be it a girl or a lad?"

"More ale! More ale!" This cry came from a drunk farmer
who was so far in his cups that he was oblivious to the scene
around him. The man standing next to him soundly boxed his
ears.

Gelina stared straight ahead as Conn halted the huge Arabian
in front of a narrow flight of outer steps leading to the
watchtower. Looking up, she could see an armed man and for a
brief instant, with the sun glinting in her eyes, a giant eagle
perched beside him. It took her eyes a long moment to translate
this into a tall man in a feathered cloak. She blinked and stared

at the ground. The last three feverish days had passed in a blur, and she feared the tricks her mind might play upon her.

Conn dismounted and turned to pull her down with him. Her height became apparent as she slid stiffly down, causing some to speculate again on her sex.

To the crowd she appeared a frightened gremlin. Her hair glinted red in the bright sunlight and stood on end, tousled by the wind and the hood that had covered it. Dark circles lay beneath her eyes, emphasizing their wide, terrified dominance of her thin face.

She balked as Conn inexorably pulled her toward the steps. Their eyes met, and his hand tightened around her wrist, gripping it in silent warning until the skin around her lips blanched. His eyes were unreadable, their only message a tense warning. Gelina bowed her head in submission but could not hide the subtle straightening of her back as she followed him up the stairs. He inwardly shuddered, knowing if she tried anything, it would destroy his plan. Running a hand down his leg, he felt the familiar contours of the dagger strapped above his knee and breathed a sigh of relief.

They reached the top of the tower, Mer-Nod stepping aside to let them pass. The cheers built to a new crescendo as Conn stepped forward and raised his arms. He surveyed the crowd until silence prevailed and every eye was on him.

"Your king has returned in triumph!" he cried. A fresh round of cheers cut through the crowd.

"What of the creature?" a woman's voice cried out.

Conn nodded. "When I left here, I promised to return with the murderer's bloody head." The crowd nodded approvingly.

Gelina closed her eyes, waiting for the moment when he revealed her, beheading her in front of them all. She could envision her head flying from the top of the tower, mouth opened wide in surprise as it smashed on the cobblestones below like a bloated pumpkin.

Conn continued, hearing a quick intake of breath behind him. "Yes, I slayed the creature who defeated our men. I am here to tell you that when the creature drew its final breath . . . ," —his voice lowered dramatically although it was still audible throughout the courtyard—"I went to where it had fallen and found only this!"

His voice rose and Gelina shrieked as he reached behind him

only to whip the huge, black cloak from his pack and loose it from the tower, sending it floating downward on the wind.

A woman screamed and the crowd drew in its breath and gave the cloak a wide berth as it landed. Two soldiers of the Fianna drew the cloak out to its full length; the poets ran forward to measure it. Mer-Nod stepped forward just in time to put a steadying hand under the girl's arm as he saw her weave.

With attention diverted from Conn, Mer-Nod hissed, "Surely you are not given to fantasies of cave fiends melting in thin air. It is not like you."

Conn turned to face Mer-Nod's questioning frown, eyes guarded. "Perhaps I only choose to give you food for your meals of poetry."

The edge to his voice was sharp enough to wound, and Mer-Nod watched him through narrowed eyes as he reached out both hands and drew the girl in front of him on the dais. She moved as if sleepwalking, her eyes glazed.

As the mysterious stranger reappeared, the crowd grew quiet again, all eyes fixed upward. Conn's hands flexed on Gelina's shoulders as if daring any man to dislodge them. His broad fingers traced her collarbone in a gesture as strangely tender as it was protective. Fighting exhaustion, Gelina leaned her head against Conn's shoulder and waited for the denouncement she was sure would follow.

"I found something else on this journey." Conn's voice carried through the courtyard. "Trapped in the cavern with the monster and kept a prisoner was this young woman who was stolen from her murdered parents."

Murmurs of sympathy echoed from below. Gelina turned to Conn, the disbelief in her eyes meeting only compassion in his. She turned back to face the crowd, tears streaming down her face.

Conn placed a strong arm around her waist and continued, "We will make her welcome here." Mer-Nod frowned, noting an almost defensive note in Conn's voice. "The enemy of the people is dead! Let the celebration begin!"

As the crowd dispersed with a steady hum of joy, Conn pushed open the door and called to the plump woman who stood wringing her hands within the chamber, "Moira, fetch some broth." His eyes avoided Mer-Nod's as he swept up the girl in his arms and disappeared into the fortress.

There had been a warning in those eyes. Mer-Nod stood, his brow furrowed. Nimbus came racing up the stairs, and Mer-Nod put out a knee to block his passage.

"Get yer bloody leg off me, ye wretched owl! I'm going to see Conn."

"I think you should wait, Nimbus." Mer-Nod's eyes gleamed in speculation. "Let him be for a while."

Nimbus crossed his arms and leaned resolutely against the door, glaring at Mer-Nod. "Then ye're going to let him be, too."

The poet shook his head ruefully. "I think I would rather."

Gelina mumbled in her sleep as she tried to pull the coverlet wadded at her feet over her shivering body. It resisted her pull until she opened her eyes in vexation. She swallowed a shrill shriek as she met the twinkling brown eyes of a leprechaun with an equally strong grip on the thin linen. Coverlet twisted in his hands, he crouched at the end of the bed, a sly grin on his little face. Gelina could not say how much this upset her.

Gritting her teeth, she sank her nails into the coverlet and gave one immense jerk, sending it and the leprechaun flying over her head into the wooden headboard. She pondered the wisdom of her action as muffled curses arose from underneath the blanket and a small fist punched out to wave threateningly in the air. She crawled to the foot of the bed, fists clenched to bash the top of the squirming bundle if the need arose.

The waving fist became an outstretched hand as the coverlet was pulled back from the leprechaun's face, leaving a thick hood to ward off further attacks.

"And how do ye do? I am Nimbus, jester extraordinary. Pleased to make yer acquaintance." The words were spoken with great caution and more than a touch of sarcasm.

She was surprised to find the voice deep and pleasant. She took the outstretched hand and shrugged an apology.

"I thought you were a leprechaun seeking to do me mischief." She found her hand raised to the midget's lips and a genteel kiss planted upon it. She jerked it back. "Now that I think upon it, you were doing me mischief. Why wouldn't you let me sleep?"

It was his turn to shrug. "Ye have been sleeping for hours."

He pushed the blanket off his head. "I wanted ye to wake up and talk to me. Did ye know ye drool in yer sleep?"

Her mouth opened in an enraged circle. "I beg to differ with you, sir. I do not!"

"'Tis quite charming really. I drool sometimes when I'm awake." Nimbus patted the area beside him on the feather pillow. "Come sit with me. We can talk."

Eyes narrowed in mistrust, Gelina yawned and crawled to the head of the bed to sit beside the intruder. Her hands plucked at her woolen shift.

"It's too hot for wool. Perhaps he put it on me for punishment."

Hearing her mumbled words, Nimbus asked, "If 'tis too hot for wool, why were ye trying so desperately to get the blanket? And who is this cruel tyrant who would imprison ye in wool?"

Gelina gave him a guarded look. "You know—him. Your benevolent liege. Where is he now?"

"My benevolent liege is downstairs at the feast, being recognized as the hero he is," Nimbus replied, surveying her suspiciously.

"Ah, yes, my savior," Gelina said, irony coating her words like poisoned honey.

"He did save yer life. Ye seem rather ungrateful considering the circumstance of yer rescue."

"Yes," she said quietly. "He did save my life."

They sat in companionable silence for a few minutes, listening to the echoes of merriment that drifted up from the hall below.

"Shouldn't you be down there regaling the crowd with your wit?" she asked.

"Probably. Shouldn't ye?"

"I can't go down there. I am not a jester. I can't juggle or tell jokes." She wrinkled her nose in confusion.

"The crowd wants to see ye. They want to hear yer tales of captivity and murmur in sympathy over yer pale skin. Conn has refused all requests that ye join the celebration, saying only that ye are too ill and have suffered a memory lapse."

"He has, has he?" She took her bottom lip between her teeth, her curiosity piqued. "Find me something to wear. I'm famished."

His enthusiasm evaporated. "Wait a minute, lass. Ye're ill. I can't just prance ye down there against Conn's wishes."

"Surely he would be delighted to see his charge so quickly recovered. Jester, where is your sense of adventure?"

" 'Tis in me head, which I'd like to keep on me shoulders."

Her bottom lip protruded, and she stared sadly at the hands folded in her lap.

His lips curved upward. "Are ye truly hungry?"

"Starved. I've eaten nothing in a month." As his eyes widened, she amended, "Nothing in three days anyway."

"Conn sent yer garments to be burned but I'll go and filch something for ye to wear."

He clambered off the bed, sliding sideways until his feet touched the floor. Her smile spread to her eyes, lighting up their depths for the first time. Nimbus paused, dazzled by the promise of beauty that sparkled in her shadowed eyes.

"One question before I go." He reached up and took her hand in his. "Do ye have a name, princess?"

Her smile faded. "Anything but princess. You may call me Gelina. I am afraid my memory lapse has obliterated my clansname." She squeezed his hand and freed him to scurry off on his mission.

He returned with a bundle and a hasty whisper of instructions before leaving her alone. She slid out of the bed, every muscle in her body crying out in protest. Her hands clutched the wooden canopy, seeking to straighten her wobbly legs.

"Maybe Conn did not lie. Perhaps I am too ill," she murmured.

The very thought gave her the will to stand tall and straight. She slipped the woolen shift over her head and made her way naked to a huge mirror of polished silver that crouched in the corner. She reached out a tentative hand and touched the gilded frame. Five years had passed since she had seen beautiful metal like this. Her eyes were caught and held by her reflection.

She was pale. The bones stood out of her ribcage; the cheeks, which had been so pinchably fat in childhood, were sunken as if sculpted by her sharp cheekbones. Her auburn hair was short, barely covering her ears in front and just resting on the nape of her neck in back. It stood at attention in all directions. She turned and gingerly touched the wound on the back of her shoulder. Although still shiny, it had lost the scarlet of infection. She heard an echo of her own scream and saw blue eyes burning into hers. She closed her eyes and shuddered, moving her hand away from the wound.

Shaking her head in disgust, she examined the silk shift and dress that Nimbus had brought. She washed her face, combed water through her hair and reluctantly donned the offensive garments, wishing for a nice snug pair of breeches and her own leather jerkin. The dress fit poorly, hanging straight over her small bosom and missing the floor by several inches at the wide hem. She twirled in front of the mirror, nearly losing her balance as her knees betrayed her.

The sound of applause came from the door. She turned to find the midget's head poked shyly into the room. "Sorry about the fit. I fear Cook's daughter is as plump and short as ye are slender and tall."

"Slender is a kind word, sir. I fear I am skinny." She turned back to the mirror with a smirk. "Couldn't you find me any breeches?"

He choked. "I didn't look. Conn would have me head if I trotted ye down there in his breeches." He circled her. "Ye look . . . well . . . less deathlike."

"Thank you, leprechaun. 'Tis the sweetest compliment I've had in months. You have truly mastered the art of flattery."

"Bend over," he commanded.

She followed his instruction only to find what he could grasp of her cheeks pinched soundly between his fingers. She howled and straightened, shaking him loose.

Rubbing her cheeks, she said through clenched teeth, "What in curses are you doing?"

"If ye're going to convince Conn ye miraculously regained yer strength, ye must have some color in yer cheeks."

"I'm going to put some color around your eyes if you do that again," she threatened.

He looked truly offended, bowing his sandy head and sticking out his lower lip. She squatted beside him and placed his hands on her cheeks.

"Go on. I know you have my best interests at heart."

His smile was blinding. She stood still, allowing his ministrations as he fluffed up her hair with both hands and found a sash for the ill-fitting dress. Hiding a smile behind her hand, she watched as he combed his own hair and observed himself in the mirror. Straightening his jerkin, he turned to her and offered her an arm. She stretched out a hand and placed it on his arm, the most she could do from her height. They walked gracefully from the room.

Nimbus had not exaggerated. Crouching behind a curtain on a platform high above the crowd, Gelina watched the scene below with wide eyes and clenched fists. The hot heaviness of the day had been replaced by a cooling fog, and two blazing fires erupted from the immense fireplaces at both ends of the hall. The room was awash with golden light. Torches glowing yellow and orange lined the walls in golden sconces, their cheery light reflected by goblets, sword hilts, jewels, and gleaming golden plates. At one end of the hall, the hands of five jugglers blurred as they tossed swords, golden apples, and balls into the air with flawless rhythm.

"Child's play," Nimbus whispered. "I could do it blind-folded."

The cupbearers filled empty flagons with a never-ceasing flow of ale at the moment of another toast that lifted the goblets high in the air. Cheers echoed through the rafters. The servers struggled to keep the massive trestle tables against the wall groaning under their burden of stewed meats, boar's head, capons, and roast heron. Gelina's nose wrinkled at the rich, unfamiliar aroma of the steaming meats. Her stomach churned dangerously, its only memories of fish caught deep in the recesses of the cavern. She pressed her hands over her rumbling belly.

Deafening noise rose from the hall. The harps and mandolins struggled to make themselves heard over the din. A huge man in ragged clothing belted out a bawdy ditty about a wench named Kathleen that set Gelina's ears to burning. Finally the musicians conceded and joined in the tune. The crowd cheered. Jesters bounded in and out among the reeling dancers, mocking them with their acrobatics and ribald mime. Gelina watched in amazement as a huge pig pranced nonchalantly through the crowd, stood on his hind feet and began to dance a jig in the midst of the merriment.

"'Tis Murphy. 'Tis not a real pig," Nimbus assured her.

He watched her as her eyes were drawn to a table on a raised platform. The color in her cheeks paled as she recognized Conn in the central seat, head thrown back in laughter as he leaned toward a swarthy brunette whose hand rested intimately on his arm.

Gelina nudged him, nearly unbalancing his precarious stance. "His wife?"

Nimbus shook his head, feet shifting to regain his balance. "No wife. 'Tis Sheela, the Dark Rose, widow of Ryan Ó Brosnahan. She finds the king an ample comforter in her grief."

A green tint replaced her pallor as she recognized the name. Her gaze traced the table where Conn sat. Laughing, cheering, and raising their goblets in toast after toast were the king's favored men-at-arms. Tall and well built, a tilt to their heads that implied, demanded, and deserved respect, they sat like kings themselves, surrounding Conn in the full uniform of their station. Their long hair lay unbraided, loose and shining on their shoulders. Soft leather vests covered forest green shirts and breeches. Around each waist was draped a belt with a name burned indelibly into it.

Ó Murchada, Ó Brosnahan, MacRuairc, Ó hArtagain. The names burned indelibly into Gelina's brain and visions of empty chairs danced in her head.

"Take me back!" She stood, rapping her head sharply on the trapeze bar hanging from a peg. Panic flared in her eyes as Nimbus reached out a hand to steady her. "I said, take me back! Now! Please, Nimbus."

"What is it?" Nimbus gripped her elbow, seeking to lead her from the alcove.

Mistaking his tighter grip as an attempt to keep her trapped in view of the scene below, she whirled around to find herself tangled in the red velvet curtain that had been waiting for just this opportunity to loose itself from its moorings and fall to the floor below, covering several dancers and the pig named Murphy.

For the second time in that endless day, Gelina found all eyes upon her as the music slowed to a halt. The huge, rough-looking man belted out a few more stanzas about Kathleen until an even huger, rougher man clapped his hand over his mouth.

Conn stood slowly, his eyes locked on the tall, slender figure above them, every muscle in his body tensed. Gelina glanced at Nimbus to find his eyes as panicked as hers.

Recognizing the murderous look on Conn's face, Nimbus

flung out an arm with forced aplomb. "Ladies and gentlemen, may I have yer attention, please!"

He halted until the group below could extricate itself from the heavy curtain, the human pig poking forth a curious snout. Only Nimbus's hand propelling her forward prevented Gelina from fleeing.

"As ye know, we have a new guest at Tara." He gestured to Gelina. "A young lass who was rescued from great distress by our Ard-Righ."

A tentative cheer rose from the crowd as they turned to Conn, unsure of what their reaction should be. Conn sat down and began to stroke his beard in a motion Nimbus knew only too well.

He spoke faster. "This lovely damsel, even in her weakened condition and with little recollection of her ordeal, has requested to join us and add her tribute to ours." Strong applause greeted his words this time.

Gelina plastered a smile on her face even as she hissed out of the corner of her mouth, "You carry this too far, kind sir."

He muttered, "They love it. Trust me."

As the applause died down, Nimbus gestured toward the stairs they had ascended. Gelina had another thought. Reaching for the trapeze, the child in her emerged with a spark in her eye that Nimbus didn't recognize until it was too late. She hoisted herself on the narrow bar and sailed out over the crowd. Gasps greeted her as her dangling feet nearly brushed the heads of those below.

As she sailed back toward Nimbus, she cried out gaily, "They love it. Trust me."

The midget had covered his face and was peering cautiously between his fingers, waiting for the slam of her body on the floor below. The trapeze lost momentum; she ignored a blushing youth's outstretched hand and the twinge of pain in her shoulder and slid off the bar to the floor unassisted. A path cleared through the crowd, a path to the table where Conn sat, not moving a muscle.

With a deep breath she forced her bare feet to move. Anonymous hands reached out from the crowd to touch her arms and shoulders. She shied away, unsure of their motives until she realized there was wordless sympathy in the hands that propelled her toward the king. Stepping up on the dais, she flinched as the men of the Fianna stood at attention one by one. Conn was the last to stand, and she found herself leisurely studying his leather boots, unable to meet his gaze. He extended his hand, and she could sense from its rigidity that failure to take it would have severe repercussions.

His voice remained carefully neutral as he said for all to hear, "Welcome. Tara is your home for as long as you choose to remain here."

She took his hand in hers. Folding her long body to kneel on one knee, her eyes touched the impenetrable blue of his, and she saw the beads of sweat standing on his brow. She lowered her head, lifting his hand to her lips.

"My liege," she said clearly.

A throaty cheer traveled through the crowd, and only Gelina heard Conn's words as he leaned to her and murmured, "And your allegiance?"

Without giving her a chance to respond, Conn straightened and gestured for silence. "I seek private audience with our guest. Mer-Nod will accompany me."

He continued to grip Gelina's hand, pulling her out a side door as Mer-Nod separated himself from his company of poets and followed them. The brunette who had been seated next to Conn watched them go, a gleam in her dark eyes. Nimbus sat, legs dangling off the platform and face in his hands, wondering just what he'd done.

Chapter Five

❖

Gelina also wondered what they had done as she felt the firm grip of Conn's hand around her fingers. The room they entered was austerely decorated with a low wooden table flanked by two long benches. The only touch of luxury was a richly woven tapestry that graced the back wall. In the dim light Gelina could see faint images of violent battles etched with bloodred threads. A man followed them into the firelit room, pulling the heavy oak door shut behind him. Gelina recognized him as the man she had mistaken for some giant bird of prey on the watchtower.

Conn let go of her hand and left her standing awkwardly in the center of the room. He sat on the bench nearest her, his back to the table, arms crossed. The man in the feathered mantle stood beside him. For an instant Gelina thought she saw a flicker of sympathy in his dark eyes.

"That was a charming little stunt you pulled, warrior. Just what were you trying to prove? I've been around Nimbus long enough to know when he's improvising, especially when he does it as rapidly and as badly as he did tonight," Conn said, his voice hard.

"Don't blame him. I rather charmed him into the whole idea. He tried to dissuade me."

Conn snorted. "I didn't know you were capable of charming. What did you do—hold a knife to his throat and threaten to cut his head off?"

Blinking in alarm, Gelina glanced at the man who stood beside Conn.

Conn answered her silent question. "He knows. This is Mer-Nod. He is the chief poet and judge of Tara and the ear of wisdom who will help me reach a decision about you."

The finality of his words initiated a shiver, which crawled from the base of her spine to the hair on her scalp. Noticing her imperceptible shudder, Conn gestured to the bench opposite him.

Gelina walked around the table and sat directly across from him. "Let the trial begin," she said caustically, locking her hands together to conceal their sudden trembling.

Conn stood and paced the length of the room, coming to a halt in front of the tapestry.

Turning to Gelina, he said, "I need to know everything you remember about your family. Leave no detail untold."

"Why don't you tell me everything you remember about my family?"

"I asked you first."

He could not miss the insolent tilt of her chin. "My father was a king," she replied.

He snorted. "Every peasant with two pigs and a parcel of land claimed himself king before my reign." He threw himself down on the bench across from her.

Her eyes flashed. "My father was not a peasant. We lived in a beautiful castle filled with laughter and music. We had more than pigs. We had jugglers and jesters and minstrels and a thousand pleasant ways to pass the time. My father's hospitality was legendary."

Conn passed his hand briefly over his eyes as if her words troubled him. "Go on," he commanded.

She smiled bitterly. "One visitor came often and feasted well. He was young and always laughing, so Rodney christened him the man with the laughing blue eyes. He brought my brother a small sword and sheath and he brought me a gem to match my eyes." Those emerald eyes met Conn's, and for a fleeting second the hint of a real smile softened her lips. "Aside from my father, I thought you were the kindest, most handsome man in all the world."

Conn and Mer-Nod exchanged a glance before Conn rested his head on his hands, rubbing his throbbing temples with tense fingers.

The smile that had transformed her face tightened into a sneer. "Then one day you quit coming. Everyone quit coming or went away. My mother cried, and my father locked himself away and refused to see any of us. It was winter before anyone came back. Rodney and I were playing in one of the secret compartments off the main hall. Nobody cared what we did anymore. We heard a banging at the main door so fierce I thought it was thunder. The door burst open and hundreds of men ran into the hall. The man with the laughing blue eyes had returned. Only his eyes were not laughing anymore.''

She hugged herself, fingers digging into the tender flesh of her arms until it reddened and began to purple. Conn did not move.

"We watched. You forced our father to his knees, slapped him, said terrible things. Then you left on your big black horse." Her words fell like chips of ice in the silent room. "Rodney held his hand over my mouth so I would not scream when they beheaded my father. The men . . . hurt my mother again and again. Then they embedded a sword in her breast. The one jester that remained was tortured and hung from the rafters until his legs stopped kicking. When the men fled with my father's head hanging from one of their bridles, we took his sword and ran until we came to the cave.''

Conn sat unmoving, his head still buried in his hands. Mer-Nod stood mesmerized at her bitter words. Gelina continued to stare, eyes focused on a dark fog in a distant cave. The fresh pain of Rodney's death pounded over her in waves.

Conn stood and went around to face her, placing his hands on her shoulders until the spell was broken and she looked up as if in surprise at his presence.

He spoke, his voice low and firm. "I want you to listen to me. While I speak, I do not want you to reject or accept what I tell you. Just listen. Will you do that?''

She felt unbearably weary. Her wound began to ache, and she gave in to the firm pressure on her shoulders. She nodded, seeing for the first time through her haze of exhaustion the lines of laughter and kindness on his face.

"Your father was a traitor," he said. Her eyes darkened, and he squeezed her arms, silently reminding her of their agreement. She did not speak. "It was true that he was a dear friend to me at one time until I came to realize that to leave your back unguarded to Rory Ó Monaghan was an open invitation for his sword to dine on your backbone. Even his peasants deserted him when they found his promises empty and his protection inept. He betrayed me more than once. I accepted his stammered excuses for as long as I could. But the time for retribution had come and gone.''

Gelina looked away, but he took her chin in his hand and forced her to meet his gaze. "I never said he was not a good father. I did not order him killed or your mother . . . hurt and killed. I wanted them taken and brought to me. But this was before the days of the Fianna, and the men I left that day were a little careless and very bloodthirsty. The men under my charge now would never have committed the atrocities you describe."

Her eyes met his unflinchingly. "Were they punished?"

It was his turn to look away. "'Twas a less civilized time. Many brutal acts went unpunished."

The gleam of triumph in her eyes reminded him eerily of the look he had seen glittering from underneath the cowl of the cave fiend. Anger tightened his jaw.

"Do not forget you are a murderess yourself, my precious little princess. You killed innocent men, some with wives and children. You killed them in unfair fights, cutting out their hearts and leaving them to rot in the woods. Do you know that Kyle MacRuairc was found with his hand still clutching his sword? But the hand was not attached to his wrist anymore."

Gelina shook her head, eyes glazed. "I did not . . . I could not . . ."

Mer-Nod cleared his throat meaningfully, and Conn took his hand off her face, leaving two angry spots where he had gripped her.

He swallowed his anger and took her hands. "Then your brother did it. I know what he meant to you, but he is dead and you are free of him. You can go on with your life, Gelina."

Her confused eyes fixed on his face in a mute plea.

He stood abruptly and began to pace again, unprepared for the jolt of emotion her desperation gave him.

"Have you ever heard of the Lex Talionis, Gelina?" Mer-Nod asked.

She nodded, then shook her head. "I've heard of it. I know 'tis a law. But I know not what it concerns."

"'Tis a law," Mer-Nod said. "A law established by Conn's father, Feidlimid Rechtmar, who was known as the Lawgiver. The Lex Talionis gives one man the right to extract vengeance from another in equal portion according to the severity of the wrongdoing."

"An eye for an eye," she murmured.

Conn knelt in front of her, his large fingers softly caressing her hands. "I have a proposition for you. You blame me for the deaths of your family—and perhaps rightly so. I blame you for the deaths of my men. According to the Lex Talionis, justice has been served. If I took your family from you, it is my duty to replace them. I will become your fosterer. You will live here as my honored charge and grow to womanhood."

She stared at him without comprehension.

"There is one condition," he added. "You must swear allegiance to me here and now. And you must mean it. If your words are empty like your father's were, your fate will be the same. I will not be constantly looking over my shoulder waiting for your dagger to slide between my shoulder blades. I will not tolerate it and I will not tolerate your betrayal. You are young. Your scars can heal here as my charge. You will have the best care I can afford you. But I must have your pledge here tonight with Mer-Nod as our witness. Then I will introduce you to my court. You will be greatly honored. You may speak."

Gelina was silent. In a dark choice between blood ties and life, only one question surfaced in her mind. "And if I refuse your offer?"

The two men exchanged glances. It was Mer-Nod who spoke, his well-modulated voice outlining her fate dispassionately. "You will be sent tonight on a ship bound for Britain, banished forever from Erin. Conn cannot afford traitors at Tara, but has agreed to let you leave alive if you choose."

Conn stood and lowered his head in defeat, anticipating her decision. She stood, her eyes on Conn's bowed head with an odd sensation of sympathy.

For the second time that night, she knelt on the wooden floor, brought his warm surprised hand to her lips and murmured, "My liege." His other hand cupped her chin, raising her eyes to meet his. "And my allegiance."

Chapter Six

❖

Visions danced like mist in the corridors of her dreams. Tall, strong, a fiery sword of retribution clutched in her hand, she towered over the heads of her enemies, her brother's strong shoulders gripped beneath her legs. Wielding Vengeance like the natural extension of her hand that it had become, she swung again and again, hacking and stabbing at hordes of featureless blue-eyed warriors until the blood ran like a river over the floor of the cavern. Too much blood. Her exultant battle cry turned into something else as Rodney swayed beneath her, his feet slipping in the gore. No. Rodney never stumbled, never faltered. He had borne her weight like his own for hours and days and years. He would never, ever drop her.

The foundation of her life vanished, and she was falling. Down, down, a thousand leagues into blackness, a moment suspended in time until the river of blood sucked her into a hazy world, tinged with pink.

Her brother swung her around and around. Sparkling black eyes, raven black hair, his warm hands clasping hers as they danced in the great hall of their father's castle. He swung her faster, his grin widening with each turn. She was ten years old and she was afraid.

She wanted to beg him to stop but knew he would laugh and chide her for being a baby. She knew also that the back of his hand would reach out and gently wipe away the tears caused by his taunts and almost make it worth it. But not quite. So her tiny bare feet crunched over the floor, the fear growing with each step. The room whirled in a swirl of color and light, Rodney's hands the only solid thing in a treacherously changing landscape. A rush of vertigo attacked her, and her eyes found the floor in a silent prayer to stop the spinning of her stomach.

The sweet smelling floor rushes had vanished. Human bones,

bleached and ancient, carpeted the floor from wall to wall, the brittle fragments cutting her feet to bloody ribbons.

A scream was ripped from her throat as bone rose and joined bone in a creaking, macabre dance of death until an army of skeletal warriors faced her, swords dripping blood held in clattering fingers. Her eyes traced the path from her arms to Rodney's fingers but found the hands she clasped to be bony appendages devoid of flesh. Her brother's jawbone dropped open and shrill laughter rolled forth, raising the gooseflesh on her arms. Dark blue eyes glistened from deep within the void of his eyesockets and she screamed and screamed and could not stop.

Conn was strolling toward his chambers laughing at the jests of the two soldiers who flanked him when the terrified screams reached his ears. He paused, then broke into a run. His men followed, swords drawn.

He burst into the room, his eyes searching the shadows. The dim glow of the half moon through the open window revealed an empty bed, a twisted coverlet. His eyes found Gelina, and he thought briefly that he would give his kingdom never to see that look on her face again.

She crouched in the farthest corner, eyes wide but unseeing, long tallow candle gripped in both hands like the hilt of a sword.

"Leave us," he curtly commanded his men.

They exchanged a look, sheathed their swords with some reluctance, and backed out of the room. Conn did not spare them a second glance. He knew they would obey.

"Gelina," he said softly, approaching with one hand outstretched.

Her eyes focused on him with all the desperation of a trapped animal. Her fear was a palpable, terrible thing and he flinched at the intensity of it.

She hurled the candle with both hands, and he thought with a chill that if it had been a sword, it would have gone right through the arm he raised to ward it away. In two strides he covered the distance between them and caught her wrists in his hands, gently but with strength. He wanted to avoid a full-fledged brawl at all costs. His men had withdrawn from the chamber, but he knew they waited in the corridor outside, speculating on the girl's curious behavior.

The flatness in her eyes warned him that she saw him but did not see him. Before she could open her mouth to scream again, he pulled her face into his shoulder and rocked back and forth on his knees until he felt the resistance leave her body. The air left his own body when her arms crept up to encircle his neck and he felt the tears soak through the linen of his tunic. He stroked her shoulders, feeling the tensed muscles relax beneath his fingertips.

Her words were muffled into his chest. "I was afraid."

"Nightmares again?" he murmured.

She nodded. He scooped her up in his arms and deposited her on the feather mattress, the lightness of her body compared to its length surprising him anew. She pulled away from him as soon as her body touched the bed. The last traces of the nightmare left her eyes, and a look of annoyance passed over her brow only to be replaced by a poorly concealed look of dread.

She sat up and wiped her nose with the back of her hand. An unfamiliar desire to protect mingled with exasperation as he saw that the dress she had worn for the evening had been replaced by a faded jerkin and well-worn breeches.

"I feel better. Thank you. You may go," she said, her polite smile stopping just short of her eyes.

Conn raised an eyebrow. "Am I being dismissed?"

She shrugged. "Can one dismiss a king without the risk of execution?"

He suppressed a sigh. "If I was going to execute you for dismissing me or avoiding me, I would have had a multitude of opportunities in the past few weeks."

"I swore my allegiance, sire, not my affection," she said, her voice sounding childish and shrill. She cleared her throat.

Conn leaned forward with his hands on both sides of her legs. Squirming sideways only brought her closer to his muscled forearms. Gelina found it impossible to resist his level gaze. The moonlight disarmed the more dangerous planes of his face, softening the fluid lines into a loving concern that set her heart to hammering against her ribs.

"I want to be your friend, Gelina," he said softly.

She stared at a spot just below his beard. "And I suppose you're accustomed to having what you want."

Conn recoiled from her acid tone with a noise that sounded suspiciously like a growl and ran a hand through his hair. She settled back with reluctance on the pillows as he made no move to leave. Locking her hands together, she surveyed him through veiled eyes, their brightness shadowed by the thick fringe of lashes that framed them.

"I meant no offense, sire. But I can hardly expect you to neglect your raping and pillaging to amuse a homeless waif."

Conn exhaled through pursed lips, torn between the desire to laugh or box her ears. "I am sorry to disappoint you but neither I nor the Fianna indulge in raping or pillaging. Rapine and mayhem have sadly lost their charms for the Fianna."

"How tragic for you!"

Conn dropped all pretense of forced politeness and laughed. "You are a contrary little wretch, aren't you?"

Gelina blinked sweetly. "If it pleases my king to think me so. Does His Highness believe he can correct such a fault?"

"Well." Conn stroked his beard. "I dare say I cannot beat it out of you, for that would only enhance your dreadful expectations of me. Roll over on your stomach, please."

Her eyes widened in alarm at his sudden command. "Pardon me?"

"Don't fret. I've no intention of taking my hand to your backside, however much you might deserve it. I want to see your wound."

With a scowl Gelina rolled to her stomach and rested her head on her arms. Conn's hands deftly stripped the jerkin from her shoulder. Gelina flinched at his touch, acutely conscious of the muscled thigh pressed against her hip. His thumb gently brushed her shoulder, and she wondered how many enemies those powerful hands had throttled.

"Must you quiver like a frightened rabbit?"

She glared at him over her shoulder. He caught her gaze and held it until she was forced to look away.

"I'm not frightened of anything," she said, her chin protruding imperceptibly.

Conn hid his smile behind a cough. His fingers gently traced the raised scar that had slowly faded to healthy pink.

"I nearly skewered your heart, Gelina. I shiver to the bone to think of it," he murmured, more to himself than her.

Gelina closed her eyes for a moment, shaken. In unspoken agreement, neither of them had mentioned the cavern. Anyone who dared to question her about her past bit back their words quickly, silenced by the blue ice in Conn's eyes.

His fingers lightly massaged the taut skin around the scar. "If your brother hadn't turned his back on me when I wounded him, you could have dodged my blow, couldn't you? How did you see through the cloak?" he asked.

"I beat the cloak against the rocks until it was sheer. We kept the torches in front of us. And you didn't wound my brother. You killed him," she added flatly.

"You're very adept with a sword," Conn said, ignoring her last statement. His fingers glided over a shoulder blade that was losing its jutting angles to become gently rounded. "It must have taken years of practice to get that good."

"Time was never something we lacked." Gelina pushed a stray curl out of her eyes and stared over her shoulder at him. "I practiced and practiced until I believed I could beat any warrior without the illusion of being a monster or a giant."

"Do you still believe that?"

She could not be sure if it was a challenge she saw in his level gaze but she met it with candor. "Yes."

A cool breeze from the open window lifted the hair from Gelina's scalp. The companionable silence between them deepened as the flat of Conn's palm rubbed away the last tense hints of the nightmare from the nape of her neck.

Her voice softened under his tender ministrations. "Your hospitality has been generous. Forgive me if I displeased you, milord."

Conn searched for any trace of sarcasm in her words but found none. His hand wandered down her back with a will of its own, tracing each bump and hollow of her spine with the pad of his thumb. The silky flesh rose and fell beneath his hand. He knew she was a breath away from slumber. The folds of the jerkin halted his dazed exploration, and he was reaching to draw it down farther when he realized what he was doing. He stared at his trembling hands.

He jumped to his feet as if catapulted off the feather mattress. "There is no need to address me as milord," he said, his voice sounding strained and imperious even to his own ears. "You may call me Conn."

Gelina threw herself onto her back, her temper not improved at being bounced away from a promise of a sleep untainted by nightmares and protected by the soothing warmth of his hands. "Do I fail you at anything else, milord? Eating or breathing perhaps?"

His laughter rolled out in hearty waves, dispelling the tension between them. "From what I've seen, you eat like a piglet. You're already starting to fill out."

He brushed the back of his hand across her soft cheek, and she struggled to hide a real smile. "You have Nimbus to thank. He threatens me with a song and dance unless I eat a dozen oatcakes a day."

"I would grow fat myself to avoid his squawking and gallumphing," he agreed.

His eyes traveled the room, and he frowned as if displeased at the scarred table and straight-backed chair he found. Ashes grown cold winters ago were heaped in the dusty fireplace. Cobwebs festooned the low rafters. His foot tapped on the wooden floor to hide the unfamiliar tension that stretched his body taut.

"Tomorrow night," he said, "meet me in the great hall. I will teach you to play chess. I believe you will like it. It involves much warring and conquering."

"I'm familiar with the game. My father had many formidable chess opponents."

From somewhere in the mists of his memory, Conn remembered an inquisitive pair of tiny green eyes peering over an elaborately carved chessboard. "So he did," he murmured, squeezing her hand before walking to the door.

He opened the door. The torches from the corridor threw his face into light as he turned back to her.

"You cannot stifle your smiles forever, Gelina. My charm is almost as renowned as my fighting abilities."

"And your humility?"

"Equally legendary." He bowed deeply from the waist and stepped into the hall with a wink, pulling the door shut behind him.

Conn would have been gratified to see the smile that played around her lips as she rolled to her side and pulled the coverlet over her shoulders. He leaned against her door for a long time, waiting for the hint of a whimper or moan from the silent room and afraid to admit that he was disappointed when none came.

Gelina awoke the next morning with a sated yawn and a catlike stretch that pulled her muscles past the boundaries of comfort and back again. It never ceased to amaze her that the first waking breath that filled her lungs didn't reek of the damp, stale air of the cave. The sunlit room resounded with the early morning birdsongs of larks and robins.

She sat up and threw her long legs over the side of the bed, starting as her feet were cushioned on soft wool instead of meeting the chill resistance of hard wood. Rubbing her eyes, she peered around the room, wondering if dreams still pursued her.

A fire blazed cheerily on the hearth, the morning chill eaten away by the blazing logs. She rose from the bed, sinking her toes into the luxuriant faces of sneering slant-eyed warriors that decorated the rug beside the bed. Her feet carried her to the wooden table in the corner to find its splintered top covered with a brightly flowered tablecloth. Steaming pastries dripping apples and peaches and smeared with honey sat on a golden platter. She poked one curious finger into a pastry and brought it to her mouth, savoring the sweetness that coated her tongue.

On the chest beside the earthenware basin and pitcher lay an ivory brush and comb she had never seen before. She picked up the brush and tugged it through the rumpled hair just starting to curl at the nape of her neck.

Peeking behind an ornate screen that blocked off a corner of the chamber, she discovered a tub full of warm, scented bathwater poured by some silent servant while she slept. Without hesitation she slipped off the jerkin and stepped into the tub, crinkling her nose at the overwhelming scent of gardenias. She sank into the water, her eyes closing.

One hand reached around to touch the wound on her back in unwitting imitation of Conn's caress. She twisted to look at her image in the mirror. The scar had faded like the memories of her nightmare. Only Conn's kindness seemed tangible in the bright morning sunshine of the cozy bedchamber.

She dried herself and donned one of the simple cotton dresses hanging behind another screen. The material hung gracefully on her tall frame. She folded the leather breeches Nimbus had stolen from a sleeping soldier at his own loudly proclaimed danger to life and limb and placed them under her pillow. Conn would be pleased to see her wearing the dress. It was suddenly important to please him.

She wound her way through the corridors of the fortress. The sun shining through the unshuttered windows cast delicate patterns on the whitewashed walls. She hummed softly and whirled around, delighting in the unfamiliar way the skirt billowed around her ankles. The tune caught in her throat as a hulking figure appeared in front of her.

The face was in shadow but there was no mistaking the ragged braids billowing out from his head. He stood over six feet and seven inches tall, with one fist outstretched. Gelina backed speechless against the wall.

Stepping from shadow into the sunshine-checkered area of the corridor, the apparition spoke. "Don't be afraid, lass. I brought you these." His gentle brogue belied his size.

For the first time she saw clutched in his hairy paw a dainty bouquet of azaleas.

She reached out a trembling hand to take them as he said, "My name is Goll MacMorna. I'm the chieftain of the Fianna. Remember my name if you should need me." Ducking his head shyly, he disappeared down the corridor as silently as he had appeared.

"Thank you," she mumbled as she slid down the wall to a sitting position, her hands clutching the sweetly scented wild-flowers.

She lay awake in her chambers that night staring blindly into the darkness. The memory of her nightmare reached out with icy fingers to pluck at the strings of her guilt. Rodney, his black eyes accusing and furious, seemed to stare back from the dark.

She was surrounded by the Fianna, was well-fed and clothed by the very man they had sworn to destroy. Her days were spent with Nimbus in merriment and game playing until she fell exhausted into the carved mahogany bed imported from a land she had never seen.

And Conn. The blue-eyed monster they had hated until they were blind and sick with it. He had been everywhere she had turned in that long day, seeking her out for a tour of the stables, excusing himself from Sheela for a hasty chess lesson. She found her tongue and her shyness gradually loosening beneath the obvious delight he took in her company, the gentle nurturing he gave their friendship. What would Rodney say?

She answered the question aloud the only way she knew how. "He can't see me. He can't."

The thick, sweet scent of azaleas wafted through the room as she drifted into sleep.

From the hill overlooking the courtyard, Barron Ó Caflin watched the scene below, his nose wrinkled in disgust. The sound of laughter floated up to him as he shifted position on his horse. The midget and the brat had rigged an outdoor trapeze from a heavy, wooden post that stretched over the courtyard. The fool gestured wildly with his hands, trying to coax the girl to somersault off the safe perch to the hay below.

Barron's scowl deepened as his gaze fell on the dark-haired man who leaned against a bale of hay with arms crossed, his head thrown back in laughter. His tunic lay discarded in the hay. He wore only his leather breeches. With his white teeth flashing against his dark beard and swarthy skin, the king of Erin looked as earthy as any peasant on a hot summer day.

Barron watched as the laughing girl gained momentum, the swing sailing higher into the air with each pass. He wished the rope would break, leaving her to sail into the air and smash against the side of the barn. She balked once, catching herself with her knees to prevent the somersault. The midget tugged at his hair in frustration. Conn taunted him until he smiled. Starting again, the girl completed the somersault, coming to land in the soft hay on her feet for an instant and then tumbling to her knees, barely missing the midget. Conn applauded and said something that sent them both into gales of laughter. They tugged him into the hay, clutching their stomachs.

Barron spurred his horse toward the north, loathing the cozy scene below. He had no eye for the beauty of the day. The gorse's yellow blooms were trampled under the horse's hooves without a glance. He had watched the orphan grow from an emaciated waif who seldom smiled to a laughing girl whose fattening cheeks were flush with color.

He snorted in disgust. There was something amiss with the foundling, and he knew it. The strange tension between her and Conn on the night she had been presented to court sent needles of suspicion up and down his spine. Only an idiot would have missed it. Conn had made it clear that she would be treated as his daughter. The arrogant bastard gave no explanation.

Barron did offer one snippet of prayer to the druid gods he so casually worshiped. He gave thanks that Conn's mysterious orphan was a girl. Had she been a lad and suitably strong, she might have presented a challenge to the throne once Conn met his imminent fate. As it was, she was only a nuisance. He also gave thanks that no bastards had crept out of the countryside to claim the king as their sire.

Since Mer-Nod had revealed his knowledge of these rides, Barron had arranged for one of Eoghan's men to meet him in the north at the tiny village of Ballybay. He rode into the village with an imperious nod for the peasants he passed. The sun felt warm on his golden hair as he dismounted before the limewashed tavern. A sign hanging from the eaves creaked in the wind. A wolf's head, its shaggy fur matted with blood, grinned at him from the sign. He smiled back, his grin not unlike the wolf's.

Tossing the reins over a post, he swaggered into the tavern and slowly made his way to the farthest table, allowing his eyes to adjust to the shadowy gloom. Blinking in surprise, he saw two figures sitting at the table instead of one. His eyes nervously traveled the long cloak and hood surrounding the stranger. He glanced at the man he knew, a question in his eyes.

Standing, the large man gestured toward the stranger who kept his head bowed. "Eoghan sent him. He wanted you to meet. You'll be working together in the next few months."

The thin figure slipped the hood back, and Barron found himself staring into the blackest eyes he had ever seen.

Chapter Seven

❖

Gelina cursed softly as the knotted embroidery unraveled in her hands for the fourth time. Conn dropped the map he was studying and gently tugged one of her auburn curls. She grinned up at him, softening his rebuke to a hopeless shake of his head. He raised the map to hide his face, and Gelina shifted at his feet until her skirts wadded beneath her and her tanned and knobby knees poked out on both sides. Nimbus muttered to himself a few feet away, rendered immobile by the bright skeins of multihued thread Gelina had wrapped around his hands and feet.

"I detest sewing," she wailed, making a great show of dropping the long, golden needle in her cushion and being unable to find it.

"Me, too," growled Nimbus, gnawing at the threads tangled around his elbows.

"I cannot begin to understand why Moira insists on teaching me the womanly arts when I've proved I'm totally inept." Gelina arced a crimson loop of thread around Nimbus's neck in an attempt to rescue him but only succeeded in tightening it around his throat. She ignored his tiny gagging noises and turned hopeful eyes to Conn. "Isn't there some useful task I could set my hands to? Perhaps I could rub your boots or sharpen your dagger?"

Conn did not lower the map. "My boots are soft, thank you, and my dagger in your lovely paws is not a sight I care to see."

A log crashed on the hearth in a shower of sparks. Conn lowered the parchment to find Gelina staring into the leaping flames. The firelight cast pensive shadows across her face, banishing all traces of insolence and softening the sharpness of her features. He frowned, strangely discomfited by the fleeting glimpse of the woman she would become. He leaned forward and tilted her chin with his callused fingers. The green eyes that met his shone with such utter trust and lack of reproach that Conn felt his heart wrench and remorse flooded him.

"Forgive me. I spoke in haste," he said, his voice a caress soft enough to elude even Nimbus's practiced ears.

"I dare say 'tis rude to whisper when a fellow can't even sidle close enough to overhear," Nimbus said, bursting from his bonds with a jerk that sent thread flying through the air.

Conn picked a strand of green from Gelina's hair with a wink. "I was just telling Gelina of a task that might be more to her liking. The festival of Midsummer is only a few days away. As soon as the goldsmith finishes beating out my mask, I shall need a fierce face painted upon it."

Gelina sat up and seized his knees. "Oh, Conn, a masked revelry? But I suppose I shall be too busy with my own mask to paint yours. Perhaps Nimbus could do the honors."

Conn's dark eyebrows drew together. Gelina sank back on her heels with a disappointed sigh.

"I am sorry, my dear," Conn said, "but the festival has been known to sink into chaos and rapacious merriment after the first few hundred kegs are tapped and drank."

"Indeed it has," Nimbus agreed with obvious delight. "I remember last year when Colum the beekeeper woke up with the masked beauty he had thrown over his shoulder and carried off to the woods only to discover he had bedded his own wife. And enjoyed it, no less. I don't know who was more . . ."

Nimbus sputtered to a stop as Conn cleared his throat. Gelina pulled her rapt gaze from Nimbus with reluctance, hoping he would finish his tale when they were away from Conn's disapproving gaze.

"So you see, Gelina," Conn said, "a young girl roaming Tara on the Eve of Midsummer would be easy prey for a prowling satyr."

"Like yerself, sire?" Nimbus said sincerely.

"Yes, like my . . ." Conn shot Nimbus a glare. "As I was saying—you may join in the games of the day but by nightfall I want you safely in your chamber with the door locked like a good child."

The set of Gelina's jaw warned Conn that he had blundered.

"I don't know why you persist in treating me like a child. Why Cook says I'm far too old to be fostered!"

Conn raised an eyebrow. "Cook told you that?"

"Well . . . no. She told one of the serving girls when I was underneath the tablecloth waiting for the tarts to come out of the kiln."

Conn glanced at Nimbus, who stared pointedly at the rafters. "Do honor us with the remainder of Cook's wisdom."

Gelina's anger faded beneath Conn's level gaze, but it was too late to bite back her words. "She said that most girls my age are betrothed or married. Or kept."

Conn stroked his beard. "Kept?"

"Kept," she said forcefully to hide the fact that she didn't have the faintest inkling of the word's meaning.

Conn steepled his fingers under his chin. "And would you care to be betrothed or married, Gelina?"

"Oh, no. I suppose I'd have to wear dresses all the time then." Her hands plucked at the threads in her lap. "I don't suppose being kept would be dreadful if you were kept by the proper person. Would you keep me, Conn?"

Conn caught Nimbus's bright-eyed gaze over her bowed head. The hand that reached to cup the curve of her cheek was withdrawn before she ever saw it.

A stern frown deepened the lines around his eyes. "I would keep you safely in your chambers on the Eve of Midsummer. Do you understand?"

"Yes, milord," Gelina said, bowing her head in demure surrender. She gave Nimbus a sidelong glance from beneath her lowered eyelashes.

Nimbus scrambled to his feet, still scattering bits of thread. He bowed. "If ye would excuse me, sire, I believe I shall retire. It proves to be a busy morrow."

Nimbus paused at the door, his eyes drawn back to the tranquil scene before the hearth. The fire bathed Gelina's face in its gentle glow as she bowed her head to the task of picking out the tangled stitches. Conn's hand stroked the soft cap of curls that had sprouted from her cropped hair. Nimbus had to strain to hear his murmured words.

"Do not think me too harsh, Gelina. I would never forgive myself if more harm came to you."

Conn returned his attention to the map, his hand still toying with one of Gelina's tousled curls. Nimbus blinked and turned away from the halo of light that held them, his brow furrowed. He slipped into the shadows of the hall, tucking his small hands deep into the pockets of his jerkin.

The shadows of darkness fell on the warm and windy Midsummer's Eve. Gelina opened her door a crack and peered into the torchlit corridor. Her eyes dropped to the horned apparition standing outside her door. Two ragged holes in a linen sheet revealed an ear and an unblinking brown eye. The eye traveled Gelina's costume; the sheet rustled with a disapproving shake that set the tiny bells on top of the horns to tinkling.

"'Twill never do," came Nimbus's muffled voice from beneath the sheet. "I did hope that disguising ye as a girl was well thought."

"I am a girl, Nimbus."

"Oh. Sorry."

Gelina spread her red velvet cloak in a sarcastic curtsy. "Your mastery of flattery blooms with each passing day." She stepped into the corridor, pulling the door shut behind her.

Nimbus circled her slowly, grunting and mumbling beneath the sheet. "'Tis your height I fear will give ye away. Try squatting."

Gelina bent her knees beneath the heavy folds of the cloak and waddled a few steps down the corridor.

The bells tinkled with renewed violence. "No, no, no. Ye put one in mind of a crippled goose."

She straightened with hands on hips. "I'm certain that no one will recognize you, either. Perhaps they will mistake you for Goll MacMorna or Large Bob the butcher." She jerked his sheet around until the ragged eyeholes revealed part of his nose and the other twinkling eye. She sighed. "I suppose we shall get no better than this."

At the sound of throaty giggling on the stairs, Nimbus scurried to the landing and waved her forward. "Just remember," he whispered, "keep yer hood up and yer head down."

Gelina drew the velvet hood over her hair until it met the thin, beaten gold of the mask resting on the tip of her nose. She glided after Nimbus with head bowed. They slid past the merging shadows on the steps and found themselves jostled into the laughing crowd in the great hall.

The torches melted into their sconces as night fell, leaving the great hall a shadowy and alien world where masked and cloaked strangers floated with mysterious grace. Gelina and Nimbus moved around them, careful to stay on the perimeter of the crowd lest they be recognized.

Gelina nudged Nimbus as they were drawn into a boisterous circle of men. "They play a game, Nimbus," she whispered. "Conn gave me his leave to play games."

The bells tinkled violently. "These were not the games he spoke of."

Gelina scanned the inner circle, peering around the cloak of a soldier. "What is its object? Why do the women stand around like sheep, giggling and blushing?"

"If the man with the blindfold touches them, they must surrender a kiss," Nimbus explained. "And if he guesses their name after that kiss, they must surrender another."

"I have no desire to play that game. Why I'd stomp any man who dared to kiss me," Gelina declared passionately.

"Ye'd be hard put to stomp that one," Nimbus said, his sheet shaking suspiciously.

For the first time Gelina's gaze fell on the man prowling the inner circle with hands outstretched. A coarse linen blindfold covered his mask and his cloak was that of a peasant but there was no mistaking his deep laughter as one of the soldiers caught his shoulders and spun him around in a dizzying circle. Gelina's mouth fell open.

"See how the demure widow Ó Brosnahan keeps leaping in front of him while pretending to stand still," Nimbus hissed.

"If he sees us, we're done for," Gelina said.

Conn's hands came within an inch of Sheela's craning neck. Gelina tugged on one of Nimbus's horns.

Nimbus resisted her pull. "He cannot see us. He's blindfolded."

A soldier stepped forward to spin Conn, ignoring his laughing protests. The soldier in front of Gelina raised a drinking horn to his lips. As his head tilted to drain the last drop of ale, his body followed in a perfect arc. He crashed to the floor to the

cheers and jeers of the crowd. Gelina was still staring at his
snoring visage when Conn stumbled out of the circle. His wiry
fingers closed around her wrist.

"She was not in the game but she is now," shouted a man,
raising his goblet in a sloshing toast.

Nimbus groaned and Gelina caught a glimpse of Sheela's
pout as Conn drew her into the circle.

"At last, I've captured a beauty," Conn cried in triumph.

Her body stiffened as his hands closed on her shoulders. She
considered fainting but knew she would be unmasked or worse if
she slid to the floor. The crowd cheered as Conn cupped her
face and leaned forward. He paused as if he sensed something
deeper than reticence in her tense posture. Gelina closed her
eyes as his warm, dry lips brushed hers, lingering with a
paralyzing sweetness that drew the breath from her trembling
body.

She would have fled when he drew away if his hands had not
dropped to her shoulders and tightened their grip.

"Name her, Conn," shouted a soldier. "Have you tasted her
before?"

"Name her and taste her again," came another cry.

"Who are you?" Conn breathed so softly that only she heard
his words.

"Name her or free her, Conn. Them's the rules."

Gelina sagged in Conn's arms as she recognized Nimbus's
voice. Conn's hands cupped her elbows to steady her and she
jerked away, dodging the hands that reached for her. She darted
through the crowd, knowing that by the time Conn unworked
his blindfold, she would be gone. She heard the patter of
running feet and glanced down to find Nimbus at her side. They
spilled out of the fortress into the warm summer night.

Bonfires sprang up around the courtyard, whipped into
chaotic flame by the warm winds racing in from the plains.
Leaping shadows cavorted around the fires to the sultry beat of a
drum.

Gelina pressed herself to the wall, trying to steady her
breathing and cool her burning cheeks.

"Forgive me, Gelina. I meant to put ye in no peril," Nimbus
said, collapsing beside her.

She shook her head with a shaky laugh. " 'Twasn't your fault,

Nimbus. The games of the Fianna have always proved too dangerous for me."

Nimbus jerked his head toward the door. "They may pursue us. Follow me."

Gelina followed him along the bushes, unable to pull her eyes away from the leering masks and flapping capes of the dancers. She started as a full-throated moan sounded from the darkness of the rustling bushes. An imploring whimper followed and the sound of scuffling grew in the night. A woman's sharp scream was silenced as quickly as it came. Gelina stood staring at the bushes until Nimbus's hand protruded from the sheet to catch her cloak. He cleared his throat in an exact imitation of Conn and set her feet in guilty motion.

"I cannot believe I let ye talk me into this," Nimbus muttered. "Conn will have me head if he knows what ye've seen and done tonight."

"I've seen nothing and anything I've done was his fault," Gelina protested, unable to hide the trace of disappointment in her voice as she followed Nimbus's merrily bouncing horns.

She longed to throw back the smothering hood and let the warm winds tear through her curls. Her heart beat in time with the drum, forcing curious, young blood through every channel of her body. The suffocating weight of the velvet skirts wrapped around her legs.

"Don't take me back to my chamber now, Nimbus. I shan't be any more trouble. I promise." She stopped and tugged the corner of her cloak out of his hand.

He whirled on her, his one visible eye narrowed. "Ye've never seen Conn truly angry or ye would not dare risk it again."

His words gave her pause. She fell into step behind him, biting back a mutinous pout.

She stumbled into his back as he came to an abrupt halt with a muttered curse. Dancers swarmed around them in a buzz of laughter and drunken snatches of song. Gelina watched helplessly as Nimbus was lifted between the shoulders of two men and swept away.

". . . to yer chambers," came his voice before it was lost in the squeals of the women and roaring laughter of the men.

But the soldier who lurched out of the bushes still tying the leather strings of his jerkin had other thoughts. He gave her forlorn figure a stumbling bow; a golden mask painted with dragon's eyes loomed in her vision.

"Deserted so early, my love?"

Gelina drew back as the sour smell of ale slapped her in the face.

"I am a bit weary at the moment," he said, his speech slurred, "but if you shall give me time to recoup my strength, I will prove myself an ample comfort in your solitude."

Gelina drew herself up to her full height. "I do believe your comfort is spent for the night, sir."

"Nonsense. I've enough comfort for more than one lass on such a hot Midsummer's Eve."

His hand closed around her wrist with alarming strength. He tugged her toward the shadows of the bushes. From the corner of her mask Gelina caught a glimpse of leaping flames and wildly gyrating couples driven by the drumbeat into a nightmarish caricature of passion. Her eyes went by instinct to the soldier's waist to find he wore no sword. She drew back her fist and drove it into his stomach with all of her strength.

He doubled over with a howl. She whirled to run and was so intent on peering over her shoulder to see if he would pursue her that she did not see the man who stepped in front of her until she slammed into his chest with enough force to stun her. She raised her eyes to stare at lion's whiskers she had painted with her own hand.

She turned around, stepping on his toes and smoothing her hood forward. Her heart pounded in her ears, drowning out the rhythm of the drum. The soldier staggered toward them, rubbing his belly.

Firm hands rested on her shoulders; his voice was a deep and gentle whisper at her ear. "Does he trouble you, my lost beauty?"

Gelina nodded, not daring to speak or flee lest he follow and unmask her.

The soldier stopped short as he saw the man standing behind her. His mouth fell open.

"There are surely enough willing women to go around tonight, Liam. There is no need to prey on the unwilling. We are not savages."

The soldier ran a sheepish hand through his hair. "I was just having some sport. I would not have harmed her."

"I shall feel more assured of that when you are safe in your bed . . . soon."

"Yes, sire. Forgive me." The soldier yawned loudly and backed into the night. " 'Tis late. I am weary of the celebration as I was just telling the young lass. I do believe I will . . ." His voice faded in the darkness.

Conn chuckled. Gelina could feel the heat of his hands on her shoulders through the velvet cloak and dress. His grip changed subtly; his fingers slid along her collarbone with strength and tenderness. She breathed a silent prayer of thanks for the darkness, knowing it would hide the color of her hair as he eased the hood back. A shiver ran through her as his broad thumbs stroked the smooth column of her throat, coming to rest against the pulse that beat wildly there. His warm breath stirred the curls at her ear.

"Your heart beats like a captive bird. Now that we are rid of him, beauty, will you come with me?"

He mistook her silence for surrender, and she had no choice but to follow him as he folded her hand in his and pulled her toward a door well hidden by a swinging curtain of ivy. She jerked the hood over her hair with a desperate hand as they ducked inside a long corridor. A crowd of laughing men and women rounded the corner. Before Gelina dared to protest, Conn slid aside a secret panel and pulled her into a deserted tunnel away from the prying eyes of the crowd. The tunnel curved far ahead of them like the belly of some great beast. A single torch sputtered low in its sconce.

Gelina balked as Conn pulled her inexorably toward the flickering light. She pressed herself to the wall, knowing he could see the curve of her flaming cheek in the half light. He leaned forward, his hands supporting his weight on either side of her. There was a deliberate grace to his movements that warned her he had drank his share of ale on this Midsummer's Eve.

His hand cupped her face but she resisted his gentle effort to tilt her face to the light.

"So shy and sweet," he murmured. "You must not fear me."

"I heard the soldier address you. I know you are . . . the king," she said softly, not trusting herself to say his name.

"Today I was a king. Tonight I am only a man."

His lips brushed hers. Her lips parted in a gasp, and his mouth closed on hers with gentle insistence, the taste of ale warm and sweet and dark against her tongue.

His mouth moved against hers. "I was afraid I'd never find you and the sweetness of your kiss would haunt me forever."

His hand cradled her chin. His fingers coaxed her shy lips farther apart. His lips molded and tugged with teasing expertise until she was open and vulnerable to the full ardor of his kiss. His other hand slid down her arm and gently cupped her breast. Hot blood flooded her cheeks. The velvet that separated his thumb from the tingling peak of her breast melted to a shimmering conductor of his heat and will. The burning blood deserted her cheeks and rushed through her body in a dizzying current. She could feel the taking, entering motions of his mouth and hand on every inch of her flushed skin.

Her head reeled as he bore her against the wall with the strength of his kiss and his warm hands on her shoulders beneath the cloak. He pressed the hard length of his body to hers in a caress he would have never given an innocent girl.

He drew back and she struggled for breath, the faint light of the tunnel going dim before her panicked eyes. Only his arms kept her from falling.

"So you know who I am," he whispered. "'Tis only fair for me to know who you are. I cannot bear to lose you again."

Before she could speak, both of her wrists were gently caught in one of his hands. He reached up to unmask her. Gelina did not have time to think of the consequences. She pressed her lips to his in a trembling kiss, feeling them part in surprise at the apparent fervor of her passion. With a muffled groan Conn forgot the mask and wrapped his arms around her, lifting her off the floor until every curve of her body was fitted to his. Gelina went weak as a tide of feeling as terrifying as it was exhilarating swept through her, the sharp pain of danger a double-edged sword in the expertise of Conn's hands.

She opened her eyes to true darkness and the faint tinkling of bells at the curve of the tunnel.

"The torch," she breathed.

"To hell with the torch," Conn said, his voice strained with a hoarseness Gelina did not recognize. "I need only the darkness and you." He bore her toward the floor with gentle persistence.

Her hands clutched his tunic; she buried her burning face in his familiar shoulder. "Please . . . , Conn."

She would never know if it was the whispered plea of his name on her lips or the renewed vigor of the jingling in the darkness but Conn loosed her with a sigh.

His lips brushed her temple. "Stay here. I shall return."

He melted into the darkness, leaving Gelina to sink against the wall, feeling oddly lost. The secret panel slid aside. A small hand beckoned frantically. Gelina caught the hand and dove through the widening opening. Nimbus slammed the panel shut, ignoring Conn's muffled cry of dismay. They sprinted down the corridor, hand in hand, Nimbus's knees pumping to his chin to match her long strides.

He tripped over a moaning peasant stretched across the entrance to the great hall and went sprawling. Without slowing, Gelina hauled him across the peasant's mound of stomach— thump, thump, thump—and to his feet. The peasant rolled to his side with a gurgling snore.

Two more strides and their path was blocked by a masked woman on the arm of a stumbling soldier. Gelina stared mesmerized as the man sprawled in a grimy pile of hay and pulled the woman on top of him. They rolled over, his grunts mingling with her squeals until he sat astride her. With a flourish he threw her skirts over her face to reveal plump, squirming thighs and fell upon her with a cry of triumph and wildly gyrating hips.

With a definite lack of gentleness Nimbus grasped the hood of Gelina's cloak and jerked her toward the stairs. They took the stairs two at a time, fear and relief escaping in breathless laughter. The door of her chamber slammed behind them. Nimbus turned the key in the lock with a flourish. They leapt onto the bed and collapsed in a giggling heap amidst the feather pillows. Gelina rolled over and propped herself on her elbows, hurling the mask into the ashes on the hearth.

"Did ye think I had deserted ye?" Nimbus asked, casting the sheet aside and running a hand through his wispy hair.

"I had my qualms. I thought I was lost when Conn pulled me into that tunnel."

"I fear 'twas my fault. He saw me in the crowd that approached and knew there'd be no mercy from me if I saw him hauling a nubile, young lass around. Gave me quite a fright when I saw who it was. Ye're certain he had no inkling it was ye."

She did not reply. Nimbus stared at the abrupt change in her demeanor. A flush of rose touched the cheeks she held cupped in her hands. Her lips parted in a half smile.

He passed a hand in front of her misty eyes. She did not blink.

"He didn't know it was ye, did he?" Nimbus repeated. "I'm doomed for the dungeons if he did."

Gelina's head snapped up. "Of course he didn't know it was me. I was masked so he mistook me for someone beautiful."

Nimbus started to speak, then thought better of it.

Gelina rubbed her aching temples with the tips of her fingers. "I am weary, Nimbus."

"I'll go," he said, sliding off the bed.

Nimbus turned to bid her goodnight. She sat staring at nothing as if he had already left. He pulled the door shut softly behind him.

Gelina touched her lips. They felt hot and swollen beneath her trembling fingertips. She buried her burning face in her pillow, unable to understand why she was crying.

Morning found Gelina sitting in the kitchen staring into a bowl of broth with her chin resting in the palm of her hand. Unable to bear the silence of her chamber and the loudness of her thoughts, she had crept down the stairs and over the snoring bodies that littered the great hall to seek the dubious comfort of the kitchen and Cook's company.

"I've no sympathy for the lousy sots. Brung it all on themselves, they did. Fill their cursed bodies with poison and then expect dear old Cook to dish up broth all day like a bloody wet nurse. Got another thing coming, don't they?"

Cook punctuated her speech by slamming a naked chicken on the hearth and twisting its guts out with a wrench that would have put fear in the heart of the bravest of the Fianna. The rolls of fat on the back of her arms quivered in moral outrage.

Gelina murmured an agreement and twirled the wooden spoon in her broth. She glanced at the doorway and then back into her broth as Nimbus entered followed by a scowling Conn.

"Good morning, pet," Conn said, rumpling her hair. "Yours is the first face I've seen this morning untouched by the hardships of the night."

Gelina knew the ways she had been touched did not all show in her face. She ducked her head and stammered a good morning.

Conn leaned back in his chair, one hand rubbing his beard. "I hope you slept well. I trust the noise did not trouble you."

She raised her eyes to meet his piercing gaze, nodded, then shook her head. Her gaze fell, noticing for the first time how the crisp, dark hairs curled on the back of his hands. She brought the spoon to her mouth with a trembling hand.

Nimbus scrambled into a chair, his legs dangling. "I slept like a babe. The only noise that troubled me was someone stomping up the stairs and slamming into his room . . . alone."

Conn glared at him. Gelina kicked him under the table. Cook sloshed a steaming bowl of broth in front of Conn, muttering under her breath, then slammed an iron pot to the hearth with a ringing crash.

Conn gripped his head in both hands and bellowed, "Must you wake the dead, Cook?" He grimaced. "I'm going to have that woman beheaded someday."

"Temper, temper," Nimbus said. "And to what do we owe the charming state of yer temper this fine morn?"

"At least I'm conscious," Conn snapped, "which is more than I can say for most of the Fianna."

"More's the pity," Nimbus murmured.

Gelina watched Conn from beneath lowered eyelashes, unable to pull her eyes away from the tiny lines around his eyes. The merciless sunlight beaming into the kitchen stole nothing from his good looks. The deceptive boyishness of Conn by torchlight had vanished, leaving in its place six feet of male strength and determination wrapped in a lifetime of experience she could never match. Gelina felt herself go pale and small beneath the force of it. She stared at the mat of dark hair curling over the smoky linen of his tunic, knowing that if she was pressed to string two words together in a coherent sentence, she would fail.

Conn ran a hand through his tousled hair with an oddly pensive frown. "If you must know, I found the softest little beauty last night only to have her stolen from my arms before I could even discover her name. I would seek her out this minute if I knew where to find her just to gaze upon her sweet lips."

Gelina choked a mouthful of broth back into her bowl, having never heard the words *soft* or *little* applied to her before.

Nimbus rounded the table and slapped her heartily on the back, knocking a bowl of broth into Conn's lap with his elbow.

Conn rose with a curse, swiping broth from his lap with his napkin and never seeing Gelina's color go from red to purple. When he looked up, she was as pale as a bolt of fine linen. The shadows beneath her eyes stood out like bruises.

Conn leaned over the table and peered into her face. "Are you ill, child?"

His fatherly concern was more than Gelina could bear. She threw her napkin over her face, burst into tears, and fled the room.

"Women!" Conn cried in exasperation.

He sank back into his chair and slammed his elbow into the new bowl of broth Cook had slid in his place. He let out a slow breath and met Nimbus's smirk of triumph with a black glare.

Chapter Eight

❖

Conn had been roaming with the Fianna for almost a month when Gelina awoke from a forgotten dream one night, her body aching and tingling in ways she could not understand. She sat bolt upright in bed, clutching the coverlet to her tight throat. Her hands flew up to cup her wet cheeks. She scrambled out of the bed and ran to the window, dragging the shutters open with shaking hands. She leaned into the night; cold air rushed over her burning brow.

A lone horse plodded into the moonlit courtyard. Gelina drew back into the shadows of her chamber, fighting her first impulse to lean forward and cry out a welcome.

Conn dismounted wearily, running a halfhearted hand over Silent Thunder's haunch. He tethered the horse to a post and started toward the faint light shining from the kitchens. He stopped and turned. His gaze lifted to her window.

Gelina hugged herself farther into the darkness, knowing he could not see her but feeling the searching caress of his eyes to the marrow of her bones. He stared at her window for a long time, his eyes shadowed. When he finally bowed his head and melted into the shadows of the hall, Gelina closed the shutters and pressed her forehead to the rough wood. Conn had come home for the winter.

A light snow dusted the ground one evening, giving off a dazzling brightness. The full moon hanging low in the sky seemed to rest upon the land as if lowered onto the unsuspecting snow by an unseen hand. Sitting with a woolen shawl pulled around her shoulders, Gelina regarded the chessboard with a newly practiced eye. Conn sat across from her with a predatory smile. A fire danced on the hearth, stealing the sharp chill from the air without obliterating the cold itself.

"Ah!" Gelina gave a short cry of triumph as she placed her knight between Conn's king and queen.

Conn frowned, and she licked her lips in anticipation, blithely ignorant of the difficulty he was having keeping the corners of his mouth turned down. He reached for the marble chessman, his eyes never leaving her face. In one movement he whisked his rook in the place of her knight.

Smiling triumphantly, he leaned back and crossed his arms. "Checkmate."

She stared at the board for a moment, then raised her eyes to him, fighting to hold the frown on her face. Faced by his dazzling smile, she surrendered and laughed, swatting him with a corner of her shawl.

"I must admit, Gelina, you become a more challenging opponent every day."

"What can I say? My teacher was the finest in Erin." She grinned at him and stood to sashay across the room.

"Flattery will get you nowhere. You look very lovely in that dress," he said. She turned to smile at him; his voice lowered to a growl. "It suits you far better than those oversized breeches I saw you meandering around in this morning."

She turned to the luxurious tapestry on the back wall, seeking to divert him and avoid another lecture.

"Look at these fierce battles! There's a man with his head chopped right off. I'm surprised they didn't run out of red thread."

Conn came up behind her and laid his hands lightly on her shoulders, pulling her slender body against his in a casual motion. " 'Twas the battle of Loch Erne." A frown touched his features. "A friend swore his allegiance to me, promising to send five hundred men to my assistance with the dawn. Eoghan Mogh surrounded us. We heard the trumpets and watched the reinforcements arrive. You can imagine our horror when the men my friend had promised turned their swords against us. They outnumbered us fifty to one but we defeated them. The rivers of Erin ran blood that night. I lost a thousand men."

It was suddenly very important that Gelina speak, that she say anything to keep him from telling her more. Loch Erne. The name sounded an off-key note in her memory, like a harp crashing to the stones.

She twisted away from him. "Do my breeches truly displease you? I should hate to abandon them for skirts forever."

"How shall I ever get you betrothed when all of your suitors persist in thinking you one of my soldiers?"

She bowed her head, unable to meet his teasing gaze. "You jest. I have no suitors. Who would want such a tall horse of a girl?"

Conn tilted her chin until she raised unblinking eyes to his. "Any man with an eye for a fine mare." His lips brushed her brow. "But it will take a fine stallion indeed to steal my girl away from me."

Gelina laughed to hide the thrill of joy that set her hands to trembling. She hooked her arm in his, and they sashayed back to the chessboard.

Setting up the pieces with care, Gelina asked, "This spring, Conn, can we go on a picnic? Just you and I and Mer-Nod and Nimbus? Moira will pack a lunch and we shall find the softest, grassiest hill in Erin." She lowered her lashes over shining eyes. "You may bring Sheela if you like."

"Why? You detest her."

Gelina shrugged. "I just don't fancy weak, simpering females." She devoted her attention to figuring out which square the king and queen should be placed on, switching them three times.

"You just don't fancy women who wear dresses consistently. And she only simpered when you and Nimbus put the ants in her rice powder." He swapped the position of her king and queen. "This picnic may never take place anyway. I'm going away in the spring."

Raising startled eyes to his, she sat back in her chair. "Away? On a raid?"

"I'll be gone longer than that. I am going to Britain."

"Why? The Romans hold Britain."

"That is precisely why I'm going. We are going to ensure that they get no similar ideas about holding Erin." Conn's gaze avoided her face, unsure of the naked emotion he saw there.

"How long will you be gone?"

"For three months. Maybe longer." He sighed. "I don't wish to discuss it."

Gelina wisely clamped her lips together although she ached to question him further. They played in silence for a while.

"Then the first warm day, we will go on my picnic before you go."

Conn shook his head and laughed. "How I pity the man who must face those pleading eyes someday. As you wish, Gelina."

"Do you give your word?"

"Have I ever broken a promise to you?" His gaze penetrated her concentration, forcing her to lift her eyes from the chessboard.

"No, you haven't," she murmured, averting her eyes downward. Casually moving her queen, she blinked and added, "Checkmate."

On that same winter evening in another firelit room, a different kind of game was being played. Barron Ó Caflin sat with forehead resting in the palm of his hand, an oddly pensive look on his face. Two men sat across from him, awaiting his answer.

He finally rose and began to pace in front of the fire. "'Tis a serious thing you're asking. Murder is very different from just keeping him out of the way."

The hooded figure Ó Caflin had come to know only too well said, "'Tis not necessarily murder. The Romans might be lenient." He tossed off a careless laugh to the man in the other chair.

"What the Romans do to the men of Erin is not a lenient thing," Barron replied. "It won't just be Conn floating to his death. It will be men I've known for years. Some of my own clansmen will be on those ships."

"Sentimentality has no place in wartime. Leave it to the poets and the women," a well-modulated voice interrupted,

seeking to soothe his misgivings. "We will spare as many lives
as we can. The necessity of the action even a child can understand. Conn must be banished. I must receive the crown. Lives
lost along the way will be lost for a worthy cause." The man
who spoke unfolded himself from his chair. "Will you stand
with me as we planned or with Conn and your . . . childhood friends?" His sneer turned the phrase into something
dirty.

Barron met Eoghan Mogh's eyes with a grimace. "I stand
with you. You will be Ard-Righ of Erin and sit upon the throne
at Tara."

He could hear the hooded man's laughter as it echoed shrilly
through the small room. He clenched his fists to keep from
slapping out in blind rage.

Spring would not be long in coming. Gelina threw open the
shutters of her window and leaned out, inhaling deeply. The
cool, sweet air filled her lungs. The mornings were her favorite
times but this morning she missed the jovial knock on her door.
Nimbus had ridden north, sent by Conn to the rocky coastline
where the ships were being prepared to sail for Britain.

Tara hummed with rumors. Some said that Conn was seeking
to conquer Britain while others insisted that he sought to aid the
Romans in their conquest to procure a part of the prize himself.
Gelina did not care to speculate or even think about the long
months when Conn would be gone.

This morning she had her own mission. She bathed and
donned the soft leather breeches and vest that had become a
familiar sight around the fortress in the early morning hours.

Opening her door, she searched both ways for any sign of
Conn. He had already threatened to take her makeshift uniform
away if he caught her roaming in it. The corridor was deserted.
Jamming her hands deep in her pockets, she stepped out and
strolled down the hall, winding through the corridors until she
stood outside a massive double door.

As she reached out and gave the handle a hard tug, she was
startled to hear a voice behind her. "So you're the boy who's
been stealing my clothes. I should thrash you where you stand!"

She found her arm caught in a bruising grasp as she swung
around to face a flushed soldier. His mouth fell open below the
chocolate of his mustache as he recognized her. His grip
loosened, and she flattened herself against the door. Her

emerald eyes widened, their dark fringe of lashes catching him unaware.

Gathering his last shred of composure, he said, "I am sorry. I had no inkling it was you."

She slumped against the door in relief. "You were right. They are your clothes and I did steal them."

He wiped his sweaty forehead with the back of his hand. "I've never seen a woman in breeches before. And I've certainly never seen a woman in my breeches."

Gelina would have sworn he blushed a tiny amount under his tan. She spoke quickly, trying to ease his embarrassment. "I'm more comfortable in breeches. Of course, that doesn't justify stealing them. I'll return them posthaste."

He stretched out a restraining hand as if fearful she would disrobe right there in the corridor. "They're old and worn. You may keep them."

Gelina started to ask if she could keep the vest, too, then decided not to push his generosity. He was staring at the door behind her with a puzzled look.

She hastened to explain. "Nimbus has shown me most of Tara, but I've yet to see the weaponry room. I fear that except for juggling them, Nimbus has no interest in swords."

The soldier arched an eyebrow, longing to ask about her interest. "'Tis locked you know," he said. Her face fell in disappointment. "But . . . I happen to have the key."

He pulled the iron key from his pocket, noting with pleasure the grin that spread across her face. He opened the door, pausing only to tell her, "I'm Sean Ó Finn."

She nodded, biting her lip to keep from telling him that Nimbus had already described his appearance to prevent just this meeting.

The double doors swung inward, revealing a hall as spacious as the great hall of Tara. Gelina gasped. Mounted from floor to ceiling were instruments of battle and death. Swords, battle axes, picks, maces, morningstars, and javelins coated the walls in a gleaming layer of gold, silver, and bronze. Fresh pine torches hung in iron brackets from the high, vaulted ceiling.

"'Tis said the light keeps the weapons shining and sharp," Sean whispered, the hallowed atmosphere of the room adding a solemn note to his voice.

Gelina walked into the room, wondering if she'd ever seen anything so lovely. Sean followed her, mystified. He'd never seen a woman respond this way to the weaponry room. But he silently reminded himself that he'd never seen a woman wearing his breeches, either.

Crystals of light cast by the flickering torches burnished the edges of the weapons fiery orange like the ghost of blood shed long ago. Their soft footsteps echoed in the deserted hall.

Gelina asked, "Are any of these ever used in battle?"

Sean nodded. "In peaceful times such as these, only three battalions of the Fianna stand active. That leaves four inactive battalions that could be summoned in the event of war. The weapons would be distributed accordingly." He took her arm and led her to the far wall. "My favorites. Conn has retired them in honor and memory of our ancestors."

The weapons bore the stain of age. Gelina read the inscription below a huge ax, painfully sounding out the words as Rodney had taught her to do. "The Battle Ax of Macha Mong Ruad, Daughter of Red Hugh. Oh, Sean, could it really be?"

"As far as we know. Look at this one." He pointed to a sword with the form of a serpent entwined around its golden hilt. "Sword of Cathbad, Son of Ross, and Wizard. It is said that the sword was stolen but reappeared in the exact spot where we see it now after the thief met an untimely end . . . from the bite of a serpent."

Gelina let out a slow breath and shook her head.

Sean pointed to an open space on the wall. "Someday Conn's sword, Deliverance, will hang there. His sword will hang above the swords of the enemies he has vanquished to show his supremacy to the coming generations."

Gelina nodded, then froze, her eyes locked on the spot he indicated. Her smile faded as she saw in front of her a sword with crooked, awkward lettering engraved on its hilt . . . *Vengeance*. Reaching out a hand, she traced the familiar hilt, the cold metal like an old friend to her fingertips. The memories hugged her heart, stealing her breath away.

Dueling with Rodney, thrusting, parrying away his carved wooden blade until she couldn't raise her arms another time.

"'Tis the sword Conn found in the cave with the monster he slew," Sean told her, watching her movement.

"I know," she replied, not removing her hand or eyes from the sword.

Growing in two summers to a height that nearly equaled

Rodney's own. Galloping through the woods, perched on his shoulders. Slamming into a branch as he ducked a second too late. Sailing into the woods, sword still gripped in her hand.

He coughed and turned away. "I'm sorry. I forgot."

She reached out her other hand and removed the sword from its mounting. Her eyes were glazed, her movements stiff and mechanical.

Running forward with a high-pitched scream. Driving the sword through the chest of the soldier they ambushed for his cloak. Pulling the sword from his sternum with a grating twist. Giving Vengeance to her brother and begging him to cut the waist-length auburn curls that had lured the man to his death.

She lifted her eyes to Sean's, a familiar grin appearing in place of the glazed look. "Would you care to duel, Sean Ó Finn?" She leapt backward, crouching in a battle stance.

"I hardly think that would be appropriate."

"Pilfering your clothes wasn't appropriate, either. I fear I am a very inappropriate person." She made a quick feint to his chest, and he stared to find her blade quivering an inch from his belly.

"Milady, you force retaliation. Your challenge is accepted." He pulled his sword from its sheath, parrying from a safe distance.

He was shocked to find her an apt and worthy partner. He could see the muscles in her lean arms knot as she sought to disarm him without threatening the sanctity of his skin. They both laughed as she ducked his thrust with skill, setting him off balance.

"Where did you learn such skills, milady?" he asked breathlessly, throwing his body to the side.

"I do not remember," she said cryptically.

Gelina only had time to see Sheela's shocked face in the doorway before she found herself slammed against the wall, the breath knocked from her lungs. She slid to a sitting position; Vengeance clattered to the floor. A familiar pair of angry blue eyes cut into her. She struggled to catch her breath as those steely eyes swam before her vision, blocking out the rest of the room.

Sean sheathed his sword, mouth open wide in shock. "Conn, what are you doing? 'Twas just a game." He stretched out his arm in a plea. "Why did you do that?"

Conn turned to him, his clenched fists and harsh breathing a sign Sean knew well. "Her games can be deadly." His eyes traveled the length of the room to rest on Sheela, who stood with her hand on the doorframe, frightened eyes on him. "Get out! Both of you! Now!" he bellowed.

Sean made one last attempt. "Sire, I don't understand—"

"Out."

His voice was quieter but more deadly. Sean knew it was the last time Conn would ask them to leave. Mystified, he took Sheela's arm in his and led her from the room without a backward glance.

Gelina closed her eyes, waiting for the pounding in her head to cease and trying desperately to swallow around the lump in her throat. The silence became unbearable. She opened her eyes to find Conn standing a few feet in front of her, his arms crossed and his gaze locked on her face.

His voice was cold. "Go ahead and cry."

Her muffled voice replied, "I wouldn't give you the satisfaction."

Something akin to shame flickered across his face, but he didn't speak.

"He was telling the truth," she began hesitantly. "'Twas just a game."

"How do I know that? How do I know you weren't waiting for just the right moment to run him through?" He paced in front of her.

"I've been at Tara for almost a year, Conn. How many of your men have I run through in that time?" She shook her head in silent frustration.

"It was like my worst nightmare, Gelina. I walk in here and find you dueling with one of my best fighters. I recognize your moves, the way you handle the sword. I remember what it was like to have you coming at me."

Her voice surged with anger. "You must still hate me a lot then. Admit it. You walked in here and assumed the worst."

He did not reply. Letting out a huge breath, he watched her struggle to keep the tears out of her voice and eyes. Looking at her, he did not see a tall, skinny girl huddled against the wall. He saw laughing emerald eyes challenging him across the chessboard. He saw whirling satin skirts and hands clasped in his in the midst of a rollicking dance.

He knelt beside her and placed a gentle hand at the back of her head. He found one small lump. She shrank from his touch.

"You think I hate you?" he asked, his voice quieter.

"Yes. No. I don't know." She sniffed.

He stood, running a hand through his shaggy curls. "I should have never brought you here. I brought this on myself. 'Twas not fair to expect you to face the Fianna every day of your life."

"You wish you had left me for dead in the cavern?"

"Of course not. I could have sent you to Rath Crogan, my fortress in the north. The Fianna do not venture there."

"And neither do you," she murmured, too softly for his ears to hear.

"Perhaps it would be better for you if you didn't have to see them every day . . . or me," he added. He pretended to stare at the weapons on the wall to mask the cost of his words.

"Perhaps," she said coldly, her face emptied of emotion and color. "May I take my things with me?"

He could not stop himself from turning, shocked at her abrupt surrender. He struggled to match the toneless quality of her words. "Of course. I can make the arrangements today."

"Thank you, sire."

He did not know how to halt this avalanche of wrongness that had slid between them. To hide his helplessness, he strode to the door, unable to meet the glassy green of her eyes. He pulled the door shut behind him and collapsed against it, a peculiar mixture of emotions draining the strength from his body.

With a solid thunk, seven inches of steel appeared beside his cheek. He recognized the sword's silver tip protruding from the door where it had been hurled with furious strength.

"The wench is trying to kill me," he breathed.

He threw open both doors, stopping to pull the still vibrating sword from the thick wood. Gelina sat a few feet from where he had left her, her face buried in her hands. His numb mind realized that she could not have known that he stood on the other side of that door. The tears inside her had freed themselves in hoarse sobs.

He walked across the room until he stood directly in front of her. She raised brimming eyes to him, staring at the sword in his hand.

"Your weapon, milady. Perhaps you'd like another try at skewering me."

Gelina's eyes widened and instead of taking the sword, she stretched out full length on the floor, sobbing even louder, head buried in folded arms. Conn sighed, rolling his eyes to the ceiling.

"Do stop, Gelina. You'll rust the weapons if you go on like this."

She bawled louder, pausing only long enough to drag her nose across her sleeve.

He knelt beside her, pulling her up until he could rest his chin on her head. Her curls felt like silk beneath the scratchiness of his beard. She cried hoarsely into the rough linen of his shirt.

"I shall not send you away, Gelina. I never wanted to anyway." He could think of nothing to add that would quiet her bitter sobs. He continued to talk, hoping to soothe her with the sound of his voice. "Soon, Gelina. Soon we'll go on your picnic."

There was sudden silence below his chin. "Do you think Moira will make us some tarts?"

He chuckled softly. "Leave it to the mention of food to cheer you." His voice became serious again. "I have one thing to ask you before you raise those damned eyes and make me guilt-ridden again." She tried to raise her head but he kept his chin firm upon it. "Please, Gelina, stay out of the weaponry room." He stroked her arm. "And please, Gelina . . . , forgive me."

There was only a subtle nod to indicate she had heard him but it was enough for Conn. He rubbed his cheek against her hair, his eyes pressed shut.

Chapter Nine

❖

Bounding out of bed, Gelina ran to the window and threw open the shutters. This was the day. The warm sun slanted across her cheeks in a fresh way. Beneath the shield of night the world had melted to green. It was not the deeper green of summer that clung to the grass, but the minty green of new leaves unfurling, shiny and wet, a green that could be blown away by a strong breath. A light mist blanketed the mountains in the distance, covering its final victim before being deposed by the warm sun. From far away Gelina could hear the resonant cry of the bittern echoing her joy.

She dressed, pulling on a simple linen dress that laced up the front and fell to mid-calf on her tall frame. Standing in front of the mirror, she ran the ivory brush through her curls, then leaned forward to examine her image. Had it been her imagination or had the dress been more time consuming to lace this morning?

She ran a curious hand over her chest and murmured, "Surely I'm not developing bosoms."

"Why not? 'Tis about time, is it not?" Nimbus stood in the doorway, a cocky smirk on his face.

"Oh," Gelina shrieked, drawing back her arm to hurl the brush at him. "Haven't you ever heard of knocking at a lady's chamber?"

He stretched out his arms in a plea, also prepared to use them to ward off the brush. "Now, Gelina, I was only jesting."

She lowered her arm, waiting until he lowered his. As he relaxed, she tossed the brush underhand, hitting him soundly in the solar plexus.

"Oof!" He doubled over and stretched out on the floor.

Gelina rushed over, fearful her surprise blow had killed him. Kneeling, she shook him by the shoulder.

"Aye, from this angle I'd say ye're definitely developing bosoms." His grin caught her off guard, and he grabbed her hand before it could reach the hairbrush. She succumbed to his pleas and helped him to his feet.

"Is Conn still abed?" she asked, knowing Nimbus made morning rounds of the castle to find out just who was sleeping in which chamber with whom.

"He's been up since dawn. Surely ye don't forget he leaves on the morrow." Nimbus watched her from the corner of his eye.

She shrugged as if Conn's departure was the furthest thing from her mind. The shrill sound of a rising female voice shattered the quiet of the corridor as they approached Conn's chambers. With the mutual consent of conspirators, they exchanged glances, unable to resist the temptation. Gelina pressed her hand over her mouth to suppress the giggle that threatened to expose them. Nimbus grimaced as Sheela's enraged voice grated across his nerves.

"I find it hard to believe you choose to spend your precious time with that foundling instead of me."

Gelina cocked her head, unable to hear the words in Conn's deep murmur.

Sheela's voice rose again. "My late husband would have never treated me this way." Sheela's voice sank to a nasal whine. Nimbus placed his hands around his throat and made tiny retching noises.

Gelina doubled over, hearing only silence in the room. Evidently Conn had found a different way to silence Sheela for no sound was heard behind the cracked door for several minutes.

"But she is such an odd creature. More like a lad than a girl. What do you see in the child?" Sheela said, swinging the door open without warning.

The child she referred to drew herself up to her full height and towered over Sheela's pout of dismay by a good six inches.

"Oh." Unable to think of a clever word, Sheela stomped her foot and stormed down the hall, ignoring Nimbus's protruding tongue and bugged eyes.

Conn entered the hall himself, trying to look severe as he surveyed the guilty partners from under arched eyebrows. Gelina flashed him a blinding smile and took his hand in hers. Nimbus followed suit with the other hand. Conn resisted their pull; then his face cracked in a reluctant smile, and he squeezed Gelina's hand.

"Come, foundling, let us picnic."

Nimbus pouted. "You always pay more attention to the foundling than me," he said in perfect imitation of Sheela's shrill falsetto. He ducked, barely avoiding Conn's swat to his ear.

Mer-Nod stood in the courtyard, struggling to look dignified beneath the burden of the burlap haversack hung over his shoulder. Nimbus danced behind him, making grotesque faces until Mer-Nod dropped the bag on him with a sly smile.

Conn took advantage of Nimbus's loud curses to tell Gelina,

"I had to invite a bodyguard. I couldn't take any chances on my last day here."

Gelina sighed. "You mean one of the Fianna, don't you?"

"Yes, but I think you'll approve."

As if on cue, Sean Ó Finn strode around the corner. He smiled awkwardly at Gelina, remembering their last meeting. She turned to Conn and nodded, her eyes giving him the answer he sought.

With a last kick to Mer-Nod's shins, Nimbus skipped in front of them and led the procession through the gates. They wandered over the grassy hills, a cool breeze drying the sweat on their brows. Gelina flew from hill to hill, pausing to pluck luxuriant bouquets of violets and bluebells. Conn's gaze followed her lithe figure, his ears tuned to her throaty laugh. He felt the small shadow of Nimbus sidle up beside him and slowed his long strides until they fell behind the others.

"I have to go away, Nimbus," he said, without looking down.

"I know."

"A man like myself—a man of the Fianna—is too restless to bury himself in the comforts of home and hearth and children."

"Of course, ye must go. I've seen that gleam in yer eye, Conn." Nimbus followed Conn's gaze to Gelina's upturned face as she draped a garland of bluebells around Sean's neck. "That hunger for something fresh and young and untried."

Conn stared down at him, startled.

"Like Britain, of course," Nimbus finished.

Conn's jaw tightened. He returned his gaze to Gelina.

"You'll take care of her for me, won't you, Nimbus?"

"Always."

"She's just a child in so many ways."

Nimbus pulled a flute from his pocket. "Who are ye trying to convince? Me or yerself."

Before Conn could reach for his collar, Nimbus had danced ahead, playing a merry tune. Sean found a grassy knoll free of the prickly gorse, and Mer-Nod sat, resting his back against a tree.

Nimbus continued to play, and Gelina danced beneath the spreading branches of the elm. Her bare feet kicked in the air. With the linen whirling around her tanned legs, she danced like a wood sprite, as elusive as the dew that dried on the grass. Conn grabbed her hands and danced with her as Sean clapped along. They whirled faster and faster. Conn could not tear his eyes away from the sunlight glinting through her auburn curls.

Sean wrestled the flute from Nimbus, and a tune he had practiced on many lonely nights camped on a distant hill rose into the air, plaintive and sweet. Nimbus took three fat apples from the sack of food and tossed them into the air, one by one. Gelina stopped dancing and held up one hand. Tossing them high in her direction, he laughed as she caught one. The other two sailed into her grasp. They hummed in the air as she juggled them until they were a blur above her palms. She sent them in the direction of Conn, Nimbus, and Mer-Nod who caught them in amazement. A rare, honest smile crossed the poet's face with no trace of sarcasm.

The noon sun found them eating beef and cheese spread on thick hunks of freshly baked bread. Golden chalices of mead rested beside them. Conn gently poured half of Gelina's into his own, ignoring her frown.

He leaned over, his breath warm in her ear, and whispered, "I dare not let my charge stumble tipsy into the hall. Moira would have my head."

She whispered back, giggling as the mead spread warmly through her veins, "Moira did pack the mead, did she not?"

He reached into the sack and pulled forth a flask. "She also packed the goat's milk."

Gelina frowned. "Do I have to drink it?"

"Certainly." But even as he spoke, he loosened the cork of the flask and watched the yellow milk dribble to the ground in a steady stream.

Nimbus was asleep and snoring loudly. Mer-Nod and Sean were deep in conversation over an ancient piece of poetry.

Gelina touched Conn's beard absently, the drone of a nearby honeybee deepening her sleepy reverie. "Conn?"

"What?"

"I don't think I've ever been so happy." She rolled over on her stomach in the soft grass and plucked a long blade, running it along her chin.

He understood. Not even in that fallen castle so far away had she been this happy.

He took his hand in hers and sighed, "What shall I do without you these long months, warrior?"

She pulled her hand away and smiled. "You must bring me a gift."

He growled, "Just like a woman. And what does your heart crave, milady?"

"I would like a dress."

Conn's eyes widened in real amazement. "Surely a handsome pair of breeches would be more to your liking."

"No. I want a red, gold, and green dress."

"Leave it to you to choose the most garish colors in the spectrum," Conn laughed. "Has Nimbus got you signed up for the traveling fair?"

The midget's sleepy voice came from behind the tree. "She's good enough for the fair."

". . . or the Fianna," Sean said softly. Conn sent him a warning glance.

"The sun is waning, Gelina. We must return to Tara," he said softly, pulling her to her feet.

They stood together, their hands entwined, a heartbeat away from moving together or apart. Nimbus had to look away as an unfamiliar sting touched his eyes.

As he turned away, a silhouette of a man appeared over the hill, the sun behind him hiding his features. He loomed over the group like a specter. Only Conn did not seem surprised at his appearance. Mer-Nod turned to Conn with questioning eyes.

Barron Ó Caflin called to the man below, "Conn, the ships await us. The men are aboard."

Gelina studied her dusty feet, a joyless, knowing smile crossing her face.

Conn turned to the silent group. "I wanted to avoid the ceremony tomorrow. I am leaving now. Mer-Nod will act as regent."

The chief poet nodded. The matter had been discussed many times since the journey had been birthed in Conn's mind. Gelina continued to study her feet.

"Sean will remain here as Gelina's bodyguard since Mer-Nod will have his hands full with managing Erin." A frown crossed Sean's face, but he struggled to hide his disappointment as Conn flashed him a grateful smile.

"Your mount is waiting over the hill," Barron called. He

ached to interrupt the scene below. He could not hear the words spoken but he could sense the mood.

Nimbus settled himself against the tree, arms crossed. Gelina did not meet anyone's gaze. Mer-Nod drew himself taller, feeling the cloak of responsibility settle soundly on his narrow shoulders. Conn looked somber, and Sean Ó Finn, Barron's childhood friend, looked only resigned. He was not aware that Barron had made the suggestion that he remain at the castle.

Conn clapped his hand on Nimbus's shoulder. "You, my friend, must rally the spirits of the people. Make sure they keep believing I will return. If they stop believing, it will only be a matter of time before Eoghan conquers Tara."

Nimbus nodded, aware of his importance as few men were.

In silent agreement the men began to walk toward the fortress, which was barely visible through the hazy afternoon sky. Barron disappeared over the hill. Gelina and Conn stood alone. She raised her head and stared toward the mountains, away from the shadow of Tara. Her eyes were dry. A breeze lifted the hair from the back of her neck.

"You will come back, won't you?" she said. Her eyes still rested on the distant hills.

"I have to bring you that dress, don't I?"

"Red, gold, and green." It was a statement of fact, not a question. He nodded. With a tired motion she brushed a lock of hair from her eyes. "You should take your leave."

Reaching out his hand, he turned her face to meet his gaze. Her eyes were strangely cold, the light within them extinguished. Something flickered in their emerald depths. For a fleeting instant he saw the woman she would become, saw the past reflected in the glistening green. Her parents died before his eyes . . . her brother fell to his knees, sending her crashing to the stone . . . and now he left her.

In a moment of sudden clarity he drew in a sharp breath, feeling her pain like a dagger twisting in his vitals. She watched him guardedly as he knelt on one knee, pressing the back of her hand to his lips. He said nothing, and she reached out her hand and stroked his hair, unsure of the unaccustomed gesture. He rose without a word and walked toward the hill without looking back. Watching him disappear over the horizon, she lifted her hand in a halfhearted wave he never saw. Then she turned and sprinted toward the fortress until her breath came in ragged gasps and her side ached.

A cool wind washed over her as she fell to her knees and for the first time heard the thunder rumbling in the distance. She was still on her knees when the rain came. It swelled over the green hills until it surrounded her. Waves of the rain scent broke over her. Her dress clung to her body. She raised her face to the rain, letting it wash into her mouth and eyes. Making small animal noises, she let the rain flow over her, mingling with the tears and banishing them to oblivion as if they had never existed.

The rain had stopped. Conn was sitting in the curragh waiting to be rowed to the ship when Nimbus came sliding down the rocky hill, more on his rear than on his feet.

A soldier stepped forward to block his path. Nimbus darted between his legs. Hearing the soldier's cry, Conn yelled, "Let him pass."

Nimbus waded into the sea and caught the rim of the bobbing curragh in his small hands just before the waves washed over his head. With one arm Conn hauled his dripping form into the boat.

"And to what do I owe the honor of this visit?" he asked, ducking as Nimbus shook the water from his hair like a dog.

Nimbus gave him a sly smile. "I've a message for ye."

Conn arched an eyebrow. "And what might that be?"

Nimbus scratched his head absently.

"Unless you are interested in sailing to Britain, I'd suggest you remember."

"Well . . . , I do believe the young lass's words were—"

"Young lass? What young lass?"

". . . tell the king that I understand. Today he was only a man. Tonight he must be a king."

Conn sat back on the bench and stared into the thin layer of water in the bottom of the boat. His throat tightened at the memory of a golden mask, shadowed eyes, lips crushed like rose petals beneath his. He reached for Nimbus's collar just as Nimbus dove over the side of the curragh and beneath the waves like a sleek seal.

"Nimbus!" he bellowed.

A small head surfaced a few feet from shore.

"Who was she? You must tell me." Conn stood. The curragh rocked in the foaming surf.

Nimbus rolled to his back and kicked toward the shore, paddling cheerfully.

"Who gave you the message, Nimbus? If I could get my hands on you . . ." Conn waved a fist in the air.

Nimbus crawled out of the water and danced a little jig on the rocky beach.

Conn put his hands on his hips, his lips compressed to an angry line. "As king of Erin, I command you to tell me who gave you that message."

Nimbus stared up at the two soldiers who suddenly appeared on either side of him. With a small bow of surrender he cupped his hands around his mouth and yelled, "Why Gelina, of course, sire. Who else?"

Nimbus grinned as Conn sat down so abruptly that the curragh overturned, dumping the king into the chilly sea.

As the soldiers dove into the water after him, Nimbus clambered up the steep hillside, whistling all the way.

❖

PART TWO

SUMMER IS GONE

I have but one story—
The stags are moaning,
The sky is snowing,
Summer is gone.

Quickly the low sun
Goes drifting down
Behind the rollers,
Lifting and long.

The wild geese cry
Down the storm;
The ferns have fallen,
Russet and torn.

The wings of the birds
Are clotted with ice
I have but one story—
Summer is gone.

—Author unknown
9th century

❖

Chapter Ten

❖

The weather continued mild throughout the long summer. The seas yielded no word from Conn, and the fortress fought valiantly to maintain its fragile equilibrium. Three battalions of the Fianna patrolled Tara and the outlying area, keeping a watchful eye for Eoghan Mogh and his men. To everyone's relieved surprise no attack had reared its ugly head. The farmers returned to their *buailtean* to camp, watching over their cattle with increased vigor. The crops grew tall on the flat plains of Erin. Sheep scampered over the rolling meadows, their coats growing thick and strong as shearing approached.

On a hot day with the sun beating down on her head, Gelina sat in the courtyard, her bare feet dangling from the trapeze. The swing was motionless; not even a wayward breeze stirred it. Her body was as still as the swing, a familiar brooding look on her features. She gasped and clutched at the ropes as she found herself sailing into the air. Hearing a familiar laugh, she dropped to the ground in a low crouch and spun around.

"Curses, Nimbus! Are you trying to kill me?"

"No. But I'm sick of ye mooning around like a ghoul." Fire lit his eyes as he shook her shoulders, which were at just his level when she crouched. "Let us play, Gelina," he said grimly.

She had to laugh. "You make playing sound as much fun as the grave, you fool."

He let a grin replace his frown. "Can ye still do somersaults?" He clambered up on her shoulders and caught the trapeze in his small hands.

"Oof! If you'd quit walking on me, it would be easier." She stood, giving him a boost onto the narrow bar.

"What we need," he said, "are two trapezes. I could let go of one and ye could catch me from the other."

"Or vice versa," she added with a nasty grin.

He ignored her, executed a double somersault and landed flawlessly on his feet. Gelina caught the bar and hoisted herself upon it. The trapeze gained momentum with each swing of her legs. She dropped and hung upside down from her knees to find three giggling faces watching her.

Righting herself, she looked down guardedly at Conn's paramour who stood with two girls who couldn't have been much older than Gelina herself. The golden balls fastened to the ends of their spiral curls tinkled as they shook their heads in laughter.

A short plump girl with eyebrows died a startling black against her ivory skin called out. "Are you sure Conn did not foster a son instead of a daughter?"

They cackled loudly as Gelina's face flushed red in a response she could not stop. She put an awkward hand to her short curls, longing to tear out the girls' elaborate combs and pins.

"Now, girls"—Sheela's simpering voice chided them— "we must not make sport of those less fortunate than ourselves." She shook her head in mock sympathy, her dark curls bouncing. "With so little to work with, 'tis no wonder the waif wears men's clothing."

They burst into new peals of laughter. Gelina's right hand itched for a sword.

"Bitch." She spoke the word in her normal tone of voice, hardly aware she had said it aloud until she recognized the silence that greeted her.

The three women stared appalled, their mouths circles of shock. Nimbus's applause broke the silence. He stepped out from the shadows to stand before the uninvited audience.

"The fair is over, Sheela. Move on."

To Gelina he suddenly appeared a giant as he stood with hands on hips, facing the women. Sheela smirked as if she itched to say something but she herded the girls forward. Their laughter echoed back to Gelina as they disappeared into the fortress.

She sat silently on the swing as Nimbus turned around. "Where did you learn a word like that?" he asked.

Her eyes narrowed dangerously. "Would you care to hear more?"

Her legs began to swing, letting the trapeze gain dangerous

momentum as her voice swelled. A stream of obscenities, some of which Nimbus had never even heard, poured from her lips. He watched, his eyes round saucers of disbelief, as she finished her tirade with a triple somersault and landed with arms outstretched on the hay, breathing heavily.

He walked over to her prostrate form and softly asked, "Are ye well?"

Her eyes flew open but she halted her abrupt reply, remembering his timely disposal of Sheela. "Nimbus?"

His voice was softer than usual as if he was afraid of setting off an explosion he could not stop. "What, Gelina?"

"Will you teach me to fix my hair?"

"Ye don't need baubles and combs. Ye're just fine as ye are."

He extended a hand and breathed a sigh of relief when she took it. A quick heave was all it took to pull him into the hay on his head. Repeating a few curses he had heard her use just minutes before, he emerged with straw poking at all angles from his hair.

"Teach me to fix my hair, Nimbus!" He did not miss the note of pleading in her voice.

He climbed to his feet with a gallant bow. "How could I refuse a child of the king?"

Gelina smiled at his reply.

Darkness. The murky blackness surrounded him like a coarse blanket, muting all sound except the swell of the ocean beneath his ear. Splintered wood pillowed his head, the rough fragments scratching bloody furrows in his cheek. The coarse rope binding his hands and feet had long ago stopped tormenting him as numbness replaced the excruciating lack of blood in his limbs. He had lain there in darkness for so long that he had no idea when his weary eyes flickered open or shut. There was only more darkness, billowing out and drowning his own stench and the smell of whatever else had lain in this filth. His mouth was free but made no sound although he sometimes ached to cry out loud. Conn of the Hundred Battles lay wearily, his only thoughts of the days preceding these.

Two ships had set sail from Erin that day of the picnic. The lightweight sailing boats had carried scores of the Fianna. Conn had captained the foremost ship while an enthusiastic Barron Ó

Caflin stood in charge of the other. Excitement spread through
the men as they set sail from the wild and rocky coast, the spray
of the sea against their faces whetting their appetites for
adventure. Many a moon had come and gone since the men of
the Fianna had taken to the sea. Conn joined in the rolling sea
chant as they left behind the untamed coastline of Erin.

Standing by the rail, he watched the sun dip lower in the sky.
A cool breeze fraught with the smell of salt washed over him as
he stood leaning on the rail with chin in hand. His eyes were
distant, and his lips would not lose the ghost of a smile that had
haunted him since Nimbus had delivered his message. He
wondered how Gelina would fare in his absence, then shook his
head to crush the memory of lips pressed to his in innocent
surrender, knowing the first thing he should do when he
returned to Tara was thrash her for disobeying him on Midsummer's Eve. Every drunken caress, every touch of his lips on her
warm flesh, came back to him with blistering force. He was
lucky she hadn't been carrying a sword beneath that cloak.

He laughed aloud. He should have brought her along. He
chuckled to think of the Romans' reaction to that woman-child,
sword-wielding warrior of Erin. A light rain began to fall as the
sun disappeared behind the horizon.

A call interrupted his reverie. A man perched high on a
catwalk yelled, ''Ó Caflin has signaled there are kegs below the
deck. May we?''

Shaking the rain from his curly hair, Conn called back,
''Only if I get the first mug.''

Some of the men huddled under makeshift canvas shelters
while others stood openly in the rain as the barrel of ale was
carried from below and tapped to the cheers of the men. Conn
turned up the first mug with the others following suit.

The pleasant warmth slid down his throat and into his
stomach. A dullness settled in his brain, nestling there like a
dragon with its tail wrapped around his neck. His eyes narrowed
as he watched his men drop one by one to the deck in a
motionless sleep. A dizzy laugh escaped his lips, and he
wondered what sort of game they were playing. The laugh faded
into an echo as the deck reached up to receive him.

Running his tongue over cracked lips, he had pried open his
eyes to find himself facing a blazing sun. He shook his head to
clear it of the remaining fog, wincing as a shooting pain flew up

his neck to his brow. He had stared incredulously through pained eyes at the vista that surrounded him. Water surrounded the tiny boat he lay in on every horizon. No ship's mast broke the fine line between water and blue sky. Anger began to boil through his blood as the harsh realization of the betrayal flooded him. They had been drugged.

"More like poisoned," he growled, as he stared in the bottom of the boat to find evidence of his own sickness sometime in the drug-induced stupor.

He had raised a hand and gingerly touched his sun-scorched forehead, trying to gauge how long he had been adrift. The sun loomed high in the sky. While he had examined the brilliant cobalt blue, a mast had appeared on the horizon. The flag that rippled proud above it had sent a sigh through Conn's lungs.

"Gelina, ye look divine."

"Very funny, Nimbus."

Standing in front of the full-length mirror, she felt less than divine. Her hair, which now curled past her shoulders, stood on end, each strand painstakingly wrapped in rags by an oddly patient court jester. She awaited the fruition of their efforts. Her silk shift felt soft and cool against her sun-darkened skin.

"I look like a fool." She stomped her foot.

"I resent that." Nimbus turned away, arms crossed, lower lip protruding.

"Oh, I am sorry, Nimbus. I forget that you are a fool!" She looked truly repentant; his lip protruded another inch.

"Curses, I do seem to be making it worse. Did you get the dress from Moira?"

Nimbus forgot her careless choice of words. He scampered to the screen and poked his head both ways before tugging out a wooden box. Gelina hid a smile, fairly certain there were no spies behind the screen. Struggling under its weight, he heaved the box to the center of the floor. Breathing hard, he threw back the carved lid. Gelina knelt beside him, a gasp escaping her as she beheld its contents.

Fold after fold of diaphanous gold floated up from the confines of the box. A faint whiff of sandalwood wafted up from the satin as Gelina grasped it with eager hands and stood, holding the dress in front of her lean figure. The dress was cut low in the bodice but gathered at the waist. Billowy sleeves narrowed at the elbow, ending in a delicate tatting of lace at the back of the hand. Slender, black ribbons laced up the front.

Nimbus shook his head in awe. "'Tis just like Moira said—the most beautiful dress in the world." He skipped around Gelina, clapping his hands. "Came from across the sea, she said."

Gelina pivoted until she faced the mirror; the wide skirt fell to mid-ankle as she held it in front of her tall frame. "It really belonged to his mother?"

"Moira said it was a gift from his father, never worn for some reason." His eyes narrowed, taking in the gap between the hem and the floor. "Moira can add a lace ruffle if ye like."

She laughed. "I would like that. This court has seen the last of my bare feet."

Moira poked her familiar dark head with its impeccable widow's peak around the door. "Give me the dress, lass, if ye want it readied for tonight."

Gelina reluctantly handed it to her. Moira examined it with loving eyes and spoke more to herself than to the others. "She should have worn this. That boy came, ruining it all."

Gelina and Nimbus exchanged mystified glances. "What boy?" Gelina asked, knowing she had a better chance of getting an answer than Nimbus.

Recalled to the present, Moira shook her head briskly. "Just babbling to meself. I'll get to work on this." She bustled out of the room, leaving Nimbus with a puzzled frown on his brow.

Gelina shrugged. Her head pounded. "When can I take my hair down?"

He examined her scalp as she knelt in front of him. "Soon. Very soon." She sighed in relief. "In at least three hours," he finished.

Groaning, she swatted him as he ducked out of her way.

Visions. They haunted him in the darkness projected in the deepest recesses of his eyelids.

Kevin Ó hArtagain's bloody corpse taunted him, appearing so close to him that he could not escape. "You are a fool, Conn. When will you learn not to trust everyone? You were far too naive to rule Erin and now you will never rule again. You did not use your power. So you lost it." The mocking laughter circled him as the half-rotted corpse dissipated into the air. A fever spread through his veins, its sick odor permeating his dulled senses.

Gelina danced in front of him as she had at the picnic, her eyes misty with tears behind the shadows of a golden mask. She wore a smock, long and gathered red silk with a border of green and gold. Her dusty feet pirouetted before him. He reached out a feeble hand to unmask her and kiss away her tears, knowing his lips would find hers even if he did not want them to. She whirled so fast that she blurred, leaving him with only the green satin of the border draped over his eyes, setting him on fire.

Green. The glittering green of emerald eyes. He was pinned against rock. He could not move. He saw the sword embedded in his chest, pinning him to the rock like an insect. The silver slowly turned, setting his heart on fire to match his eyes. Following the sword up to the strong hand that twisted it, he saw a woman's face. It was Gelina's adult face and twisted cruel mouth he saw, her mocking smile pinning him more effectively to the rock than her sword ever could.

It was cold. Chills racked his body with a violence that shook the bonds he had long ago stopped struggling against. There was snow. He lay in the snow, gagged and bound not twelve feet from the window where he and Gelina had gazed at the full moon a lifetime ago. She stood there now. Pensively staring at the snow with one arm resting on the sill, her forehead pressed against the cool wood of the open shutter.

Fighting against his ropes, he saw the glow of the fire behind her. He felt the warmth in her eyes and knew somehow that she was searching for him. A low growl came from beside him, raising the hairs at the back of his neck.

He turned. A jackal with black matted hair grinned at him, its gaping mouth revealing jagged, bloody teeth. The animal nodded knowingly. He watched in horror as the jackal turned away from him and raced for the window. It leapt, crashing through the shutters, ripping out Gelina's throat with a single motion as Conn struggled against his ropes. The vision disappeared, and for the first time in his adult memory Conn cried, the tears choking him as they ran into his mouth.

Light. Screwing his lids tightly shut, he heard in another vision a man's commanding voice. "Great Jupiter! Look what you've done! It is him! He's alive! Get over here, you fool, and lift him out of there!''

Feeling his body carried up an incline, Conn struggled to open his eyes. The bright light of the sun hit him like a mace between the eyes, and he fainted from the pain, slumping in the arms of those who carried him.

Eoghan Mogh was a patient man. In his southern stronghold he awaited word of Conn's capture, amusing himself with plans for his new kingdom. The waiting had just begun. The two ships once outfitted with the finest of the Fianna were manned by his own men now. Conn's soldiers were dead, their bloated bodies floating in the sea. Barron Ó Caflin was out of the way, for now.

In twelve months Conn would be officially declared dead. Eoghan chuckled, picturing the cairn that would be erected in memory of the vanished Ard-Righ, Conn of the Hundred Battles. Then he would step in. He would organize Tara, creating order out of chaos, becoming the high king of Erin without lifting one sword.

Time. It was his only enemy now. And his only friend.

Nimbus avoided Gelina's eyes, something he had done often this fall eve. ''I regret that I'll be busy tonight. Big show to put on and all that rot. I've procured another escort for ye.''

''You mean after you've gone to all this trouble, you won't be accompanying me to the festivities?'' Gelina asked, her voice reflecting her dismay.

''Afraid not. I must go.'' He opened the door to her bedchamber to reveal Sean Ó Finn, looking somewhat abashed. ''This fellow will take good care of ye.''

He pushed past Sean and strode down the hall, struggling to hide his newborn feelings. When he was out of their earshot, he mumbled to himself, ''Can't let a beautiful woman hang around with a midget forever, can I?''

He blessedly missed the expression on Sean's face as the soldier took a long, appreciative look at Gelina. It had taken Nimbus's loving eyes to see the woman beneath the childish exterior she flashed so carelessly. He had allowed the dress to stand on its own as the most ornate part of her attire, leaving her own simplicity to complement it. The soft curls he had fashioned tumbled around her shoulders, a simple gold comb in the shape of a seashell sweeping them upward over her right ear. Her height and straight shoulders gave her a dignity and grace that was the antithesis of the soft plumpness of most of the women at court.

Her eyes sparkled, thin outlines of kohl below them; her cheeks glowed under the gentle touch of red juice squeezed from berries. Her color deepened as she stood before Sean's perusal. She resisted an overwhelming urge to crawl under the bed.

Clearing her throat, she caught Sean's eye. He had the good grace to look sheepish.

He offered her his arm and said warmly, "Shall we go, milady?"

She lay one hand on his arm, the newly dyed crescents of her fingernails a brilliant crimson against the green of his tunic. A new shyness gripped them as they strolled to the great hall.

Gelina wracked her mind, trying to think of something to say. "'Tis warm outside, is it not?"

He looked at her oddly, and she flushed as she realized that the men had already began to talk of snow as the cool wind blew out of the mountains. "I was jesting, of course," she quickly amended. "Conn said I brought the snow with me. He said there had been no snow for years until I came to Tara."

Sean laughed. "If you brought the snow, Gelina, you also brought the sunshine. I've never seen less rain and fog." He silently congratulated himself on his chivalry.

They had reached the door of the great hall. Taking a deep breath, Gelina closed her eyes for an instant before Sean swept open the door. The din that met their ears provided a moment's comfort. She had been fearful of sudden silence. Now it seemed that she and Sean would be able to melt into the crowd.

A trumpet's fanfare sounded, cutting through the conversation and laughter. Looking to the platform, she saw her familiar playmate brandishing a horn.

As the people turned in his direction, he called out in his most booming voice, "Ladies and Gentlemen—Lady Gelina, daughter of the Ard-Righ."

No matter how hard Gelina prayed, the floor would not open up and swallow her. She was left with no alternative. She raised her head and met the eyes of her king's people. With head held high, she smiled and nodded. All eyes were drawn to her in the complete silence of the hall. After a few seconds of looking embarrassed, Sean drew himself up proudly, not oblivious to the envious stares of his comrades.

"Shall we dance?" Sean said loudly enough to cue several musicians to their left, who struggled with their instruments and a few discordant notes before finding the lilting melody they sought.

Gelina took his arm. She counted the rhythm under her breath until they fell into step without a flaw. The evening passed in a blur. More dances followed, some with the men of the Fianna, another with a bold farmer who handled her like a piece of rare glass. Dexterous dancers linked hands and wove around the room. A small shiver went through her each time she clasped hands with one of the familiar braided figures, but it soon disappeared as she became comfortable with their teasing banter and graceful moves. Sean waited impatiently on the sidelines for his opportunity to whisk her away again.

Finding herself alone during a break in the music, she massaged her tired calves and searched for a familiar face among the cavorting jesters. She did not find it. The platform was empty although the velvet curtain seemed to move a fraction of an inch even as she watched. She frowned as Sean approached with a goblet of mead in each hand.

"I thought you might need this," he said.

"I needed this an hour ago."

He laughed. "I thought you were going to scale the wall and pitch Nimbus to the floor when he pulled out that trumpet."

"Quiet, Sean. Not everyone knows I could have."

She took a sip of the mead, and through her veins spread a sweet sensation of warmth that seemed to be related more to the warmth she saw in Sean's sparkling brown eyes than to the sweetness of the mead.

"Someone seems to be less than pleased with the caterpillar's transformation." Sean pointed toward the corner where a pouting Sheela watched them with narrowed eyes. "I do believe I promised the good widow a dance tonight, but I just can't seem to tear myself away."

"You must. We must not disappoint the king's lady." Her smile faded, but Sean didn't seem to notice.

"I shall pass tonight. I've no stomach for her teasing." He glanced at Gelina, realizing he'd forgotten he was talking to a lady, not a comrade in arms.

She spoke rapidly, trying to cover the effect his words had on her. "These jigs are tiresome. Tell them to play the tune you played at the picnic, and we will show them how to dance."

He nodded, a glint in his eye. "You must promise me one thing."

"Anything, kind sir." She batted her eyelashes, fixing her mouth in a pout that made Sheela's look amateur.

He shook his finger at her. "No juggling."

The first plaintive strains of the flute flew through her heart like needles. Her feet joined the dance as Conn's face appeared in her memory which it had never really left. The other dancers backed off the floor, leaving it to her and Sean.

She whirled with primitive grace until even Sean was left standing still. Her vow to remain shod flew across the hall with her sandals. No one knew that the brilliant emerald of her eyes glistened with unshed tears. The twirling golden skirt blurred around her ankles. The music ended, and she sank to the floor in fold upon fold of diaphanous material, head bowed.

There was only silence until a farmer began to clap his callused hands, nudging the man next to him who stood with mouth open. He clapped, too, and soon the whole court had joined in the thunderous applause.

She opened her eyes to find Sean's hand extended to her. She smiled weakly. "Well, I did not juggle."

That was only the beginning. She spent night after night in the great hall, seeking the stubborn cheer of Conn's people. Although still more comfortable in Sean's pants, she folded them aside and wore the skirts Moira fashioned for her. But she persisted in wearing an oversized man's jerkin to bed, a garment she had pilfered from Conn's chambers with her own hand.

Nimbus became increasingly hard to corner for any sort of sport, and she found herself spending less and less time in his company. Despite her newfound popularity her loneliness deepened as the months without Conn wore on.

The light winter snows came just as the poets had predicted. Eight months had passed since Conn's departure. A fleeting glimmer of doubt was seen in the eyes of the men and women of his court although they strove to cover it with a joke or a song.

On a cold winter night Gelina pushed open the door of the chess room, leaving the laughter and music behind. The ashes in the fireplace lay cold and forgotten. The dusty chess board sat untouched on the table. The room was awash with the gentle glow of a new moon. She sat down on the bench and propped her legs up on the table in a pose she was seldom allowed. With a deep sigh she rose and went to the window.

Placing one arm on the windowsill, she threw open the wooden shutter and leaned into the chill night. The snow had begun to fall again. Soft flakes brushed like feathers against her face. The scant dusting lay like a thin blanket on the earth, bathing the land in a luminous glow reflected in the moon's face. A tear slid down her cheek and into her mouth where its saltiness tasted somehow both foreign and comforting. She stood there for a long time, unaware of the hungry eyes that watched her from the darkness of the night.

Chapter Eleven
❖

The ship moved slowly down the coast of Erin, cleaving the blanket of mist. The steady breaking of the waves against the ship's bow cut through the dense fog. A solitary figure stood at the rail, marveling at the silent world before him. The bearded, caped man watched the rocky coastline grow clearer through narrowed, hungry eyes, his mouth set in a tense line. He did not feel the splintered wood that sought to embed itself in his fingertips as he grasped the rail with both hands. He was going home.

Gelina stared at the crumpled piece of paper in her hand, her whole body shaking. She did not need to read the message again to remember the words—*Help to dethrone the bastard king*.

She had opened the artfully sealed parchment lying on her bed without a second thought. She searched the scrawled message for clues but found nothing. The heavy bonded parchment could be found anywhere in the fortress. She paced the room in long strides, a habit she still clung to when distressed.

"It will hardly be necessary to dethrone him. He is to be declared dead within the month," she said to the silent room.

A white kitten with a darkened face and paws watched her passively from the foot of the bed. Gelina had practiced saying "declared dead" so many times in the past month that the cat found nothing odd in her behavior except a slight confusion that no epithet or hurled vase followed her words. It did not have to remain puzzled for long.

"Behl and thunder!" Running a nervous hand through her hair, she tousled it into the very style she fought so hard to tame.

Who could she tell of this missive? She could not tell Sean for he had no inkling of her background. Not knowing what Nimbus did or did not know, she did not dare reveal more. Mer-Nod was her only possible confidant, and he was a very busy man. He had dispatched envoys to Britain two months ago. They had returned with discouraging news. Neither Conn nor his men had ever been sighted in Britain. Two ships, over three hundred men, and the high king of Erin had vanished without a trace over ten months ago.

With the frequent comings and goings within the fortress, anyone could have left the missive. Clans were coming from leagues away to offer last respects for the missing king and advice on the future of Erin. The great hall broke into a new altercation every night. Even Sean had breathed thanks that the weaponry room was kept locked according to ancient tradition.

The men of the Fianna held lengthy conferences marked by disagreement. Who would be king? Were the men sent with Conn also dead? Was Mer-Nod capable of making the decisions at hand? Was Conn truly dead?

All of these questions circled Gelina's mind as more and more dark evidence was presented. In the past few months the only peace of mind she had came from her rides on Silent Thunder, Conn's own steed. With Sean locked in meetings, she would steal away to the stables with an old cap covering her hair and Sean's clothes covering her body. All of her concentration and frustration would be spent in controlling the headstrong Arabian. She would have sought the horse's solace now in her confusion had it not been for the fog.

It had rolled in from the coast in huge billowing clouds, covering the land in an impenetrable mass. The dampness had penetrated the castle until she sought the haven of the fire in her bedchamber. She went to that fire now, holding the note in the flames until a corner of it flared into destruction.

She would bide her time. Whoever had left the message could not be far away. She went to the corner and opened her chest. Buried beneath the folds of linen dresses was a short scabbard and a small, sharp dagger.

Lifting her skirt, she strapped the weapon to her thigh and felt an immeasurable sense of reassurance. Pausing in front of the mirror, she ran an ivory comb through her luxurious hair, eyes thoughtful. She would go downstairs and scout for Conn's enemy who was unknowingly her enemy, too.

Nimbus sat on the steps, chin in hands, observing the scene below. Gesturing hands and moving lips filled the great hall. Every man and woman crowding Tara seemed to be voicing an opinion of earth-trembling importance. He sighed in disgust, unable to avoid hearing some of the thoughts uttered.

"Some say a sea monster et the whole lot of them."

"He was a good king." A drunk farmer slid down the wall, each word bringing him closer to the floor. "He was a very good king."

"I think our next king should have to stay home and not go gallivanting off, sticking his nose in others' affairs."

The Fianna joined in the boisterous row, their voices carrying over the crowd in deepened tones. "Goll MacMorna should be king. He is the largest."

"How idiotic. He is as gentle as a puppy."

"Not when he's ripping a man's head off—and I've seen him do it, too!"

Nimbus longed to clap his hands over his ears and scream until he could hear no more of the nonsense that had settled over the fortress like some dimwitted plague. Anarchy was swiftly replacing the ordered system of government Conn had established. Even the most practical of his subjects seemed to be falling under its spell.

"Perhaps I should present meself as king. I'm sure they would agree," Nimbus muttered to himself, shaking his head at his own whimsy.

He bowed his head in shame as he thought of the charge Conn had left him with on the day he sailed for Britain. The saddest thing of all was that Nimbus himself had stopped believing that Conn would return. No amount of joking or juggling could stop the spread of darkness through his heart as he saw hope flicker and extinguish itself.

Hearing footsteps on the stairs behind him, he turned to see Gelina. Her once-galloping gait had been replaced by slow, ladylike steps, the effort of which occasionally flickered across her face. He smiled as she sat beside him on the steps, arranging her skirt around her feet. The green of her skirt matched perfectly the green of her eyes but he could not help noticing the trepidation he saw there. A new air of maturity graced her bearing but it seemed to be an air born of sadness.

"Milady." He swept off his feathered cap.

"Spare me the theatrics, Nimbus. 'Tis Gelina, not Sheela."

He started to tease her but stopped, noting a tenseness in her voice like a harp string stretched to the snapping point.

"Sorry." He reached out his small hand and placed it over hers in an unfamiliar gesture.

Smiling at him gratefully, she took his hand, and they sat watching the hall. Gelina did not know what she searched for but hoped she would know it if she saw it. Two fires burned in the fireplaces, seeking to dispel the dampness of the foggy night. To Gelina the fire gave light but no warmth. The hall was devoid of warmth. Cold faces made unintelligible noises. Chill music was ground out of the instruments like chaff in the wind. The notes hung in the air as if on the verge of falling into a thousand brittle pieces. The Fianna seemed reduced to a mob of quarrelsome boys. She saw Sean himself gesturing to a group of men in the corner, some of whom were shaking their heads violently. She and Nimbus exchanged glances, each reading despair in the other's eyes.

They both saw Mer-Nod stride into the hall and climb onto the dais where Conn's empty throne sat. The feathered mantle rested heavily on his shoulders. The year had not been kind to him; it had etched new lines around his eyes and mouth. He lifted his arms for attention, waiting for a feeble trumpet blast to stop the babble.

Lowering his arms, he stood for a moment in the silence, as if hesitant to proceed. Gelina felt a serpent slowly uncoil itself in the pit of her stomach, and she fought an urge to retreat up the steps. Nimbus grasped her hand and she found herself surprised to see Sean standing just below her as if to shield her from an invisible threat.

Mer-Nod's voice shot through the crowd. "A member of the expedition has returned."

A murmur rose to a roar, and Nimbus hardly felt the nails that stabbed him as Gelina clutched his hand, not allowing herself to hope.

Mer-Nod continued, refusing to be daunted by the uproar. "I will let the returning soldier tell his story."

He stepped aside to let a bearded man with straggly blond hair take the stage. Gelina closed her eyes and fought the bile rising in her gorge as she recognized him. Barron Ó Caflin stood on the dais, body emaciated and skeletal, hair mangy and lank.

He raised one hand, its tremble effectively silencing the hall. "Both ships were lost in a storm on the night we left Erin." He punctuated his sentence with a feeble cough. "I awoke the morning after the storm clinging to the broken side of the ship that Conn was captaining. I floated to an island where I was marooned until rescued yesterday by a fishing boat. To my knowledge there were no other survivors."

A voice cried, "Then the king is dead?"

Barron nodded slowly as if the knowledge were breaking his own heart. Gelina rose to her feet in a trance, never feeling Sean's hand on her shoulder.

"You cannot know he is dead. Not for certain. We thought you were dead and you're not." Her voice shot high and clear across the room like a slap that passed as a flicker of annoyance across Ó Caflin's face.

"You cannot know what it was like. We thought the skies were cracking open. The thunder was deafening. Lightning surrounded us like a web. Waves three times the size of the ships crashed over the bows. The ships were crushed like driftwood." He spread his hands in a silent plea for belief, ignoring the tall girl who refused to sit down.

"But there is still a chance that Conn lives. At least for two more weeks! If one man sent on that voyage is alive, then another man could be."

"Silence! I shall tell you then. I sought to protect the ladies from the grisly truth, but if I am forced to reveal it, then I shall!'' Barron's voice was ugly and shrill. "I saw the king. I saw his bloated body float past me after the storm." He shot a vicious glance at Gelina.

The strong clipped brogue echoed through the hall. "What storm? There was no storm."

The tall, caped figure stood just inside the doors. Barron's face went three shades paler as he recognized the mocking voice. Sheela slid to the floor in a swoon in front of the dais. A huge cheer rose from the crowd as a beautiful auburn-haired creature flew down the steps and threw herself into the arms of the man who stood there. He swung her around and around, letting her tears wet both of their faces. Conn of the Hundred Battles had come home.

Chapter Twelve

❖

"I was only away for a year, lass. What ever did they do to you?"

Conn and Gelina stood alone in his chambers. He held her at arm's length, his hands warm on her shoulders. She could not erase the grin from her face.

"With a few suggestions from Moira, Nimbus took it into his head to turn me into a girl. Are you pleased with the results?" She stepped back and turned slowly, arms spread wide.

The warmth in his blue eyes gave her the answer she sought. He stared at her as if believing she would vanish from his sight.

"I am lucky the Fianna did not desert their posts for the pleasure of squiring you around."

She searched his face for any shadow when he mentioned the Fianna but found only unabashed happiness. "I see a few changes in you, too, milord." She patted the silver wings that graced his temples, highlighting the unruly dark hair. "Perhaps the question should be, 'What did they do to you?'"

His smile faded and he looked away. "'Tis over. I do not

wish to discuss it. The dog responsible for the tragedy will be executed, and his name will be stricken from all records of history.''

''You're proceeding with your plans?'' She walked slowly to the shuttered window.

''You do not approve?''

''As someone who was once threatened with the same fate, I find public beheadings distasteful.'' She met his steady gaze with candor.

Conn sighed. ''An example must be made. I will not tolerate betrayal.''

''I know.'' Her lips twisted in a sardonic smile.

He stirred the fire. ''If what happened to me were his only crime, perhaps I could be more lenient. But, Gelina, three hundred of Erin's finest men perished because of Ó Caflin's misguided loyalties. I am sworn to avenge their deaths.''

''Couldn't you just banish him or imprison him?''

''If I banished him, he would find a way back to Eoghan Mogh's camp before the morrow. To imprison him would be worse than death. You cannot understand.''

''You seek to do him kindness by beheading him publicly?'' She arched an incredulous eyebrow.

He pulled her down to sit beside him on a cloth-covered lounge. ''Once a man has tasted the sweet spring waters of Erin and slept under a thousand stars, life in a dismal cell would be no life at all. I have a heart, Gelina. I watched Barron Ó Caflin grow from a scrawny, charming boy into a valiant fighting man. The only thing I missed was watching his heart turn black as midnight. I will end it cleanly and quickly.'' He clasped her hands in his, searching her face for some hint of understanding.

Looking up from her lap, she smiled winsomely. ''We've been together for only minutes, and already we disagree.''

Conn laughed, happy to let the tension seep from his body. As he stared into her sparkling eyes, he was reminded of his plan to chasten her for disobeying him on Midsummer's Eve, but the teasing words died on his lips. His broad thumbs caressed the trusting hands entwined in his. How could he chastise her for offering even in error what he had been only too willing to take? His ale-hazed memories of that night were vague at best, but the sharp clarity of his moments with her were enough to wake him in the night with a longing deep in his gut for something he could not name. He opened his mouth, then closed it again, no more certain of a lecture coming out than an apology.

Overcome by a strange shyness, he shook his head. "Look at you. You're a woman grown. I don't think I've ever been so proud as I was when I walked into that hall and saw you standing up to Ó Caflin. Your eyes glowed green fire and you pointed at him as if you already knew he was the liar."

"Did I point? All I remember was your voice coming from nowhere like magic."

His fingers teased a stubborn curl at her earlobe into submission. "Surely you do not believe in magic. I think even Mer-Nod has given up on his heritage of Cesard the magician."

"Who knows? Perhaps it was Mer-Nod who conjured you back to me."

"I regret to disillusion you, Gelina, but a real ship conjured me back from halfway around the world."

A wistful look crossed her features. "I would like to go to Rome someday. Was it so terrible once your friend rescued you?"

"No . . . , it took me a full moon to recover from my time on the slave galley, but Demetrius was an able host and he made my stay as pleasant as possible. You can imagine my shock when I regained consciousness in Rome, thousands of miles from Erin. But I promised you I would come back, and here I am."

Gelina stretched out her arms to him and rested her head on his shoulder. He was shocked to discover how pleasant her sweet-smelling body felt against him. His broad hands flexed on her slender back, fighting the urge to draw her into him, the fear that she would not protest frightening him more than the fear that she would. When a sharp rap came on the door, he stood, feeling unaccountably guilty.

Sheela flew into the room, dark hair disheveled. Gelina rolled her eyes and turned her back, staring into the fire.

"Oh, my love! I would have come to you sooner. Didn't you see me in the great hall? I swooned when you appeared there just like a ghost. I tried to come to you as soon as I recovered but that infernal jackass of a jester sat on me!"

Gelina's shoulders shook suspiciously. Sheela shot her a venomous look.

"Sat on you?" Conn queried, eyebrows raised politely.

"Indeed! He said that in my weakened condition, I did not

need to be walking about. And then he sat on my chest! Everyone was milling around. No one noticed and there he sat for what seemed like hours on my delicate chest. I nearly swooned again.''

She allowed her legs to fold beneath her and pressed her delicate chest to Conn's arm. He steadied her and led her to a chair. Watching from the corner of her eye, Gelina saw Sheela bestow a hearty kiss on Conn's lips, looking far from faint. She stood and cleared her throat loudly, which only seemed to intensify Sheela's grip on Conn. He disentangled himself with difficulty.

"I shall take my leave now. I ate earlier and find myself feeling a bit . . . queasy," Gelina said, smiling sweetly.

"I think the lass is insulting me. Is she insulting me?" Sheela turned wide brown eyes to Conn.

He shrugged, refusing to commit himself as he struggled to hide a smile.

"They prepare a feast in the hall. I will see you there, Conn," Gelina called back as she exited the room.

Pulling the door shut behind her, she leaned against it, her elation mixed with a sick feeling deep in her gut. Looking down the hall, she saw Nimbus leaning against the wall with arms crossed smugly.

"You sat on her?" she said.

Nimbus dragged her around the corner as they both doubled over in paroxysms of laughter.

He sat huddled in the corner, his head between his knees. His lank, filthy hair hung past his shoulders like a faded, moth-eaten mantle. The stone floor radiated a chill that traveled through his bones to the top of his skull. Licking his chapped lips, he ran his hand through his once-glorious hair. Staring into the darkness, his eyes focused beyond the dungeon walls.

Barron Ó Caflin had become a learned man in the past months. He had learned of exile. He had learned of broken promises. He had learned of doubt and uncertainty for the first time in his life. And now he had learned of fear. The men on Conn's ships had been murdered, their throats cut while they lay in the throes of the vicious illness induced by the poisoned ale. Few awoke in time to offer a feeble struggle to Eoghan Mogh's soldiers. It had taken every ounce of wit and cunning Barron possessed to stop the men from murdering him at the sides of his companions. As Barron had stood surrounded by the corpses of his friends and comrades, a creeping numbness had settled in his mind. Things were not supposed to happen this way. But they had.

He was home now. Locked in a dingy cell without even a hint of light. He sat with head bowed. He held no illusions that Eoghan Mogh would storm the castle before his impending execution. He spared himself that maudlin hope. Conn had visited his cell already. With the light from the open door framing him, he had appeared as an avenging spirit sent by the gods to torment him.

His plans had gone awry from the very moment that redheaded wench had stood to confront him. She had thrown a shadow of doubt on his words, turning the crowd against him, though that had hardly mattered when Conn's voice echoed through the hall. He sat in the airless cell remembering other days. His pride in the Fianna had died long ago in the flames of his twisted ambition but the memory of it stung him now. The laughter of young men haunted him and he bowed his head, learning the one lesson that had eluded him all along. Conn of the Hundred Battles was not a man to betray lightly. The silence closed in around him.

Tapers were lit from one end of the hall to the other. Glowing faces added to the shining light. In one corner the musicians deftly tuned their instruments. There were to be no ribald ditties sung tonight. The chief minstrel would assure the music of his flutes and harps was so beautiful that it would wring tears from hearts of stone.

The bustling activity halted and a hoarse cheer rose as Conn strode into the room. Waving a hand in recognition, he let an almost boyish grin cross his face as he approached the throne.

He had ignored Nimbus's whispered suggestion that he make a grand entrance after the people had been waiting, saying only, "They have waited long enough."

His white shirt shot through with golden threads was covered by a crimson coat that fell to the floor in wide folds. A golden girdle set with emeralds and rubies encircled his waist. A torque of gold was fastened around his throat by a brooch of sapphires that matched his eyes. Unruly dark hair fell to his shoulders, the new silver wings gleaming in the light of a thousand tallow candles. He sat on the throne and stretched his long legs in front of him, watching the frantic preparations with poorly concealed delight.

Cook appeared from the kitchen bearing a boar's head on a platter precariously balanced between hand and hip. "Get out of me way, ye arseholes! I'll drop this meat on yer heads if ye don't!" she announced, scattering the serving girls and cup-bearers.

"Perhaps we should recruit her for the Fianna," Conn whispered as Mer-Nod joined him on the dais.

Catching sight of the king, Cook stumbled backward, nearly dropping her burden. She heaved it to the nearest table and backed out of the room, bowing all the way.

As word of Conn's arrival spread through the fortress and surrounding *raths,* the hall filled. No one cared that the hour approached midnight. Children were snatched from beds and thrust into clothes despite their groans. Conn welcomed hand-clasps from the men and accepted shy pecks on each cheek from some of the bolder women.

Standing with arms outstretched, he had little difficulty gaining the rapt attention of everyone in the hall. "I have come home!"

"And about time it was!" one of the soldiers called out laughingly.

Conn smiled. "Yes, it was time, was it not? I sat many nights on a rooftop staring out over the city of Rome, a city whose beauties you can only imagine unless you've seen them. I was surrounded by hospitality, exotic women"—a whoop rang from the corner—"and an abundance of rich, incredible food." He paused. "And do you know what I craved?" He lowered his voice as expectant faces awaited his answer. "A fresh-faced lass of Erin and a mug of ale." Laughter rippled through the hall.

The minstrels struck up a rollicking jig, and a jester led the dance, grabbing from the sidelines a comely girl who squealed in mock dismay.

Conn sat back on the throne, searching the crowd as more dancers joined in the reel. "Where are Nimbus and Gelina?" he shouted to Mer-Nod, struggling to be heard over the music and laughter.

Mer-Nod shrugged. "Up to some mischief, no doubt." He scanned the crowd. "Sean is absent. That might account for Gelina's whereabouts."

Conn frowned and leaned forward to question him further as Gelina appeared in the doorway. A ballad singer's sweet alto rose in a gentle melody as Gelina stood peering through the crowd. Against his own volition Conn rose to his feet as the room narrowed to hold only the slender figure in the doorway. Her gaze halted on the dais, and she spun in a full circle, spreading the golden satin of her skirt, eyebrows arched for his approval.

His expression did not change. He stepped off the dais and made his way through the crowd. A path cleared before him. The dancers paused, and it was only Nimbus's vicious pinch and frantic gesture that kept the chief minstrel directing his musicians in the lilting melody. Gelina smiled uncertainly as Conn faced her. He saw the familiar flicker of fear that he hated cross her features.

Offering her his arm, he said softly, "Shall we dance, milady?"

"Better than we used to, I think," she replied, breathing a slow sigh of relief that did not go unnoticed by her partner.

"You still fear me." It was a statement that Conn made as he swung her into the dance, not a question. Her bare back felt warm and silken beneath the gentle pressure of his fingers.

"I feared you were angry because I wore your mother's dress. Do you still fear me?" she asked.

He looked deep into her eyes and replied, "Perhaps more than before."

She looked away and then returned his gaze steadily. "No sword hides beneath this dress."

He laughed despite himself at her serious words. "The way you fill that dress, I doubt there would be room for any weapon save the beauty given you by nature."

Blushing, she trod hard upon his toe. He laughed harder even as he stumbled.

"I wish you would not laugh at me. There are some who hardly find me as hilarious as you seem to."

"Quit pouting, Gelina. I find you far more lovely than funny, and I'm very proud of the way my foundling has bloomed."

His teasing words stung her, and she pulled away, tossing her head. "If you will excuse me, I believe I promised this dance to someone else."

He stood in the middle of the room in unfamiliar bewilderment as she flounced through the crowd, disappearing by the long tables. Straightening his shoulders, he sauntered back to the dais where a smirking Nimbus greeted him.

"What ails ye, Conn? Lose yer touch with the ladies in yer travels?"

Swatting him out of the throne, Conn replied, "What lady? I was dancing with Gelina."

Rolling his eyes, Nimbus muttered something unintelligible.

Eyeing him suspiciously, Conn asked, "What did you say?"

"Nothing, sire. But someone else seems to think Gelina is quite a lady."

He gestured to the floor. Conn watched as Sean Ó Finn led Gelina into the dance. Her laughing face was turned to him as if they shared some private joke. A strange knot curled in Conn's stomach as he watched with open mouth. Nimbus studied him, eyes narrowed.

"They've become friends. That is wonderful," Conn said wanly.

"Spectacular," Nimbus hissed in his ear before clambering off the dais and vanishing in the crowd. Conn felt very alone as he watched the scene below him.

Gelina spun around the room with Sean, all of her attention focused on forcing her long narrow feet into the petite steps of the dance. Her overt concentration and studied smile was wasted on Sean, who glowed with excitement and talked incessantly.

"Who would have thought it was Barron? He and I grew up together. We've played together since we were wee babes. I suppose that's why he ensured I would be left behind when those ships sailed from Erin." He shook his head in amazement. "How can you know the depths to which a person can sink? He dropped hints about Eoghan Mogh, said he admired his strategy, but I never guessed his intentions were so deadly."

Gelina heard enough of his speech to interject, "If one of you had listened to Nimbus—" before Sean interrupted her.

"Conn himself had no inkling. And he is a shrewd judge of character. At least he came home in time to avert a catastrophe."

At the mention of Conn's name Gelina glanced at the dais to find the throne empty. From the corner of her eye she saw a door at the side of the hall slowly close. Pushing away from Sean, she mumbled an apology and ducked through the dancers. She opened the door and peered into the room. Conn sat at the window, staring into the misty midnight.

She stepped into the room and closed the door, dulling the music to a delicate echo. Conn held something in his hands, turning it over and over. Reaching out her hand, she gently took it from him and found herself holding the precisely carved figure of the white queen from the chess set that still rested in the corner as they had left it the last time they played.

"I dreamed about you once," he said softly without looking at her. "I dreamed you were in this room waiting for me."

She sat down on the wide windowsill, her back against the wooden siding. Laughing softly, she said, "I probably was. I came here often."

"I am sorry if I hurt you out there." He looked at her, his eyes unguarded. "I forget you are a big girl now and I mustn't banter with you like I used to."

"If you didn't tease me, I'd be devastated. I guess I've become too used to the ways of the ladies of the court. 'Tis essential that you bounce off at least once a night with an offended pout," she told him sheepishly.

"And do you try to do everything the ladies at court do?" He looked momentarily alarmed.

She quickly reassured him, "Oh, no! Not everything." Conn breathed a sigh of relief as she continued, "I refuse to drop my gloves just so some bumbling idiot can scoop them up. And I still ride bareback."

Laughing loudly, Conn asked, "How is Bluebell?"

She quickly recovered from the baffled look that flashed across her face. "The mare you left me to ride? Gentle as a kitten. I ride her often."

"I cannot wait for a jaunt on Silent Thunder. I hope the stable boy exercised him well."

Clearing her throat, she replied, "Every time I've seen Silent Thunder, the horse has looked in prime condition."

"I brought your present."

Her eyes widened in delight. "Under the circumstances I assumed you had forgotten."

"As much as you annoyed me about that damned red, gold, and green dress? I didn't dare return without it. Why do you think I went to Rome? It was all a ploy to attain the infernal garment. I had a maidservant leave it in your chamber."

Gelina's smile faded as she remembered the note that had been left in her chamber earlier. The confusion she had felt then seemed years away instead of only hours. Conn studied her face, mystified by the abrupt change in her demeanor.

"Gelina, does something trouble you?"

Quickly recalling her smile, she answered, "Nothing at all. I was thinking how badly the evening was going until your return." She made a rapid decision not to tell Conn about the message, determined that nothing would spoil his homecoming.

The plaintive strains of a flute floated in from the great hall, and Conn cocked his head to listen. He met Gelina's grin with one of his own, and they both recalled a warm spring day, cheese melting in the sun and the sweet taste of mead on their tongues.

She stood and curtsied, offering her arm to him. He faced her for a moment, an unfamiliar sensation of longing dancing through his body. Then he took her arm and led her to the door. Opening the door with one hand, he put his other arm around her and they danced into the crowd as if they had never left.

It was impossible for them to be as inconspicuous as they thought they were. Gelina was almost tall enough to look him in the eye and moved with the athletic grace of a young lioness. They spun faster and faster. She threw back her head, laughing out loud.

Standing by the tables, Sheela watched with open mouth, allowing the goblet of mead she held to dribble down the front of her silk dress. In the entranceway to the kitchen Cook nudged a young serving girl and pointed to the king and his partner, smiling broadly. Sean paused in the dance to watch. A nagging sensation pricked the back of his neck, and he remembered a young girl in men's clothing slammed against a wall in the weaponry room, the breath knocked from her lungs. Frowning, he continued in the dance, dismissing the memory and its implications from his mind.

"The gods be cursed! 'Tis just like that bastard to come crawling out of the grave to destroy our plans." Eoghan Mogh sat in the saddle on his nervously prancing horse, staring into the fog, a muscle twitching in his cheek.

The rider who had brought him the news sat stoically on his mount wondering if he was going to be run through for his trouble.

"I am beginning to think he is immortal myself. Perhaps he is one of those gods you are cursing." The cloaked figure perched on the third horse shook his head in disgust.

"He may be a god but he will not be Ard-Righ of Erin when this year is out. Do you know what must be done?" Eoghan studied the dark-haired figure, hands clenching the reins.

A roguish grin spread across the sharp features of the cloaked man. "I know. And I am ready. I've been ready."

Remembering the silent messenger who watched them, Eoghan shook a handful of gold pieces out of a linen bag and tossed them to him. Without another word the rider disappeared into the fog toward Tara.

Eoghan Mogh bit his lip, deep in thought. "We must have her."

"Oh, we will have her. You need her. I need her. We'll have her. I promise you that much."

The look in his companion's dark eyes troubled Eoghan. It was as if a dark abyss lurked just below the surface of those eyes.

He forgot the sensation as quickly as it had come when the man laughed out loud and said, "I can just picture the look on that sniveling Ó Caflin's face when Conn walked into the hall."

Eoghan shook his head. "He certainly didn't turn out to be of much use to us, did he?"

"We'll do better next time."

"I hope you're right." Eoghan shivered. "We'd better flee this dampness if there's going to be a next time."

He spurred his horse into motion, heading south. His companion stared in the direction of Tara with eyes narrowed. A slow grin traveled across his face, and he laughed out loud as he kicked his mount and followed Eoghan Mogh into the mist, galloping hard.

Chapter Thirteen

❖

Nimbus sat on the hearth in the kitchen with legs crossed and lips clamped together.

"Laugh if you must, Nimbus. I want your honest opinion." Gelina stood in front of him with hands on hips, modeling the dress Conn had brought from across the sea.

His face became instantly serious. "'Tis just different, Gelina. 'Tis lovely on ye."

"I have to admit I feel silly. 'Tis like running about in my shift."

"Does it have a name?" Nimbus asked.

"Conn says it is called a tuga."

She stared down at her body trying to gauge the effect of the straight, flowing silk gathered over one shoulder, leaving the other shoulder bare. The gauzy fabric circled her waist unevenly, dropping to the floor in a line marred only by a single slit which revealed a glimpse of shapely calf when she walked. True to his word, Conn had ordered the dress fashioned from green silk with a red and gold satin border.

Nodding, Gelina said, "I think I like it."

"Try liking it elsewhere. Cook and I have a meal to prepare." Moira interrupted Gelina's self-perusal as she bustled past with a large vat filled with steaming stew.

Nimbus scampered off the hearth. "Come, Gelina. Let us go where we are wanted."

"Good luck finding such a place for yerself, runt," Cook called after him.

As he passed by the table, he stealthily knocked a dozen plum tarts into his pocket. Gelina followed, waiting until they were outside the kitchen to scoop a hot tart from his pocket and shove it into her mouth.

"Where is Conn this morning?" she asked.

"He's been shut up all morning in the study with Mer-Nod. I think they speak of politics," he answered, struggling to speak through a mouthful of juice and berries.

She sighed. "How dull. I wanted to show him the dress."

Gesturing to the figure that strolled toward them, Nimbus said, "There walks yer chance for a second opinion."

Gelina snorted as she recognized the bouncing spiral curls.

Sheela said, "What sort of garment are you wearing, Gelina? 'Tis ghastly."

Smiling wanly, Gelina grabbed Nimbus's balled fist to stop him from punching Sheela in the nearest area he could reach, which would have been quite awkward. "'Tis called a tiga. It came from Rome."

Sheela's face paled as Gelina had anticipated. "I suppose 'twas a gift from Conn. He is a generous man, even to orphans with whom he is burdened." Her tongue traveled over her ruby lips in a consciously catlike gesture.

"He is a generous man. His kindness to elderly widows is unsurpassed. What did he bring you?"

With eyes narrowed Sheela replied, "He brought me himself. What better gift could there be?" With a final withering examination of Gelina's attire, she gathered her skirts and flounced down the hall.

Gelina remained staring after her. "What does he see in her, Nimbus? She and three of her cronies put together wouldn't make one human being."

Nimbus shrugged. "Perhaps beneath the sheets a man does not seek a human being."

"Then let him get a sheep," she said crossly. "I've made one decision anyway. I don't like the dress."

"No?"

"I love it." She scooped another tart from his pocket and flipped it into her mouth, head held high.

The day came and went with Conn still closeted with Mer-Nod and other chosen soldiers. Only one decision leaked from beneath that barred door. Barron Ó Caflin's execution had been postponed another day. No head would roll in the courtyard that evening.

Gelina left the great hall late that night and ambled to her bedchamber with restless feet. The mirror captured her reflection as she entered the room, and she made a terrible face, laughing at her own foolishness. She ran one hand down the slender column of her throat, wondering pensively what another's hand would feel like in its place, then ran to the window.

The full moon hung bloated in the sky. The wind had whipped away the mist of yesterday, and now it tossed the high grasses of the moor, battering them with its fury. A cloud darted across the face of the moon, masking its brilliance for an instant before being blown onward to blight the stars that braved the windy sky. The night looked as restless as she felt. With a heavy sigh she picked up a vial of sandalwood perched on her chest and dabbed the scent on her wrists and throat.

A wicked grin lit her face. Striding to the screen, she reached into the farthest recesses and pulled out her breeches and shirt. She dressed quickly, pulling a jaunty cap over pinned curls and stuck out a defiant jaw to rub the last of the rouge from her lightly freckled cheeks.

She slipped out the second story window on a rope kept handy for nights such as these, leaping the last five feet to the ground. The winds were warm, boding spring. Excitement built within her; her heart raced in time with the wind.

She ran to the stable, shivering with anticipation. The dim-witted stable boy was nowhere to be found. Silent Thunder whinnied a greeting as she stepped into his stall. She blew gently into his nose to quieten him.

"Sorry, boy. No apple for you tonight. I did not dare sneak into the kitchen," she murmured, leading him out of the stable by a single rope draped around his sleek neck. The huge Arabian followed her docilely.

She mounted him bareback by retreating several feet and running until she gained enough momentum to vault upon his back. It took two tries but the horse did not twitch a muscle. Holding tightly to the rope, she kicked him into a gallop.

The landscape was lit as if by daylight with the brightness of the moon. The wind whistled past them until the horse seemed to capture it and surpass it. Timeless silence surrounded them. She bent low, clinging to the sinewy body of Silent Thunder until she herself felt part of the powerful rhythm that propelled the horse into the night. They flew over the moors, the horse's hooves barely touching the tall grass. Gelina opened her mouth in a soundless yell of sheer joy as they galloped into the rolling hills. She guided the horse in a wide circle and they thundered back toward Tara.

The wind evaporated the sheen of sweat that covered both of them as she slowed the horse to a trot. Entering the fenced stableyard, she halted the steed and slid off its back, exhausted but happy. She tethered the horse to a post and started inside for a cloth to rub down the animal. She was shocked to find herself firmly gripped by the collar and lifted off the ground.

"You fool! I knew you were dim-witted but I didn't think you were stupid enough to risk your life and the life of my horse out there in the dark!" It was Conn's furious voice that spoke. Gelina said a silent prayer and fought to keep her face in shadow.

"I told you to exercise the horse, not drive it to an early grave. Have you taken leave of your senses, boy?" Conn shook her for emphasis, and Gelina thought she was going to choke to death and rather wished she would.

"Answer me when I ask you a question! I know you're not mute, too."

The only sound she could utter was a small gagging noise so Conn lowered her feet to the ground, and she nearly collapsed with the wonder of being able to breathe again. She mumbled something unintelligible and apologetic and pulled the cap forward over her face.

"Speak up, you little jackass. I've a good mind to give you the thrashing of your life!" She didn't have to get a good look at Conn to know when he was serious, and she flinched. "Come outside. Let's take a look at the damage you've done."

She knew if he got her outside, she wouldn't stand a chance of camouflage in the bright moonlight, so she planted her feet firmly in the ground and refused to budge as Conn tried to drag her out the door. With a sudden jerk he uprooted her feet, and she grasped the doorframe, holding on with all of her might as he grabbed her around the waist and tugged. He let go as quickly as he had grabbed her. She closed her eyes and laid her cheek against the doorframe, wishing her parents had never met.

"Fine. You can take your thrashing in here." His voice was quiet but deadly.

With a firm grip on her arm he jerked her around to face him and drew back his hand. Having been on the receiving end of his anger before, she made a frantic choice and with her other arm knocked the cap from her head and faced him, eyes wide with trepidation.

"I was wondering if you were going to let me beat the hell out of you or reveal who you were." His voice remained soft and dangerous.

"You knew it was me?" She breathed a sigh of relief, then wondered if she should have as she saw the anger still burning bright in his eyes.

"You are a little softer than the stable boy, and I've yet to notice him wearing a sandalwood fragrance!" His voice rose to a low roar, and she took a step backward, unable to stop herself.

He glared at her until she began to squirm. "I've never taken the horse out on a bad night," she started. "Why 'tis like daylight out there tonight."

"So you've taken my horse out before, have you?" She grimaced, realizing her mistake. "Just where in the hell are the people who are supposed to be watching you in my absence?"

" 'Tis not Sean's fault. I climbed out the window. He could not have known." She incriminated herself further while attempting to extricate her bodyguard. "I would never hurt Silent Thunder. You've got to know that." She raised her palms in a plea.

"Silent Thunder be cursed! What about you?" He paced the length of the stable, barely controlling his anger.

"Me?" she said weakly.

He turned to face her, eyes merciless. "Do you think I've been locked up all day for nothing? Do you think I have patrols circling this fortress for no reason? We have enemies out there." He gestured to the darkness outside. "Do you have any idea what Eoghan Mogh's men would do to you if they captured you?"

"I guess I never thought—"

"I guess you never think! If you didn't step in a bog and break your neck out there, you could be captured and held hostage . . . or worse." He searched her face to determine if she knew what was worse.

Biting her lip, she slid to a sitting position and fought to keep the tears welling in her eyes from spilling over. "Go ahead and thrash me. I guess I deserve it." She looked up at him, a stubborn set to her jaw, a mute challenge in her eyes.

"Don't tempt me. Come. I shall escort you to your chamber where you shall be spending the next few days." She refused his outstretched hand and climbed to her feet.

He walked to her chamber without a word, stopping there just long enough to jerk the rope dangling from her bedpost. He tossed it out the window with a meaningful glare.

"You're to stay in here for three days. Moira will bring you your meals. If I catch you outside, I shall give you that thrashing I promised." He slammed the door in her face.

She stood in the middle of the room for a moment, staring at the closed door. Walking to the chest, she picked up the ivory hairbrush and hurled it toward the wall where it crashed with a satisfying bang.

She stared at her tousled reflection in the mirror and began pulling the pearl pins from her hair, sending it tumbling to her shoulders.

Conn walked slowly to his chambers, feeling cheated of the midnight ride he had anticipated throughout the long day. The fight with Gelina had drained him. Coming back and finding a beautiful, accomplished woman in place of the waif he had left had given him hope that perhaps she had abandoned her less disciplined ways. So much for that hope, he thought, pouring himself a goblet of ale in his bedchamber. He stripped himself of the heavy clothing he had worn all day and wrapped a single piece of linen around his waist.

The day had been a trying one. He had been closed away for long hours compiling a list of any possible traitors to his kingdom. In the thirty days he had spent chained in the hold of the Roman slave ship, he had learned the value of mistrust. With the events of the night fresh in his mind, he sighed as he thought of another name that would be added to the list if the others knew the truth—Gelina Ó Monaghan, murderess of five men of the Fianna. The thought gave him great pain, and he closed his eyes, taking a deep swig of the ale. The numbness it afforded his brain was welcome.

He thought of summoning Sheela but decided that listening to her prattle would not be worth the forgetfulness he would find in her arms. Settling his tired form on the backless couch, he took another deep drink. He was startled when he heard the soft rap on the door.

Opening the door, he took a step backward and put his hands on his hips.

Gelina faced him unblinkingly. "I wanted to show you how I looked in my tiga and I wanted to apologize."

He poured himself another goblet of ale. "'Tis a toga and I would value your obedience more than your apologies," he said sharply.

She stepped into the room. Following in his footsteps, she picked up a goblet, blew the dust out of it and held it out for him to fill.

Staring, he said, "I didn't invite you in, and I certainly didn't offer you any ale."

She shrugged and set the goblet down. Her gaze traveled the room, searching for a focal point. His broad chest covered with curling dark hair was making her nervous. Conn watched her, puzzled. The toga draped her tall, lithe form. Her unbound hair fell softly past her shoulders. The gentle fragrance of sandalwood floated toward him, unmarred by the scent of horse. She smiled uncertainly, and he found himself relenting despite his lingering anger.

"Here, drink this," he commanded. He poured a golden liquid from a separate flagon and handed it to her.

She sipped the mead gratefully, sensing that some of the anger had slipped from his demeanor.

"Conn, I really did come to say that I was sorry. I shall remain in my chamber for three days if you wish, but I cannot bear your anger. I was so restless tonight. I wanted to see you all day but was never allowed to."

He almost smiled. "It was a dreadful day. You got to the horse before I did. I'm still so tense that I ache all over."

He sat down on the couch. She sat behind him and began to rub the knotted muscles at the back of his neck. He moaned softly and chuckled. "The gods must have read my mind. I was just wishing for a wife to do that." Her eyes lit up, and he continued, "I guess a daughter will do just as well, even a stubborn one." He did not see her smile fade.

She ran one gentle fingertip down his bare back, tracing a fresh scar that marred the muscled flesh. With a soft moan of sympathy her lips brushed his shoulder. Conn was completely unprepared for the shock that traveled down his spine. Standing abruptly, he turned and faced her. She stared at the spot he had vacated, eyes distant.

"Gelina?" he said softly, unsure of her attention.

Looking up at him as if awakening from a trance, she smiled, completely disconcerting him with the unguarded emotion he saw in her face. He strode across the room and stared out the window. A hint of dawn lightened the sky.

"You had better go." Even he wasn't sure if it was a warning he heard in his husky voice.

"Yes. Come visit me if you get a chance in the next three days." She smiled wanly. "Goodnight."

He did not turn but continued to stare at the fading stars until he heard the door softly shut. He looked down at his hands. They were trembling.

Gelina felt disoriented as she entered her own room. It was as if some sort of impasse had been reached. Her eyelids grew heavy even as pink clouds began to separate from the blackness of the sky. She headed straight for the bed, not bothering to remove the toga.

Pulling back a coverlet of the softest fox fur, she stared at the round gray object resting on her pillow. Puzzled, she picked it up, turning it over in her hands. It was a pendant made of the finest, grayest metal she had ever seen. The locket flew open as her hand inadvertently tripped a spring along its side. A single word had been engraved inside the locket—*Remember*.

Awakening early the next afternoon, Gelina felt something soft hit her repeatedly in the stomach. She groaned and opened her eyes with growing suspicion. Nimbus's twinkling eyes greeted her over the down pillow he was using to batter her. She grabbed the end of the pillow and jerked it out of his hands.

"This is getting redundant, Nimbus. Can't you let a lass get a decent night's rest?" She rubbed her eyes irritably.

"A night and half a day's, you mean. The sun climbed high and started its descent an hour ago."

"I didn't get to bed until the sun started that climb."

"I know."

She searched his face for laughter but found only concern. Averting her eyes, she wondered what he had concluded.

He clapped his small hands briskly. "I came to get ye. A commotion begins in the courtyard."

Thankful for the change in subject, she was half out of bed and grabbing for the hairbrush, which still lay in the corner before she stopped. "What am I thinking of? I cannot go out for three days."

"Why not?"

She stuck out her lower lip. "I was a bad girl."

"Who said?" He scowled, ready to slay the villain who had slighted her.

"Our dear lord and master." Nimbus stood deep in thought, started to speak, then stopped. Gelina continued, "Conn said I must stay in my quarters for three days. You could be in trouble for visiting me."

"I don't understand. Conn is the one who sent me to fetch ye."

Running the brush through her tangled curls, she mused, "Why would he relent? Just what is going on down there?"

He took the brush from her and worked it through her hair. "Ye do not know?" She shook her head, struggling to clear away the fog of sleep. "Let me give ye a hint." He ran the brush across his throat and made a slicing noise.

"Oh, no. 'Tis Ó Caflin's execution." She paled. "I don't wish to see that."

Nimbus shrugged. "I was sent with orders to fetch ye. Ye're no swooning female. Ye've a strong stomach. 'Tis all for sport."

Her stomach churned as she remembered another sport she had experienced with sword in hand. Reaching under the pillow, her fingers touched the cool pewter, and she breathed a sigh of relief. The pendant was where she had shoved it with exhausted fingers in the early morning light. Knowing Conn needed to be told of the mysterious gift was not making it any easier. With the relationship between them already on shaky ground, she was hesitant to recall painful memories.

"I'll wait outside. Hurry and dress." Nimbus interrupted her thoughts as he left the room.

She dressed as slowly as possible, slipping on a long green skirt and matching blouse that laced up the front. Her routine was punctuated by short raps on the door. Nimbus practically jerked her out of the room when she finally opened the door.

True to his word, there was a commotion in the courtyard. A scaffold had been erected in its center and hordes of men, women, and scattered children milled around it. A deafening din arose as they pushed and shoved, vying for better positions. A towering figure stood passively on the scaffold, a black hood covering his features. The hood did little to disguise his bulk.

Nimbus whispered, "Goll MacMorna is chieftain of the Fianna. They wish to denounce Ó Caflin publicly, so Goll performs the execution."

Gelina remembered a ragged bunch of wildflowers clutched in a hairy fist and felt the sickness in the pit of her gut increasing. Hysteria threatened her as she thought of Conn's own words to her once, "I'll have you beheaded." She gripped Nimbus's hand tighter, hardly aware that she did it. He looked up at her, the strain of worry showing on his small features. He considered ignoring Conn's orders and getting her out of the bloodthirsty crowd.

He heard a cry from the tower above them. "Nimbus, bring Gelina." Sean beckoned them upward. A path cleared before the stairs as the crowd parted to let them through.

Mer-Nod and Sean stood together at the top of the stairs. The poet grumbled as they approached, "You may watch from below, Nimbus. Just leave Gelina with us."

Nimbus smiled a falsely sweet smile. "Drop dead, eaglehead."

Conn stood alone at the corner of the tower, staring at the crowd with arms crossed, his face a brooding mask. Gelina pried her hand out of Nimbus's with a reassuring pat and approached Conn. She touched his arm, and he looked startled to see her.

Choosing her words with care, she said, "I shall gladly return to the confines of my chamber if you will allow."

Conn shook his head with regret. "Forgive me, Gelina. I need everyone here."

He touched her cheek in a silent plea for understanding. The pain was sharp in his eyes, and she realized what this execution was costing him. She nodded, resolutely clamping her lips together, and returned to Nimbus's side. Conn turned his attention back to the crowd.

An ugly roar rose at one corner of the courtyard and crossed like a wave until the crowd seemed close to rioting. The reason

soon appeared as Barron Ó Caflin was led into the courtyard.
He stumbled but found himself pulled upright by the guards that
flanked him. He never saw the sunlight. A blindfold covered his
eyes. Gelina flinched as a rotten tomato spattered across his
face, hurled by an anonymous hand. He held himself straight.
Even Nimbus looked sickened.

Angry cries flew through the crowd like missiles. "Traitor!"
"Bastard!"

"Eoghan Mogh's dog!"

As he was led up the scaffold steps, an old woman spat in his
face before the guards could pull her down.

Conn raised his arms and roared, "Halt!"

The crowd fell silent and faced the tower. Conn's words were
short and clipped. "This man's execution will stand as his
punishment. The other abuse will cease." Some looked
abashed but others continued to watch Ó Caflin with open
hostility. Conn took a deep breath. "It pains me greatly to see a
man of the Fianna meet such a death. But Barron Ó Caflin chose
this path for himself. He chose to betray our kingdom. He chose
to let his brothers die." His voice hardened with anger. "I
know that many of you have lost young men of your clans
because of Ó Caflin's betrayal."

Gelina felt tears start in her own eyes as she saw a burly
farmer standing below them with tears streaming down his face.

"I cannot bring back your men. They were my men, too, and
I grieve with you. Justice will be done today, and it will be done
publicly, so that anyone else who seeks to betray Erin may
observe the fate that awaits him. You may proceed." Conn
gestured to the men on the scaffold.

The guards did not force Barron Ó Caflin to his knees. He
knelt before the crowd like a lamb prepared for sacrifice and
placed his head on the wooden block. The hooded executioner
picked up the bronze ax. Its blade glinted in the sunlight. Gelina
fought the scream rising in her throat and looked at Conn. She
was the only one who saw the tension that knotted every muscle
of his body and knew he wanted to scream as badly as she did.

The crowd grew silent as the heavy steps of Goll MacMorna
echoed through the courtyard. He approached the chopping
block and hefted the enormous ax in the air.

Gelina forced her eyes away from the grisly scene and found
them drawn to a tall, cloaked figure who stood at the back of the

courtyard. A hood was drawn toward his face, obscuring his features but she could not rid herself of the impression that the man was watching her.

He raised one hand and slipped the hood back just enough to reveal his features. She never saw the ax fall. She never heard the whistle it made as it severed Ó Caflin's head. She never saw the decapitated head roll off the scaffold. The only thing she saw was laughing dark eyes and features she loved as well as her own before she slid to the floor of the tower, her world going dark around her.

Chapter Fourteen

❖

Opening her eyes, Gelina found Conn's concerned face a scant foot away from hers. He sat beside her on the canopied bed peering at her as if afraid she would evaporate. With no conscious thought, she stretched out her arms and pulled him close, hiding her face in his shoulder and savoring the sweet manly smell of him. His arms circled her for a sweet moment, then he pushed her back on the pillows, reluctance in his fingertips.

"Forgive me," he murmured. "I should have never made you watch the execution." She looked away, her eyes unreadable. His voice was filled with unfamiliar remorse. "Sometimes I forget what hell you've been through."

She still did not trust her voice to speak, knowing that if she admitted to him and to herself what she had seen, all was lost. The life she had found at Tara was over. She held her silence, preserving the only happiness she could remember.

"Gelina, can you speak? My physicians tell of those who have been so frightened they lost their voices."

"You couldn't be that fortunate, Conn." She managed a weak smile, and he laughed aloud. "What happened?"

"You fainted on the tower. Mer-Nod caught you, and I

carried you to your chamber. You've been unconscious for several minutes.''

"How humiliating. Did Sheela see me swoon?" She sighed in mock shame.

Shaking his head in exasperation, he said, "Is that your only concern?"

"Well, no. I didn't crush Nimbus, did I? He is such a dear little fellow.''

"You scare me half out of my wits, and all you can do is jest. I've a good mind to box your ears." Conn brandished his fist in the air, fighting to keep the scowl on his face.

She caught his fist and brought it to her lips, smile fading. "Did I really frighten you?"

He pulled his hand away from her soft lips as if it had been burned and planted a brisk kiss on her brow. "You frightened someone else more. I should go and assure them of your health. There is one hysterical midget running around out there. I want you to stay in your room tonight."

"As punishment?" she could not help asking.

He shook his head. "For your health. I shall send Moira up later with some broth."

She grimaced and he pointed at her, not needing to say another word. She settled among the pillows without complaint. The door closed behind him.

Bounding out of bed, she ran to the window. To her relief no caped figure lurked below. She hugged herself, fearing the solitude and the thoughts that came with it. She considered calling Conn back and begging him to send in Nimbus or Sean for company but she knew there was no need to whet his suspicions.

The chest in the corner beckoned her. She fished out a fine piece of linen. Dangling threads and bulges marked it as her work. Finding the needle, she began to painstakingly rework the embroidery, focusing all of her concentration on a task she detested.

The afternoon passed, measured by the tangled stitches and the tiny, bloody pricks of the needle in her finger. A knock came on the door.

"Come in, Moira." She didn't look up. The embroidery was beginning to blur before her exhausted eyes.

The door opened slowly. When only silence greeted her, she

raised her head, her eyes growing as round and frozen as saucers as she saw her brother standing in the doorway.

He was taller than she remembered. His black hair stood on end. Black eyes watched her with an intensity that shook the breath from her body.

"They keep you heavily guarded, do they not, Princess?"

"Guarded?" she croaked.

He took a step toward the bed, and she instinctively flinched against the headboard.

He stretched out his hand, speaking as if to a startled animal. "I am not a ghost, Lina. I've come for you. I've come to take you away from him."

"He told me you were dead."

"Do I look dead? Have we ever known him to speak the truth?" The hatred etched on his sharp features was ugly. When she didn't answer, he said, "I've found people like us, Lina. People who hate him as badly as we do. We are fighting to rid Erin of his tyranny."

She studied him with eyes narrowed. "Why did you wait so long to come for me?"

"At first I didn't know you were alive. I was sick for a long time. The wound he gave me festered. Some men found me and nursed me back to health. I could not come for you until we had the power to do what had to be done."

"You have that power now?"

He laughed, the sound an unpleasant one. "Yes. We will see Conn of the Hundred Battles rue the day he stole the throne of Erin." He approached her where she crouched on the bed and caressed a tousled curl. "Lina, 'tis Rodney. You belong with me." His voice was a gentle whisper, and she fought the urge to reach out her arms to him.

"I cannot go with you," she said, turning her face away.

"Why not? I've come to rescue you. I don't care what he has done to you. I shall make it better," he said, a note of desperation stretched tautly in his voice.

She laughed bitterly. "He has done nothing to me except give me a home and a family.

A lullaby floated into the room from the stairs, borne by the sweet wind of Moira's soprano.

"I must go." Rodney's words were clipped, and he put a strong hand on either side of her face and stared into her eyes.

"Meet me at sunrise. Ride south to the drumlins. I will be waiting for you."

Then he was gone before Gelina could shake her head, the tormented denial caught in her throat. Moira bustled in seconds later, bearing a steaming bowl of broth.

She put a perfunctory hand on Gelina's forehead. "Ye're as pale as a ghoul, lass. Perhaps 'twas an oncoming illness that made ye swoon. Conn's physicians can look at ye tomorrow if ye feel no better."

The broth sat untouched on the plate long after Moira had gone, although the mead disappeared shortly thereafter. The room darkened, the shadows of night descending without mercy. Gelina did not stir from the bed to light a candle. She remained staring into the darkness for hours.

Midnight approached. She unfolded her long body and put her feet on the floor. She was going to Conn. She would confront him and try to understand why he had deceived her. She knew him too well to convict him without a trial.

She straightened her rumpled skirt and padded barefoot to his chambers. The door stood ajar so she knocked softly before pushing it open. She sighed, finding the room empty and the bed untouched. If he were with Sheela, it could be hours before he returned. She would wait.

She yawned and climbed up on his feather mattress, the long day's events tugging at her eyelids. Her eyes closed of their own volition as she lay back on the bed. A cool breeze floated in from the gentle night. She reached to the foot of the bed and pulled the down coverlet over her, leaving the troublesome day behind.

Conn trudged up the stairs. He was haunted by the nagging sensation that something was amiss. Gelina lacked the learned artifice employed by most of the women he knew and the fear in her eyes that afternoon had been real. Her teasing could not hide it. He longed to discover what troubled her with an urgency foreign to him.

He had started for her room twice and then returned to his chair, unsure of his motives. The fire in the study had held no answers. The dancing flames only reflected the apprehension in his eyes, mesmerizing him until sleep had come.

He stopped in front of her chamber now, his hand on the

handle. The silence was deafening. The fortress slept around him. He drew back his hand and sighed, trying to shake off the fancy that something was frightening her, attributing it to his own perplexing feelings. Perhaps something was frightening him.

Opening his own door, he felt the chill of the room deep in his bones. He slammed the shutters and cursed aloud the manservant who had neglected to lay a fire. He jerked off his garments. A low mumble came from the bed, startling him.

A well-bundled figure nestled underneath his coverlet, burrowing deeper into the warmth of the bed. Smiling, Conn shook his head. He should have realized that Sheela was not a woman to be ignored, and in the time since he had returned, there had been scant opportunities for attention. He approached the bed, hoping she would provide the warmth he craved.

Sliding underneath the coverlet, he felt the heat radiating from the body next to his before he even touched it. Reaching for her shoulder, he gently turned her to her back. With an arm on each side of her, he lowered his lips and body to hers. The scent of sandalwood hit him like a fist, but he could not stop the descent of his lips any more than he could willfully stop the beating of his own heart.

The shock of Gelina's young, lean body against his own sent a shudder through him as her lips parted beneath the onslaught of his kiss. His body covered the full length of hers, crushing her into the soft feather mattress in cherishing urgency. The small corner of his mind that was still rational tried to pull him away, but when her arms circled his neck, desire thundered through his soul, rendering him deaf to the pleas of his mind.

His hungry lips sought her temples and throat, gliding across the heated velvet of her skin. Gossamer strands of hair caught in his mouth like spun sugar. His hand traveled the length of her body, probing the softness beneath the thin blouse and skirt. His breath came raggedly as he once again captured her lips, drinking of the sweetness within. One hand cupped her neck even as the other pushed her skirt upward to reveal a silken thigh.

The heat of her tender thigh against his possessive fingers burned him to the core, and he flew out of the bed, jerking a cloth around his waist.

Resting on his knees, he struggled to gain control of his

breathing. Gelina sat bolt upright in the bed, her eyes luminous in the moonlight.

"What in the name of Behl do you think you're doing?" he bellowed between breaths.

"Perhaps I should ask you that." Her body trembled and she could not seem to catch her own breath.

"Since I did find you in my bed, I think you should answer the question first." His eyes were furious, but Gelina heard a new emotion in his voice—stark fear.

She swallowed. "I came to talk to you. I guess I fell asleep."

"Were you going to reveal your identity before or after I ravished you?" He got to his feet, tucking the cloth around his waist, and strode to the ale flagon.

"You knew who I was," she said, straightening her neck proudly.

He stared into his mug. "I did not. I thought you were Sheela."

"You're lying." Her voice carried crystal clear in the silent room.

His eyes narrowed as he approached the bed, and Gelina fought the urge to flinch. He stared down at her and shook his head. "You just can't seem to stay out of danger, can you?"

"I saw no danger in awaiting you here. You knew it was me." She stared sadly at the coverlet and mumbled, "It wouldn't be the first time you lied."

"I did not know it was you," he repeated. "I have no interest in bedding a child."

She averted her eyes so he wouldn't see how deeply his words cut her. "You're angry, are you not?"

"You're damned right I'm angry. I almost raped my foster daughter!" His hoarse words shot out at her like missiles.

She shook her head but didn't dare voice her opinion that what had happened had little to do with rape. He scratched his head, studying her.

"Conn, please—"

"Hold your tongue, Gelina." He cut off her words before she was even sure what they were going to be. "I am trying to decide what must be done with you."

The finality in his quiet words frightened her more than all of his ranting. The cold eyes of a stranger assessed her. She felt a flush rise to her cheeks. She sat in the center of the huge bed, looking very small with her hair tousled and her face tightly drawn.

He turned to the window, refusing to meet her eyes. "I fear there is only one answer for you. You shall marry Sean Ó Finn before the week is over. I will grant a generous marriage portion, and he can take you away from Tara."

"I do not love Sean. You cannot do that." She leapt out of bed and ran to face him, placing one hand on his arm.

He shook her hand off. "I can do anything I bloody well please. I am the Ard-Righ."

"Is that the attitude that earned you such an inflated reputation for fairness?"

"Do not scream at me. It annoys me," he said through clenched teeth.

She made an elaborately exaggerated curtsy. "Forgive my rudeness, sire. It grates on my nerves when I am forced to marry a man I do not love."

"Sean is quite fond of you. He told me so. Every woman desires a Fiannic soldier for a husband. Perhaps a passel of brats will keep you out of trouble."

"It will take a hell of a lot more than a passel of brats to keep me out of trouble if you persist with this absurd idea!"

"It is no more absurd than you thinking I would care for you in my bed," he said disparagingly.

Her hand rose in the air of its own volition only to be caught in an iron vise as he said softly, "Don't even think about it. Don't let the thought cross your mind." The threat was real. Darkness held his eyes, a darkness she had struggled to forget.

"Marrying me to Sean is not going to change the way you felt a few minutes ago, is it?" she whispered.

He didn't speak but crossed to the door and opened it. She walked out, refusing to give way to the bitter tears until she reached the end of the corridor. She sank to the floor and cried like a baby. Hearing another door slam, she ducked into a muddy garden, stumbling over her own feet as tears blinded her.

Falling to her knees, Gelina faced a firelit window. The scene in the room was achingly clear, as if she herself stood within. Conn crossed the chamber in long strides. The question died on Sheela's lips as Conn's hand caught in her dark web of tangled curls, bending her backwards. His lips captured hers with battering violence. Her arms rose to circle his neck, and they sank from view. Gelina's fingers dug into the wet soil as if to grasp what was already out of her reach.

Having never dreamed that her heart was located so low in her stomach, the physical pain amazed her, doubling her over with its intensity. Her breath came in ragged gasps sucked in through clenched lips. She knelt in the garden for a lifetime. Her sobs grew infrequent and muffled. The cool mud beneath her knees soaked into her skirt. The tears on her face dried to grimy tracks. For the second morning in a row she watched the sky pinken in the east. Searing, white-hot anger began to replace the pain, and she could breathe with a semblance of normality. Morning was coming.

She darted along the corridors of the sleeping fortress until she found the bedchamber. Sean sprawled across the top of the coverlet, mouth open in sleep. She watched him fondly for a moment before rifling his clothes and producing a key.

The weaponry room was as she remembered, still lit with the eerie rows of torches reflected by the gleaming instruments of death. She returned to her chamber with the sword hidden in the long folds of her skirt. She stripped. The morning air from the open window caressed her skin before she slid the man's jerkin over her head and the breeches up her legs. She cinched them with trembling fingers. Digging through the wooden chest, she tossed things right and left until she found the cap. She tucked her long hair into it, then stopped, catching her reflection in the mirror.

The dagger lay where she had hidden it. Her breath came unevenly as she lifted it. The curls fell limply to the floor like a dying dream, leaving her with short-cropped hair that refused to lie flat. The pendant went around her neck. She wrapped herself in a huge cloak with a hood, much like the one her brother had worn.

With the familiar weight of the sword clutched in her hand, she opened the door. A lone figure leaned against the wall at the top of the stairs, arms crossed and no trace of laughter in his eyes.

She froze as he spoke. "He'll not let ye go."

"He has no choice, Nimbus. I am going now." Her voice held both a warning and a plea.

"Ye're crazy to do this." He moved toward her with arms outstretched.

"Yes, I'm crazy. He's crazy. We have all gone a little bit crazy." Her hissed whisper traveled to him on a note of desperation.

"Stay, Gelina. Marry me. I love ye, ye know."

"Oh, Nimbus." Tears welled up in her eyes as she took his small hand in hers. "I love you, too, but not that way. You've got to let me go."

He nodded and looked away for a long moment. When he looked back, his eyes were clear and dry. "Do ye have somewhere to go?"

"I think so."

They studied each other in silence, then Gelina knelt beside him and put her arms around him. It was Nimbus who reluctantly pushed away.

"Take care and hide yerself well. He'll be coming after ye."

She couldn't resist a bitter laugh. "I doubt that. He'll be glad enough to be shed of this foundling." Nimbus shook his head as she stood. "I must go. Daylight grows."

She gave him a final sad smile, then turned and ran down the steps, her hand on the sword hilt, the cape billowing behind her. Nimbus stood for a moment after she disappeared, then slid to a sitting position, staring at nothing.

The stable was deserted without even a snoring stableboy to block her way. She examined each stall before pausing in front of the stall that held the Arabian. A grim smile twisted her lips. She mounted the horse in one attempt, vaulting to its back. The bleary-eyed guards threw open the fortress gates without so much as a blink. They had seen her ride through at odder hours in the months of Conn's absence. A battle cry caught in her throat. Silent Thunder galloped through the gates of the fortress and ran for the southern hills as the sun rose over the eastern horizon.

Conn awoke with a bitter taste in his mouth and a bad feeling deep in his gut. It took only seconds to remember why. The bitter taste was a reminder of the large amount of ale he had drunk after slamming into Sheela's room last night. Sheela lay beside him with one arm thrown over his chest, snoring delicately. He moved her arm and slid out of bed, suppressing a groan as his knees hit the cold wooden floor. He dressed and stepped into the hall. The silence proclaimed the newness of the

morning. He had to see Gelina. He cursed himself as their
encounter came back to him in full force, complete with the
bitter words spoken.

Her door opened with a creak. He stopped in his tracks as he
faced the havoc of her chamber. The chest had been emptied,
and dresses were scattered from one end of the room to the
other. The bed was empty, untouched. The table had been
cleared in a single swipe, ivory combs and earthenware bottles
shattered on the floor. The scent of sandalwood overwhelmed
him. He took a step backward, a horrible suspicion dawning in
his numbed mind.

A few stragglers snored in the great hall around the dying
fire. The kitchen was deserted as was the study. He paused at
the chess set, something puzzling him. Drawing in a sharp
breath, he realized that the white queen was gone, her space
empty.

He ran to the weaponry room, opening it with his own key.
His worst fears were confirmed. He touched the empty wall with
icy fingertips, mouthing her name in silent prayer.

He flew to the stables, searching stall after stall until he stood
before Silent Thunder's stall. He flung the door open. A narrow
strip of leather hung from a nail on the wall opposite him. He
jerked it from the wall. It was a belt of the Fianna, engraved
with his own name. He slammed it to the ground, cursing
furiously.

"She's gone."

He whirled around. Nimbus leaned against the wall behind
him.

"Where is she?" he roared.

"I told ye. She's gone."

Conn turned on him, lifting him off the ground by his collar
until he could look him in the eye. "Where did she go?"

"Go on, Conn," Nimbus yelled. "Bully me, too. Destroy
something else today!"

Conn lowered him to the ground and turned away, fighting to
control his breathing.

"Just what did ye do to her?" Nimbus demanded.

"I didn't do anything to her." Conn laughed bitterly. "I
think that was the problem."

"She loved ye, ye know." Nimbus spat out the words.

"Of course, she did. I was her fosterer."

"Are ye blind?" Nimbus asked, eyebrows raised. "She loved ye like a woman loves a man. She loved ye before ye ever left for Rome." The jester turned away, pacing the floor.

Conn slumped against the wall, all of the energy drained from his body. "She's young enough to be my daughter."

"Ye wouldn't be the first king to raise a foster daughter to be his bride."

"That is ludicrous, Nimbus. I told you. I've always thought of her as my daughter."

"I'll wager that ye have," Nimbus said with a snort.

"Do you know where she went?" Conn asked softly.

"I thought maybe ye would since ye're the only one who knows where she really came from."

"I'll find her." Conn straightened his back, his eyes narrowed. Nimbus wasn't sure he liked the look he saw there. Conn scooped up his belt from the ground where he had thrown it. Looping it around his waist, he repeated the words, "I'll find her."

❖

PART THREE

Pity the woman loves a man,
When no love invites her;
Better for her to fly from love.
If unloved, love bites her.

—Author unknown
9th century

❖

Chapter Fifteen

❖

Twilight descended around him, settling in with the eerie lavender stillness of summer. Darkness gathered on the horizon in the east. He galloped over the deepening emerald hills, the muffled crunch of the horse's hooves in the long grass the only sound. His thoughts darted to and fro, steeped in the desperation and weariness of the long ride. Having felt despair in the hold of the Roman slave ship, Conn knew that what he felt now had been pushed beyond the brink of despair. In the distance he heard the howl of an animal and thought again of the jackal in his vision.

He had ridden forth from Tara each day, sometimes not returning in a night's time. Villagers welcomed the forlorn figure who rode into their midst. At times he was accompanied by soldiers but more often, he was alone. They honored him, fed him, received him in their simple cottages but they could not offer the one comfort he sought above all others—news of Gelina. She had vanished without a trace. When a week had crawled by, he had been forced to give up the notion that she had gone away to sulk, perhaps to return cold and hungry, prepared for reconciliation. When a month had passed, he had been forced to give up many other notions, too.

Always in the summer the Fianna were dispatched throughout the island to live under the stars, acting as a peace-keeping force and defending areas still threatened by the ever-annoying presence of Eoghan Mogh. Now they had been dispatched with another mission. Gelina must be found. Explaining her disappearance as just that, no one was certain whether she had been stolen or left of her own volition. No one who sat in the presence of Conn's gaunt, tormented eyes dared to ask why or how she had gone.

Only Nimbus, the jester whose jokes became more bitter with each passing day, knew the guilt that Conn felt as he sat in the study, face buried in his hands after a night's ride and a futile day's search. Nimbus sat with him often, both of them staring into the fire until it faded to ash. Nimbus tried to cheer him, offering to make use of the dusty chess set that sat deserted in the corner. Conn's haunted eyes as he raised them were enough to make the jester pardon himself and leave the room.

To Conn, summer had always meant long forays into Erin's countryside with the Fianna. It had meant nights of song and poetry under a starry sky as they feasted on meat cooked on hot coals over open pits. It had meant warring when necessary and long drills when there was no one left to fight. It had meant the camaraderie of men who shared a dream. Now the summer meant riding and searching, nothing more. The days were endless and the nights longer.

He halted the chestnut stallion on top of a hill as the blackness of night soundlessly replaced the purple of twilight. Sliding to the ground, he pulled out a bag filled with stale rations and sat on a flat rock, staring into the night. He ate methodically, thankful that he was too tired to taste the cold meat.

He studied the stars that hung over the vast land, marveling at his loneliness. He had never felt the sting of the empty night like he did now. The brightest star only reminded him of laughing emerald eyes that shone more brilliantly than any star.

The cruel words he had said to her echoed through his mind, bitterly erasing another memory of sweet parted lips and gossamer curls. Reaching into his pocket, he pulled out the soft strand of auburn hair that had hit him like a kick in the gut when he had found it discarded on the floor of her chamber surrounded by others like it. He held it between his fingers, feeling very close to her. It was almost as if he could reach out his hand and touch the warmth of hers in the cool night. He knew with certainty that she was alive.

"Where are you?" he murmured hoarsely.

The night gave him no answer, mocking him with its silence. He stood, calling her name to hear it float over the hills, returning to him a faint echo. Mounting the horse, he wondered if he was taking leave of his senses. He spurred the stallion toward the fortress as if the demons of hell pursued him. The wind drew his hair back with its force. He rode faster and faster, driving the stallion into the endless night. The wind dried the tears on his face before he even felt them.

The fortress lacked the bustle of summer on this hazy summer night. With the soldiers dispatched to all corners of Erin and the herdsmen camped in the buaile with their beasts, only a few stragglers remained at the fortress. No fire blazed in the great hall. A warm breeze blew through the open doors.

Mer-Nod and Nimbus sat in the courtyard, the jester perched on a bale of hay while Mer-Nod reclined comfortably in his poet's chair, which he had had carried outside in a fit of self-importance. They watched each other warily, neither speaking. The sun had disappeared an hour ago on this slow night, and they both awaited Conn's return, knowing there was no guarantee that he would return that night or the next. They started nervously at the sound of hoofbeats in the distance, only to relax in disappointment as Sean Ó Finn pounded into the courtyard and leapt from his horse.

"Has Conn returned?" he asked them breathlessly.

"Would we be sitting out here if he had?" Nimbus retorted.

Mer-Nod shot him a cold look and said, "We would be much more comfortable sitting out here if some of us would retire."

Nimbus poked his tongue out at him, and Sean threw up his hands in exasperation. "You two sit here babbling like children while I bring important information to Conn."

"Ye have news?" Nimbus sat bolt upright.

Sean shrugged. "That is for Conn to decide." He pulled a piece of hay from the bale Nimbus sat on and tucked it in the corner of his mouth, struggling to appear casual.

"I suppose you would rather not divulge this information until Conn arrives," Mer-Nod said.

"Ye won't have to wait much longer for here he comes." Nimbus's voice was barely a whisper, and they all looked up to see Conn walk his horse into the courtyard, head bowed in utter defeat. He raised his hand in a lackluster salute.

Sean and Mer-Nod exchanged a glance, and it was Mer-Nod who spoke, breaking the tense silence. "Conn, Ó Finn desires an audience with you. He has something of importance to impart."

"You found her. She's dead, isn't she?" Conn slipped off the horse and tossed the reins over a post without even raising his head.

"N-no, Conn. Can we step inside?" Sean said.

The two men started inside with Nimbus fast on their heels. Mer-Nod reached out a long arm and jerked him back by the collar, ignoring the vicious kick aimed at his shin.

Conn led Sean to the study and closed the door. He leaned on the table and faced him. "What is it?" His hooded eyes were unreadable.

Sean cleared his throat, wondering at the wisdom of his words. "There have been new raids in the south."

Conn snorted. "That isn't news. Eoghan Mogh seems more tempted to stretch his muscles in the warm summer air."

"They are plundering the villages, demanding booty. They attack in the dead of night, catching us unaware." Sean struggled for words.

"You think I do not know this? I am still king, even though I have been otherwise occupied in the past few weeks."

Sean saw no trace of anger in Conn's face, only weariness.

"I was not insinuating that you were uninformed, Conn. The reports I have received from the southern provinces indicate that the same band is responsible for all of these raids. A man in a long black cloak has been seen on several occasions. He seems to be their leader." Sean paced across the room, pausing to gaze out of the open window.

"That is still not news. 'Tis probably one of Eoghan Mogh's cronies. If you've something to say, Sean, spit it out. I long for a soft bed and strong ale."

Sean turned to face him. "There is a woman." Conn froze, his eyes daring him to continue. "They say she is almost as tall as a man and fights like one." Sean's eyes shone with something akin to admiration. "She scouts for them and wields a mighty sword with her hair shining the color of blood in the moonlight. Some say her features are familiar. Others say they are obscured in the darkness of the night. She is becoming quite a legend."

Conn stroked his beard. "When was she first spotted?"

"Two, maybe three weeks ago. I would not have brought the matter to your attention, but I've been to the weaponry room. I know the sword is gone."

"You've done well to tell me this." He turned away from

Sean and murmured, "So it has come to this." His shoulders
began to shake.

Sean moved to him and stretched out a tentative hand, placing
it on his shoulders. "Sire, perhaps I am mistaken. Do not grieve
yourself so."

Conn turned around, tears streaming down his cheeks. Sean
took a step backward, thinking that perhaps his king had taken
leave of his senses, the shock too much for him to bear. Conn
stretched out his hand and struggled for words but was unable to
manage anything but a quick intake of breath before new waves
of laughter convulsed his body, doubling him over.

Sean nervously snickered, unsure of his mirth but thinking it
might do him well to join the king in his hysterics. Soon he
found himself guffawing. Conn lay across the table, clutching
his sides, and Sean stumbled across the room to lean on the
wall. Taking deep breaths, they both gained control only to
meet each other's eyes and dissolve into fresh roars of laughter.

Mer-Nod and Nimbus crouched outside the door listening
mystified to the muffled cacophony. Nimbus had to smile. He
hadn't heard Conn laugh for a long time. The door was jerked
open, sending them both tumbling into the room. Mer-Nod
stood, straightening his mantle with wounded dignity. Conn
leaned against the table, arms crossed and chuckling.

His voice booming through the room, Conn said, "It hasn't
taken our little girl long to show her true colors. Close the door,
Nimbus. Conn of the Hundred Battles has returned ready for
war. We've plans to make."

Chapter Sixteen

❖

Every muscle screamed in protest as she fell back upon the hay,
a low moan escaping through clenched teeth. She sighed and
closed her eyes, letting her arms fall beside her weary body. Her
nose twitched at the sweet smell of the new mown hay. Her

weary hand would not lift to scratch it. Taking slow deep breaths, she felt the tension float from her body and rise above the roof of the low-slung barn. Today would be a good day. The exhaustion would blanket her, protecting her from the piercing pain that threatened to discover her even in rest. Her sleep would be dreamless. When she awakened in the evening, there would be time, perhaps even a few minutes, when the pain could not find her. The afternoon sunshine would fall across her face through the loft window and the cleansing air would burn her lungs. There would be time before she remembered why she hurt.

Eoghan Mogh studied his well-trimmed nails with interest. "Your sister is not a happy woman, you know?"

"Of course, she is happy. We are together again. 'Tis what matters to her," Rodney said defensively, plucking an apple from the bowl on the table.

"No. 'Tis what matters to you. There is a difference," Eoghan replied.

Rodney snapped a bite out of the apple and chewed ferociously. "That bastard has bewitched her. She's doing her job, isn't she?"

"I can hardly complain about her scouting abilities. I would hate to meet her on a moonless night myself."

Grinning, Rodney said, "I trained her, you know. I told you long ago that she would be an asset to us."

"That is still not the issue. She is not happy. I would even say that the girl is miserable." Eoghan enunciated each word precisely as if explaining the metrics of poetry to a child. "Talk to her. See if you can make her happy."

"I could always make her laugh when she was a little girl." Rodney's eyes focused beyond the walls of the simple hut, a gentle sadness haunting them. "Perhaps we've pushed her too hard too fast. A week of drills and three weeks of raids might be too much. You didn't see her at Tara. She was a real lady."

Eoghan turned away from his hungry look, refusing to meddle in an affair that was not his concern. "I want her ready for the fortress in a month. We work our way north. The closer we get to him, the harder it will be for her. She must be prepared."

"A month is not very long," Rodney said, doubt in his voice.

"It will have to be long enough. 'Tis all we have."

"I shall make her happy." Rodney strode out the door, tossing the apple core to Eoghan with a cocky grin.

He walked to the barn where Gelina slept, whistling a jaunty tune. The loft was empty, the hay still warm where her body had nestled. He swung down from the loft and started for the stream where she bathed each afternoon.

He stepped furtively through the woods until he came to the small clearing where the stream giggled over the flat rocks. Gelina sat on the bank, her breeches pushed up past her knees, feet dangling in the water. Rodney slid down a tree to a sitting position before he spoke.

"This reminds me of the time we picnicked in the forest outside the cavern."

Gelina looked back at him, startled. "I remember it well. You told me to eat the eyeballs in my fish. Said they were good for me. Picnics seem to be my specialty," she said dryly.

He rose and went to sit beside her with legs crossed. "I am so happy you are here with me."

"And I am happy that you are alive." She smiled a genuine smile, something he'd seen few of since she'd joined him that morning on the Arabian, riding as if pursued by a nightmare.

"You really thought I was dead all that time?" he asked.

She picked up a stone and tossed it into the stream, her face devoid of emotion. "'Tis what I was told."

"Conn told you that, didn't he?"

She shrugged and tossed another stone where the water ran deep, skipping it across the surface and shattering the reflection of the afternoon sun.

"He's posted a reward for your return—a thousand gold pieces," Rodney said softly. When no reply came, he continued, "The rumors fly over Erin. Some say he wants you because he cares for you. Others say he wants you because you took something that belonged to him and he wants it back. Some say he wants to kill you." She shook her head and rolled her eyes but remained mute. "Some say he wants you for another reason entirely."

She met his eyes briefly before slamming a stone that missed the water and bounced violently off the opposite bank.

Rodney sighed. "I guess the rumors were laid to rest yesterday when the reward was changed."

"Changed to what?"

"Five thousand gold pieces for your return. Dead or alive."

The trees spun in front of Gelina's eyes, although she made no motion to indicate the sudden whirling of the world. The eyes she raised to Rodney were as dark as night. He struggled not to flinch under their steady gaze.

"What did you say?"

"I am sorry, Princess, but you had to know. We must kill him before he kills you. Once Eoghan Mogh is on the throne, we shall be rich and favored. We shall have our rightful places back. The name of Ó Monaghan will stand forever as a name of honor." He spoke quickly, afraid to stop the torrent of words. "Why we'll be—"

"Dead or alive?" Her voice cut through him, the words crashing like icicles to the ground.

Nodding, he reached out a hand to her as she stood, almost losing her balance on the muddy bank.

"Curse him!" she said hoarsely.

Rodney ducked as she unsheathed her sword, nearly lopping off his ear with the clumsy motion. Wielding the sword over her head, she swung at the branches of a rowan tree. Muffled sobs and muttered curses blended as twigs and brush flew through the air. Rodney crawled backward until he was no longer in the line of destruction. A steady thump drew his attention as her sword found a solid target. She chopped at a huge linden tree, sending bits of bark skyward to catch in her hair.

"Great Gods, Lina. 'Tis not a battle ax!"

He waited for the precise moment when the sword would hang in the stubborn wood of the tree and grabbed her around the waist, hurling her to the ground and letting the sword clatter to the foot of the tree. Hardly daring to breathe, he held her until her ragged sobs subsided to silence. He pressed his face to her hair, relishing its softness.

She sat up and he followed, his arm still anchored firmly around her waist. Rubbing her eyes like a spent child, she turned her tear-stained face to his coat and cried. Stroking her hair softly, he began to hum a lullaby they both remembered from childhood, a soft lilting tune sung in their mother's gentle brogue.

"Rodney?"

"Yes?"

"You're a very bad singer."

"Thank you, Lina. I love you, too." He brushed his lips against her temple, feeling the gentle pulse that beat there.

Late that afternoon Rodney sat alone at the top of a small drumlin facing an open meadow drenched in the gold of summer sunset. Below him his sister rode the huge ebony monster she called Silent Thunder. Charging back and forth across the field, she thrusted the sword in front of her, screeching a hideous battle cry and sending an imaginary enemy to a gruesome death. Hearing laughter behind him, Rodney turned to see Eoghan Mogh standing with arms crossed.

"She is quite a girl, your sister. Did you make her happy?" he asked Rodney.

Rodney's own smile faded as he answered, "I did the next best thing."

"And what is that?"

"I made her angry."

They watched in silence as Gelina thundered across the field, a bloodthirsty snarl on her delicate features. Her shrill battle cry floated past them and into the night sending a chill down Eoghan's spine.

It was the first of many battle cries they would hear in that long summer. With her hair covered by a cap and her long cloak flying, Gelina led them into the villages at midnight to catch the sleeping watch unaware. On some nights as many as a hundred men would accompany them, traveling from door to door to demand the treasure of that cottage to support the reign of Eoghan Mogh. The victims were offered their lives in exchange. Gelina would stand guard outside the cottages on her huge, black mount. Few of the men were even aware that she was a woman.

As they rode north, their gold coffers spilled over with ill-gotten plunder. On more than one night, Gelina, Rodney, and Eoghan would share a toast of ale while the gold coins spilled through Gelina's fingers to land in a shining heap in the floor. There was no stopping them now.

Gelina was trapped in a hazy dream with no beginning and no end. The cool coins that flowed over her fingertips matched the spreading ice that captured her spirit. Greed took root in her soul, its tendrils smothering the flashes of guilt and nostalgia that threatened to engulf her.

One hot night she sat perched on Silent Thunder awaiting the marauder who lingered inside the whitewashed cottage. Sweat trickled down her sides under the heavy cloak and she shifted in the saddle in a vain attempt to stop the tickling sensation. She jerked the reins at the sudden noise behind her.

The horse pranced around to face the soldier who stood with sword in hand. One look at his stature and braids and she knew who had sent him. She groaned, wishing him far away to a country she had never seen. He did not disappear. Seeing no choice, she pulled forth her sword in one fluid motion and brandished it in the air with a fierce growl. He still did not disappear.

"Stand and fight, hooligan!" he cried, his cracking voice revealing him to be little more than a lad.

She leapt off the horse and crouched in a fighter's stance. The young warrior jabbed his sword at her. He found his attempt a vain one as she parried his attack neatly, stepping aside and nearly knocking the sword from his hand with a deft blow from her weapon. She became dimly aware that the man she awaited had returned and was watching the fight with a smile, a sack of gold in each hand.

The swords crossed again and again, the clang of cold metal echoing in the heat of the night. She met each thrust with an equally clever parry. Taking her sword in both hands, she caught the soldier off guard by leaping sideways and whirling in a circle, catching his wrist with the blunt side of her sword. His weapon sailed through the air as he knelt and grasped his wrist with a cry of pain. She turned to mount her horse.

"Watch it!" It was only the hissed words of the man with the gold that sent her spinning around with sword outstretched.

The soldier impaled himself on the sharp point of her sword, the dagger in his hand clattering to the cobblestones. A thin stream of blood trickled from the corner of his mouth. She watched him slide to the ground in numb horror.

"Nice job, mate." The admiring words of the man who had warned her accompanied a hearty slap on the back, which drove the air from her lungs.

As he moved to the next cottage, she knelt beside the dead

man. Her fingers reached for the familiar leather belt without feeling.

Closing her eyes, she said softly, "Not another MacRuairc."

She sat on the dirt floor of the hut, arms wrapped around her knees. Dawn had not yet arrived, and the night was still fraught with darkness. Since they had taken to sleeping during the day and raiding at night, she found sleep elusive with her nerves still on the tenterhooks of darkness.

Eoghan Mogh ducked through the tiny door bearing an earthenware flask. "Rodney went to fetch some veal. I am ravenous."

He settled his burden on the table, surprised by her silence. "What is it, Gelina?"

"I killed a soldier of the Fianna tonight." She stared up at him, eyes wide and filled with the demons of doubt.

Before Eoghan could reply, Rodney stormed through the door, whooping. "I heard about it, Lina. 'Tis magnificent! Martin saw the whole thing. He's been telling the men what a warrior the little guy is. Let's have a toast, shall we?"

He dropped three mugs on the table with a horrible clatter and poured the ale, spilling a generous amount over the rims. Practically dancing, he spun around, a mug in each hand. They stared at him mutely.

"What is it? You look like grieving clansmen of the bloke," Rodney said, baffled.

"Gelina is a little disconcerted," Eoghan explained, taking the overflowing mugs from his hands.

"Oh." Rodney's face fell like a small boy's, then quickly recovered its grin as he knelt in front of Gelina and took both of her hands in his. "Lina, you should be proud. The world can only be bettered by the loss of one of his men. You did what you had to do."

"Did I?" she asked coldly, jerking her hands away.

"It was inevitable, Gelina," Eoghan said. He truly liked the girl, and it grieved him to see her distraught. "As soon as the men from Castile arrive, Tara itself will be placed under siege."

"What men?"

Rodney grinned. "Eoghan has a dark-haired Castilian beauty tucked in the wildlands—his wife Beara. Her father, Heber Mor, who just happens to be the king of Castile, has promised us five thousand warriors to arrive within the month." He clapped Eoghan heartily on the back, congratulating him for his cleverness.

"It hardly seems right to involve foreigners, does it?" Gelina asked, her brow furrowed.

"Right?" Rodney's grin faded. "Was it right for Conn to have our parents butchered? Was it right for his men to string our jester from the rafters? Was it right for him to tell you I was dead?"

Gelina closed her eyes. They flew open as Rodney grabbed her by the shoulders and shook her. "Was any of that right, Lina?"

Eoghan reached out a hand to restrain him but stopped when Gelina's voice rang out.

"Stop! Take your hands off of me. I will not let you bully me. If you try, you're no better than him!" She scrambled out the door and into the night.

Rodney started after her only to find Eoghan's hand tight on his shoulder. "Leave her be. Give her time."

Gelina paced outside, eyes dry and burning, too angry to spill tears. A huge bonfire blazed in the center of the clearing. Eoghan's men gathered around it. Gelina's nose twitched. Lacking both the neatness and intelligence of the Fianna, even the cleanest of them seemed to permeate the air with the sour odor of unwashed flesh. Matted hair hung over their shoulders. None of them noticed Gelina as she paced a few feet away from the fire.

"Good haul we got tonight. Don't ye think so, Martin?" A large man wearing a jerkin emblazoned with a skull and crossbones spoke.

"Best yet. I got an even better haul when I stumbled on a sweet little milkmaid in one of the cottages."

Gelina recognized the man who spoke as the one she had been waiting for when challenged by the soldier. She spat on the ground in disgust.

The men laughed as another one said, "Ye always were the lucky one, Martin. Must be those pretty teeth that the ladies like."

Martin grinned, revealing two huge gaps where his front teeth should have been. "She liked me tongue more than me teeth. I just offered to leave her a couple of coins, and she was more than happy to show her gratitude in a number of ways.'' He leered, eliciting guffaws and envious congratulations.

Still outside the circle of light cast by the fire, Gelina pulled off her cap and threw it on the ground.

''Bastards,'' she breathed, unaware that her sudden movement had revoked the protection of the darkness.

''Well, what have we here?'' The men's eyes were drawn to her, and she nervously ran a hand through her hair before resting it on her sword hilt. The burly man who spoke pointed. ''No wonder that fellow is always closeted with Ó Monaghan and Mogh. That's no fellow.''

Two of the men rose, lustful eyes locked on her. ''She wouldn't be a bad-looking little piece if she had more hair.'' They laughed, their grins hungry and unpleasant.

''She looks good enough for me.''

Gelina held her breath as one of the men started toward her. Pulling her sword, she hefted it defiantly in the air. ''Take another step and meet your maker, blackguard.''

The man chuckled and looked back at the others in disbelief. Several of them shrugged.

The man they called Martin spoke, his voice halting the man where he stood. ''She means it.'' All eyes turned to him. ''She's the one I told ye about. She slew the soldier of the Fianna.''

''Ye must be jesting. This''—he struggled for words, gesturing toward Gelina—''little girl slew one of Conn's fighting men?''

''That's what I said.'' Martin stared into the fire, a muscle twitching in his cheek.

The man studied Martin's face for a moment, then turned his gaze to Gelina, who stood locked in position, feet spread wide in a battle stance, eyes narrowed in warning. The sharp blade of her sword gleamed in the firelight.

Eoghan's commanding voice sneered at them from the doorway of the hut. ''I will not have my men fighting amongst themselves. Or my women, either. If you do, how can you expect to unite and help me capture Erin itself?''

''And the first one of you who threatens my sister again is going to find his head severed from his shoulders before he draws another breath.'' Rodney's furious form sailed into their midst, sword drawn.

"I can take care of myself, Rodney." Gelina replaced her sword in its scabbard with dignity and moved toward Eoghan.

Eoghan studied her, his laughing, speculative look striking a familiar chord she could not place. He put his hand on her shoulder, turning her around to face the men. His voice rang out in the night.

"Gelina Ó Monaghan is one of us. She will be treated with the same respect and more than you give to one another. She is courageous and dedicated to driving the tyrant Conn from Erin."

Gelina met his dark blue eyes, hesitating only a second before pulling her sword and calling out, "Death to the tyrant!"

The men exchanged wary glances and then pulled their swords one by one. Even Rodney joined in, forgetting his anger as the sweet, pure hatred of Conn rushed through his veins. Their cries rose into the night sky and echoed through the drumlins. "Death to Conn."

The Castilians joined them a week later. The five thousand warriors Heber Mor had promised shrank to only two thousand before their ships reached the rocky coast of Erin. Eoghan welcomed them without rebuke, and they moved north, conquering whole villages in the darkness of night. As Eoghan predicted, the number of soldiers Conn sent to halt them doubled and then tripled in the next month.

Eoghan set up sprawling camps. The dark-eyed, foreign-speaking Castilians mingled with the men of Erin, causing utter confusion. There were women among them now—camp followers who sought both gold and prestige as their numbers grew. Gelina spent days closeted with Rodney and Eoghan, mapping their plans on unwieldy sheets of parchment. She transcribed their plans in her neat, narrow writing, revealing an uncanny head for strategy.

She sat inside the tent one sultry day mapping their path for the week before they would arrive at Tara. The tent felt airless and the ink kept running off the page onto her breeches.

"Hey, Ó Monaghan. I've brought ye something." A man poked his head into the tent.

She cursed as the pen slipped for the thousandth time. "Sorry, Martin. I am having a bit of a time here. What is it?"

She'd become rather fond of the toothless soldier after he had discouraged the other men from assaulting her, discovering he wasn't quite the ogre she had imagined.

"A man left this for ye and then rode away. Said it was to be delivered to you in person." He handed her a small burlap bag tightly cinched at the top.

"What man? What did he look like?"

She struggled with the strings, finally jerking open the bag and pouring its contents into her lap. Three golden apples spilled out.

Martin shrugged. "He was riding a jackass. He was a midget."

Chapter Seventeen

❖

"Are you daft? Can't you understand?" Gelina grabbed Rodney by the jacket and shook him violently.

"I understand that you're hysterical." He firmly removed her hands from his lapel. "For Behl's sake, Lina, quit screeching and get control of yourself."

Sighing in disgust, she paced back and forth in the narrow confines of the tent. "He knows, Rodney. He knows where I am. He's coming after me."

"You've got it all wrong, Lina. We're going after him. He's not interested in you. If he's after anyone, it will be Eoghan Mogh, the man who almost killed him a few months ago." Rodney threw himself into a small carved chair and propped his feet up on the table. "He's probably forgotten you already."

Gelina shook her head, her voice deepening with fear. "You are the one who's wrong. Eoghan has always been his enemy. I am the one who betrayed him. He told me he would kill me if I ever betrayed him. He is a man of his word."

Rodney snorted. "You should be the last one to believe that."

"If he finds me, I'm dead, Rodney. You've got to help me."

Gelina stood with her palms turned upward in a plea, the

baggy pants she wore emphasizing her vulnerability. Rodney rose and led her to the chair, sitting her down with firm pressure on her shoulders. He knelt at her feet.

"If you and this jester were friends, isn't there a chance his contact could mean something good? Perhaps he wants to join us. If you'll look outside, Princess, you'll see that we are surrounded by people night and day. Even if Conn was after you, he couldn't possibly reach you. Right?"

"Wrong. If Conn wants me badly enough, he'll find a way to get to me. And Nimbus would never betray Conn."

"Surely some little fool wouldn't harbor that kind of loyalty to a king. You overestimate the dwarf," Rodney said with contempt.

"And you underestimate Conn." She shielded her face from him, covering her eyes with her hand. "What kind of man was our father, Rodney?" she asked, stealing a surreptitious glance through her fingers.

"Rory Ó Monaghan was a good man. He was a fine warrior, and he fought for the noble Conn in many a battle. Don't you remember the stories he used to tell us?" Glaring at her, he stood and poured himself a mug of ale. His hands shook.

"You are certain he was a good man?"

Slamming the earthenware mug down on the table with enough force to shatter it, he turned on her. "Of course, I'm certain. I suppose you're prepared to believe something that bastard told you instead of what your own brother tells you!"

"Your hand is bleeding," she said quietly.

She rose and took his hand. A single shard of pottery protruded from his palm. She worked it out with gentle fingers, then wrapped his hand in a makeshift bandage torn from her jerkin.

He stroked her hair with his free hand. "I won't let him hurt you, Lina. I'll never let him hurt you again."

Her eyes met his unflinchingly. "I hope you mean that. Because he's coming after me."

"No. On Midsummer's Eve we are going after him."

Light billowed out from the fortress in shimmering waves. The gates had been flung open, and torches blazed from every portal and window. The Midsummer's Eve of Tara beckoned them with its glow. Gelina sat astride Silent Thunder, her lower lip caught between her teeth. She pulled her misty eyes away from the familiar walls with effort, lifting them to the starry sky. The warm winds blew across them, clearing them to brightness and teasing the tendrils of hair at her temples with a whisper of force. She remembered another warm and windy summer night, loving hands on her shoulders, gentle thumbs tracing her collarbone, unwitting lips plundering her mouth and her heart for the first time in a kiss that might as well have been a kiss farewell. A deep sadness gripped her as she reached into the pocket of her jacket and pulled forth the golden apple that had found its way there.

Rodney shifted on his horse, biting back the words he longed to say. Setting her lips in a grim line, Gelina shoved the toy deep in her pocket. Her other hand pushed back her cloak to find the sword hilt at her waist. Silent Thunder pranced nervously as she drew back the reins.

Exchanging a dark glance with Rodney, she spurred the horse forward. Three men followed them, the black cloaks they wore flapping behind them like giant birds of prey as they thundered down the hill. They left behind over two thousand men who awaited the flash of their signal torch in the darkness of the night.

Slowing the horses to a walk, they plodded through the gate. Gelina sensed Rodney's presence at her left flank and felt the mantle of leadership settle on her shoulders. She knew the inside of the fortress, and it was she they would follow. She gestured sharply for Rodney to move forward. His eyes darted over the deserted courtyard.

They dismounted, tossing the reins over posts without tying them. Gelina hissed orders to the three men, and they disappeared around a corner. Running a shaking hand through her hair, she pulled Rodney along until they reached the wooden door hidden behind a sweeping curtain of ivy. She pushed the ivy aside; the door creaked open. They ducked into the darkness of the passageway.

A sliver of light at the end of the corridor drew them forward. They crept toward the light, Gelina in the lead, the wall at their backs. The door to the weaponry room lay before them. Gelina shook her head to find the door slightly ajar. Rodney frowned, unsure of her hesitation. With a trembling hand, she pushed the heavy door open, widening the circle of light in the dim corridor.

Her eyes widened. The torches in their iron brackets shone on black and empty walls.

She took a step backward, her mouth a circle of dread. "'Tis a trap," she hissed. Rodney stared at her without comprehension and found himself shoved down the hall, her desperate hands driving him forward. "Flee!"

They stumbled down the corridor to the door they had entered only to find it latched from the outside. Gelina rubbed her hands raw against it, slivers of wood tearing her palms. It would not budge. She turned to lean breathlessly against it.

Her words tumbled over one another, the fear in her voice palpable. "There was no noise, Rodney! I should have known! There was no laughter, no music, only that cursed light! We've got to find the others and get them out of here."

Rodney stood mesmerized in front of her. She shoved him. They flew through the mazelike corridors toward the center of the fortress as fast as their shaking legs would carry them. With their hands on their weapons, they stumbled into the great hall.

A thousand tallow candles lit the deserted hall. In the distance Gelina heard the sound of battle. Swords clashed in the night. Rodney froze beside her, hearing the cries of men and thundering horses at the same moment. The nightmarish din grew nearer by the second.

"Follow that corridor, Rodney. I sent the men in through the tower. Find them. I'll meet you outside with the horses."

Obeying her without question, he disappeared, and Gelina found herself alone in the great hall. The eerie sound of battle echoed through the hall like the memory of a conflict fought long ago. Shivering, she drew her sword and started down a narrow corridor. The tramp of heavy footsteps down the stairs at the end of the corridor froze her in her tracks. Her frantic hands found the protruding panel on the wall. Drawing in a deep breath, she ducked into the secret tunnel. A flickering torch set midway on the wall cast long, wavering shadows over her path.

Gelina ran toward the torch, the sword a cold comfort held rigidly in front of her. The dank air filled her nostrils. She rounded the corner, then backed up just as rapidly.

Conn stalked her, his eyes blue fire as he forced her against the wall, his sword an inch from hers. She drew in a ragged breath, her desperate eyes fixed on the vicious hatred she read in his face. He tapped the end of her sword with his, and she felt the shock reverberate through her fingertips to her pounding heart.

"Found at last, my lost beauty," he breathed, his voice as smooth and deadly as a black velvet noose, tightening her throat with its mocking intimacy.

Gelina took a step away from him, her back still pressed to the wall. He tapped her sword again.

"What stops you, Gelina? You have proved you could best a soldier of the Fianna in a fair fight. Have you lost your nerve?" He slammed his sword against hers; the sound of metal against metal echoed in the deserted corridor.

She held her tongue, knowing silence was her only weapon.

A cruel smile twisted his lips. "Are you going to let me kill you without a fight? Why, I do believe you would!"

She leapt to the side as Conn's sword whistled past her throat and raised Vengeance to block his thrust at her chest. Her emerald eyes widened; her chest heaved with a shuddering breath.

Conn laughed, the sound hollow and empty in the tunnel. "You defend yourself but you do not raise your sword to me. You are a fool, Gelina Ó Monaghan."

His arms fell to his side, his sword barely gripped with the tips of his fingers. "What are you waiting for? Attack, Gelina. Prove what a fine warrior you are. Avenge the noble name of Ó Monaghan."

He stepped forward, pressing his broad chest to the quivering blade of her sword. His sapphire eyes fixed on her trembling lips.

"Drive it home, beauty, or I will," he said, his voice a caress belied by the unyielding fury in his eyes.

The tip of her sword pressed into the leather of his tunic. A plea died on her lips as the mouth she had so often seen curved in a loving smile twisted in a malevolent sneer. The hand that held Vengeance slowly lowered until the blade touched the floor. Conn turned away from her with a short laugh, then whirled back, placing the point of his sword at her soft throat.

"Drop your weapon," he commanded.

Gelina swallowed, feeling the sting of the cold steel against her aching throat. She lowered her arm, her fingertips uncurling from the hilt of the sword with agonizing reluctance. In the same instant that Vengeance clattered to the wooden floor, the sharp end of a sword appeared through Conn's shoulder, its tip stained with bright red blood. Conn sank to his knees, dropping his sword. Gelina stared into Rodney's black eyes as he coolly withdrew his blade from Conn's back.

"Now, Conn. Your time has come." He drew back his sword, the keen edge of the blade aimed at Conn's neck.

Conn raised his head slowly, lifting his eyes to Gelina. A cryptic message was mirrored in the pain she saw there.

"No!" Her hands flew out to grip her brother's wrist.

Staring at her in disbelief, Rodney said, "What are you doing? Have you taken leave of your senses?" The thunder of footsteps approached the corridor. "It won't take long to finish him off. Out of my way," he shouted, struggling to pull away from her viselike grip.

"I said no!" she roared, scooping up her sword and sliding past Conn, who followed her every move with his icy gaze. "They come. We must flee." The shouts of men filled the passageway.

"This is our last chance, Lina!"

Even as he spoke, Rodney took a step backward. She started after him, then stopped, turning to face Conn. She dropped the sword and knelt beside him, frantically tearing a narrow strip of linen from her tunic, trying to staunch the steady stream of blood spilling from his wound. Swallowing hard, she avoided his eyes, which reflected a hatred as black as the night.

"What are you doing, Gelina?" Rodney called to her from the end of the corridor. He waved his arms wildly.

Turning toward him, she replied, "I'll be right there."

It was all Conn needed. Strong arms circled her, pulling her against his chest. For the second time that night she felt cold metal at her throat as Conn pressed a razor-sharp dagger to the smooth skin. His arm locked brutally under her breasts.

Rodney stared in horror, his eyes darting between the two of them and the passageway where voices rapidly approached. Conn's warm blood soaked her back as he sank to the floor with her, his grip still deadly. She relaxed against him, closing her eyes. A peculiar peace claimed her as she leaned away from the cold dagger, pressing her body to his.

"Go, Rodney. Leave me. You must," she called to him, eyes still closed.

"I cannot leave you." The voices grew louder as Rodney took a step toward them, his face twisted in impotent rage.

"Go. He won't hurt me," she whispered.

Rodney backed away from them.

Only she felt the warm breath in her ear and heard the hissed words as Rodney disappeared around the corner. "Don't count on it, my sweet beauty."

Then her world went black as pain shot through her arm and to her brain, blocking all the signals mercifully.

❖

PART FOUR

The world is running out
　　　like the ebbing sea;
fly far from it,
　　　and seek safety

　　　—Author unknown
　　　7th century

❖

Chapter Eighteen

❖

The chill floor felt rough beneath her cheek. Astonishment that she was still alive pierced her foggy mind. Lifting her head a fraction of an inch, she shook it, trying to clear the cobwebs from her brain before daring to open her eyes. She made a vain attempt to stretch her limbs away from her curled body. None of them seemed to be functioning.

Opening her eyes gingerly, she saw Conn standing over her.

He was dressed in the brown and forest green of a Fiannic warrior. Soft leather boots laced up to his knees, matching the leather belt looped around his waist. He wore no sword, only a wicked-looking dagger strapped to his thigh. He gazed down at her with a look that drew the breath from her body.

She frowned, her voice barely a whisper, "Your wound?"

"Your brother is a less than competent swordsman even from the back." His words were clipped.

"So much blood," she murmured.

"I'm thankful my loving daughter was there to staunch the bleeding." His voice dripped sarcasm as thick as honey.

Gelina blinked, bringing the room into focus. Moist rock walls circled them, their dripping surfaces pocked with craggy hollows and overhangs.

"Where are we?"

"You mean you don't know?" He peered around the high-ceilinged chamber in mock puzzlement. "'Tis so similar to the rock you crawled out from under that I assumed you would recognize it."

She bit back a sharp retort.

He paced beside her, hands locked behind his back. "We are in a cavern, my dear."

"I expected a dungeon, not a cave."

He whirled on his heel. "Then you expected too much, didn't you?"

"I fear I've always had that problem where you're concerned," she murmured. "Why are we in a cave?"

He pointed at her. "Because I wasn't brooking any interference from anyone. Nimbus found you for me, but he'll not tell me what to do with you. He still holds the illusion that there may be something redeemable in your wretched little heart."

"And you hold no such illusions?" Gelina asked, her mouth tightening in a challenge.

"None whatsoever. That's why we're here. Alone and isolated, away from prying eyes and hearts."

A chill ran down the length of her spine as Conn stared down at her, an awful light glowing in the depths of his eyes.

She spoke, prattling like a child to hide the fear spreading through her veins. "I'm not afraid of you. The worst that could happen has happened. You've found me. There is nothing to be afraid of anymore."

Conn knelt beside her, tangling a powerful hand in her short curls. He brought her face close to his. "If you think the worst has happened to you, my dear, you have a very limited imagination." His fingers tightened, and tears of pain sprang to her eyes.

"I cannot feel my arms," she said, seeking to hide the sudden trembling of her limbs.

He loosed her hair disdainfully. "You're bound well, milady, much like the way I was bound when your crony Eoghan Mogh tried to sell me into slavery to the Romans." He smiled pleasantly. "Quite uncomfortable, is it not?"

"You tell me," she snapped, his little games beginning to try her frazzled nerves.

With a swift move he pulled the dagger from his scabbard and cut the bonds from her arms. The tingling began, intensifying in her right arm until she cried out in pain.

"Oh, what did you do to me?" Gelina doubled over the arm, blinking back tears.

Conn jerked her to a sitting position. With one hand cupping her neck, he poured a burning liquid down her throat. She coughed and sputtered in a desperate attempt to catch her breath. Sticky amber dribbled down her chin.

Her eyes watered as he said coldly, "I wanted to make sure that you wouldn't be using a sword for a while. Don't fear. The bone isn't broken."

"Thanks a lot," she sneered.

"I won't break it unless I have to." Conn sat back on his heels and took a deep swig from the canteen. "Did the whiskey help?"

"About as much as it did the time you lanced my wound. Not at all."

She focused her blurred vision on a rock, unwilling to reveal how close the sobs were to spilling forth. The warmth burning in the pit of her stomach unleashed a wealth of regrets as she listened to the stranger's cold voice beside her.

"And how is dear Eoghan?"

"Do you know him?"

"We've met." Conn's veiled eyes refused to reveal more.

"Maybe you should tell me how Eoghan is. You're the one who probably knows if he and Rodney are still alive." She sniffed. "Not that you would tell me the truth."

He shrugged. "If they survived the battle with five thousand of my men, I'm sure they still walk the earth. We both know your brother has an unfortunate capacity for survival."

"Not as unfortunate as yours." Gelina bit the words off, fury making her careless.

Conn's hands closed on her tunic. He lifted her off the floor and slammed her to the wall in one fluid motion. She struggled to catch her breath and stared at the dark hair curling over his whitened knuckles. He loosed her; his hands flexed on each side of her. He leaned forward, his knee bent between her legs. She could feel the heat radiating from his tensed body.

"Take care, milady," he said softly. "You may pay dearly for every word you speak and every black deed you've done."

His face was the face of a stranger in the dim light. Gelina met his glittering eyes, something inside her awakening and dying in the same breath as she realized for the first time what his fury made him capable of. Her eyes dropped to her own waist where a leather belt engraved with the MacRuairc name hung as a condemning admission of guilt.

She slid slowly to the floor, her back pressed to the cave wall. He crouched beside her and retied her wrists in front of her, his head bent only inches from her face. She stared at the dark curls interspersed with gray and fought an absurd desire to lean her head on his shoulder and beg for his forgiveness, plead for his mercy. He glanced up; the unguarded need in her eyes caught him unaware. Without another word he rose and stalked out of the chamber. Lying back on the cold stone floor, she closed her eyes wearily, making her mind a careful blank.

Conn stepped outside the cavern and collapsed against the rocks. Covering his face with both hands, he wondered what had possessed him to bring her here. It had been an effortless assumption that once he got his hands on her, the rest would come easily. It was unbearable to admit to himself that he wasn't even sure what the rest was. The murdering bitch that had haunted his dreams through the heated summer lay inside the cave at the mercy of his every whim.

But her smooth skin was tanned honey brown from the sun. She struggled to hide her fear of him behind eyes fringed with dark lashes. Her wide mouth spoke without words of a beauty he could never deny. Even the auburn brilliance of her short-cropped hair could not hide it. Beneath the dusty leather of her garments lay the sweet flesh of a woman.

She brought out the worst in him. Never had he dreamed that he would break the Fiannic oaths he held as dear as his own life. He had sworn to avenge the deaths of his fellow warriors, but he had let her live in a moment of weakness. And now she had killed again. For the thousandth time he wondered what he had done to her that had driven her away from him that cool spring night. He stared at the stars, choking back a curse. He could not deny it. Conn of the Hundred Battles was afraid.

"Conn!" The voice floated out to where he dozed on a note of desperation.

He untangled himself from his bedroll and flew into the cavern, his hand on his dagger. Gelina lay where he had left her, muscles rigid and teeth clenched, staring at her leg.

"Get it off me!"

Her wide eyes watched in terrified fascination as a huge spider inched up her thigh, its fuzzy legs the span of a man's hand. Unspilled tears welled between her sooty lashes.

An unpleasant smile crossed his features. "You have no fondness for spiders, eh?"

Shooting him a look of pure hatred, she commanded, "Take it away."

Crossing his arms, he said softly, "Say please, and I shall give it some thought."

"Please." Gelina choked out the word, despising herself even as she said it but despising him more. Her eyes never left the spider.

Conn leaned over and flicked the spider from her leg with the point of his dagger. Her body sagged in relief.

"I need to get up," she said.

"Why?" he asked, sheathing the dagger.

A faint pink graced her cheeks. "I have . . . needs to attend to."

Conn feigned ignorance. "Needs?"

Her flush deepened. "Must I spell it out?"

"Perhaps." He smiled innocently, enjoying her discomfiture.

She turned her face to the floor and shook her head. With one hand, he grabbed the back of her jacket, pulling her roughly to her feet.

His voice held no trace of laughter. "I shall untie you. You have three minutes. If you try anything stupid, it had better work because if it doesn't, I'm going to call back your furry, little friend."

Gelina swallowed as he unknotted her bonds and shoved her out of the cave.

In barely a minute she reappeared, the moonlight behind her throwing her lithe figure into silhouette. She approached him, holding out her wrists in surrender for the bonds to be replaced. Conn took both of her hands in his and turned them upward, his broad thumbs tracing the roughened skin. Gelina bowed her head in a vain attempt to still the sudden trembling of her lower lip.

"I guess I don't have to ask what you did with your summer," he said.

Her palms were scarred with a fine line of calluses from long nights of gripping sweaty reins. She met his eyes evenly. Capturing both of her hands in one of his, he reached up and ran a finger over her grubby, tearstained cheek. His thumb traced the curve of her lower lip.

"Your wound is bleeding again," she said mechanically, unable to bear the mockery of his tender touch.

He loosed her as if she had burned him, placing a surprised hand on the stain spreading over the shoulder of his tunic.

"I would dress it for you but I don't think my arm would work that well."

"I would just as soon let a viper dress it, thank you." Even as Conn spoke, he removed his tunic and ripped it into narrow strips. He wrapped a strand of it around his shoulder, trying to knot it under his arm.

Gelina crossed her arms to stifle the growing desire to help him as he struggled with the awkward bandage. Her lips twitched as he tied it for the third time only to have it slide to the floor in a defiant heap. He cursed loudly and imaginatively.

"You'll bleed to death before you get it tied."

Without awaiting his protest, she snatched the bandage with her left hand. His eyes narrowed in a silent dare to strangle him with the innocent scrap of cloth. Biting her lower lip, she looped it around his shoulder, tangling it hopelessly around her fingers. Shooting pains traveled up her right shoulder and down her side. They both sighed in exasperation.

An idea crossed her mind. "Kneel in front of me," she commanded.

"You'd love that, wouldn't you?" He stood even straighter, ignoring the blood trickling down his bare chest.

"Bleed to death then. See if I care." Gelina shot the words back at him, her patience reaching its limit.

He stood for a moment longer, then got to his knees, back straight and eyes furious. "Finish it."

With both hands working at that level, she fashioned a neat little bandage, securing it with a vicious jerk. A low growl from Conn's throat made her wonder if she had gone too far.

He sat on the ground, stretching his long legs in front of him, his eyes never leaving her. She sat in front of him, crossing her legs, fighting to convey a calm she was far from feeling. She wondered what thoughts lurked behind his opaque eyes but did not have long to wonder.

"Your brother is insane," he said as if commenting on the weather.

"'Tis a lie," she replied, controlling her voice with effort.

He spoke deliberately. "If you were my sister, I wouldn't have left you with me."

"He had no choice."

"Didn't he? If you were a nodding acquaintance, I wouldn't have left you with me."

The quiet assurance in his voice sent a shiver down her spine. She averted her eyes, refusing to let him see the fear nestled within.

"How did Nimbus find me?"

"It wasn't difficult. 'Tis hard to be subtle with a thousand Castilians trailing you about the countryside. Nimbus even traveled with you for a few days, following your every move."

"I never saw him."

Conn shrugged. "When Nimbus doesn't want to be seen, he generally isn't."

"Does he know you captured me?"

Conn snorted, the familiar grin sending a pang through her heart. "If he did, he would undoubtedly be here hanging off my legs, begging me to give you another chance."

"That, of course, is impossible." Gelina didn't bother making it a question.

"Completely." The dangerous gleam reappeared in his eyes.

She refused to look away, searching in vain for some trace of the friend she had known within their recesses. Finally she lowered her eyes in disappointment. He stood and paced in front of her, each step carrying him further away from her into the black void of his anger.

"Do you know I am sworn to avenge the death of a Fiannic soldier without mercy? I am also sworn to provide gentleness to all women."

"Gentleness has always been a problem with me, hasn't it, Conn?" The venom in her words stopped him in his tracks.

"Perhaps it wouldn't be if you broke the unfortunate habit of murdering my soldiers." His palm itched as he fought the urge to slap her, the insolence in her taut mouth daring him. "If you were a man, I would have killed you with my bare hands by now."

"If I were a man, you would have never had the chance. I guess you were going to let your men do the dirty work for you again. 'Tis why you offered that reward." Gelina's fear dissipated as her anger grew.

"I offered a reward for your return. Your safe return."

"You're lying. The truth isn't in you. Rodney told me himself that you wanted me returned to Tara dead or alive. Offered a nice lot of gold coins, didn't you?" Gelina couldn't stop the words that spewed from her wounded heart. "You've got a nasty habit of lying. You lied about Rodney's death. You probably lied about my father. The only thing that surprises me is that you're man enough to admit you sent the rutting pigs who killed my father and raped my mother. You're a bastard, Conn, who pretends to be an honorable man when it suits him.''

She stood, hands clenched at her sides, her chest heaving. With her eyes darkened in rage, she reminded Conn painfully of her brother. If a sword had been gripped in her hand, he knew they would have repeated the conflict of their first meeting.

His quiet voice broke the taut silence. ''Sit down, Ó Monaghan. Now.''

Disobeying his command was a fleeting thought as Gelina threw herself down, slamming her back into the wall, welcoming the pain it brought. Her white knuckles revealed the depth of her anger.

''For twenty-four hours a day I have thought of you, searched for you.'' She looked up, shocked at the raw pain in Conn's voice. ''I didn't know why you ran away until I found out your brother was alive. Then I found out you had allied yourself with Eoghan Mogh.'' He ran a hand through his shaggy curls. ''I plotted ways to trap you. I lay awake at night staring into the darkness, thinking of ways to get revenge on you. The things I thought of . . .'' he said hoarsely, running a hand across his eyes.

''I left because you lied. My brother was alive. My place was with him, not with some hypocritical king who soothed his conscience by playing the noble patron.''

Turning away from her to hide how deeply her callous words cut, he sighed. ''Then I am left to believe only one thing. You were in contact with your brother from the beginning. You knew when I left for Britain that I was being sent to my death. Perhaps the night I caught you in the stables, you were returning from a rendezvous with Eoghan Mogh.''

His accusation drew a gasp from her. '' 'Tis not true! I did not know Rodney was alive until the day I ran away.''

''I believe you.'' His sarcastic laugh belied his words. ''Nimbus told me all about your dear brother. He told me how he watches you, the look in his eyes, the way he touches you.''

''What are you trying to say?'' she said through clenched teeth, beads of sweat standing out on her forehead.

''Perhaps you and your brother are closer than you lead me to believe, Princess. Perhaps you are closer than your tainted blood should allow."

The full implication of his words hit her like a slap in the face. Icy white wrath shot through her veins resulting in a pure energy that propelled her into Conn like a mad creature. She pummeled him with her fists, seeking to take him down any way she could. Scalding tears coursed down her cheeks. Her nails raked bloody furrows down his arms.

Conn's arms went around her, slamming her to the ground where they rolled, locked in a desperate tangle of arms and legs. The length of his body covered hers, his weight pressing her to the floor, stilling even the barest hint of movement. His eyes gleamed a scant inch from hers, and for the first time Gelina wondered what she had done.

Conn wanted to kill her. He wanted to tear her to shreds, to silence forever her accusing young voice. Some cruel facet of him wanted to push her over the edge, beyond the boundaries of the past she eluded so boldly. He raised his dagger from its sheath with his powerfully muscled arm, and Gelina squeezed her eyes shut, awaiting the death blow to come.

With a single practiced flick of his wrist, he severed the flame from the torch ten feet away, leaving them in darkness. The tautly stretched rope of his control snapped as the darkness shielded him from her only weapon—her wide, terrified eyes.

The blue of his eyes blocked out the darkness as his mouth descended on hers without compromise. He caught her chin in his hand. His thumb forced her tender lips apart, forging a bruising trail for his lips to follow. His tongue took the deepest corners of her aching mouth, spreading and stroking, leaving her with neither the breath nor the means to protest. Shame and fear flooded her at his merciless rape of her mouth. Her eyes filled with hot tears. As the tears splashed on his hands, his grip loosened.

She wrenched away from him with a cry of despair and stumbled toward the mouth of the cavern. He called her name. She stopped, her face turned to the moonlight. She never heard his footsteps, but he stood behind her, his body barely touching hers.

"You have no right to refuse me. I'm your king."

Conn had never used those words against a woman before and never thought he would. He knew it was the cruelest thing he could have said, but he couldn't stop himself from saying it. The exquisite pain of wanting her filled him, driving all traces of honor and compassion before it.

His hands closed on her shoulders. His fingers slid beneath the tunic, pushing it aside and baring her shoulders to the caress of the moon and his lips. Her head fell back as his mouth glided upward along her throat. A shudder wracked him as he felt her moan against his lips before he heard it. She stood as still as a statue in his arms as he gently drew the tunic over her head. He tugged at the drawstring of her breeches and eased them down her hips, feeling the gooseflesh rise on her smooth skin to prick his fingertips.

The pressure of his knees against hers was all it took to fold her against him. They sank together into the folds of his bedroll. His mouth closed on hers in a fierce kiss, drawing her into the abyss of fire that spurred him on.

Gelina spiraled downward into the darkness of his desire. Stripped of her sword and her will, she knew that tonight they fought a new kind of battle and Conn held all the weapons. The damp heat of his mouth against her parted lips, the callused palm cupping her neck, the rough softness of his chest teasing her bare flesh—these were his weapons, and he possessed the expertise to use them to devastating effect. Even through her haze of inexperience she knew the burning sword he pressed to the soft hollows of her body would be swift and merciless, fashioned to invade and conquer her childish arrogance. She clung to his shoulders, shivering and afraid. His kiss sent a sweet fire spreading through her veins, as heady and exhilarating as the whiskey she could taste on his tongue.

Without missing a stroke of his kiss, he untied his breeches. He lifted himself from her, his breathing harsh in the silence. Gelina stared up at him with eyes as opaque as the moon reflected within them. The back of his hand traced the curve of her cheek. Terrified by the web he wove with his mocking travesty of tenderness, Gelina caught his hair in her hands and drew him down to her, her eyes blazing to remind him of the battle to be fought.

His pent-up fury erupted in a lust so violent he never had another thought beyond his hunger for her. Feeling the heat of her young body trapped beneath his, he parted her legs with a relentless knee. Gelina clenched her eyes shut and saw the moon burst into flames behind her eyes.

With one splintering movement he drove himself into her. He halted, his world narrowing to her sharp intake of breath and the fingernails that dug like tiny daggers into his back. He could not turn back. His need drove him deeper, deafening him to her low cry of pain. With each brutal thrust, he brought himself closer to the point where he could forget, retreating to a mindless place where no thought would follow until her body lay still and conquered beneath his.

Having been taught to kill with his bare hands in over a hundred different ways, Conn had risen from many prostrate, broken forms in his lifetime. He had never faced the dread he faced now. He sat back on his haunches, spent and afraid.

The narrow stream of moonlight caressed a face in sweet, childlike repose. Only the even rise and fall of her chest assured him that she lived. With a trembling hand he touched between her legs, then stared without comprehension at the blood on his fingertips. Having no more will to face what he had wrought, he tucked his jacket around her, donned his breeches and stumbled into the warm summer night.

Unable to face the glittering stars, he sat with his back against a rock and stared into the mud. Black despair gripped him as he contemplated what he had become. An eternity of dark time passed.

"The stars have been plentiful this summer."

The familiar, matter-of-fact voice jolted him like a ghost from the past, and he looked over to see Gelina emerge from the shadows, hugging his jacket around her. It hung halfway to her knees. Her face was ashen in the moonlight.

She studied the stars for a long time before daring to shoot a glance at him. His haunted gaze held hers steadily. Some instinct told her that if she cared to slit his throat at that second, he would gladly offer her his dagger.

"I suppose it was inevitable, Conn." She turned her eyes back to the sky, biting her swollen lip.

"Don't comfort me," he hoarsely replied.

"It hardly matters." He shook his head at her words, then buried it in his arms as she continued. "My mother was not a strong woman, you know. She wasn't like me. After the men had finished with her and left, she rose and stumbled around the hall, muttering and whimpering like a beaten dog.'' Gelina looked at Conn to find his eyes locked on her.

"I wanted to go to her. I wanted to tell her that Rodney and I were alive. I tried to call out, but Rodney just held his hand more tightly over my mouth. It was as if he knew what she should do under the circumstances.''

"The soldiers didn't kill Deirdre?'' Conn asked, horror shining bright in his eyes.

"They did many other things to her but they didn't kill her. When she found my father's body, she took his sword, placed it at her breast and fell on it. She never even looked for us. I don't know if I'll ever forgive her that. I think the dishonor drove her to her death, not the grief. So she was weak.''

Conn stood, weaving on his feet. Even in the moonlight, his pallor was unmistakable. Gelina stared in alarm at the dark stain rapidly spreading across his chest. Blood dripped to the waistband of his breeches, soaking into the dark material.

"Do something for me, my Gelina,'' he said, his speech slurred. "I am going to fall down. After I do, I want you to do one of two things. Kill me, or leave me.''

Before he could finish speaking, he slid to the ground. She threw herself behind him, trying to break his fall as he faded from consciousness.

Sitting in the cold mud with his head awkwardly cradled in her lap, she leaned down and whispered, "Since you're probably going to die, you might as well know—I love you nearly as much as I hate you.''

His eyes fluttered just once as he murmured, "Me, too.''

Chapter Nineteen

❖

Nimbus's short legs flopped like rags; his hands clutched at Sean's side as they galloped over the drumlins. After a day of riding this way, he could feel the matter between his ears turning to pudding along with his now boneless legs.

"Whoa!" With a bellow belying his size, he jerked the reins from Sean's hands and pulled back on them with clenched fists.

"What did you do that for, you runt?" Sean yelled as the horse stumbled to an awkward halt, nearly unseating them both.

"Because I'm exhausted. There must be a hundred caverns along this range. We'll never find them!" Throwing a leg over the horse's back, he neatly kicked Sean in the elbow as he slid to the ground, landing on the balls of his feet with as much aplomb as he could muster.

Rubbing his elbow, Sean dismounted, resisting the urge to shove his companion off the cliff they traveled along. With a snort of disgust, he unpacked a flagon of goat's milk and a round of cheese.

"You're nearly as tiresome as Mer-Nod said you would be. First you're begging to go look for them, and now here you are, acting the fool. I guess you can't help that, though." Sean chuckled at his play on words.

"Perhaps ye should have been the jester and not I, Ó Finn. Ye're a real wit—a dimwit."

Sean refused to rise to the bait, choosing instead to seat himself against a rise in the land and take a ravenous bite of the cheese. Nimbus approached with outstretched hand.

"Get that hairy little paw away from me. I refuse to reconcile with you after that last insult." Sean choked out his words from a cloying mouthful of cheese.

"'Tis not reconciliation I'm interested in. 'Tis the cheese."

Knowing how vicious the midget's kicks could be to a man his size, Sean decided it would be wiser to yield than to argue. He tore the round of cheese down the center and handed the smaller half to Nimbus. Nimbus stared at it for a long moment, then turned narrowed eyes to Sean. Without a word Sean handed him his half and took the smaller half cradled disparagingly in Nimbus's fingers.

They ate in silence, the morning rays lulling them into tranquil drowsiness. The sun danced on the plains below. A warm breeze blew from the west, stirring the tall grasses. In the distance a forest shimmered in the heat, the dark green of its leaves spun from the richness of the soil. Nimbus sighed, wondering how everything could be so wrong on a morning that looked so right.

"I don't know why we seek them. They've probably killed each other by now," he said, more to himself than to Sean.

"I seek Conn. I am here on a mission of state to obtain instructions as to the disposal of a prisoner of war." Sean's words were clipped.

Nimbus applauded. "Well said. I suppose ye have no interest in the disposal of another prisoner of war—Gelina."

"Realistically speaking, Nimbus, disposal is probably the correct word. You didn't see Conn leave the fortress with her. I have never seen him so . . . resolute. Conn has never raised a hand to me, but I saw death in his eyes when I stood before him that night. He came storming down that corridor with blood all over him, carrying her in his arms like a child. Her neck hung limp and she was so pale I can't swear she wasn't already . . ." His words faded to an awkward halt.

Nimbus rose and paced to the edge of the cliff, hands on hips, lips clamped together. He stared blindly down the hillside.

"Forgive me, Nimbus. That was brutal. I wish I understood his feelings for her."

"I'm afraid I do," Nimbus muttered.

Sean's appetite deserted him, and he tossed the rest of the cheese away. "I cared for her, too, you know. I don't desire to discover that he's killed her or worse. It doesn't make my life any better to know she's probably lying dead on the floor of one of those caverns."

Nimbus's mouth opened and closed but he couldn't manage more than a squeak.

"I didn't mean to grieve you, Nimbus." Sean went to stand beside him, placing a hand on his shoulder.

It was he who needed the support as his mouth fell open at the sight on the cliff below them.

Floating through the blackest tunnel in a stream of warm water with only his head above the surface, Conn went limp and surrendered to the joy of unconsciousness. No light and no pain; delicious warmth surrounded him. He was a small boy again drifting through life without a single flaw to mar his virgin honor. He would stay forever. Then came the voice.

It wasn't a bad voice but it droned on, talking incessantly. He longed to silence it, knowing it was the only thing holding him back from drowning in the sweet water with only the broken surface to mark where his head had been. But still it continued.

It was his father's voice. "Hold the bow steady. You shall never hold the kingdom of Erin if you cannot hold a bow." Its very severity was comforting.

"Of course, I love you. You are my only son." He was pulled to his mother's bosom; he breathed in the scent of sandalwood.

A boy's voice taunted him. "You're only a bastard. You will never be a real man."

There was silence. The water closed over his head.

Then came the midget's voice, the very sharpness of it buoying him out of the water with a jolt. "She loved ye like a woman loves a man. She loved ye before ye ever left for Rome."

His own voice was the worst. "I shall let you choose between two just punishments. I will either turn you over to the clans of the men you killed . . . or I will have you beheaded."

Hearing a rhythmic splashing in the water beside him, he dared to open his eyes. They adjusted to the blackness; he turned to follow the sound.

Paddling beside him was the jackal. Its sleek muscles gleaming in the water, it followed him effortlessly downstream. Ragged jaws parted in a smile, sharp fangs dripping crimson blood. If he could, at that moment, he would have pulled the water over his head like a blanket, destroying the jackal forever. But the voice began again, and the jackal disappeared.

It was a girl's voice, sparkling with the nuances of youth. It spoke of dancing barefoot and which berries made the most brilliant rouge. It spoke of horses traveling faster than the wind and jealousy in a muddy garden. Good swords were distinguished from bad ones by their weight. Lentil soup was compared to steak in the value of warming a cold, empty stomach. The voice continued, speaking of the most trivial and most important things in life as he floated downstream.

Each time he began to sink, the voice grew louder and faster, speaking of life's pleasures so intensely that he would begin to fight the weight of the water himself. His journey was as endless as the voice. At last he dared to sleep, knowing that he would awake and the voice would still be holding him up.

When he opened his eyes again, there was light and the worst-looking bowl of soup he had ever seen in front of his face.

"There are eyeballs in that soup." His voice was weak but not nearly as weak as his stomach as he faced the offending bowl.

"They will make you very strong. I ate lots of them when I was younger and look at me."

He struggled to focus on the blur behind the bowl, squinting at the young cannibal who held the steaming soup. "Whose eyeballs are they?"

A joyous laugh rippled through the air. "No one's, silly. They come from the fish the soup was made from. I won't make you eat them. Just take a sip of the broth."

Before he could protest, a spoonful was sent tumbling down his raw throat. The taste was not unfamiliar. He wondered just how many bowls of eyeball soup he had eaten.

The face behind the bowl came sharply into focus as the fog lifted from his eyes, blown away by the steam from the soup.

"Gelina," he breathed.

"In the flesh. I fear I've been disobedient again. I haven't gotten around to killing you or running away. You shall have to be patient. Perhaps the soup will kill you."

She sent another spoonful down his throat as he attempted to sit up. A shock wave of pain sent his head reeling, and she pushed him back down. Shaking her head, she reached for a flagon and poured a few drops of the amber liquid onto the spoon. He took it without argument.

"I am afraid 'tis the last of it," she said. "I've had to give you a lot in the past few days."

"Days?"

He struggled to remember, seeing that she still wore his

jacket with a narrow rope cinching it shut in the front. Her slender legs appeared tanned in the shadowy cave.

"Three days. You nearly bled to death." She busied herself with cleaning the spoon and bowl in a still pool.

Blood. He remembered blood. Her blood on his fingertips. "Why . . . ?"

She interrupted him. "You must rest. I'm going to dry these things in the sun."

She disappeared before he could croak another word. Her voice had been hoarse; dark circles had smudged the pale skin beneath her eyes. He sighed, knowing whose voice had pulled him back from that dark stream of death.

The sun bathed his body in its forgotten comfort. With much effort and giggling, Gelina had dragged him outside inches at a time until he could sit on the sun-drenched rocks in front of the cave. Closing his eyes, Conn wondered if he had ever felt so content. Even the bad fish soup had begun to taste good once he insisted that Gelina remove the eyeballs from his portion. Three days had passed since he had regained reluctant consciousness. He was still as weak as a child, but he could feel the stirrings of strength deep in his belly. He stretched his rusty limbs like a drowsy lion.

Pretending to nap, he watched Gelina beneath lowered eyelids as she bustled around, moving their scant belongings outside. She paused at the makeshift spit that settled over a small pit close to the edge of the cliff. A frown of concentration nestled on her features. She cursed softly as the sticks collapsed for the third time, stubbornly refusing to balance on the uneven rocks. She peered around the clearing until she found a large flat rock to support the sticks, then surveyed her handiwork with a smile.

"I know men of the Fianna who know less about living outdoors than you do," he said softly.

She beamed at him. Her smile faded as she was caught and held by his intense gaze. She glanced away shyly, wondering what thoughts lurked behind the sapphire of his eyes. Seeking any chore to end the awkward silence, she started for the cave.

"Come here."

She stopped in her tracks, sensing a note of command in his voice. She stood in the entranceway with her back to him for a long moment before turning to face him.

She moved toward him, mouth tight and eyes carefully veiled. "Yes, sire."

His eyes revealed nothing but she sensed a brief flare of anger at her words. She knelt beside him.

He took her hand in his; his fingers played across her palm in a tender caress. "You saved my life."

"I confess to that. Perhaps you can give me a medal of honor to wear on your jacket." Attempting a wan smile, she stared at their entwined hands as if they belonged to someone else.

"I hurt you." His gaze raked the sunlit valley below them, but his hand traveled gently up her arm. "I took you for all the wrong reasons."

Color stained her cheeks. Her words tumbled over one another. "They say it hurts anyway. It would have hurt even if you hadn't intended it to."

"Oh, I intended it to," he said huskily. "You must know I could have made it easier for you. Or maybe you don't." His eyes caught and held hers with the hurt bewilderment of a child. "I would have died for you, Gelina. What did you want from me that I denied you? Why did you betray me? If anyone had tried to tell me I would ever force my will on you, I would have killed them where they stood."

He bowed his head. It was she who tilted his chin and saw the remorse in his eyes. It was she who placed her lips on his without thought, attempting to draw forth his pain. His lips parted against hers, guiding her inexperienced kiss. Unable to pull away, she put her hands around his neck sensing a promise of tender sweetness foreign to her. Conn's strength surged. He wrapped his arms around her, pulling her body to his.

A mocking voice cut through them, abruptly breaking their embrace. "So this is how the high king of Erin spends his time while his favorite jester is out busting his ass searching for him!"

Conn groaned, wasting no time on his reply. "My ex-favorite jester, thank you."

Chapter Twenty

❖

Nimbus stood with arms crossed and legs akimbo, a smile twitching on his lips. Sean surveyed the view from the cliff with mock interest, poorly hiding his consternation at their untimely interruption. Gelina scrambled to her feet and stalked into the cave without so much as a look at Nimbus. Exchanging an uneasy glance with Conn, the jester followed her.

The king's posture and pallor were not lost on Sean. He knelt beside Conn, his practiced hands examining the bandage on his shoulder. "Are you all right, Conn?"

He shrugged. "I live." Not missing Sean's glance at the cavern, he added, "It wasn't her. Her brother ran me through from the back."

"Did you get him?" Sean's handsome features twisted in uncharacteristic bloodlust.

He shook his head. "I guess that means you didn't get him either."

Sean bowed his head, suppressing a grin. "No. But we got someone else." In answer to Conn's raised eyebrow, he said, "Along with about three hundred Castilians, a certain Eoghan Mogh is languishing in our dungeon."

Conn laughed bitterly. "Dear Eoghan. Death is too good for him. What shall we do with the blackhearted traitor?"

"You know the law of De Denann as well as I. A maimed man may never sit on the throne of Erin."

"You make a worthy point. Perhaps I shall tear out his eyes and make the last sight he sees the throne he will never have."

Sean rose and stood at the cliff's edge, his back to Conn. "I regret to bring you another difficulty."

"What is it?"

Sean turned, hesitant to continue. "'Tis Gelina. There are those who say she aided and abetted the rebels. They say Eoghan Mogh's fate should be hers."

Although Sean would have sworn it impossible, Conn paled a shade whiter. "Who dares to say this?"

"Nobody knows where the rumors began. I told you that the woman on the black steed was becoming a legend."

With his mouth drawn in a tight line, Conn asked, "Do they know I have her?"

"No. I told them exactly what you told me to tell them. That you were in the south with the third battalion helping them round up the last of the Castilians." Sean met his eyes with candor. "Now, I have a question for you."

"Proceed."

"Do you also think Eoghan Mogh's fate should be hers?"

Nimbus's eyes adjusted to the dim light of the cavern. Gelina sat with her back to the wall, hugging her knees. Her jaw jutted out in an expression he knew too well.

"Gelina . . ." Her name was a whisper on his lips.

She turned her face away from him.

"Please," he said, not even sure what he was asking for.

"Didn't you know, Nimbus?" Her voice erupted in venomous outcry. "When you hunted me down for him, didn't you know he planned to kill me?"

"Ye're alive, are ye not? I knew he could not harm ye."

Her accusing gaze caught his, and he turned away with the gut-wrenching knowledge that she had known harm at his king's hands.

He drew in a shaky breath. "Ye don't know what it did to him when ye ran away. He was devastated. He searched for ye day and night. He would ride out for days at a time. He did not eat. He barely slept. He drank too much. He even sent Sheela away."

"Poor man," she said scathingly.

"When he found out ye were riding with Eoghan Mogh, he changed. I believe he hated ye. I knew he wanted to kill ye. But I also knew he couldn't."

"You took one hell of a chance."

"Ye belonged with us, Gelina. I had to get ye back for him."

She snorted. "So you hunted me down for my own good."

He stood in front of her, forcing her to raise her eyes and meet his gaze. "I thought of not telling him I'd found ye. For the first time in me life I thought of lying to Conn. 'Tis why I traveled

with ye. I wanted to see if ye were happy without us." He
sighed, reluctant to continue. "One night ye sat in front of the
fire. Yer eyes were haunted. 'Twas as if the light within them
had been extinguished. Then I saw him. Yer brother. He
followed yer every move with the look of a hungry animal just
waiting to strike. He was biding his time. So I quit biding mine
and rode home to tell Conn of yer plans."

Gelina's trembling hand fluttered upward to wipe the sweat
from her brow.

Nimbus leaned forward, daring to take her chin in his small
hand. "From what we just witnessed, I would say ye're a lot
closer to what ye wanted than ye were when ye ran away."

He loosed her and strode away.

"Wait."

He stopped in his tracks as her voice cut through the musty
air. "I believe these are yours."

Tossing the golden apples upward, she drew an elaborate
pattern with the whirling gold. They went hurtling through the
air, stopped only by the quick reflexes in the jester's stinging
palms.

"Thank ye." He stared down at them, hoping she would say
more.

She scraped at the dirt with her bare toe. "Did you bring any
food?"

"Do I live and breathe?"

He waited for her smile but none came, so he bowed and
stepped outside. He returned with a worn burlap bag and pulled
forth three loaves of bread, two rounds of cheese and six fine
strips of dried meat. She nodded in approval. The raised voices
of Conn and Sean grew subdued as they carried their feast
outside.

Sean quickly volunteered to hunt for some live game. He
returned as the sun was setting with two small rabbits.

"'Twill make a meal for me but what will the rest of ye eat?"
Nimbus asked.

"I would do battle with all of you for a taste of fresh meat,"
Conn called from his seat.

Gelina did not reply or meet his eyes but handed him a bowl
filled with lukewarm fish soup. He groaned and smiled at her,
but she just turned away and disappeared into the cavern.

Bewildered, he stared into the growing darkness that en-

croached on their cozy circle of light. Gelina reappeared in a
suit of Sean's garments and moved gracefully around the camp,
helping Nimbus spear the rabbits and turn the spit. The aroma
of roasting meat floated into the night.

Conn could not take his eyes off her. Her short curls caught
the firelight in a tantalizing auburn web. She never once glanced
in his direction. He began to wonder if his memory of the warm,
clinging creature he had held in his arms so briefly had been a
product of his fever. To his chagrin he was discovering feeling in
parts of his body he had been too weak to think of until now.

He was hardly aware that he was scowling violently until he
caught Sean's puzzled glance. Smiling sheepishly, he thanked
him for the plate he held out.

They ate in companionable silence until Nimbus broke it with
a satisfied belch. Sean groaned.

"Sorry," Nimbus said with the smallest amount of cheerful
penitence he could manage.

"A good meal among friends is no reason for apology,"
Conn said.

He sought Gelina's eyes, but she turned away and stared into
the darkness. Nimbus raised his canteen in a silent toast, brown
eyes shining.

"I hate to disturb our borrowed serenity, but I feel the need to
call a meeting of state," Conn said with a sigh. "Sean and
Nimbus sought us for a reason, Gelina." He saw the hardened
veil of self-defense lower over her eyes and despised himself for
causing it. "A prisoner awaits my sentencing in the dungeon.
Eoghan Mogh."

"Is he well?" she asked before she could stop herself.

"I would say the traitor fared better than our king," Sean
said, anger surging in his voice. "The Fianna do not take to
stabbing men in the back."

Gelina closed her eyes briefly, unable to face the unfamiliar
ire in the soldier's eyes. Conn raised his hand for silence.

"Sean has brought another matter to my attention," he said,
his voice recapturing its command, daring anyone to interrupt.
"It seems that there are those at Tara, Gelina, who know you
aided the rebels. They want you to stand trial with Eoghan."

"The game is up then. I cannot hide behind your robes
forever, Conn. 'Tis time for the old head to be lopped off."

Even Nimbus flinched as she stood and paced the length of the clearing, draining her canteen in a single swig.

"Things can be mended, Gelina," Conn said.

"Ha! When are you ever going to learn, Conn? You cannot mend everything. Once some things are broken, they can never, ever be mended." She spat the words at him, their eyes locked in silent battle. He had to look away.

"All we have to do is convince them that you were coerced," Sean said calmly. "We don't ask them to believe you did not aid Mogh. We just ask them to believe you were kidnapped and held hostage, forced to do the things you did."

She plopped down on the ground and stared into the fire.

"What would you prefer? Would you prefer to confess to being a traitor? Would you rather ride out of here tonight and run forever?" As he spoke, Conn struggled unsteadily to his feet, ignoring Nimbus's outstretched hand. "We will take you back, Gelina. We will help you. Isn't that what you want?"

"I am guilty of what they accuse and more. I deserve to be punished as much as Eoghan does." She faced their questioning circle of faces. "I don't know what I want. I just want a new life. And I'm not sure I want any of you in it." She stood and fled down the narrow pathway into the night.

The moon was waning when Gelina returned to find Conn sitting alone before the dying embers of the fire. He glanced up as she walked into the flickering light, then returned his gaze to the object he held in his hands. She saw no sign of Nimbus or Sean.

"They're gone," he said in answer to her silent question.

"How did you know I would be back?"

He chuckled grimly. "I've never known you to run away without your sword." He stared into the waning flames for a long moment before saying, "Did you understand what I was offering you earlier, Gelina?"

"I don't know."

"I was offering you my protection."

"At what price, Conn?" she asked coldly. "The price was loyalty last time, and I failed at that. What is the price for your protection this time? Or have I already paid?"

"We shall never know, shall we? The offer has been withdrawn." His eyes rose to meet hers; a chill shot down her spine. "Do you need to be punished, Gelina? If that's what you want, I will punish you."

"What are you talking about?" she queried softly, afraid of his answer.

"Kneel beside me," he commanded. She followed his order without thought. Running a hand through her soft hair, he began, "I revoke your citizenship. I revoke your freedom, Gelina Ó Monaghan. From this moment on you are one of the *fuidir*. You are my serf. You belong to me. You will serve me without questioning. You will do my bidding without protest."

He spoke with such tenderness that it took a long moment for his words to register. When they did, she pulled away in rage only to find her hair caught in his iron grasp. Tears of pain sprang to her eyes.

"You will bake my bread. You will wash my clothing. You will be my slave."

"But the *fuidir* are . . ." She stopped, horrified comprehension dawning.

"That's right, dear. War captives. Fugitives. They give up their freedom to right a wrong, pay a debt. There is not a man at that court who will dare to argue with me on the justice of it."

"You cannot take away my freedom!" She stopped struggling as his fingers tugged cruelly at her hair.

"The hell I can't! I should have never given it to you in the first place. You can run me through while I sleep if you choose, but you should remember that the death of your master will not release you. Sean has been sent ahead with news of your capture and punishment. If anything happens to me out here, you will be hunted down to the four corners of the earth."

He pulled her face close to his, his strong hand cupping her neck. He held up the object he had been toying with and pushed it into her line of vision. The familiar carved object danced before her eyes.

"Face it, Gelina. I have captured the white queen."

Chapter Twenty-one

❖

Gelina smoothed the linen of her skirt with icy fingers, oblivious to the bustle of the serving girls and cupbearers behind her. She didn't even raise her eyes when Cook's large bulk backed into her with a frown. The unfamiliar darkness of her garments held her rapt.

She was clad in black from head to toe. A dress that was too small pressed against her bosom and fell to mid-calf. The frayed ribbons of the black sandals laced up her legs over opaque black stockings. Conn could not have proclaimed her to be a slave any more effectively if he had carved the word *fuidir* into her forehead. She pushed her hair away from a face that was pale and drawn against the blackness of the linen. Laughter floated into the kitchen from the great hall. In a moment she would face them all. She wished she were as invisible as she had felt in the past few days.

Conn hadn't spoken two words to her since he had revoked her freedom although she often looked up from some task to find his eyes on her with an infuriating mixture of amusement and triumph. In the days they had remained at the cavern he had demanded only that she prepare his meals and help him to his feet as his strength returned.

More than once she had been tempted to shove him over the cliff as he paced the confines of their camp. He would turn a knowing grin on her as if reading her thoughts from her thunderous brow, infuriating her further. The truce between them was fragile. She refused to hold onto him as Silent Thunder carried them back to Tara and he took great delight in choosing the rockiest terrain, reaching around at the fortuitous moment to grab her and keep her from sailing off the horse in a fit of stubbornness.

The fear that had grown in her heart as they approached the

shadow of Tara flourished now as she stood inside the kitchen door, not even feeling the heat of the kiln. Conn had whisked her through the tower into Moira's waiting arms. There had been no Nimbus or Sean to greet her. Moira had averted her eyes and handed her the infernal dress with a terse command to bathe and come straight to the kitchen. Her bathwater was not hot and sweetly scented in a long wooden tub. It was lukewarm in a chipped earthenware basin in a tiny cell in the servants' quarters.

Cook bumped into her again. And again. This time Gelina had to raise her eyes and take the golden tray loaded with thick slices of honeyed bread that Cook held out to her.

"Yer to serve the king's table," she commanded, and Gelina wondered if anyone would ever look her in the eyes again.

Suddenly bold, she put her hand on Cook's arm, marveling at the muscles rippling beneath the layers of fat. "What have the people been told?"

Cook pulled away. "They've been told enough."

Gelina felt rather than saw all activity stop behind them, and knew eyes that were not unkind, but curious, bored holes in her back. She drew in a deep breath, trembling hands tight on the tray, and ducked out the swinging door into the great hall.

For an instant she could pretend that nothing would change. That the ballad singer would not choke on her last throaty word. That the flutist would not hit a shrill, false note before lowering his instrument and his head. That the great hall would not fall into a stunned, embarrassed silence as the tall girl in black wound her way among the trestle tables. But it was only pretense that let her hope. The silence was a choking, cloying monster wrapping itself around her legs, nearly making her stumble.

A plump serving girl smiled brightly at her as she passed, a smile Gelina would remember for the rest of her life. She climbed the steps to the table where Conn sat surrounded by his men. Her knees almost folded in relief as several of the soldiers resumed their conversations at the same time, filling the terrible silence with words.

Conn's gaze flicked across her face with the scant interest of a stranger as she laid a thick slab of the bread on his plate. He leaned toward the man next to him, appearing engrossed by his words. Nimbus sat on the other side of Conn, brown eyes flashing. When Gelina met the jester's eyes, it was she who had to look away, fearful he might find an answering thread of anger in her eyes to match his own.

The night settled into a comfortable, if unfamiliar rhythm. She carried out food. She took back empty trays. She carried out more food. The steps to the dais grew longer and steeper as she climbed them for the twentieth time, struggling under the burden of a steaming boar's head.

She did not have time to protest when Nimbus leapt out of his chair and came around the long table, his arms outstretched to relieve her of the tray.

"Nimbus." Conn said it softly but the word was more of a command than if he had bellowed it. The table fell silent.

The jester turned to the king, and Gelina thought for one breathless moment that he was going to defy Conn. His small shoulders slumped; he returned to his chair. But he did not bother to hide the fury that burned in his eyes when he looked at Conn.

Gelina lowered the tray to the table and busied herself with carving the meat, her ears tuned to the name she had heard as she approached the dais.

"So you sent the gibberish-speaking foreigners back to Castile, Conn. What of Eoghan Mogh? Have you decided his fate?" asked Goll MacMorna.

"Should have hung the whole lot of them if you ask me. That would teach the filthy pigs to get involved in an affair that's none of their concern," a fair-haired soldier interrupted.

Conn leaned back in his chair, sipping ale from a silver goblet. "I saw no need to execute the Castilians. They were following the orders of their king, just as you would follow my orders should I send you to Castile. Eoghan Mogh is another matter."

"What of the cloaked one? Did you discover his identity?"

Gelina thought Conn's eyes rested on her for a fleeting moment, but they had moved on before she could look up from her task.

"No. He slipped through my grasp . . . this time."

The knife slipped in her hand. She tucked the nicked finger into her mouth.

"But what of Eoghan?" A soldier leaned eagerly toward

him. "Shall you blind him? Castrate him? Cut off a hand or an arm? What shall your justice be, Conn?"

"I believe I shall give Eoghan time to ponder his actions. He can languish in our dungeons for a while," Conn replied, watching Gelina beneath lowered eyelids.

"Would a thousand years be long enough?" Goll MacMorna cried out, raising his goblet.

Conn laughed, and the other men raised their goblets in a toast to justice that rang through the hall. Gelina stumbled down the steps, thankful to remove herself from their laughing jests. She was halfway back to the kitchen when a rough arm circled her waist and a callused hand snaked up her skirt to clasp her tender thigh.

"Serving wench, fetch me some brew as tasty and filling as what ye've got underneath them skirts?" a voice bellowed in her ear, stinking of ale and rotting teeth.

She barely had time to draw in a gasp of outrage before she was loosed. She stumbled against the wall, the sudden silence pounding in her head, and turned to find the burly shepherd flat on his back with Conn's foot on his chest and a gleaming sword's point at his throat. Even as she watched, a thin line of blood trickled from his throat where Conn gently pressed his blade, his eyes blue fire. The man dared to raise one trembling hand in a silent plea.

Before Gelina could cry out, a sallow-faced woman separated herself from the crowd and threw herself at Conn's feet, spreading her skirts wide about her.

"Mercy, milord, I beseech you," she cried, tears coursing down her cheeks. "My husband has been in the north with his flocks for some time. He did not know."

Conn gave no indication that he heard her; the tip of his sword did not waver. For a long moment her broken sobs were the only sound in the room. Conn's icy gaze pulled away from the pallid shepherd and traveled the muted, frightened faces until he found Gelina pressed to the wall, skirt twisted in her hands, a mute plea in her eyes.

He lifted his sword from the man's throat. A collective sigh of relief traveled the hall like a wave.

"I would like to have a word with you outside, sir," he hissed.

A wide path cleared through the crowd as he turned and strode toward the door, sword still clutched in his hand. The shepherd breathed a silent prayer with eyes closed before reluctantly clambering to his feet and following.

Gelina stared at her shaking hands, not hearing Cook's sturdy approach.

"Quit yer woolgathering, girl. There's serving to be done," she scolded.

Gelina pried herself from the wall and gratefully followed Cook's white-garbed form into the kitchen, away from the curious eyes.

On the dais Nimbus folded a napkin over his mouth to hide his smile.

Gelina kneaded the stiff, white dough with a fury, her hands pounding it into submission. The autumn sun was warm on her back. She scratched the end of her nose leaving a smear of flour at its tip. Suppressing a groan, she watched Cook carry in another huge vat of the dough.

"As soon as ye finish these, there are rugs to be beat," she said, lowering the vat to the table.

Nodding meekly, Gelina cursed as the last of her cracked fingernails snapped off into the gooey dough. After a second of thought, she continued kneading without bothering to extract it. Perhaps Conn would choke on it. She set aside the first vat and pulled the new vat to her. Long streaks of flour stained her black linen. She pushed up her kerchief with one finger as it slid over her smooth curls to cover her eyes.

She left the finished vats to rise in the sun and approached her next chore with trepidation. Four thick rugs were piled outside the kitchen door. Placing both arms under the heap, she tried to propel them upward. To her chagrin they didn't budge. She glanced around the courtyard to see if anyone had witnessed her folly but found it deserted. She wished for the familiar sight of Nimbus, although Conn had reached out a restraining hand a dozen times to stop him from helping her.

She dragged one rug through the dirt with both hands. Her face fell as she saw the high rope strung from building to building. Setting her chin, she gave a tremendous heave on the rug. It sailed over the line and to the ground on the other side, the momentum of her swing sending her to the ground with it. She shook her head. On the third try the rug landed on the rope.

She picked up the giant wooden spoon and smacked the rug. A cloud of dust swirled around her head, choking her. Backing away, she poked at the rug. She held the spoon like a sword. Her feints and jabs elicited little dust but the task was more bearable.

A solitary figure watched her from a latticed window on the second level of the fortress, drinking in her every move. He laughed out loud at her mock battle. Her room was far from his now. Late in the night when sleep eluded him, the door of her old room would beckon him. He had opened it only once, the lingering fragrance of sandalwood sending him back into the corridor with his whole body aching. She was everywhere. She was in the courtyard, her lithe body bent over a tub of dirty linen. She was in the great hall, head bowed as she struggled with a tray loaded with tankards. She was in the corridor, polishing the baseboards. Her eyes would catch his for a brittle second, making a mockery of her subservient pose as fire flashed in them. His hand clutched the window ledge as he watched her.

He jumped and turned guiltily away from the window as someone cleared their throat behind him. Nimbus stood in the doorway, a smirk on his small face.

"I request an audience with ye, Conn."

Conn moved away from the window, hands clasped behind his back. "Since when must you request an audience to talk to me?"

Nimbus did not reply. His eyes did not leave Conn's.

"I know you've been less than pleased with me lately, Nimbus. You've made that clear. I would be happy to grant you an audience. Do proceed."

Conn sat on the edge of the couch. He saw that the jester's worn burlap garments had been replaced by a short red jacket and a dark green kilt. He hid a smile, wondering what could be so serious that Nimbus would resort to wearing freshly laundered clothing.

He didn't have long to wonder. Nimbus crossed his arms and said, "I want to wed Gelina."

Conn stared at him for a long moment. He swallowed the

chuckle that rose in his throat, realizing as he faced the man's resolute brown eyes that if he laughed, their friendship would be over forever. He cleared his throat, thankful that he was already sitting.

Biting back a hundred words, he steepled his fingers beneath his chin and asked, "Why?"

Nimbus flung his arms outward, calm deserting him. "Because I cannot bear to see her creeping around here like some captive spider in that dreadful dress. She deserves better than that."

"She is well-fed. She is not mistreated. You know that," Conn replied, a fine line appearing between his eyebrows.

Nimbus's voice rose. "She is humiliated. She is degraded. I will not stand for it. Ye had no right—"

"I had every right." Conn's words were spoken quietly; his eyes dared Nimbus to continue.

Nimbus lowered his eyes with difficulty and repeated, "I want to wed Gelina. I desire no marriage portion. I will take her as she is."

His words stirred Conn to rise and pace to the window. He stared down into the courtyard, hands clenched behind him in some hidden emotion.

Nimbus took two steps toward him, then stopped, his legs refusing to carry him further as realization dawned. "I'm not the first to ask, am I, Conn?"

"I've been approached by others."

"And yer answer, sire?"

Conn struggled for words. "I couldn't ask anyone to take Gelina. She isn't suitable for marriage."

"Why not?"

Nimbus refused to look away. Conn could feel his gaze boring a hole in his back until he was forced to turn around.

The jester cursed furiously. "I knew it. Ye ruined her, didn't ye? Ye spoiled her yerself." Nimbus turned away, fighting the churning of his stomach. "'Tis true, is it not?"

Conn ran a weary hand over his eyes, not bothering to answer.

"Ye didn't just ruin her, did ye? Ye hurt her. Ye and all yer fine talk of chivalry and gentleness to women! Ye make me want to puke." Nimbus turned back to him, drawing in a breath through clenched teeth. "Tell me, Conn, how was it? Did ye take her like a peasant wench? Did ye give her the courtesy of spreading yer cloak for her to lie on while ye were spreading her legs? Or did ye just take her on the ground like a common—"

"Stop it, Nimbus," Conn bellowed.

"Ye don't understand, do ye? I did this. I gave her to ye. I made her beautiful for ye. So that ye would cherish her and love her like she deserves to be loved. Like I could never . . ." He sputtered to a stop, unable to continue without crying.

"You cannot understand all the circumstances, Nimbus."

"I understand one thing," he said quietly. "I understand that Gelina is still suitable to be me wife. Let me take her away from here."

"My answer remains the same."

Nimbus chuckled, the bleak sound a bitter travesty of his rolling laughter. " 'Tis all very handy for ye, Conn. Ye spoil her for any other man but keep her right here under yer thumb for yer use. Will ye visit her in the servants' quarters or have her serve ye in yer chambers? Yer first try didn't get her with babe. If yer spilled seed finds its mark the second time, will ye marry her off to some other man then?"

Conn paled, visibly shaken. "That is not fair, Nimbus. I haven't laid a finger on her since we returned to Tara."

The jester shrugged. " 'Tis only a matter of time though, isn't it? Ye'll reach beneath the skirts of a serving wench and what a surprise. 'Twill be Gelina."

Conn took a step toward him, eyes blazing. "You push me, Nimbus. You push me beyond the limits any other man would dare."

Nimbus bowed with a flourish. "I beg yer pardon, sire. I have not forgotten ye're the king. Ye're beyond reproach."

Conn pushed past him and strode from the room. Nimbus stared after him, his mocking smile fading. He paced to the chest and snatched up an earthenware mug. It shattered against the wall with a satisfying crash.

In the courtyard below, Gelina stared up at the window to hear the sound of voices raised in anger replaced by the shattering of pottery.

Music and laughter floated up from the great hall, the din grating across Gelina's frayed nerves as she dragged the scrub brush across the wooden floor. She hummed faintly, trying to

drown out the festivities below, where she was no longer
welcome. As her voice found the words she sought, it rose,
booming out the words to a ditty Nimbus had taught her about a
man and his goat. Her unmelodic tune was accompanied by the
rhythmic splashing of the brush across the rough floor. Drops of
dirty water spattered the walls unheeded. Also unheeded was
the door that flew open at the end of the corridor.

"What in the hell is all this caterwauling?"

Conn's furious voice startled her. She jumped to her feet,
dropping the brush into the bucket with a splash that wet them
both.

"I thought someone had skinned a cat and left it to die in the
corridor," he bellowed, ignoring her arched eyebrow and
twitching lips. "Can't a man get a decent night's rest in his own
chambers?"

Gelina stood with her back straight for a long moment before
remembering the obligatory curtsy due the king. "I beg your
pardon, sire. I assumed you were below enjoying the merriment."

"As you can see, I'm not. I've been trying to sleep for hours.
Just when I begin to drift off, I awake to the nightmarish sound
of your"—he paused suggestively, searching for the right
word—"singing."

He turned on his heel and strode back to his chamber.
"Come with me," he tossed over his shoulder.

Gelina looked behind her. "Who? Me?"

He did not dignify that with an answer, and she followed him
into his chamber with trepidation.

"Close the door," he commanded. Seeing her hesitate, he
added softly, "Please."

She shut the door slowly, mistrusting his gentle plea more
than his bullying commands. He pulled his tunic over his head
and she took a step backward, replacing her hand on the door
handle. He ignored the wide eyes fixed on the crisp mat of dark
hair that covered his chest.

"Rub my shoulders, please," he said, as he straddled the
couch.

"Yes, sire." She let go of the door and curtsied again.

"And would you quit bobbing up and down? I find it very
distracting."

She approached the couch with all of the enthusiasm she

might show in approaching a lizard. She settled herself behind him, jumping when he turned his face to her.

"You aren't armed, are you?"

Her lips twitched. "No, sire."

His gaze remained on her face with a warmth that sent a flush shooting upward to the roots of her hair. "But you're always armed, aren't you?"

"I don't understand."

"That is fortunate. You would be even more dangerous if you did," he said, presenting his back to her.

"My hands may be rough," she said. Her palms curled around his warm shoulders.

Conn shifted his weight to hide the shudder that traveled the length of his body and grunted an answer that was no answer. Her hands kneaded his broad shoulders and moved downward, her gentle fingers finding the knotted muscles of his back with uncanny accuracy. He stifled a groan of delicate agony as her fingertips probed his tingling skin into slumped submission.

Gelina swallowed a yawn, the long hours since Cook had shaken her out of bed a blur in her mind. Her touch against Conn's skin grew soft, her own muscles betraying her exhaustion. The teasing caress of her fingernails brought gooseflesh to Conn's arms. Her hands stopped their motion, and he twisted around, a burning question etched on his tense features.

Her eyes were closed; her dark lashes lay against her pale cheeks; her small breasts rose and fell evenly. Conn smiled at the sleeping nymph sprawled on his couch and let her hands fall gently to her lap. He reached out a hand to fondle a stray curl, then jerked it back as Nimbus's words flicked across his conscience like a whip. His smile faded.

He ached to take her soft face between his hands and kiss away the faint circles beneath her eyes. The fire that had been ignited in the cavern smote his soul, rendering him weak limbed and fearful of where his hands might touch should he reach out to her. It had been sheer torment not to touch her in the past weeks. And now she lay before him like a trusting child, stirring in her sleep with a moan that drove into his heart like a sword.

With a decision that wrenched his heart, he planted a soft kiss on her brow before shaking her awake with the cold, impersonal hands of a stranger.

Chapter Twenty-two

❖

Gelina's hands flew as she sliced the steaming loaf of bread. One hunk flew from her fingers and landed on the floor. Without glancing around, she scooped it up and replaced it on the plate.

"Gelina!"

Cook's voice grated against her nerves. She tossed the soiled bread into a nearby bin. The plump blonde filling the earthenware plates across from her giggled.

"Hold your tongue, Audren. I've seen you do the same thing a hundred times." Gelina flashed a smile at the good-natured serving girl.

"But I never get caught. Ye've got to wait till she's not looking," Audren whispered with a wink. To prove her point, she tossed a slice of the bread into her mouth without missing a stroke of her knife before carrying her platter into the great hall.

The door was open to the darkness outside, and a chill fall breeze licked at the heat from the twin cooking hearths at each end of the kitchen. Pausing in her task, Gelina drew in a deep breath. As the cool, sweet air chased the dull smoke from her lungs, she wondered what it would be like to be pounding along the moors on Silent Thunder tonight.

Cook cut short her reverie. "Hasten, girl. Hungry guts make for quarrelsome tempers."

Motivated by her second scolding, Gelina hefted a tray laden with a stew of onions, lentils, and saffrons. Audren came sailing through the door, nearly knocking her down.

"Curses, Audren. Trample me, why don't you?" Gelina snatched the bowl of pepper from the girl's tray.

"So sorry. There's such a crowd out there. I've never seen so many handsome faces attached to pinching hands." She bit her lip, knowing that the king's hand went to his sword if a man so much as looked at Gelina askance. She spoke quickly to cover the awkward silence. "The Dark Rose has returned."

Gelina squinted. "The what?"

Audren took the tray from her and set it on the table after a quick peep to see if Cook was watching. She led Gelina to the door and pointed to the table on the dais.

"Sheela—the Dark Rose. They called her that before her husband was killed." She giggled. "I've heard some say that she is rare but easily plucked."

Gelina stood frozen, fighting the urge to double over. An invisible fist planted itself in her gut. Golden balls bounced at the end of dark curls as languid eyes laughed up at Conn. A calculated blankness fell like a curtain over Gelina's features.

"Audren, you must help me." She pulled the girl away from the door and back to the table. "Trade tables with me tonight. I'll serve the common tables. You serve the king's table."

She did not know she was gripping the girl's wrist until Audren pulled away, rubbing her injured limb. Her eyes shied away from Gelina's. "I cannot trade with ye. Not even for tonight."

"Why not?"

"'Tis the king's command that ye serve his table. Ye must know that." She began to pile plates on a platter, grateful for the task to remove her from Gelina's stricken gaze.

"Curse the king," Gelina muttered, turning back to the door.

She watched the dais, biting her lower lip. Sheela wore a long velvet smock of royal blue gathered in deep folds at the waist. On her hands she wore gloves of a lighter blue. The gold of her bracelets flashed with each fluttering gesture.

Gelina stared down at the black linen of her own dress, one hand reaching up to the black kerchief that covered her hair. The dress was marked with awkward stitches from too many repairs done late at night in the faint light of a beeswax candle. The hand that smoothed the fabric was callused and workworn.

With a subtle straightening of her spine, Gelina returned to the tray and lifted it to her shoulder. Audren stared after her as she exited the double doors with head held high.

She weaved among the tables. The dais loomed before her, each soldier a giant to her gaze as the steps unfolded beneath her tattered sandals. Nimbus was squeezed between two large soldiers. His joke faded to silence as he watched her approach. He shot a glance at Conn. The king was nodding to Sheela, but his eyes followed Gelina as she lowered her burden to the table.

Nimbus climbed out of his chair and took a golden plate from her hand, ignoring Conn's frown. She smiled wanly at him. When only two plates remained, she gestured toward his seat, which he took reluctantly, a scowl on his face.

With steady hands Gelina lowered a plate in front of Sheela, saving the last plate for Conn. The men around the table were subdued. Not one of them could touch their food until the king received his plate. Gelina turned back to the platter. Sheela's voice rang out.

"I do believe 'tis the little foundling! I hardly recognized her in that dowdy black. Suits her, does it not? You should have made her a serving wench long ago, Conn." She laughed, looking to Conn for approval.

Conn sat back in his chair and crossed his long legs. A look that could have been guilt flickered across his countenance. Gelina stopped in her tracks. Nimbus's lips moved in silent prayer as he recognized the look that brewed like storm clouds in her eyes. Goll MacMorna shook his head in disgust and shot her a sympathetic look. She scooped up the last plate.

"Wench, fetch the bowl of pepper. Make it quick. My food is chilling even as you dwaddle," Sheela said.

A soldier at the foot of the table cleared his throat, bowing his head in embarrassment. Gelina returned once again to the platter and gathered the bowl of pepper with a flourish. Silence fell over the table as she traveled its length.

"I do believe I shall need another plate. After you tuck in my napkin, return to the kitchen and fetch one. My food has grown cold while you poked around the table like a snail." Sheela pouted prettily. "Perhaps a good flogging would speed up your tasks."

Conn pounded on the table with his fist. "Hold your tongue, Sheela. She is my slave, not yours."

Gelina slowed her steps as she approached Sheela's chair. An uneven smile spread across her face. "Milady would like another plate?"

"Now," the woman demanded, trying to pacify Conn with a familiar hand on his thigh.

"I would be delighted to oblige." Without another word,

Gelina dumped the steaming contents of Conn's plate on Sheela's head.

Stunned silence fell over the hall, broken only by Sheela's muffled cries of outrage as gravy dripped from her sodden curls into the velvet of her smock. Goll MacMorna choked on his ale, sending a golden spray across the table. The soldier next to him thumped him on the back, unable to hold back his hearty brays of laughter. The uproar grew as the hall's attention was captured by the spectacle on the dais.

"And as for you . . ." The din faded as quickly as it had begun as Gelina turned to Conn, whipping off the dull kerchief to reveal shining auburn curls. "Enjoy your dinner, sire. May you choke on it!"

A path cleared before her as she stormed out of the hall, skirts gathered in her hands. Conn leapt out of his chair and followed. The crowd parted further to avoid his clenched fists and thunderous brow. Nimbus tried to leave the dais only to find his arm caught in Sean's viselike grip. Sean's face held a grim warning as he tried to twist away. He quit struggling and slumped in his chair.

Gelina burst out the main door, her long legs carrying her across the courtyard. Hearing her name bellowed behind her did not halt her determined stride.

She spoke without slowing or bothering to glance back. "I don't care, Conn. Beat me. Flog me. Isn't that what one does to willful slaves? Do what you like but I quit."

Conn caught her elbow as she entered the stables, jerking her around to face him. "You cannot quit. You're a slave, you stubborn woman."

She blinked sweetly at him. "Oh, you noticed I was a woman. I thought a term like that was reserved for that gravy-covered slattern who graces your table."

Conn's lips twitched suspiciously. He grasped her shoulders and pushed her against the wall.

His voice was deceptively gentle. "Gelina, my sweet cat. I do believe you're jealous."

His thumb tenderly stroked the inner flesh of her arm. The tiny hairs at the nape of her neck stood on end as something more powerful than fear flooded her veins. She recoiled from his touch only to find herself pinned, his hands no longer gentle.

She tossed her head with a nasty laugh. "Don't flatter yourself, Conn. Just because you used me once doesn't mean I own you. 'Tis king's privilege to use a woman once and go on his way, is it not?"

Conn lowered his face until it was a scant inch from hers, his voice a brutal whisper. "What do you want, Gelina? Would you prefer I used you every night? It can be arranged."

Breathing became a task as she retorted, "You've already got one whore. Why should you need another?"

She fought the urge to slide down the wall in relief as he loosed her. He turned away. His shoulders shook as he laughed out loud.

"Sometimes I think you were sent by the gods themselves to drive me to the very gates of insanity." He turned back to her, his eyes glittering in the rushlight. "I suppose you did give the good widow the comeuppance she deserved."

She shrugged, unsure of what her reply should be. He laughed heartily, and Gelina's face folded in an impish grin. Going to the center stall, he threw open the door. Silent Thunder nickered softly, recognizing his master's scent. Entering the stall with whispered words, Conn rubbed his silky mane.

"Come, Gelina. Let us ride this windy night." He led the horse out of the stall.

"You mean"—Gelina stuttered in her doubt—"you will allow me to ride?" She could not hide the light that sprang to her eyes.

"I will allow us to ride," he corrected.

Her eyes narrowed. "You're not going to leave me strangled on the moors, are you?"

He raised a sinister brow and hissed, "Perhaps."

Gelina followed as he led the animal into the moonlit night. He watched her curiously as she backed up several feet from the horse and ran toward it. Catching her around the waist as she passed him, he halted her in mid-vault.

"That might be more difficult in a skirt. Allow me." He interlaced his fingers, providing a stepping place for her.

With a mocking curtsy she swung herself on the horse, spreading her skirts on his back the best she could. Conn swung himself behind her. He handed her the reins and placed his hands on her waist. Her body was warm as she leaned against him, the top of her head barely brushing his chin. He touched his lips to her hair in a gesture as soft as the wings of a butterfly. His arm pressed against her bare one felt the gooseflesh rise on her silky skin.

They both kicked, sending the stallion into a gallop. The clouds gusted across the moon, creating a patchwork of black and silver on the long grass. They raced through the night. Gelina laughed aloud as she guided the horse across the meadows, the laughter snatched by the wind before it became audible. Conn smiled down at her as she glanced over her shoulder, his eyes sparkling in the moonlight, the wind whipping his hair. The horse thundered over the moors, its muscles moving in careless arrogance. As they reached the foothills, Gelina reluctantly steered the Arabian in a wide circle.

She made no protest when Conn took the reins from her hands. He steered the horse with one hand, leaving his other arm nestled around her waist. She leaned against his broad chest and rested her head on his shoulder, relishing the unstable peace between them. The moon broke through the last of the clouds, bathing the night in its luminous glory.

Gelina tensed, her back going ramrod straight as Conn guided the prancing horse into a moon-dappled forest. The muscled forearm around her waist did not relax its firm but gentle pressure. She leaned back, surrendering to the hard cup of Conn's body against hers. He halted the horse beside a splintered wooden bridge that spanned a rushing brook. They sat in silence, listening to the water dance over the rocks.

Conn's warm breath, scented with ale and cinnamon, stirred the tendrils of hair at her earlobe. "Shall I strangle you on the moors or toss you in the brook?"

She giggled, not quite certain he was joking. "I'd prefer to be throttled, thank you. I cannot swim, and the last time you and I ended up in a brook, I fear you were the victor."

"You once told me you weren't afraid of anything."

"I lied."

He dismounted without a word, then raised his level gaze to her. Gelina stared at her freckled hands. They tangled in the black silky mane with a will of their own. Conn knew he would have to drag her off the horse. He turned away to hide the wrench of his heart as he realized the depth of her fear of him.

His fingers circled her bare ankle like a chain of velvet. He rubbed his bearded cheek against the satiny skin of her calf.

"I built this bridge, you know," he said softly, "when I was just a lad."

Gelina stared at his bowed head, unable to fathom the agonizing gentleness of his touch. Her trembling fingers brushed his hair. He looked up at her, and she was reminded of the night he had sat in the mud outside the cavern, begging her with his eyes to kill him.

"The bridge has lasted well," she said, her voice the murmur of a stranger.

He nodded. She felt the burning touch of his lips against her calf, coaxing a response from her heartbeat that she could not stop. His hand glided upward until his fingers found the pounding pulse sheathed behind her knee.

Gelina drew in a ragged breath, struggling to remember that his tenderness was a gift more easily snatched away than given.

"I wasn't even born when you built this bridge," she breathed.

Conn jerked his hand and lips away from her. He took a step backward. "We have more in common than I'd care to admit, milady. Neither one of us fights fair."

Without another word he swung himself behind her and urged Silent Thunder out of the forest and into the meadow. His arm circled her waist like an iron band, dragging her softness against every unrelenting inch of his body. Gelina smiled.

He slowed the horse to a walk as they saw the torches of the fortress shining below them. He loosened his grip with a sigh. Gelina's shoulders stiffened, and he tousled her curls with his hand.

She relaxed against him, tears springing to her eyes. The horse walked into the courtyard and halted in front of the stables.

Neither of them stirred for a long moment, both reluctant to break the calm. With a sigh Conn swung his leg over and stepped to the ground. He held out his arms to her. She slid into them, finding her body pressed close to the hard length of his. He loosed her, his eyes distant.

"Rub down the horse, please," he said, already turning away from her.

She nodded and started to speak only to find him already

covering the distance between the stable and the fortress in long strides. She stared after him, bewildered that she could know him so well and not know him at all.

Conn entered the castle through the kitchen door, startling Cook so badly that she almost slipped into a round barrel of dishwater as he gave her a terse command and disappeared into the great hall. He stalked through the hall without a word, although every eye followed him and the music stumbled to a halt. He went straight to his room, where a fire had been built to drive away the chill. Sitting down in the chair before the fire, he waited.

Chapter Twenty-three
❖

Gelina ambled toward the light of the fortress, reluctant to surround herself with laughter and questions. She knew Audren would interrogate her mercilessly about the night's events. She veered away from the kitchen and ducked into the servants' quarters. Audren's plump form rounded the corner, and Gelina silently groaned. To her amazement the girl brushed past her in the narrow corridor without lifting her eyes. Gelina stared after her with a frown of confusion before she shrugged and opened the door to her tiny cell of a room.

Her eyes adjusted to the light of a candle melted to a waxy puddle and knew that something in the room had altered. The narrow cot she tossed on each night remained as she had left it, a linen sheet thrown across it. She went to the table and ran her finger through the thick layer of dust that should have been partly concealed by a chipped basin and pitcher.

Perplexed, she knelt and opened the chest where her ivory comb and brush should be, the only remnants of her life as Conn's foster daughter. They had vanished. With frantic hands she pressed the latch under the trunk's lid to reveal an empty compartment. The pendant was gone. Her room was a parchment, erased by an unknown hand.

She shoved her fingers through her hair. With a vain attempt to steady her breathing, she whirled around in search of an answer. Moira's buxom form stood silhouetted in the doorway, her face in shadows. Gelina sensed rather than saw her discomfort.

Gelina was so afraid of the answer that she could barely form the question. "My things? Surely I am to be allowed to keep my meager things. Where . . . ?"

Moira said gently, "They were moved. The order came tonight."

"Moved where?"

Moira let her gaze wander the empty room. "They were moved to Conn's chambers."

Gelina's whole body began to shake, and for an instant Moira feared the girl would cry. But the emerald eyes she raised to Moira glittered with wrath, not tears.

"I shall not stand for this," she stated coldly.

She swept past without another word, leaving Moira frozen in the doorway with a silent prayer on her lips. She did not know who she prayed for.

Gelina stormed into the great hall, her face a mask of bitter fury. As she weaved among the drunken dancers, she felt a hand grasp her wrist, tugging her to a halt.

"Where do you go in such haste, milady? Are you not weary of always rushing about?" Sean held her captive, trying to pull her into the reel.

She jerked away. "Leave me be, Sean. I've no desire to dance."

When he refused to loose her, she calmly placed her heel on his instep, painfully reminding him of their first dance together. She disappeared into the crowd, leaving him to curse pleasantly as he rubbed his aching foot. She dodged other hands with equal alacrity, dispatching three soldiers and two farmers to the sidelines with throbbing shins.

She bolted up the stairs two at a time, her side aching from the effort. Traveling the torchlit hallway, she passed her old chamber without a glance, her eyes locked on the door at the end of the corridor.

Without hesitation she shoved the door open, sending it crashing against the wall. Conn sat in front of the fire, his long legs stretched out before him. The look in his heavy-lidded eyes stopped her in the doorway.

"I want my things. You cannot take them from me." Her voice came out shriller than she intended, and she fought the urge to clear her throat.

"Close the door," he commanded.

Gelina stood unmoving for a moment, then slammed the heavy door. The sound reverberated through the room. Conn did not move.

She stood in front of him, arms crossed, and repeated, "I want my things."

"I didn't steal your things. I just had them moved," he said with infinite patience.

She peered around the room and saw her brush and comb resting on his chest. The pendant Rodney had given her lay beside them, its contours gleaming in the firelight.

"Why did you move them?"

"Because these are your new chambers. Your things belong here now." He crossed his ankles and studied his leather boots.

A chill traveled her spine. His perfect calm terrified her.

"And where is Sheela? Under your bed?"

"She has departed."

Gelina struggled to keep the pleading note from her voice. "I know 'tis my fault that she left, but I shouldn't have to take her place, should I?"

"I sent her away."

His words sent Gelina resolutely toward the door before his quiet voice paralyzed her.

"There's a guard outside the door."

She turned. Without meeting his eyes, she went to the couch and sat down.

"It seems I've walked right into your latest little trick. I have to congratulate you on your cleverness. Your strategy was infallible. You didn't have to drag me kicking and screaming through the great hall. You did away with the hysterical scene." She observed him from under her thick fringe of lashes and laughed weakly. "At least you've got the good graces to look guilty."

Arching his eyebrows, Conn replied, "A man in my position has to learn to live with a little guilt."

He stood abruptly and went to the window. His eyes stared into the night as he raised a hand to either side of the window and supported his weight.

"At some point in his life, Gelina, a man has to decide how much of his power he's going to use. I decided tonight."

"Can you live with your decision?"

"Better than I can without it." He turned toward her. "When I was a boy, I wanted nothing more than to be Ard-Righ of Erin—to unite the tribes of Erin in a common bond. When I faced death with a dagger at my throat, I wanted nothing more than to live. When I faced exile in a strange country, I wanted nothing more than to feel the grass of Erin beneath my feet again."

He stood only inches in front of her. She locked her hands together to hide their violent shaking.

He tilted her chin up until she was forced to meet his eyes. "But I've never wanted anything as much as I want you."

She exhaled slowly, unable to still the sudden trembling of her lower lip. He knelt in front of her and placed a hand on each shoulder. Pulling her to him, he kissed her softly, his tongue exploring the warm contours of her mouth.

Gelina jerked away. "Is this a game, Conn? Is this your final jest on Rory Ó Monaghan? Is this how I pay my debt to the Fianna?" She grabbed the front of his shirt and twisted it between her fingers, demanding an answer.

He captured her hands in his and brought them to his warm lips. "No, Gelina. The debt is mine. I fulfilled a lust born of anger that night in the cavern. I hurt you. 'Twas not the way things are supposed to be. I must prove that to you."

"If there's a guard outside the door, Conn, there is no difference. This is still a battle, and you're still the enemy." She struggled for the words to make him understand.

He stood and pulled her to her feet. "Tonight might be a battle and tomorrow might be, but you cannot resist me forever."

"So once again I have no right to refuse you?"

Conn took a step backward, unable to face the tears of dread that welled in her emerald eyes. He reached out a hand to her cheek, then drew it back in despair. Sitting down heavily on the couch, he buried his face in his hands.

His words were muffled. "If you leave me tonight, Gelina, then you leave me forever. Nimbus has offered to take you away from here. I cannot bear to have you so near to me and not be able to touch you. It's killing me. If you're going to leave me, go now . . . or I fear I shall never let you go."

Hardly daring to draw a breath, he waited for the slam of the door. Gelina remembered another night, Conn's head bowed in defeat as he faced a skinny, frightened orphan. She had been driven to her knees and sworn allegiance to him that night. She had learned to withstand many things in her young life but Conn in defeat was not one of them.

A hand brushed his hair. Then two hands gently pulled his face upward to meet sweetly parted lips. A maelstrom of emotions broke loose in him as he wrapped his arms around her, pulling her between his knees in an embrace as painful as it was satisfying.

She was drowning in his kiss, dying in his arms, and she did not care. Even when his arms slipped beneath her knees and lifted her to the bed, she could not pull her mouth away from his tender onslaught. His kiss deepened as he felt her body move beneath his. She moaned in protest as he pulled away from her.

Her eyes fluttered open. Conn drew back, his face shadowed by the firelight behind him. She fought the fear that threatened to rise in her throat, remembering another night, a face in darkness and driven, relentless hands. As if sensing her fear, he reached out and took the softness of a velvet curl between his fingertips. He explored her face with gentle fingers, soothing away the tense lines around her eyes. His thumb traced the outline of her lips. Feeling the warm flesh part beneath his hand, he lowered his lips to hers, drinking of a wine sweeter than nectar. He pressed her into the feather mattress with the hard length of his body.

She turned her face away from his with a sharp intake of breath as his hand glided beneath her skirt to rest against the silky skin of her inner thigh. She felt the restraint curled in his every muscle as he sat up and straddled her, pulling off his tunic with shaking hands. Her fingertips moved with childish curiosity to trace a lingering path from the dark, curly mat of hair on his chest to his abdomen. His muscles contracted violently from the curious caress.

His voice was as gentle as his hands as he worked apart the worn linen frogs that held her dress together. "I thought I could hide your beauty beneath these rags. But I was wrong." His lips nuzzled her throat. "I never wanted you more than I did the first time I saw you march into the great hall, garbed like a slave and carrying yourself like a queen." His breath came faster as the ugly linen fell away to reveal a gossamer silk shift that Gelina had hoarded from a better day.

She stared up at him with wide eyes as his hands caught in the delicate silk. With a roguish grin and a neat twist of his wrists, he parted the sheer material.

Gelina gasped. The hands that flew up to cover herself were caught in Conn's gentle grip.

He collapsed against her throat with a shaky laugh. "Child, child . . ." He raised his head and met her wide-eyed gaze. "You render me weak-kneed and inarticulate with your beauty. Don't be shy with me."

Her head twisted to stare at the hands that held her captive. "I shall surrender if you will."

His hands flexed, then opened. She met his wary gaze. Her hands lay pale and still in the shadow of his. She kissed the line of his jaw and cupped his neck in trusting surrender. Conn buried his face in her curls, her name a whispered prayer of thanksgiving on his lips, before raising his eyes to a body kissed to a roseate glow by the firelight.

Gelina felt light-headed as all the blood rushed from her cheeks and followed the burning trail Conn forged with his mouth. Her hands caught in his hair as his lips brushed the aching peak of her breast. Her skin quickened beneath the teasing caress of his warm, rough tongue. Her hands caught his shoulders as a shudder wracked her body. His mouth slanted across hers again, enslaving and freeing, taming and taking with the slaking motion of his kiss.

His hands worked to free them of the last restraints of clothing that held their sprawling limbs reluctant prisoners. His eyes burned like twin coals of blue fire as his hand traveled the length of Gelina's trembling body until his fingers brushed the warm softness of her. He covered her mouth with his, silencing her tortured moan. His hand explored her, stroking out a sweet pattern until she was damp and writhing, her body spread beneath his like a wanton angel's.

Her breathing grew ragged. His kisses no longer silenced the small noises she made deep in her throat. He parted her legs and slipped between them. At the exact moment her world exploded, he drove himself deep within her. Her world diminished to the feel of his sweet thrusts rendering her captive in the firelit night. He emptied himself into her and collapsed, his face wet with sweat and tears. He buried his face in the curling tendrils of sweat-dampened hair that clung to her throat and slept.

A faint light glowed through the east window as Gelina struggled to open her eyes. From somewhere in the fortress came the hollow bark of a dog. As she tugged the fur coverlet over her shoulders, she felt a warm hand stroking her waist. She rolled over to find Conn propped on one elbow, regarding her intently.

"You are leering at me, sire," she accused, running a hand through his disheveled curls.

"No. I am marveling at you." His hand traced gentle circles at the small of her back. "Did you sleep well?"

"I wasn't aware I had the chance." Stretching like a sated lioness, Gelina let one hand fall on his chest. She studied the darkly furred area with wonder, allowing one teasing finger to follow the crisp mat of hair to his lower abdomen. She felt his muscles tighten beneath her fingertip.

Drawing in a quick breath, he caught her hand and grinned. "Now I am leering at you, milady."

"Oh, no. Not again," she groaned, drawing the coverlet over her head in mock dismay.

Conn laughed, his gentle hands guiding her over until she lay on the smooth, flat planes of her stomach. She tossed the coverlet back and stared over her shoulder at him, her eyes comically wide.

He kissed her freckled nose. "'Tis early yet, my love."

When Gelina awoke again, the bright fall sun of late morning cast its beams across the bed. She groaned as she opened her eyes. The bed beside her was cold and empty. Raising her head, she could see the last embers of the fire dying into darkness. She shook her head, wondering if the night had been only a poignant dream. That thought was vanquished as she sat up, discovering pleasant pains in muscles foreign to her. She grinned sleepily and rested her head on her knees.

The click of efficient sandals in the corridor sent her into a panic. She scanned the room for a hiding place. The door opened a crack, and she plastered herself flat on the bed and pulled the coverlet over her head. She held her breath as the swish of bustling skirts and the clang of dishes came from across the room.

"Good morning, Gelina. I left yer breakfast for ye."

"Thank you, Moira," she replied, trying to sound as dignified as she could under the circumstances. The coverlet did not stir.

After the door closed, she dared to poke out her flushed cheeks. Placing her bare feet on the cold floor, she slipped into Conn's shirt so carelessly discarded the night before. She padded to the small table where a golden tray held a plateful of pastries and pancake crisps. As the sun hit the tray, diamonds of light sparkled across her eyes.

She picked up the shining object around the goblet of goat's milk and caught her breath. The burnished gold of the *niam-lann* was beaten to a fineness so thin she could bend the tiara around her forehead with two fingers. The emeralds captured the sun's light and sent it flashing across the room like shattered glass. She dropped it guiltily as a sharp rap sounded on the door.

"Come in," she cried gaily, trying to hide her discomfort at inviting anyone into the king's chambers.

Audren's blond head appeared in the doorway. "I was told to fetch these for ye. May I enter?"

"You may," Gelina answered, stuffing a pastry into her mouth to avoid further conversation.

To her acute embarrassment, Audren entered, followed by four girls, their arms loaded with mountains of silk, satin, linen, and wool. One of them cradled a long mantle trimmed with otter fur. Gelina choked down the pastry, her throat going dry.

"Whatever are you doing, Audren?" she asked, licking cinnamon from the corners of her mouth.

The girl curtsied. "We're here to measure ye for yer new garments."

Gelina pulled her to a standing position by tugging gently on her ear. "Do not bow to me, Audren. One does not bow to slaves."

Audren shrugged and held up a bolt of lavender silk to Gelina's chest. "One bows to the best dressed slaves."

Moira rescued her from their good-natured poking and pinning hours later, herding them out of the room with firm hands, not oblivious to Gelina's thankful glance. She closed the door behind the giggling girls and turned to Gelina, who stood in the center of the room wearing only a thin silk shift. A flush rose to Gelina's cheeks under Moira's knowing perusal.

Sensing her discomfort, Moira bent and gathered an armful of satin. "This material will not do ye a mite of good tonight, but I've a trunk outside with something that might." She bustled to the door. With one hand on the handle she turned to Gelina and looked her straight in the eye. "I've known him since he was a lad. He was a good boy. He liked to fight, but he never fought unless he was provoked and he always fought fair."

Without another word she closed the door behind her, leaving Gelina to stare after her, a small smile playing around her lips.

The sun faded in the west leaving behind an evening that remembered summer in the warm, cloudless twilight that fell over Tara. The great hall was deserted. Its occupants spilled out of the fortress onto a field glowing with torchlight. The Aonach had begun. Ale flowed freely from tapped barrels as the stars claimed their places in the night sky one by one, competing with the brilliance of the smiles gathered below at the great fall fair of Tara.

At the center of the meadow played the king's musicians. Their sweet airs floated on the breeze to the foothills and beyond. Dancers locked hands and cavorted around the woven baskets stuffed with bread and cheese. Conn and Mer-Nod wove through the crowd, dodging dancers and jugglers.

"You look well," Mer-Nod shouted, struggling to be heard over the shouts of the crowd.

Conn's dark beard parted in a blinding smile. "I feel well. I feel wonderful." He kissed a crying child held in his path without breaking his stride.

Mer-Nod trotted to keep up with him only to trip over a small object and stumble to his knees. The small object was Nimbus, who received a murderous glare for his trouble. The jester fell in behind them, his short legs pumping up and down with exertion. Conn's path toward the fortress never swerved. As they neared the massive doors, the cause of his haste became apparent.

Framed in the open doorway by the light of the torches stood a lone figure. Her eyes searched the meadow, their emerald depths exactly matched by the hue of her smock. Mer-Nod heard someone take in a quick breath and knew without glancing beside him that it was Conn. Looking down, he was surprised to find that Nimbus had vanished, immersed in the line of dancers that passed within inches of them.

Conn stepped forward without his usual self-assurance until he stood in the light of the torches. Gelina's lips curved in a dazzling smile as her eyes lit on him. Gathering the sweeping velvet folds of her skirt, she started forward only to stumble as one sandal caught in the golden hem of her smock. With an apologetic shrug, she kicked the sandals off, sending them flying through the air to land upon the head of a farmer who was sober enough to eye them curiously and glare at the sky. Mer-Nod coughed into his hand, hiding a smile.

"Good evening, milord." She curtsied. The burnished gold of the niam-lann gleamed beneath the curls laid artfully across her forehead.

"Good evening, Gelina," Mer-Nod replied.

Conn continued to stare at her with hungry eyes.

Mer-Nod cleared his throat. "I must attend to those damned poets. They'll have Queen Maeve making war over a sheep instead of a bull if I don't keep an eye on them." He excused himself, feeling invisible as neither Conn nor Gelina acknowledged his departure with a word or a glance.

Conn wrapped his hand around Gelina's and pulled her through the throng of people. She felt curious eyes on them as they passed. A woman turned to the shepherd beside her, whispering and pointing. Two hefty soldiers lay in the grass, muscles bulging, arms locked in combat as the group gathered around them tossed gold pieces in their midst. The larger of the two glanced at Gelina as she flew by, breaking his concentration long enough for his opponent to pin his arm with a tortured groan. The huge face cracked in a grin. Gelina smiled back at Goll MacMorna.

Conn pulled her around the corner of the fortress, and they nearly trod upon a couple locked in a passionate embrace in the tall grass. He jerked open the ivy-covered door in the wall and ushered her into the secluded garden. The music faded to a sweet echo as he closed the door behind them.

He let go of her hand and took a step backward, his eyes drinking in her features. He pushed a hand through his hair and let out a ragged breath, looking as nervous as Gelina had ever seen him.

"I was afraid to see you today," he said.

She sat down on a slim wooden bench, suddenly shy. He sat beside her and took her hand in his. She traced the black curling hairs on his wrist.

"Why were you afraid?" she asked.

"I assumed that you had taken the time to think about last night and would hate me by now."

"I do hate you." His face fell and she smiled. "I hate you for allowing those alleged maidservants to torture me with their pins all day."

" 'Tis a fine way to show your gratitude for a new wardrobe, milady. Most of that fabric was imported from across the sea when my mother was still alive."

" 'Tis beautiful, but I would have done just as well—"

"Absolutely not. I won't have you parading around here in a pair of satin breeches."

She hid her smile behind a pout, struggling to look offended. "You would not find me comely?"

"On the contrary. If you were beautiful in that infernal black dress, you would be beautiful in anything. Or nothing." He gazed into her eyes, leaving little doubt that he meant what he said.

"You flatter me, Conn. I'm far too tall and gangly to be beautiful."

"By the time I'm through with you, you're going to believe you're so beautiful that you shall become impossible to live with." Conn cupped her face in his hand and touched his lips to hers. "But I'm willing to try anyway."

Sinking her toes into the cool mud beneath the bench, Gelina remembered another night she had spent in this garden. She pulled away from him and looked around. The plants had begun to die, their dry leaves hanging like surrendered flags from their stalks. Conn watched in bewilderment as her gaze rose above them, her eyes clouding as they rested on a darkened window.

"And shall I stay in Sheela's chambers, Conn?"

The lifeless quality to her voice sent Conn to his feet. He paced the small garden, his heart racing.

"I want you exactly where you are—in my chambers. Why should you ask such a question?"

Gelina shrugged. "I thought I might be like her now."

He fought to keep the fear out of his voice. "Sheela was just a . . . diversion. You're my best friend."

"And your worst enemy," she murmured.

He pointed a finger at her. "I was willing to overlook that if you were."

"What about them, Conn? What will they think of your slave now?" She gestured toward the garden door only to find her hand caught in his. He knelt at her feet.

He spoke slowly and precisely. "As far as the people know, you were coerced into fighting by the men who abducted you. You chose slavery as a self-imposed punishment for your weakness."

"You told them that?" In response to his smug nod, she added, "And they believed you?"

"There are certain privileges that go with carrying a large sword and being the king. Your credibility remains unquestioned by those too clever to risk your ire." He rubbed the back of her hand against the prickly softness of his beard.

"Just don't let it go to your head." She boxed his ears softly with her other hand.

"How could I? There is always one woman I can count on to question my credibility."

He left no doubt in her mind who that woman was as he pulled her to a standing position and pressed his body to hers. His lips devoured hers. His hands glided downward, over her shoulders and the slim contours of her back.

She pushed him away and backed around until the bench lay between them. "If you continue, we might as well go lie in the grass like those two out there."

He stalked her with a wicked grin. "Would that be so dreadful?"

"Scoundrel."

"Wench."

She threw back her head and laughed as he leapt over the bench and swept her up in his arms. He carried her to the inner door that led to their chambers. Staring over his shoulder, Gelina could almost see the forlorn girl crying in the muddy garden disappear as she buried her face in his neck, breathing deeply of his scent.

Chapter Twenty-four
❖

The scene shifted; the colors faded to gray, then deepened to red. Fog swirled through the narrow corridor, granting teasing glimpses of the two locked in silent combat. Rodney crept down the corridor until he faced the straightened spine of his enemy. His sister's terrified eyes spurred him to action. He rammed his sword into Conn's back, laughing aloud at the gratifying sound of metal tearing flesh. Conn sank to his knees, and Rodney faced his sister. Her loving eyes shone with gratitude.

He withdrew his sword. "Now, Conn, your time has come."

"No!" Gelina's hand flew out to grip his wrist.

With a cruel smile she wrenched the bloody sword from his hand, swung it in a high arc and severed Conn's head with a mighty blow. The head bumped against Rodney's toes; lifeless blue eyes stared into the fog.

Rodney woke up smiling, the nights he had awakened sweat drenched and shaking a vague, unpleasant memory. His sister's accusing eyes behind the dagger no longer haunted him when he closed his eyes. In a hundred nightmares Conn had jerked the blade across her throat, marring the perfection of her ivory skin with a crimson line before her neck collapsed like the neck of a broken doll.

Rodney sat up, shaking the image out of his mind. His stomach rumbled, drowning out the rustle of the dying leaves. The glade he slept in had become his dearest friend, sheltering him from the winds that blew cooler each day. He crawled to the bubbling spring. Catching a distorted glimpse of himself in the water, he smiled. His hair hung long and unkempt over his shoulders. A fledgling beard had settled on his face, its straggly hairs softening the sharp contour of his chin. His shirtless chest was pale.

He peered out between the trees. Tara, the mighty fortress, perched like a sleeping giant on the plains. He spat upon the ground.

A splash on the surface of the spring drew his attention. He plunged one hand into the cool water. A pang of loneliness shot through him, and he wished his little sister were there to chastise him about his eating habits. He glared at the fortress again.

"When I get you this time, Gelina, I shall never let you go."

His whispered words were drowned out by a splash as he grappled beneath the surface of the water and drew out a writhing fish. The fin slashed across his hand, drawing blood. He bit off the squirming head with a single bite.

Gelina sat bolt upright in bed, a cold sweat on her brow. Conn stirred beside her and laid a warm, possessive hand on her thigh without opening his eyes. In the light of the full moon pouring through the unshuttered window, Gelina watched him sleep, delighting in the vulnerability of his open mouth. She softly kissed his fingertips before laying his roaming hand on his chest. She tucked the coverlet around him and slid her feet sideways until they touched the cold floor. The fortress slept around her as she pushed open the door and padded into the corridor.

This was not the first time she had awakened from a sound sleep with her heart pounding in her chest like a captive bird. She could remember no dreams, but a sensation of dread lay curled in the pit of her stomach. Restlessness sent her to prowl the fortress, unable to return to sleep. She felt in the pocket of her long nightdress for the cold iron of the key. The weaponry room beckoned her just as it had on the night of the catastrophic siege.

She pushed open the door. A cool draft sent a chill down her scantily clad back. The torches burned low in their sconces with the approach of morning. Crippled shadows limped across the walls, transforming her shadow into a looming giantess stomping over the swords and lances. She roamed the room until she faced the far wall.

Vengeance hung where Conn had replaced it. She ran her finger over the familiar hilt, wiping away a light layer of dust. Her fingers itched to remove it, to feel the cold comfort of the metal in her hand. She placed her hands behind her back, resisting the temptation with difficulty.

"You look like a guilty child caught eyeing the tarts."

The voice snapped her out of her reverie. She turned to see Conn leaning against the doorframe, his arms crossed over his bare chest.

"I wasn't planning a revolt. I was just"—she searched for the right word—"restless."

He strode toward her, then stopped as he saw the brief flare of fear in her eyes. "Please don't look at me like that. You look as if you expect me to rush in here and pitch you against the wall."

She shrugged. "Perhaps I do."

Shaking his head, he strode past her and took Vengeance from the wall. He tossed the weapon to her. Caught off guard, she let the blade slide until it clanked against the floor.

"You are a natural warrior, but there are certain skills that you can achieve only with practice." Conn took a thin, silver sword from the wall and crouched in a fighting stance. "Have you ever fought as a partner?"

Gelina shook her head.

"I thought not. You've never had a partner worth fighting for." He glared at her from under his dark eyebrows. "But that is another matter altogether."

She fought the urge to turn as he circled her and placed his broad back firmly to hers. "If you are outnumbered and there are two of you, the best way to fight is back to back. Circle with me."

She struggled to keep up with him as he moved about the room, jabbing at an imaginary enemy.

"Tell me, Gelina. Is Eoghan Mogh as skilled a warrior as I?"

Her feet stopped at his question, but his back prodded her on. She tripped over her own feet in an effort to match his long strides.

"He shares your modesty if not your skill," she replied.

"And where do his skills lie?" His voice remained as calm as if he were standing still instead of galloping around at her back.

"Why don't you ask him yourself? He is languishing in your dungeons."

At her answer, Conn doubled his pace.

"He is a strategist, not a warrior," Gelina cried breathlessly. "I never saw Eoghan lift a sword."

Conn slowed, and she breathed a sigh of relief.

"Eoghan was truly kind to . . ."

His pace doubled again, and Gelina wisely closed her mouth.

Conn guided her through a series of drills until her arm ached with the sheer effort of holding up the sword.

" 'Tis like dancing," she gasped.

She giggled as he whirled and knocked the sword from her hand with a gentle blow. She sank to the floor in an exhausted heap only to find her arm caught in an iron grip.

"There is one more thing you must learn. If you or your partner is ever disarmed like I just disarmed you, 'tis imperative that a weapon reach your hands," he explained.

He pulled her to her feet, then went to stand forty feet away, taking her sword with him. She watched in bewilderment as he flung the sword into the air. Throwing her hands up, she ducked and ran toward the door.

The sword clattered to the floor. Conn said, "Nice catch."

She uncovered her head with a sheepish grin. The grim set of his lips did not relax as he strode to her and laid both hands on her shoulders.

"This involves a consummate amount of trust in the person responsible for getting the weapon to your hand. Your life is in their hands." She trembled beneath the warmth and strength of his hands; his thumbs gently traced her collarbone beneath the thin linen of the nightshirt. "Do you trust me?"

She nodded an assent in one beat of her heart.

He moved behind her; his arms circled her, lingering at her waist for a moment before rising to her shoulders. "Show me where you want the sword to fall. What is the most natural position for you to catch the sword and be able to swing with your next move?"

She stretched out her arm and felt his follow like a shadow.

"Stay where you are," he commanded.

He crossed the room in long strides, leaving her to still the trembling of her hands. Without a word he drew back his arm and hurled the sword in a high arc. It spun toward her, the reflection of the torches flashing from its gleaming blade. Her feet cried out for movement, but she kept them locked in place.

The sword hurtled toward her outstretched arm. Its path was cut short by the firm grasp of her palm as it landed in the precise spot she had designated for Conn. Her palm stung, but she hardly felt it as Conn rushed across the room and swept her up in his arms, swinging her around until her feet left the floor. She dropped the sword with his blessing as he laughed aloud, covering her forehead and cheeks with kisses.

The days passed in a dreamlike state for Gelina. The nights were even better. The weather mellowed to a gentle fall ideal for long rides on Silent Thunder. On days when Conn was closeted inside, he allowed her to take the horse out alone. The first day she had done this, she had returned to find him pacing in front of the stable with only Nimbus for company. As he pressed his warm lips to her temple, she realized what this extra piece of freedom had cost him.

His dark head next to her auburn one became a familiar sight at Tara. Cook declared they had all taken leave of their senses when she caught them in the kitchen at midnight with Gelina on the king's lap, clad only in their nightclothes, eating yesterday's tarts and giggling like children.

They were inseparable. Conn would touch her a hundred times a day and then move on, unaware himself of the strength he obtained from their subtle contact. A soft touch on her hand would be followed by a gentle correction of her disheveled curls. Gelina knew him well enough by now to know that it was also his way of saying that she was his just as Erin was his. To her own surprise, she did not resent it.

They existed from moment to moment, awaiting the hour when they could retreat to their bedchamber and close out the questioning eyes. Gelina would laughingly resist his advances, knowing he still reveled in the thrill of the hunt. But always would follow the tender yielding that left them breathless and sated, arms and legs entwined in exhausted slumber, her lips pressed to the thundering pulse at the side of his throat. On some nights they simply lay holding each other like children who were afraid in the darkness of the night.

Gelina awoke one night to the sound of broken sobbing, her brother's name a whisper on her lips. She felt Conn's hands stroking her and realized that the bitter sobs were her own. She began to speak softly as he kissed away the tears streaming down her cheeks, speaking of that which they had never dared to speak of.

"I dreamed of Rodney. I dreamed he was trying to hurt me. I know he would never, ever hurt me."

Conn pulled her to him; his eyes stared blindly into the darkness as he struggled to understand her broken words.

"We were so close during those poor years in the cavern. We had only each other and our dreams of vengeance to sustain us through those terrible days and nights. Somehow we made it bearable. We made it an adventure."

She paused for a long moment with only a sniff to break the silence. "Nimbus didn't lie, you know. Rodney did watch me. I would glance up to find his eyes on me. They were starving eyes, and they made me afraid. Why was he bad, Conn? I awoke one day, and he wasn't good anymore. Was it my dream of revenge that poisoned him? Was it me? Why didn't I see it coming? Why didn't I stop it?" She sobbed brokenly, burying her face against his softly furred chest.

He spoke, his eyes bitter with empathy. "You couldn't have stopped it, Gelina. I, too, awoke one morning to find Rory Ó Monaghan an enemy. I never saw it coming. He fed me. His pretty wife sang ballads for me. He confided his deepest secrets and drew mine from me. But I couldn't see. I was as blind as you were, my dear." He kissed her ear softly. "But now our eyes are open and we see only each other as it was meant to be."

He rolled her to her back and studied her to see if the accusations he made against her father disturbed her. She wrapped her hands around his neck and pulled him down to her before he could read the fear in her shadowed eyes. They kissed and, in the tender depths of their love, pushed away the doubt that lay nestled in the darkest recesses of their hearts.

Gelina was strolling through the great hall the next morning when a body dropped from a noose above her head. Tiny feet dangled inches from her nose.

An infuriated shriek escaped her lips. "Curses, Nimbus. You'll frighten me to an early grave." She pulled off a sandal and drew back her arm.

He opened one eye and winked at her. "Don't ye dare, Gelina. An accomplished jester must practice. I'm working up this routine for Eoghan Mogh's burial. Do ye like it? Fitting, is it not?"

Her only response was a black glare.

"So sorry. I forgot he was an acquaintance of yers. Be a good lass, and climb up here and get me down."

His request met pointed silence. Gelina crossed her arms and smiled sweetly.

"Please, milady?" he asked with a supplicant look from his earnest brown eyes.

With a disgusted snort she stomped up the stairs to the platform. Resting on her stomach, she hauled him up by the braided rope. She sat with legs crossed and watched him remove his gear.

"How do you do that?" she asked.

Removing his jacket, he revealed a harness fashioned of narrow strips of leather that crossed his chest. "Do ye see this?" He held out the harness and pointed to an oblong brass charm with a narrow strap pulled through it.

She turned it over in her hand. "What does it do?"

"It saves me life. It makes sure that the harness catches me before the noose does. See the engraving. I did that meself."

"What does the crown stand for?"

"Nimbus—Ard-Righ of the Jesters. What else?"

Gelina shook her head, her eyes roaming the deserted hall below. "Tell me, sire, where have all your subjects gone on this gloomy afternoon?"

"Conn did not tell ye?"

Gelina shook her head.

Nimbus stood and paced the small confines of the platform. Gelina hid a smile as he rubbed his chin in a perfect imitation of Conn deep in thought.

He turned to her with a frown. "The Fianna have just dismissed their court."

"Conn spoke of no court. What is their case?" Before he could answer, she breathed, " 'Tis Eoghan, is it not? 'Tis why Conn did not tell me. Is Eoghan well? Is he alive?"

"For now."

"They have sentenced him to death?" Gelina knelt and took Nimbus by the shoulders. "Tell me. What is his sentence?"

Nimbus sighed. "Conn and Eoghan will meet in battle this afternoon in a meadow a few leagues from here."

Gelina's eyes clouded. "That is impossible. Eoghan is no match for Conn. Conn knows that. Why, I told him . . ." She grasped Nimbus's jacket with frantic hands. "Where are they going? You must take me there."

Nimbus jerked his jacket from her hands and smoothed his lapel. "I cannot take ye there. Only the Fianna are to be in attendance. Conn would be furious."

Gelina's eyes narrowed with a wicked glint. "That's stopped neither you nor me before."

A smile rose unbidden to Nimbus's lips. He rubbed the back of his neck thoughtfully. "We must hasten to get there before they do." He stood and offered her his arm, stumbling as she jerked him toward the steps.

Mer-Nod dismounted from the mare and whipped his feathered cloak behind him. A silence as heavy and still as the damp air fell upon the meadow with only the soft nicker of a horse to break it. Gray and black clouds split the late afternoon sky. All bloodlust had been carefully erased from the seasoned faces turned to Mer-Nod. The men invited to attend the battle had been handpicked from the experienced ranks of the Fianna. They had ridden to the meadow through the shadow of a damp forest to witness the final battle between their king and the man who had been his enemy for almost a quarter of a century.

A low murmur rose as Silent Thunder pranced out from the trees. Conn sat on his back in the full leather of a warrior, his face drawn. Sean Ó Finn followed on foot, the unlined smoothness of his young brow strangely out of place. Mer-Nod studied his king, committing each detail to loving memory so his vision of this day could be recreated in a poem written by candlelight late that night. What he failed to see in his careful scrutiny were the two who perched on a sturdy branch above his head.

Gelina clutched the rough oak with one hand and Nimbus's jacket with the other. Crouched on the narrow limb overhanging the meadow, she struggled to keep her balance and hide herself

in the damp and dying leaves, a feat that was far more difficult
for her than it was for Nimbus who sat in comparative comfort
on the branch. He shot her a look of amused annoyance as she
jerked his jacket, disturbing his own balance. Her skirts tangled
around her ankles.

Her attention was drawn from her discomfort as Conn
dismounted and raised his hands in a plea for a silence he
already had. Nimbus's heart twisted as he saw the look in her
eyes when they rested on Conn. He averted his own eyes and
watched the proceedings below with interest.

Conn signaled and Sean Ó Finn disappeared into the forest to
reappear with his prisoner. Eoghan Mogh walked into the
meadow without introduction. As the voices rose, it was
obvious that he needed none.

Gelina peered at the man who had been her friend a lifetime
ago. His angular frame was thinner than she remembered. She
could read no signs of starvation or maltreatment in his pallid
face, but she could see that the weeks in the dungeon had taxed
his strength. She flinched at the thick chains binding his wrists.
Even from where she perched, she could see the raw flesh
festering under the iron links. His eyes beneath their dark brows
glittered as they surveyed the warriors with contempt, finally
coming to rest on Conn.

Conn returned his gaze for a long moment before clearing his
throat for silence.

"You know who this man is. I won't bother listing his
accomplishments. Instead, I will list his crimes." Conn pushed
away the parchment Mer-Nod pulled from his cloak, desiring no
script. "He is a traitor to the kingdom of Erin. He has
undermined every effort to unite this country. He has slaugh-
tered both my soldiers and innocent citizens who opposed his
greedy plans to conquer Tara by forcing men into his service and
stealing their gold. He has been a thief in the night and a bane
on our land."

Angry voices rose. Eoghan stood impassive before Conn's
charges, an eerie dignity clinging to his tall frame.

"He poisoned our men and cut their throats when they were
helpless!" a voice bellowed from the soldiers who ringed them.

Another soldier waved his fist. "My clan was forced to give
up a fortune in gold when Mogh's pigs came knocking at their

door. They threatened to take my brother's youngest daughter for sport if he did not yield to their demands. She was just a child!''

The man next to him nodded. ''He stole away a girl from this very fortress. Forced the fair Gelina to ride astride and join his bandits. Only our king's timely intervention saved her from a terrible fate.''

Gelina choked as she saw Eoghan meet Conn's gaze evenly. She realized with horror that Eoghan could condemn her for many of the crimes that had just been attributed to him. Conn would be helpless to defend her. Eoghan did not speak but smiled faintly at Conn's deepening pallor.

Conn drew his sword from his scabbard with an uneven movement. ''Unchain him,'' he commanded Sean Ó Finn.

Without allowing herself a second to change her mind, Gelina swung down from the branch, ignoring Nimbus's frantic clutch at her skirt. She landed gracefully on her feet before the shocked men.

She faced Eoghan and Conn. ''I beg pardon, sire. I wanted to witness the battle so I hid up there.'' She gestured to the branch where a petrified jester had plastered himself, hidden from the astonished upward glances. ''I lost my balance and fear I find my shelter lost also.'' She spread her skirts and curtsied with an unabashedly charming smile. Conn sheathed his sword.

Eoghan took two steps toward her. Conn moved behind her. His hands fell on her shoulders in a possessive grip.

She was the only one who heard the prisoner's whispered words as he leaned forward. ''You wear his love well, Gelina. It suits you.''

She smiled through the tears that sprang to her eyes, knowing as she heard his familiar, lilting words that Eoghan would never betray her. She was oblivious to the hostile looks Eoghan's apparent intimacy drew from the men. Conn turned her around to face him.

His voice was steely as he pointed to a vacant space in the crowd. ''You are here. You may as well stay.'' The ominous slant of his eyebrows left little doubt he would deal with her later. She curtsied again and stepped back.

Conn paced a few feet away, forming his words with care. ''Do you have anything to say in your defense, Eoghan Mogh?''

"I cannot be a traitor to a kingdom I have never sworn allegiance to. My desire to rule Erin is as valid as yours," Eoghan answered, his voice a chiming bell in the muted silence.

A furious roar erupted. Conn stepped forward, raising his arms once more for silence.

"I have decided to give you what you gave me when you set me adrift on the sea—a chance." Conn circled Eoghan, his hands locked behind his back. "Your men are not here now. If you want to steal my kingdom, then you'd best be prepared to fight for it yourself."

A cheer rose at Conn's words. Sean unlocked Eoghan's chains with a flick of his wrist, and the irons fell into the damp grass. Eoghan rubbed his wrists, his veiled eyes never leaving Conn.

Gelina bit her lip to keep from crying out as Sean slapped the hilt of a sword into Eoghan's palm.

Conn's hand went to the hilt of his sword, then paused. "I know many of you wanted the death penalty for this man. But I could not grant it." Knowing Conn as she did, Gelina could see that his next words would cost him dearly.

"We all know the meaning of the word *clansman*. We know the responsibility it entails." He pointed at Eoghan. "This man knows the burden it carries. When our ship bound for Britain was set upon by his pirates, he left strict orders as to my disposal. I was not to be killed. I was to be placed in a boat and cast out to sea in an area of Roman patrol. My death would be imminent, but my blood would not stain his hands." He stared at Eoghan, eyes narrowed. "He did this because he is my clansman. He is the son of my mother's sister, and if his blood must stain my hands, it will be in a fair fight."

The meadow exploded in cries of disbelief. Gelina stared between the two of them in wonder. She remembered with shock the way that Eoghan had laughingly studied her and knew whom he had so painfully called to mind.

"I want silence!"

The gleaming sword Conn brandished in the air left little question that he meant what he said. The meadow quietened.

Conn's voice was as soft as Gelina had ever heard it. "Stand and fight, Eoghan Mogh. Fight . . . or die."

Gelina felt a restraining hand on her shoulder and knew Sean had seen her step forward. Her frantic glance drew a flat shake of his head and the hand on her shoulder tightened.

She flinched as Eoghan swung at Conn with a clumsy two-handed motion. Conn ducked with a bitter laugh that sent a shiver down Gelina's spine as she remembered a hot summer night when that laugh and that sword had been for her.

"You scurvy dog," Conn cried. "Did your father never teach you to fight? Or do you know who your father was?"

Conn's sword crashed into Eoghan's. Eoghan's lips were set in a tight line, his arms extended stiffly in front of him.

"You shall die like the coward you are, swine," Conn hissed, his blade lashing across Eoghan's arm. A thin line of crimson appeared on the ragged tunic. Cries for more blood rent the air.

Through the fog of her fear, Gelina heard Sean whisper, "If Eoghan surrenders beneath the weight of Conn's insults, the battle will be done." The scene swam in front of her as tears of relief and love sprang to her eyes.

Eoghan backed toward the forest, his eyes dark and fearless. Conn stalked him. "The Castilian bitch you married is a common whore, Eoghan."

For a breathless moment Eoghan's eyes rested on Gelina, and she knew with certainty that his next words would be his last. His lips parted, then closed again. Gelina felt Sean's hands rub her shoulders in wordless support as her legs wavered beneath her.

With a wild cry Eoghan charged Conn, his sword aimed at Conn's heart. Conn easily stepped aside, disarming Eoghan with a twist of his wrist. Eoghan fell among the damp leaves and rolled over to find the tip of Conn's sword pressed to his throat.

Conn's voice shook with emotion. "You are the son of a whore, Eoghan Mogh."

"That I am," Eoghan bellowed, his clear words stunning the triumphant cries into silence. "Truer words were never spoken. Our mother was a whore, and you, my dear brother, are a bastard."

Conn drew back his shaking sword to ram it into Eoghan's throat. "Even as you die, filthy, lying words spew from your lips."

A determined bulk propelled itself from the shadows of the forest into their midst without bothering to curtsy.

There was only the sound of a gasp high among the branches of the oak as Moira's voice rang out. "Cease, Conn. I cannot let ye slay yer own brother."

Gelina buried her face in Sean's tunic as Conn sank to his knees beside Eoghan, his sword falling unheeded to the leaves.

Chapter Twenty-five

❖

Conn's lips moved, but no sound came forth. Eoghan Mogh stood and paced a few feet away, sparing a glance laced with contempt for Conn. The men parted to let Moira through until she stood in front of Conn. He raised dazed eyes to her, and Gelina strained to hear her soft words.

"Forgive me. Ye have to know the truth . . . before 'tis too late."

Sean stepped forward, clearing his throat. "Shall I send the men away, Conn?"

Conn shook his head. "They may stay. They deserve the truth. They are my brothers." His eyes fell on Eoghan, who stood with arms crossed. The blue of his eyes met the cold blue of Eoghan's glare, and he flinched. "The truth, Moira, please."

Moira nodded, the burden of thirty-six years of silence slipping from her shoulders. "Yer mother was promised to Eoghan's father when she was a little girl. They were wed, but Ulad Mogh had little time or concern for his young bride. Maureen was a gentle child, and his blustering, drunken ways terrified her. A year passed and she bore him a son they called Eoghan."

Conn did not raise his eyes.

"I cannot lie to ye. Maureen would never have betrayed Ulad or her infant son. That child was the light of her joyless existence. But one summer day, when she was bathing in a stream alone, a warrior appeared from nowhere on a huge steed as black as the night. Her comely form and timid eyes were too much for him. He forced his love upon her.''

Conn turned desperate eyes to Gelina. She ached to reach out to him.

Moira continued, ''The warrior was Feidlimid Rechtmar—the Lawgiver, king of the province of Meath. But the conqueror became the conquered. Having tasted of the joy he found in Maureen's arms, he found he could not live without her and he wooed her to win her love and soothe the brutality of his first advances.'' Moira's lips curved at the memory. ''She would return from their meetings with her eyes blazing like the sun. I was young and foolish myself and found the elaborate schemes we devised to bring them together a diverting game, never realizing the danger lurking beneath their love.

''When Ulad discovered her infidelity, he became a wild man to discover that the woman who lay so stiff and full of fear in his bed gave herself freely and with joy to another. He beat her, threatening to kill her and the unborn child she carried that was not his. Although a part of her heart remained behind, she fled with her lover, leaving her firstborn with his father. She did so with the knowledge that Eoghan was the one thing Ulad Mogh did love.''

Moira knelt before Conn, a plea for the beautiful, tormented Maureen in her dark eyes. ''So she came to the fortress of Feidlimid and bore ye, Conn. Ye grew strong in the shadow of their love. Tara rang with yer laughter. Sometimes I would catch Maureen staring over the moors, and I knew she thought of Eoghan.''

Moira ignored Eoghan's derisive snort. ''When Ulad Mogh died a drunkard's death, my sister sent Eoghan to Tara. At his own request, he was introduced as the son of a sister who had never existed.''

''We fought like wild beasts all summer,'' Conn murmured.

Moira nodded. ''Eoghan begged to return to my sister. He wanted no part in the life Maureen had found for herself in Feidlimid's arms. It broke yer mother's heart to say farewell to her firstborn son for the last time, but she sent him away. Your parents' past eluded ye and followed them to the burial cairn they share in the distant hills.''

A breeze boding rain rustled the leaves. Eoghan's bitter laughter rang out.

"What a touching tale, Moira! Why should I have wanted any part in the life of the woman who deserted me so she could raise her bastard child? Conn was so sweet. Conn was such a good child—so handsome and skilled. I was an intruder here. There was no room for legitimacy at Tara.''

Conn, who had listened to the end of her story with his face buried in his hands, looked up at Eoghan coldly.

Eoghan taunted him. "How many bastards have you sprinkled about the countryside, Conn? How many young girls have you forced to spread their legs in the name of the kingship, so you could slake your lust? 'Tis in your blood, you know. You cannot help it.''

Eoghan's bitter gaze scanned the crowd. As it rested on Gelina's stricken face, a brief wave of remorse traveled through him.

"Take him away," Conn commanded flatly.

Sean roughly wrapped the chains around Eoghan's wrist and led him to a horse. Conn did not move as the soldiers filed away, mounting their horses one by one, their faces grim.

Moira touched his arm with a gentle hand. "I never meant to hurt ye, Conn. Just as Eoghan vowed on his father's deathbed never to shame his family by revealing his mother's betrayal, I vowed to your mother that if either of ye threatened the other, I would reveal what I knew. Forgive me.''

Conn could not speak. He touched her hand with his before getting to his feet and going to Silent Thunder, his shoulders bowed in defeat.

"Conn?" Gelina breathed as he mounted. He ignored her and spurred the horse into a gallop without a word.

Dark clouds billowed across the horizon; an oppressive fog rolled over the drumlims toward the meadow. Gelina rubbed her bare arms as gooseflesh rose unbidden to her skin. She stood alone staring at nothing until Nimbus swung down to land in front of her.

"Gelina?" he said softly, touching her knee.

She lowered her eyes to meet his concerned gaze. "I have to go after him.''

"I wish ye would wait.''

She took his hand and squeezed it. "I cannot.''

"Take care. He may be in no mood to receive ye," Nimbus warned.

"It would not be the first time."

She lifted her skirts and ran to where the last soldiers mounted their horses. She could see Conn disappearing in the distance, driving Silent Thunder into the cloying fog. A soldier stared in astonishment as she ran up to him and jerked the reins from his hands.

"I must have your mount," she demanded breathlessly.

Knowing who she was, he clambered down from the horse's back, mumbling a few protests but not daring to refuse. His mouth fell open as she leapt upon the horse, paying little heed to the position of her skirt, and kicked the mare into a gallop.

The fog enveloped them in a velvet curtain of gray. Gelina slowed the horse to a walk as she approached the forest where Conn had disappeared. The mare quivered at the unfamiliar weight on its back. She ran a soothing hand down its neck. The muffled crackle of the wet leaves beneath the horse's hooves cut through the impending darkness. The foilage glistened with moisture from the fog swirling through the trees. Gelina wished for a torch as a nightbird cackled in her ear, startling her. She steadied her shaking hands with effort, murmuring to comfort both herself and the mare. They moved deeper into the silent forest.

She longed to call out to Conn but was hesitant to shatter the silence. She cursed herself for neglecting to strap on the jeweled dagger Conn had given her. Every muscle tensed as the mare picked its way through an underbrush that had yet to lose the thickness of summer. The horse stumbled as its hoof caught on a root.

Gelina grasped the mane, the reins slipping from her sweaty palms. The horse charged, and she slid from its back, landing on her bottom with a cry of despair. The mare disappeared into the fog. Climbing to her feet, she peered around, fighting the panic that rose in her throat. The fog and fallen leaves conspired, rendering it impossible to retrace her path.

Sitting down on a fallen stump, she struggled to catch her breath. Her eyes fell on the ashes at her feet. Leaning forward, she touched her fingers to them but could not decide if the faint warmth she felt radiated from her own fingertips or from some recently deserted fire.

Her nervousness grew. She scanned the trees, feeling a cold gaze that prickled the tiny hairs at the nape of her neck. Panic conquered her, and she rose and fled deeper into the protection of the forest. Her sandals flew off; branches slapped across her cheeks; her hair caught on an obstinate twig. She jerked it free, not daring to slow her flight. A relentless crackling pursued her through the woods.

As the crackling grew in intensity, she looked back in terror without slowing her driven flight. That flight ended as she came up against a solid barrier. Strong arms encircled her.

She turned in horror to find herself caught against Conn's broad chest. He stared down at her, his eyes dark with concern. Throwing her arms shamelessly around his neck, she buried her face in his jacket. His hands rubbed her back, trying to still her violent trembling. The hushed drip of the leaves surrounded them. The silent underbrush revealed no secrets.

He led her to a clearing where he had began to build a shelter of interwoven pine branches. A small fire blazed within, dispelling the gloom and chill. Settling her in front of the fire, he took off his jacket and laid it across her shoulders. He sat back and studied her, a question in his eyes.

"I followed you. I lost my horse. Well, actually it wasn't even my horse," she said lamely. She rubbed her forehead in dismay. He raised his eyebrows, leaving her to continue faintly, "I thought I was being followed. I was afraid."

He picked up a stick and stirred the fire, his voice cold and distant. "Did it ever occur to you that I came here because I wanted to be alone?"

"I didn't think you should be alone," she stammered. "You've had a trying day."

His laugh was bitter. "To find out my whole life has been a lie? You call that a trying day?"

She pulled his jacket tight around her. "Your parents loved each other and you. Your mother was a braver woman than mine. She did what she had to do."

Gelina stared into the fire. The flames cast gold highlights across her tangled hair, leaving her eyes in shadow.

When he did not speak, she continued, "As for being Ard-Righ, you know as well as I that ruling in Erin has never been a matter of lineage but a matter of the sword. Even your father was not brave or wise enough to unite the kings of Erin."

Conn rammed a stick into the fire with a scowl. "What do you know about my father's history? You're only a child."

"That is odd. You didn't seem to find me so childish last night. And I didn't seem to be a child this morning when I awoke to find you—"

"Stop!" he commanded.

Gelina cursed in frustration, unshed tears standing in her eyes.

Conn chose his words with care. "After you ran away to Rodney, Nimbus told me you loved me. I did not believe him."

"Sometimes I think Nimbus knows more than the rest of us put together," she said softly.

"And what would Nimbus say about Eoghan Mogh? What would you say about him?"

Gelina rested her head on her knees. "He was kind to me. He seemed to sense how miserable I was. I suppose he used me to further his cause. He needed me because I knew the fortress and because I knew you." She glanced up to find Conn gazing into the fire.

"Go on," he commanded.

"He is brilliant. His wit is very dry, and you are never quite sure if he is laughing with you or at you. He is persuasive and charming when the need arises. He was fair to me. In some ways he reminded me of you."

His glare told her she had said the wrong thing. She scooted around until she was next to him and touched his hand. He jerked away as if her touch burned him. She sank back in disappointment.

"I thought my mother was such a good woman. I wonder how many times she looked at me and saw that other blue-eyed baby she had deserted," he said.

"She had no choice, Conn. Don't you see? Ulad would have beaten her again, killing her or her unborn child. If she had taken Eoghan when she fled, Ulad would have followed. There could have been no peace, no happiness. Both you and Feidlimid would have ended up dead or Ulad would have. She protected those she loved with every resource she had. An evil woman could not have begot such a son as yourself."

"Do you mean a man of such pure motives?" he asked mockingly, one eyebrow raised.

She bowed her head, unable to face his sarcasm. "Could what he said be true?"

"What?" he asked gruffly.

She pushed a stray curl from her eyes. "Could you have children out there somewhere?"

He shrugged. "It's possible. Does it trouble you?" They sat shoulder to shoulder now, neither looking at the other.

"I just never pictured you rutting about the countryside."

His voice revealed no small measure of indignation. "Is that what I've been doing to you? 'Rutting' about you?"

Gelina suppressed an insane desire to giggle and held her tongue.

"Perhaps I should send you away," he stated flatly.

This drew a stricken look from her. "Are you so eager to be shed of me? Must that always be your answer?"

"Eoghan is probably right." His voice exploded into emotion, startling her with its vehemence. "I'll just hurt you. Think what I did to you once. I'll carry the image of your torn, bleeding body to my grave, but who is to say that I won't do it again?" His eyes narrowed. "Who is to say that if I wanted you now and you resisted, that I would not ravish you again? Can you say I wouldn't? Can I?"

She stared at him as he grabbed her arms, tense fingers digging into tender flesh. She fought the urge to pull away. His eyes burned with an eerie sapphire heat.

"What are you trying to prove, Conn?" she asked softly.

Without a word he shoved her down, pinning her to the ground with the weight of his body. His lips closed on hers in savage demand only to find her lips parting beneath his, her tongue meeting his with no challenge but tenderness.

He pulled back, his voice hoarse. "If my mother looked to my father the way you look to me, I can never blame him for what he did."

"Then I can never blame you," she said, trying to steady her breathing. "I can only blame you if you deny what is between us."

"I cannot deny it. There is only one thing I can do." He smoothed the tangled hair away from her face with tender fingers.

"What is that?" she asked fearfully.

"Our children will not be bastards, Gelina."

His lips parted against hers, smothering her sharp gasp. Her arms locked around his neck as the fire blazed in their small shelter.

Greedy black eyes devoured them from the darkness.

Chapter Twenty-six

❖

Gelina flew through the chamber with Nimbus in pursuit, her short curls tied up in rags. Capturing a handful of her linen skirt, Nimbus found himself lifted off the ground by Mer-Nod, who rose from the parchment he was studying to halt their gleeful chase. Ignoring Nimbus's curses and futile struggles, Mer-Nod caught Gelina by the elbow.

"Is this any way for a future bride of the Ard-Righ to behave?" he chided.

Lowering her head with a penitent pout, she replied, "I beg pardon, Mer-Nod."

He loosed them at the same time, sending Nimbus to the floor in a sputtering heap. The jester opened his mouth only to find Gelina's hand clapped over it. Smiling politely, she backed them out of the room without losing her grip on Nimbus. Mer-Nod frowned as the running steps resumed followed by a laughing squeal.

Rubbing his tired eyes, he settled himself once more before the parchment. A map of Erin lay before him, its lines as familiar to him as the lines on his palm. A new line lay across this parchment, a bold line drawn in Conn's own hand. Mer-Nod shook his head and ran his finger over the line that separated Erin from coast to coast.

Eoghan Mogh had walked out of the fortress a free man. A handful of the men who had been held in captivity with him had followed, shielding their eyes from the bright fall sunlight. He had held in his hand a treaty signed by his brother. The horses they had been given carried them south, Eoghan's proud shoulders the last sight Mer-Nod had seen as they disappeared over the plains.

Mer-Nod shook his head once more as he remembered Conn's words before an unfettered Eoghan Mogh and the same tribunal that had heard Moira's confession.

"If you want the south, Eoghan, it is yours. There is no land for grazing. There are no fields for raising crops. If you can make a kingdom there, do so. In return you must sign this treaty guaranteeing that those who inhabit that area will be protected, that you will make no further strikes over the boundary of your territory, and that you will meet here with me once a year to discuss our agreement."

Conn's words had elicited shocked gasps and protests from the men who listened. Mer-Nod had scribbled violently, trying to capture every nuance of his words even as his own mind reeled from the shock. Only Eoghan Mogh had remained impassive, sitting quietly before reaching for the parchment that Conn held out to him. Their eyes had met for a moment, not in fondness but with a certain grudging respect that Mer-Nod could have written volumes about if he could only have recorded it.

With a command to the guards to provide Eoghan and his men with safe passage, Conn had strode out of the room, leaving behind a storm of controversy.

Gelina's laughter floated through the door pulling Mer-Nod back to the present and his most pressing concern. As Conn's decision was announced, two distinct divisions of opinion developed. There were many who supported his decision, trusting his judgment and rejoicing in the announced wedding to the lovely Gelina, whom they had seen grow from a skinny ragamuffin into a stunning young woman. But dissenters sprang from the crowd, both within the ranks of the Fianna and among the others.

Word had spread of Eoghan Mogh's whispered words to Gelina in the meadow. Mer-Nod had listened impatiently to every possible accusation in the last few days. The girl was a witch, a banshee. She had forced Conn to free the evil Eoghan. She had been sent to the fortress from the beginning to arrange this perversion. She had not been stolen but had run to Eoghan, her lover. Those who dared to question Conn's decisions were few, but their accusations were ugly enough to instigate several fist fights as Gelina's honor was defamed and defended.

Mer-Nod was to soothe the people even if it meant confirming the dark rumors of Conn's parentage that had began to float in ever-widening circles from the fortress. He knew with certainty that the wedding would help to quiet the vicious tales. Guests had been arriving for days. A week of merriment and feasting had been ordered by Conn with no grandeur to be spared. With the people well-fed and full of ale, they would surely accept both Conn's decision and his new bride with open arms. Mer-Nod smiled at the prospect, his spirits lightened.

"Who are they?" Gelina asked as they studied the odd assortment who passed through the courtyard. She perched on the wooden gate, her long legs dangling.

Nimbus replied, "They're traveling acrobats, jesters, cooks, musicians, and they are all here for your entertainment, Gelina."

"Look! There's one like you!" She pointed to a dwarf dressed in garish purple pantaloons and a pointed yellow cap.

He shot her a venomous look. "I wouldn't be caught dead in that garb."

She ignored him, eyes wide as she watched the steady stream of brilliant costumes, golden instruments, and laughing strangers parade around the side of the fortress. She hooked her ankles around the wooden post and swung the gate back and forth.

Thumping Nimbus on the head, she teased, "How are you going to compete with all of that talent?"

"No challenge. I've still got me noose trick. I've yet to see it duplicated."

"What are you going to do? Swing from the rafters as I exchange vows with Conn? That will add a nice touch to the oaths."

"Indeed. Before ye ever enter the room I shall announce that any fellow who planned to marry the most beautiful girl in the world follow me example, for she is taken. Then I will step off the platform and stun the watching masses, who will include yer impatient bridegroom."

"'Tis the silliest thing I ever heard. I've yet to see any unmarried men threaten to take their lives over me," she scoffed.

"Sean is quite heartbroken. I think he rather hoped Conn was saving ye for him."

"Nonsense. Sean looked quite jolly at dinner last night slobbering in the bosom of that serving girl."

"Well, if I had room for a heart in me joke of a body, I've no doubt it would be shattered." Nimbus's hearty laugh did not reach his eyes.

Gelina looked away; the gate lost its momentum and creaked to a halt. She jumped to the ground, smoothing her skirts. She bent and touched her lips to Nimbus's dry cheek. "I'll leave ye to welcome the guests," she said, deliberately mimicking his speech. "I've got to unwind these curls before me hair falls out."

Nimbus called after her, "Don't forget. No talking to Conn. If Moira finds out I quit following ye around, she'll make mince meat of me."

He leaned on a bale of hay as she was swallowed by the main door, letting his smile fade. His jaws ached from the effort of maintaining it. The sunshine that fell on his shoulders did not warm him. He surveyed the courtyard with dull, lifeless eyes.

"Good day, stranger. You look as if you could use some cheer." A bearded man whom Nimbus did not recognize held out a wooden flask as he leaned on the bale beside him.

Nimbus studied his laughing eyes for a moment before taking the flask and drinking deeply. "Much obliged."

"Could you direct me to where the servers are sleeping? I've traveled far and would like to rest before the feast." The man took the flask back and drank from it, wiping the sweat from his brow with his other arm. "'Tis as hot as summer here. Is it always this hot?"

"It varies," Nimbus answered shortly. "Where do ye hail from?"

"The coast."

"Erin is surrounded by coast."

"I've traveled much in the past few years." The man pointed to the door. "Was that the bride we've heard so much about?"

"That is her." Nimbus again took the flask from the outstretched hand, accepting the numbing relief of the ale as it slid down his throat.

"She is beautiful," the stranger said, shaking his head. "Our king is a lucky man."

"Sometimes I think he does not realize how lucky," Nimbus said, the ale loosening his tongue. He missed the stranger's slow grin and the cold, speculative look in his dark eyes.

He handed the flask to Nimbus. "Finish it. I shall follow these others to the quarters."

He picked up his pack and started after the others. He glanced back with a friendly wave that left Nimbus with an uneasy feeling of recognition. He shook it off and drained the flask with a single swig and a loud burp.

"'Tis barbaric. 'Tis torture," Conn said passionately as he stared into the garden beneath his window.

"'Tis tradition," Sean answered, unable to hide his grin. He joined Conn at the window.

Below them Nimbus and Gelina practiced a double juggling routine that sent Gelina into gales of laughter as three of the golden balls came down in quick succession, rapping Nimbus's head.

Conn smiled in spite of himself. "I have not been with her in a week. I see her each night, but I cannot dance with her or speak to her or . . ."

". . . or touch her," Sean finished, aware of the king's restless prowling through the sleeping fortress each night. "You are to be married tomorrow. You can talk to her for thirty years. I wager you'll not be able to still her tongue even if you desire to."

"I may not be around for thirty years," he said cynically.

"You certainly followed the Fiannic oath in choosing a wife. She came to you with no dowry and only the clothes on her back."

"And those weren't hers," Conn murmured. He raised his hand in silent greeting as Gelina looked up at them and touched two fingers to her lips.

He groaned, and Sean patted him on the shoulder. "Do not fret, Conn. Tonight is the last night. I shall be outside your door to ensure you do not weaken."

"Stay alert, Sean. I might sneak up behind you and knock you unconscious."

"I shall be alert. I'm as worried about her hitting me upside the head as I am you. I would be hard pressed to knock her out." They both laughed, and Sean pulled him away from the window.

* * *

Gelina entered the great hall that evening, tripping over the trained marmosets that somersaulted across the floor at their master's command. She untangled herself and gazed around her, eyes wide with wonder.

Scattered among the faces of those she knew were strangers garbed in exotic hues and fabrics. The finest men and women in Erin would feast at Conn's table tonight. Many had been kings themselves before choosing to ally themselves with the Ard-Righ. Curious eyes gazed back at her. Her heart raced in excitement as she realized her wedding day was only hours away.

The hall was a study in joyful chaos as goblets were filled to the brim, drained, and filled again. Gelina made her way to her table, winding among the jesters and acrobats with care. Her table was opposite Conn's, close enough to allow them an occasional wink but no words. Moira's considerable bulk was already stationed in the chair next to hers to ensure that nothing more than tortured glances would be exchanged. Gelina sat, arranging the voluminous pink satin of her smock around her.

She jumped as a trumpet fanfare sounded to announce the king's entry. Conn entered, bowing as he traveled the path that cleared to his table. Only Gelina caught the silent words on his lips as he raised his goblet in a toast.

"I love you, too," she whispered only to find her leg soundly pinched between Moira's sturdy fingers. She looked away, rubbing her leg under the table.

Servers moved between the tables offering treats of seasoned shrimp soaked in butter and warm spiced ale. Gelina's healthy appetite disintegrated as anticipation settled gleefully in her stomach leaving little room for anything else. She poked at the steaming prawn on her plate with indifference and sipped the ale.

Another group of servers appeared from the kitchen bearing trays laden with steaming plum tarts. Gelina smiled as she watched a small boy fondle each tart on the platter before choosing one, his eyes wide with delight.

A haunting whistle from the table behind her drifted over her shoulder like a cloak of uneasiness. She turned, drawn by the lullaby. A server worked behind her, his back solidly presented to her curious gaze.

"Tart, milady?" He whirled around, holding out the platter.

The floor beneath her feet tilted as she stared into her brother's mocking eyes. The dark beard that covered his chin did little to hide his cold smile. Before she could catch her breath or speak or scream, he was gone, weaving back through the tables without a backward glance.

Gelina turned back to the table and drained her ale in one drink. Turning to Moira in desperation, she found her deep in conversation with the woman next to her. She sat with hands clasped in her lap for a moment, the laughing voices fading to a dim roar. She rose, ignoring Moira's curious stare and started for the door. Her eyes wide, she shot Conn a quick look before vanishing from sight in the crowd.

Conn stood only to find Sean's hand firm on his shoulder.

His man-at-arms laughed. "That trick will not work, Conn. I am sure some bit of food just disagreed with her."

Conn sat down with reluctance, certain he had seen a plea for help in Gelina's wide eyes and ashen cheeks. He shook off the chill that traveled down his spine, attributing it to jitters.

The courtyard was deserted. Gelina caught an elusive flash of white linen from the corner of her eye as a figure rounded the stable. Following it without thought, she found herself face to face with Rodney. She stopped in her tracks, biting her lip to keep silent. The eaves cast menacing shadows over the lean planes of his face. She took a step backward without realizing it. He stood with arms crossed, leaning against the stable wall.

"Greetings, little sister. I regret to disturb your feast."

She stopped in her tracks, biting her lip to keep silent.

"Whatever is the matter? Surprised to find me alive? Or didn't you bother to ask anyone what happened to me after we laid grand and glorious siege to Tara?"

"I asked. No one knew. Eoghan never saw you after you entered the fortress with me," she replied, struggling to keep the fear out of her voice. "What are you doing here?"

He spread his arms in mock innocence. "You have to ask? I could not miss the grandest wedding this country has seen. Surely you would not deny me the witness of my only sister's oaths."

"I would. I want you to go."

"I am going. I am leaving Erin. A ship awaits me at the coast.

I will not be back. Not ever. I thought you might want to go with me." He stretched out a hand and rubbed her cheek. "You cannot go through with this farce."

She jerked away from his hot touch. "I belong here, Rodney. 'Tis where I belonged from the beginning."

He cursed. "That vermin has cast some sort of spell over you. I know he makes you say these things. He has made you into his whore."

Gelina slapped him hard, the sound echoing through the empty courtyard. He stared at her in amazement with the wounded eyes of the one who knew her best, then dropped his head in defeat. Tears sprang to her eyes.

"Forgive me, Rodney. I know we have suffered through so much together, but it is time to let the old dreams die. They were wrong." She grabbed his hand and held it tightly. "You must understand. You must not destroy this. To destroy this is to destroy me. You must leave this place."

He leaned against the stable, shoving his hands deep in his pockets. "I ask one thing, Lina."

She awaited his request with dread, wiping the falling tears away with the back of her hand.

"I want to stay and witness your nuptials. I cannot bear to leave without that small memory to see me through the dark days and years ahead."

She turned away, her voice a whisper. "If Conn recognizes you, I will not be responsible."

He nodded, and she turned toward the lights of the fortress.

"Princess," he called after her. She stopped and turned, her back straight. "Remember . . ." With a sad smile he bowed to her before stalking into the darkness.

So Gelina remembered. The chamber she had occupied as Conn's foster daughter held her memories. She sat on the hard floor wearing only her shift and hugging her knees. The dark, still hours of early morning shielded her as she wracked her mind to remember.

She remembered the handsome young warrior who had visited her father. Standing on tiptoe, she would peer over the edge of her father's gem-encrusted chessboard, feeling invisible until the warrior would reach out and tweak her nose. She would run squealing from the room only to return a moment later and repeat the game.

Then the arguments began. A closed door greeted her when she sought to intrude on her father's games. Leaning against the heavy door, she would listen to the bitter words and accusations, not understanding but knowing that the warrior's eyes were like blue ice when he stormed out of the castle without a word to her or Rodney. What had Conn's orders been to those brutal men? Had he sought to close forever her small emerald eyes? With a shudder she remembered the deadly force of Conn's anger, which she had come to know firsthand.

Yet Conn had protected her again and again. He was protecting her now. Nimbus's diversions and games could not hide that there were those who believed her a traitor, could not shield her from the hostile glares. She shifted, fighting exhaustion, and wondered if Conn were still awake.

Smiling sleepily, she remembered his words to her as he pulled her into his chamber one rainy afternoon—''I've got to have you. I cannot stay away from you. I want you every way I can.'' Was this the same man who had ordered her returned to him dead or alive only months before?

''Too many questions,'' she murmured.

She slipped the rumpled satin over her head and laced it with sure fingers. Stepping into the corridor, she looked both ways. The hallway was deserted, the only sound a raspy snore that floated out from the chamber opposite hers. She crept through the corridor, suppressing a groan as she rounded the corner in front of Conn's chambers to find Sean leaning on the door. She ducked back around the corner.

''No, you don't, Gelina,'' Sean called out.

She peeked sheepishly around the corner. ''I must see him, Sean.''

He chuckled. ''He's already been out twice trying to convince me he must see you. The two of you are incorrigible. The answer is no.''

''You do not understand, Sean. 'Tis . . .''

''. . . a matter of life and death,'' he finished. ''The answer is still no. You will be married in a few hours. Surely you can wait.''

She shook her head in defeat. ''Will you be here all night?''

He nodded.

She put a hand on his arm. "Guard him well, Sean. Give him a message from me, please?"

"What do you want me to tell him?"

She frowned. "Tell him to take care."

"'Tis an odd message for a prospective bridegroom," he said, sensing the trepidation in her touch. She shrugged and turned away.

"Gelina, the reason I cannot let you see him is because it could bring down the wrath of the gods and cause terrible things to happen," he called after her.

"Terrible things?" she murmured. She laughed aloud as she rounded the corner, leaving Scan to stare after her.

Conn watched the door with curiosity as it crept open inch by inch. He made no attempt to hide his sigh of disappointment as Nimbus's tousled head appeared in the crack.

"Sean said I could come in if ye weren't sleeping," Nimbus said, pulling the door shut behind him.

"Do I look like I am sleeping?" Conn got to his feet and stretched, stifling a yawn. Taking Nimbus by the shoulders, he steered him to the window. "Look at that sunrise, Nimbus. That sun is rising on my wedding day. From this day forward Gelina Ó Monaghan will be mine."

Nimbus did not reply.

Conn studied him with concern, fearful of his uncharacteristic silence. "I have a feeling that you did not come here to congratulate me, friend."

Nimbus shrugged. "I congratulate ye, but there is another matter I would like to discuss."

Conn gestured to a chair and settled himself on the couch, pulling a tunic over his bare chest.

Nimbus ignored the chair. "It has occurred to me that Gelina has no family to ensure the right decision has been made," he said.

"We are her family, Nimbus. You know that. If you've come to speak on her behalf, then do so," Conn said with a puzzled frown.

"Thank ye, sire," Nimbus said with a trace of his old sarcasm.

Conn smiled faintly, unsure if he should be angry or amused.

"Gelina is very special," Nimbus said. "I just want to be sure ye know that."

"I wouldn't be marrying her if I didn't. Do you believe I harbor poor intentions toward her? Do you think the Ard-Righ of Erin is a poor choice for her husband?"

"If ye're asking me whether I'd rather see her as yer paramour or yer wife, I think ye know the answer." Nimbus held up a hand for silence as Conn stood. "In the past ye've shown a certain lack of insight into her situation. I don't want it to happen again."

Conn paced the length of the room before turning on him. "Thank you very much, Nimbus. I am sure a court jester is qualified to give me the wedding counsel I did not ask for." He bowed mockingly. "There are things between Gelina and me that you have no inkling of."

"Like the fact that she murdered soldiers of the Fianna?"

Conn paled. "How did you know that?"

"I didn't until just now."

Conn sat, his legs weak.

"Are ye sure it is behind ye, Conn? She was just a child. Have ye really forgiven her? Will ye treat her well as yer wife and never look at her with accusing eyes?"

Conn met his gaze, the stark emotion in his eyes giving Nimbus the answer he sought. "I love her," he said hoarsely.

A grin spread across Nimbus's face. "That was all I needed to know. Just remember, Conn"—he walked to the door and bowed; a bouquet of roses appeared in his pudgy hand—"everything is not always what it appears to be."

With an enigmatic smile he tossed the roses to Conn and slipped from the room.

Chapter Twenty-seven

❖

A beam of sunlight danced across Gelina's face. Her eyes flew open. The sluggish residue of sleep vanished as she leapt out of bed and ran to the window, drawing in a quick breath at the beauty of the morning. Not one cloud scarred a sky that was the sapphire blue of Conn's eyes. The warm sun fell across her cheeks, banishing the shadowy fears that had haunted her only hours before. Oblivious to the chill that clung to her bare feet, she danced around the room, arms extended to an imaginary lover. She stopped abruptly in front of the mirror.

Her cheeks were flushed rose; soft disheveled curls framed her face. Hugging herself, she pictured Conn standing behind her, his strong arms around her. Smiling, she turned from side to side, examining the bosom she had feared would never bloom.

A giggle from the doorway collapsed her posturing. Audren poked her head in the door. "'Tis yer wedding day, and ye stand there admiring yerself."

"I was not admiring. I was mourning my lack of certain assets," Gelina laughed.

"Conn don't seem to find ye lacking, milady." Audren smirked.

Moira entered the room, her bulk nearly buried in mounds of emerald velvet.

Audren sighed. "'Tis beautiful. Do ye like it, Gelina?"

Moira snorted. "If I know our girl, she would probably prefer green velvet breeches."

Gelina studied the dress. "Could it be altered?" She received a sharp rap on the head for her question, which dissolved Audren into hopeless giggles.

Moira turned long-suffering eyes to the ceiling. "The most

important day of me life, and I'm cursed with a troupe of jesters. Both of ye listen to me."

They struggled to appear sober under Moira's grim perusal. She took both of Gelina's hands in hers. "When the time comes, child, Audren and I will assist ye in dressing. When ye finish, Audren will escort ye to the tower in the other wing where ye will be left alone until I fetch ye. In that room ye will find a golden torque for yer throat, a jewel-encrusted girdle, and Conn's own ring of gold. These will symbolize that at the end of this day ye will reign as queen of Erin."

Gelina sat down on the bed, her face gone ashen.

"What is it?" Audren asked, fanning her with a corner of her skirt.

"I don't know. I feel overwhelmed. Being queen of Erin was never an ambition of mine." She placed both hands on her stomach, trying vainly to stifle the rumbling within.

Moira touched her cheek. "To be his wife, it will be worth it."

Gelina knew she spoke the truth. Tears sprang unbidden to her eyes. Throwing her arms around Moira's neck, she laughed through her tears.

As the hour of noon approached, the main doors were thrown open so the less fortunate onlookers could pile one on top of the other to watch the ceremony. A hundred torches blazed along the walls. The copper rivets that lined the wooden walls glowed with unearthly light.

Rodney Ó Monaghan stood on the platform high above the crowd. He pushed aside the velvet curtain just enough to watch the proceedings below with contempt. His eyes narrowed as they rested on the ruby-encrusted thrones that dominated the room. He stared at them for a long time before his gaze returned to the platform. A rope lay docile at his feet, its end anchored to the ceiling high above his head. Three shiny golden apples rested among its coils. A narrow leather harness hung from a peg on the wall. Rodney smiled and took the harness, turning it over in his hands. He parted the curtains boldly, his presence undetected in the confusion. As he scanned the crowd, one gaze caught and held his.

The midget stood below him. He gazed at Rodney, then

lowered his gaze to the object twisted in Rodney's hands. They
stared at each other long and hard before Rodney raised a hand
in silent salute and drew the curtain closed.

Audren drew together the laces of the dress, her hands
shaking violently.

"Are there many people?" Gelina cleared her throat to rid
her voice of its troublesome quaver.

"Thousands. The hall is overflowing. The courtyard is full.
Even the land around the fortress is full. I've never seen more
soldiers in one place. I might even land me a husband."

As Audren finished lacing the front of the dress, Gelina
stepped in front of the mirror. The dress was cut low in the
bodice, rising to puffy shoulders. The skirt flowed out in
graceful billows around her slender legs. Narrow green sandals
encased her feet. Without a word Audren extended a hand and
gestured to the door.

They moved through the deserted corridors to reach the tower
where the trappings of Gelina's impending royalty awaited
them. This side of the fortress was quiet. Not even a faint echo
intruded on the silence. With a final squeeze to Gelina's icy
arm, Audren closed the door, leaving her alone.

Gelina sighed, feeling oddly peaceful. The view from the
unshuttered window was breathtaking. She stood there for a
long moment, inhaling deeply the cool air pouring through the
window, then spun around, giddy with excitement.

She ran to the long table opposite the window and reached for
the slim golden torque, the smooth metal cool to her trembling
fingers. She fastened it around her throat and reached for the
girdle. Rubies and emeralds encrusted within the gold glistened
in the sunlight, casting iridescent sparkles into the air. She
hooked it around her waist, its weight unfamiliar on her slender
hips. She touched Conn's ring to her lips before sliding it onto
her finger.

Frowning, she studied the remaining two articles, unable to
recall any mention of them in Moira's tutelage. Stretching out
her hand, she picked up the oblong brass object that lay on the
table. Turning it over, she studied the tiny engraving of a crown
on its underside. Her legs began to shake. With a growing sense
of horror, her eyes rested on the last object that lay upon the
table. It was a tiny golden apple.

She hit the door running, jerking the skirt free of the splinters, oblivious to the shredding material.

High upon the platform in the great hall, Nimbus slipped the harness over his head and tightened it.

She flew through the deserted corridors, the pounding of her heart drowning out the pounding of her feet. Even as she ran, the fortress grew larger; the halls stretched infinitely before her; her breath came in gasps.

Nimbus stepped into view to the generous applause of the crowd. Conn stood and bowed mockingly to the jester.

Gelina rounded a corner and slammed into the wall, ignoring the spasm of pain in her arm and the tiny drops of blood that spattered the crushed velvet of her gown.

Spreading his arms wide, Nimbus awaited the crowd's silence.

She descended the stairs two at a time, tripping over her skirt. The applause from the great hall swelled as she neared, then faded.

"Ladies and kind sirs, may I have yer attention, please? After this day the most comely lass in all of Erin will be the wife of another. As her smitten suitor whose heart is shattered, I have decided to put an end to this game, to say farewell to love." He slipped the noose over his head. The crowd gasped. Conn nodded knowingly to Mer-Nod, hiding a smile behind his hand.

Gelina ran into the corridor that led to the great hall only to find herself immersed in a chaotic jumble of arms and legs.

Nimbus gestured to the musicians with a flourish.

She crawled, shoved, and clawed her way to the door.

The trumpets blew a lilting fanfare.

She burst into the hall, falling to her knees, her scream drowned in the gasps of the crowd as Nimbus stepped off the platform.

A smattering of applause led by Conn traveled through the crowd from those who had witnessed the stunt before. It faded quickly, the only sound the creaking of the rope as the small body swung in a gentle arc. Conn stood, eyes wide with dread. His gaze traveled over the stunned crowd until it found Gelina, doubled over and kneeling on the floor, the green velvet of her skirts rumpled and torn. The eyes of the crowd followed his.

Leaping off the dais, he ran for the steps as the outcry began.

"He is dead!"

" 'Twas no trick!"

"His neck is broken!"

Children burst into tears as their parents cried out in horror. Conn appeared on the platform, tearing down the velvet curtain with a vicious tug. As Nimbus's form passed within his grasp, he reached for it.

Gelina raised reluctant eyes to the sight above her. The noise of the crowd faded to a few solitary sniffles as Conn slipped the noose from the jester's neck and cradled the small broken body to his. He stood with his eyes closed as a new cry went up.

"She killed him!" A soldier Gelina had never seen before pointed at her. She turned her tear-stained face to him in bewilderment.

"She is a banshee!" cried a woman.

Before she knew what was happening, a soldier had pried open her clenched fist to reveal the small charm that lay in the palm of her hand.

He held it aloft, crying out in triumph, " 'Tis the jester's own buckle for his harness. He had no intention of killing himself. She murdered him!"

Gelina's eyes darted across the room in desperation as menacing threats materialized around her. The accusations faded into silence as Conn descended from the platform, cradling Nimbus's body like a child. In the sudden stillness of the room Gelina saw movement near the door. She recognized her brother's back as he disappeared, leaving her alone.

Conn took the steps one by one until he reached their foot where Sean stood waiting to receive his small burden. An icy breath blew down Gelina's neck as Conn turned to face her, a path parting through the crowd that led straight to her kneeling form.

Their eyes met across the room, hers widening in utter terror as she saw the intention in his. It was only some primitive instinct of survival that propelled her to her feet as his hand found his sword hilt. She shook her head mutely, unable to form the words that might halt his deadly advance. He unsheathed his sword with one smooth motion. She backed away from him, matching his pace step for step until the wall was at her back, and he stood directly in front of her with sword in hand. His eyes held hers, midnight blue in murderous rage. His nostrils flared.

For an eternity the sword was drawn back, its blade gleaming in the torchlight. Tears filled her emerald eyes. The sword clattered to the floor as he backhanded her across the face with his fist. She slid down the wall. Blessed unconsciousness received her, the bittersweet taste of blood filling her mouth.

❖

PART FIVE

No chain and no dark dungeon
Will hinder its course;
It laughs at seas and fortresses,
Is mocking of force.

—Author unknown
9th century

❖

Chapter Twenty-eight

❖

"She refuses to talk. She will tell me nothing." As he spoke Sean turned away from Conn and stared blindly into the night lurking outside the window. He could not bear to look into Conn's face and find it so devoid of compassion and warmth.

Conn sat before the fire. "She won't answer any of your questions?"

Sean shook his head in defeat. "No confessions. No denials. She will not admit to an accomplice. She will not utter a word."

Conn stood and paced the length of his chamber. He ran a hand through his unkempt hair. His shirt hung loosely around him, unfastened to the waist.

He turned bloodshot eyes to Sean. "Perhaps we should let her rot down there and see if she will talk."

"From the look in her eyes, I think she could stay there for a hundred years and never open her mouth."

Conn knelt before the fire and stirred the logs into vicious flame, handling the poker like a weapon. The flames cast odd shadows over his face. His eyes burned like live coals, bleary victims of sleepless nights and too much ale.

"'Tis my fault, you know. Nimbus would be alive if I had never trusted her." He threw down the poker, strode to the window and leaned out, letting the cold night air wash over him. "I've buried many friends in my lifetime, but burying Nimbus was the hardest thing I've ever had to do." He shook his head musingly. "The grave is so tiny. If I don't build a cairn, the fuchsia will bloom over it in the spring. It was odd. As we covered him with earth, I thought I heard his laughter in the distance, mocking me."

Sean placed a hand on Conn's shoulder, unable to find the words to ease his pain.

Conn's voice changed abruptly. "I'll make the bitch talk. She'll rue the day she was born."

He strode to the door only to find Sean's hesitant form blocking the way.

Sean's soul trembled inside as he opposed his king. "I don't believe it would be a good idea for you to go down there right now."

Conn laughed—a brittle, icy sound. "Are you afraid I'll kill her? Does it really matter?"

"I just don't believe it would be a good idea," Sean repeated.

"I do. Stand aside."

Even as Conn spoke, the tortured scream floated through the window, filled with nuances of pain and rage. The unearthly sound sent the tiny hairs at the back of Conn's neck erect as he recognized the jester's name locked somewhere in the scream. His hands trembled as he met Sean's gaze.

The soldier nodded wearily. "'Tis her."

Visibly shaken, Conn strode into the antechamber that bordered his chambers and slammed the door, leaving Sean standing in the center of the room, his shoulders slumped.

Conn awoke abruptly from his tortured sleep. He hugged himself, trying vainly to obliterate the pain that wracked his body from head to toe. Nimbus's voice danced in his memory, teasing words nagging at him until he tossed and turned, unable to recall the answer to a question he never asked. He sat up and stared at the dying embers of the fire. His hand brushed the cold and lifeless bed beside him. The undeniable ache in his groin tormented him until he flung aside the coverlet and slipped on his breeches.

He padded through the deserted corridors in his bare feet. The wedding guests had taken rapid leave of the fortress, leaving only a bare skeleton of its occupants behind. Most of the Fianna had chosen to withdraw to the field, preferring to gather around fires in the chilly night than face the haunted eyes of their king. Conn wound through the labyrinth of the fortress, descending into its ancient depths.

A stony-faced guard stood at attention as he approached, startled to see the familiar apparition at the heavy oak door.

Conn's burning eyes silenced any questions as the guard unlocked the door and handed him a torch. The iron keys clanked in Conn's hands as he descended the stairs alone.

He wandered past cell after damp cell until he reached the most distant door. With shaking hands, he slipped the key into the lock and turned it, pushing the door ajar. It creaked open on darkness.

He held the torch aloft, casting eerie shadows over the dirt walls. He blinked, his eyes adjusting to the darkness. The light of the torch flickered across a figure in the corner. Gelina huddled against the wall, the dirty tatters of the velvet dress hanging around her. She turned her face to the door, shielding her eyes from the bright light. As she recognized him, her eyes narrowed in dismal contempt. Her face was drawn, the smooth skin marred by a dark bruise and the swelling over her cheekbone. Conn flinched, unprepared for the black hatred reflected in her lifeless eyes.

Setting the torch in a sconce, he paced the confines of the dank cell, his eyes never leaving her.

"I want the truth," he said, struggling to keep the fury out of his voice. "Why did you murder Nimbus? Who helped you do it?"

Her steady gaze mocked him; her lips curved in a barely detectable smile.

"Answer me, Gelina. Now."

He knelt before her and took her by the shoulders. His fingers dug into her flesh. Her smile only widened, effectively hiding a grimace of pain as he shook her until her head flopped like a rag doll's.

"I want the truth," he bellowed.

He raised his fist only to halt its descent in midair as he stared into her unflinching eyes.

"Finish it, Conn," she said, her voice hoarse from disuse. "There's no one to hear me scream. There's no one to care if I do scream. Finish it," she taunted.

He lowered his fist and closed his eyes briefly. "The truth, Gelina," he said, loosing his grip on her arm as he stood.

She rested her cheek on her knees. "Ah, the truth is a funny thing, is it not? The truth is never to be believed. Nimbus would have found it amusing. He could always find humor in the saddest of situations."

"Quit talking in riddles, Ó Monaghan. Why did you kill him?"

"So now I'm Ó Monaghan again, more like Rory than Gelina. Both your affections and my name seem to blow like a fickle wind in the summer." She chuckled only to find herself jerked to her feet.

Conn was forced to support her as her legs folded beneath her. The bruise on her cheek stood out in brilliant relief as her pallor deepened. Her eyes sparkled in the torchlight. She laughed aloud.

"To what lengths are you willing to go for your answers, Conn? Will you beat me? Rape me? Kill me? I do believe that murder is the only thing you haven't tried in your miserable attempts to tame me."

He lifted her to him until her eyes glittered an inch from his. "Shall I kill you, milady? Shall I surrender my very soul for you?"

"You have no soul," she sneered.

"For once you speak the truth. I lost my soul the first day I laid eyes on you." He held her against his body until he knew she could feel every inch of him pressed to her. "I wouldn't give you the satisfaction of killing you. You would love to prove I was as terrible as you always wanted to believe," he accused.

"You are far more terrible than I ever believed." She drew back her foot and kicked him in the shin.

Conn shook his head, barely feeling her pitiful attack but amazed at her audacity. Loosing her shoulders, he placed both of his warm, powerful hands on her neck, turning her face to his.

"How would you like it if I snapped your comely little neck?"

He thought he saw a brief flare of fear in her shadowed eyes. Almost of their own volition, his broad thumbs caressed her throat, coming to rest against the pulse that fluttered beneath the smooth skin, their power coiled tightly in his control.

"If you despise me so deeply, why didn't you kill me instead of Nimbus?" he asked, his grip tightening.

Her jaw jutted out. "I wish it had been you," she hissed. "I wish you had died, swinging from the rafters, choking on your own bile like the bastard you are."

For an instant his grip intensified and the lights wavered in front of her eyes. He hurled her to the ground where she resumed the posture he had discovered her in, face turned to the wall.

"First you won't talk. Now you don't know when to stop." He went to the door, his voice weary. "If I keep you here, I don't know what I'll do to you. Sean will take you away. So far away that I'll never have to face your tainted soul again."

He slipped out the door, turning the key in the lock. Closing his eyes, he leaned on the door. No sound came from within the cell.

Gelina bit down hard on her ragged skirt until she heard the second heavy door slam in the distance. Only the lone guard heard the broken sobs that echoed through the empty dungeon.

Sean pushed open the study door to find Conn sitting in the fireless room, his back to the door.

"Sire?" he said, rubbing the sleep from his eyes. "Mer-Nod awoke me. He said you summoned me."

Conn spoke without turning around. "You must prepare for a journey in the early morning."

Sean strained to hear his soft words.

"I want you to take her far away from here to one of the crannogs. You are not to tell anyone where you are going. Do you understand me?"

"Yes, sire."

"I am not sure that you do."

Conn turned slowly. Sean struggled to keep from taking a step backward as he faced the unholy fire burning in Conn's eyes.

"I never, ever want to know where you took her."

Sean nodded.

Conn rose to his feet with a jerky movement, and Sean saw the overturned flagon sprawled on the table in a pool of burgundy. "You must swear it. You must swear that you will never, ever tell me where she is no matter how I press you."

"I swear it."

Conn took a step toward him. "Swear it by the god by whom your tribe swears."

Sean raised a hand in protest. "But, sire . . . such an oath . . . to break it would surely mean—"

"Swear it."

"As my king commands." Sean dropped to one knee, his eyes never leaving Conn's. "I swear I shall never reveal her whereabouts to you. I swear it by the god by whom my tribe swears."

Conn nodded, weariness etched in every line of his gaunt face. "You may go."

He turned away with a wave of dismissal. Sean pulled the door shut with a sigh, leaving Conn alone at the window to watch the ebony night fade into gray.

At dawn Gelina was led to a tiny chamber and left there. Drawn to the first window she had seen in days, she wrapped her fingers around the bars and pressed her forehead to the cold iron. Fog shrouded the courtyard. A dog howled in the distance; the lonely sound sent a shiver down her back. The courtyard was deserted except for two horses patiently tethered by the stable.

Gelina turned as the door opened. Garments were tossed at her feet.

"Change," was the guard's surly command as he slammed the door.

Running a hand over the coarse material, she smiled sadly as she recognized the clothes. Slipping what remained of her wedding smock over her head, she hurled it into the corner without a second glance and donned the soft, clean linen. At the bottom of the pile rested her cap. She tucked her unruly curls into it and leaned against the wall with hands in pockets.

She didn't have long to wait. The guard threw open the door and motioned her out. She drew in a deep breath of the cold air as they walked outside; the freshness of it burned her stale lungs.

Sean Ó Finn stood beside the motionless horses. He refused to meet her eyes as he interlaced his hands to help her mount the small roan. The other guard stood nearby, his lips pursed in open hostility.

"Give me your hands," Sean commanded without emotion.

A question flickered across her face and she wondered what would be done to her if she refused. She stretched out her arms, face sullen. He bound her wrists, slipping a finger underneath to ensure that the rope wasn't too tight. He mounted the other horse and waited as the guard handed him the rope that led to Gelina and the rope that led to her horse.

He led them out of the courtyard at a walk. Gelina's shoulders straightened as she stared back at the shadow of Tara for the last time. A lone figure in a second story window caught her gaze. Her eyes narrowed in contempt. She met his gaze unflinchingly for a long moment, then averted her eyes in disdain as they moved through the gate. She never saw him sink to his knees and bury his face in his hands.

Sean felt resistance on the rope as they crossed the hillside. He turned, stopping his horse, and followed Gelina's gaze to the small mound of newly turned earth that scarred the grassy knoll. Sean thought he detected a subtle nod toward the tiny grave. He spurred his horse into a gallop, nearly unseating her. She grabbed the rope as it cut cruelly into her wrists, gripping the horse's back with her knees as they thundered away from the fortress.

Sean's stiff back remained presented to her as he led them galloping over the open meadows and walking through the thick underbrush. The sun made its appearance late in the morning, its dull glow doing little to warm the chill air.

They stopped when the pale sun hung high above them. Sean untied her and issued a terse command to dismount. Her gaze was drawn to his hand, which rested on his sword hilt. He stood beside the horse, still avoiding her eyes as she knelt beside the small pond. Cupping her hands, she splashed cool water on her face. She touched her tender cheekbone, feeling the swelling. Peering into the water, she caught Sean's reflection. He was staring at her.

Whirling around, she saw him avert his eyes.

"Look at me, Sean," she commanded.

He raised his eyes to hers, not bothering to hide the contempt in them. She turned away, unable to face what she thought she was prepared to see.

"Why did you do it, Gelina?" he asked, his brow furrowed.

"You asked me that in the dungeon. 'Tis the wrong question. Until you find the right one, I will not answer."

"There will be no more questions where you're going." He crossed to where she stood and bound her hands, not bothering to check the rope for tightness.

"Why did he choose you to make this journey, Sean? Wouldn't it have been easier to send someone who didn't know me?"

He helped her mount the horse, then stood looking up at her. "He sent me for two reasons. I know what you're capable of doing."

"And?"

He didn't look away. "He knows what I'm not capable of doing."

He mounted his horse without another word and kicked it into a canter. Gelina breathed a prayer of thanks for the rush of wind that dulled the bitter stinging in her eyes.

As the long day faded into night, Sean halted his horse and pulled Gelina off the roan. Leaving her bound, he gathered brush for the fire. She stood beside the horse, her legs cramping from thigh to toe.

Sean whirled on her with dagger drawn before she had taken two steps.

"I was just stretching my muscles," she said, holding her bound hands in front of her in feeble defense.

"You don't move unless I say you can."

He sheathed his dagger, small beads of sweat standing out on his forehead. She stood motionless as the branches and twigs crackled into flame.

"You may sit now," he told her, unfastening the knapsacks from his horse.

Her legs folded under her. He unbound her hands, and they ate in silence.

"Why didn't he kill me himself or have me executed?" she asked, breaking the strained silence.

"He was merciful."

Gelina snorted.

Finishing the lean strip of meat, he rose and approached her, rope coiled around his hands. "I must bind your hands and feet while you sleep."

"Why?"

"Those were my orders." He wrapped a length of rope around her ankles.

"What were you ordered to do if I tried to escape? Chop my head off?" Her lips curved in a cold smile.

"I might as well." She thought she saw a flicker of pity in his eyes.

An unwilling sigh escaped her. "Why do you say that?"

"Because if you try to run, I've been ordered to return you to Conn. He'll deal with you himself."

Without another word, Gelina flopped over like a sack of meal. She stared into the fire, her lower lip protruding. Sean watched her for a long time until weariness closed his own eyes. He awoke only once during the night, sitting bolt upright as an agonized whimper cut through his troubled dreams. He looked over at Gelina to find her eyes closed and her chest rising and falling evenly. Shaking his head, he threw himself down, seeking again the black solace of sleep.

Gelina awoke without drowsiness, yawning, or stretching. She simply opened her eyes. The dim sunlight of morning blanketed her face in its meager warmth. There was little difference between sleeping and waking. Even with her eyes open, Nimbus's tiny body swung back and forth between her brows until the furious blue eyes blocked it out. The dreams were worse than the nightmares. Conn stood behind her, encircling her with his powerful arms, his head thrown back in laughter and love shining in his eyes.

She had the dim sensation that she had been weeping. The rope constricted her hands as she lifted them to check for tearstains. She prayed her face was clean. No one must see her cry.

Sean gathered their belongings and helped her mount the roan. Shadows of darkness lay beneath his eyes, and she knew his rest had done little to renew him.

The second day passed in bitter imitation of the first. Darkness was fast approaching when Sean slowed his mount to a walk. The dim sun faded in the west, leaving a faint moon in its wake. Gelina nodded at the rocking pace, her chin almost to her chest as she fought the seductive sleep of exhaustion. The lulling motion ceased, and her head flew up to find Sean sitting motionless on his horse, his gaze locked on the valley below. He seemed to have forgotten she was behind him and did not protest when she nudged her mare to his side.

The hill sloped away into a treeless plain unrolling to the foot of shadowy peaks blacker than the night sky. Gelina suppressed a shiver as a gust of wind whipped the loose tendrils of hair away from her face. Desolation as powerful and silent as the wretched face of the land swept her pounding heart clean, leaving only dread in its place.

A nervous laugh escaped her. "With the moon shining on the rocks, that cottage looks as if it's sitting in the middle of a lake."

Sean didn't turn around. "It is."

Gelina squinted at the dark blot on the land, hearing in the vast silence the whisper of waves licking the stony shore. A thin film of sweat coated her palms. The tiny island looked as if it had risen from the depths of the lake a century ago. The moon shone on a thatched roof, round and solid in its center.

"'Twill be a good place to pass the night, I suppose," she whispered.

In answer, Sean kicked his roan into a canter. Gelina's legs flopped as her mount followed, her knees shaking too hard to grip the horse's sweaty coat. The basin of the windswept plain cupped them in the impersonal fingers of the sky. Sean jerked his mount to a halt and flung himself to his feet; his fingers unknotted two bulging knapsacks with uncharacteristic violence. He pulled Gelina from the mare, his mouth set in a hard line. She stared at the splintered nightmare of wood and rope that stretched from the shore to the island.

Sean stepped onto the bridge, oblivious to its tortured swaying. He turned back to find Gelina rooted to the rocks, a hint of a plea buried deep in her eyes.

"I cannot swim, you know," she said softly.

He fixed his eyes on the island and tugged on the rope until she was forced to follow or splash into the lake. She flinched as chill water rushed over her boots, hardly feeling the dubious comfort of the creaking wood beneath them. She clutched the frayed rope. By the time Sean pulled her to the shore of the island, her eyes were squeezed shut. She resisted the urge to fall on her knees and kiss the mud.

Sean dumped the knapsacks on the ground and untied her hands without a word. She rubbed her chafed wrists.

He busied himself with coiling the rope around his hands. "You'll find lentils behind the hut and dried meat and grain in the sacks. There are torches and blankets and everything you should need inside. I shouldn't have to tell you where to find the water."

He started for the bridge. Gelina clutched his arm. "You're going to leave me here? Just like this? In the middle of the night?"

He shook off her grasp. "I'll return before your supplies run out to bring you more."

"And when will that be, Sean? A week? A month? A year?"

He strode onto the bridge and started across the lake.

Her voice rose in panic. "What if marauders or bandits find me?"

"Then the gods had best help them."

Gelina stood with hands on hips, her whole body shaking in anger. "And what is to stop me from just walking right out of here and returning to plunge a sword in your precious king's heart?"

She heard the crunch of rocks as Sean stepped off the bridge to the shore. He turned and stared across the lake into her eyes. His sword flashed three times in quick succession and Gelina watched forlornly as the bridge sank into the fathomless lake with hardly a bubble to mark its passage. Sean mounted his horse and gathered the rope leading to the mare.

"What if he changes his mind, Sean?" she cried. "What if he doesn't let you return? What if he decides to let me rot here at the end of the world? But oh, no! He's too cruel to let me die. He'll send you back, won't he? He'll send you back until you're old and gray and I am begging for death. The heartless son-of-a—"

Sean urged his horse into a canter. Gelina's curses rent the velvet curtain of the night as he galloped out of the valley and over the hills until the bitter words died in his ears.

Gelina attacked the hut, tearing out ragged handfuls of muddy wicker. Hot tears coursed down her face like blood. She screamed until she couldn't recognize her voice as her own. She sank to the ground in a hoarse heap, her curses fading to sobs.

With a soft hiccup, she sat in the mud hugging her knees, her back pressed to the hut. Sparse stars scattered across the vast sky winked mockingly at her. Silence closed in around her, broken only by the chirp of a cricket on the shore and the gentle lapping of the waves against the rocks.

Chapter Twenty-nine

❖

Gelina wrapped a scrap of linen around her hand and scraped the smoldering turf from the iron lid. The aroma of fresh baked bread filled the hut as she dumped the coarse, yellow loaf from the pot to the table. She tore off a hunk and wandered out of the shadowy hut. She turned her face to the sun, her eyes drawn to the purple peaks that ringed the plains. Her dripping breeches and vest hung across a rope stretched from hut to shed, leaving her garbed in a shapeless linen dress she had found crammed into the knapsack. She tucked the ragged hem under her knees on the bench and wondered, as always, if she were losing her mind when the sun felt warm on her face and the bread crumbled in her mouth in grainy goodness.

The days since Sean had left faded one into another, as seamless as her emotions. She could have been alone on the crannog for a week or a month or a year. Her days were spent fishing, digging peat, and sitting in the sun or the afternoon rain. Her nights were spent staring into the flames that danced on the open hearth and sleeping a dreamless sleep on the creaky bed.

She sighed, hating the fall sun for the healing rays it spread across her soul. She finished the bread and licked her fingers, waiting for the waning of day, when the last rays of the sun would strike the distant slopes until they flamed into the sapphire blue of Conn's eyes.

The black clouds billowed toward Tara, as dark and menacing as the scowl drawn over Conn's features. Sean and Mer-Nod watched from the window as Conn drove Silent Thunder across the meadow and back again. He jerked the horse around with a savage rear that nearly unseated him.

Mer-Nod turned away from the window with a muttered curse. Sean drew the shutters closed as the first raindrops spattered on the sill.

Mer-Nod pulled a scroll from a pigeonhole under the table and tucked the end of a quill between his lips. "I cannot say what is the worse torment—losing Nimbus and Gelina or keeping Conn in this terrible rage."

Sean nodded. "We have more reason to grieve for the king we knew than for those who are truly gone."

"He stormed in here last night and commanded me to erase her name from all records of history. He threatened to destroy my personal poetry if I didn't hide it where his eyes could never chance seeing it."

Sean shook his head, the burden of dread settling visibly on his shoulders. "It'll be time for me to return there in a few days."

"He has never asked you about her?"

"Never."

"How many times have you been?"

"Three."

"In what spirits did you find her?"

"She looked well enough."

"That wasn't my question."

Sean threw open the shutters, oblivious to the rain that slanted across his face. "She refuses to talk to me. All that time alone and she won't even exchange a cross or reproachful word with me when I come."

"Her rage is locked inside," Mer-Nod said.

"That may be true but I don't turn my back on her lest it surface again. I have no desire to be another Nimbus." He leaned against the window frame and watched Conn pound across the meadow, as driven as the sheets of rain that pursued him.

Sean awoke with a start, believing the frightful apparition at the foot of his bed one of the gods come to claim him. Relief eluded him when he realized it was Conn, his hair tousled as if raked by a thousand agonized fingers. Sean sat up, desperate to pretend the next words would not come.

"Where is she?" Conn asked hoarsely.

"But Conn . . . , I cannot—"

Conn cut off his stammered words with a terse command. "Tell me where she is."

"The oath, Conn. I swore."

"Break the oath."

Sean stared at him, aghast. "Sire, you cannot ask me . . ." He swallowed as the icy tip of a sword was pressed to his throat.

"Break it," Conn repeated.

Conn's burning gaze followed him as he sank back into the pillow, a choked protest dying on his lips.

Gelina ladled the steaming broth into the bowl and moved the kettle away from the iron grate. She sat cross-legged on the open hearth, relishing the warmth that kept the night outside at bay. The rain had stopped. As night fell across the crannog, mist rose from the lake in swirling tapers to permeate everything in the hut with a bone-chilling dampness. After a moment's thought she pulled the damp dress over her head and sat clothed only in her shift, her long legs pressed to the warm, flat stones.

The earthenware bowl was hot beneath her fingers. She had to alternately blow and lick her fingers to keep from burning them. A splash drew her eyes to the shuttered window.

She poked a spoonful of broth into her mouth, knowing it was not the first time an errant fish had flopped from the swollen lake to the muddy shore. Perhaps if the night had been clear, she would have gone outside and tossed the poor, gasping creature into the water. But she had no desire to open the shutters and peer into the wounded creature of a night. She was too afraid the wildness strangled by the enveloping mist might find an answering agony in her heart.

The bowl fell to the floor as the door flew open with a mighty crash that shook handfuls of wicker from the walls. Conn stood in the doorway, mist swirling around him, water pouring from his mane of dark hair to his boots in a muddy cascade. His gaze moved from her disheveled curls to the thin cotton shift. His breathing was audible. Gelina tugged the shift down over her thighs; her fingers closed around the warm iron of the poker nestled in the fire.

"I banished you to this hell to punish you, and how do I find you? Languishing on the hearth, licking your fingers like a satisfied cat." Conn slammed the door.

Gelina jumped to her feet with a mocking curtsy, not bothering to hide the poker clenched in her fist. "Do forgive me, sire. Wasting away gracefully was never my strong suit. Perhaps it would have pleased you if I had succumbed to the call of the lake in a ladylike fit of despair. My bloated body could have floated up to greet you in the course of your swim."

Conn stared at a body that was anything but bloated. The months at the crannog had softened Gelina's girlish angles. The reddish glow of the fire behind her threw her gentle curves into aching relief. The shift molded to her body like a second shimmering skin. Conn struggled to remember how old she was, then wished he hadn't. Her hair curled past her shoulders, gleaming in the firelight like spun gold. He took a step toward her without realizing it.

Gelina raised the poker; her eyes blazed. "If you touch me, I shall kill you. I swear it."

Conn stopped, recognizing a new determination in her low, flat tone. He clasped his hands behind his back with a small smile. "You always were a stupid child. I suppose you came by it honestly, though. Your whole family was cursed with a lack of natural intelligence probably caused by all that inbreeding on Deirdre's side of the family."

He ducked. The poker came sailing past his ear as he had anticipated. His lips curved in satisfaction as he straightened. A clay bowl shattered off his temple. Gelina shrieked as he lunged across the hut with a growl. A broom and a copper kettle followed the bowl in quick succession.

Gelina bounced off the wall, staying just out of Conn's grasp and keeping a steady stream of objects in the air, all sailing toward his head with enviable accuracy. She scooped up an iron spoon and was jerked to a halt by a powerful hand wrapped in her hair. Brutal fingers twisted until tears sprang to her eyes, and she was forced to her knees at Conn's feet. She stared up through misty eyes at a face that could have been set in granite, so cold was its intent and so merciless its expression. She closed her eyes, knowing she could trace every line of laughter on that face and had done so a thousand times in the last three months.

"Was this in your plan all along?" she whispered. "To come here when the whim strikes you and hurt me." She opened her eyes to find his face very close to hers.

His voice shook. "If that had been my plan, I would have

kept you chained to my bed at Tara and had you until I tired of
you. My plan was to never lay eyes on your sweet, freckled face
again.''

His lips brushed the bridge of her nose. He jerked away,
stabbed by the tenderness of his own touch. Without loosening
his grip on her hair, he forced her to kneel over the side of the
feather mattress and pressed the hardness of his body against her
rounded softness with a heat that seared through the thin cotton
shift. The stiffness left her back in a tortured sigh as she felt his
other shaking hand fumble behind her and knew he drew apart
the drawstring of his breeches.

''I know what you believe,'' she said in a very small voice.
''But I don't deserve to be taken like this . . . like an animal.''

He loosed her hair. It fell across her face in a cascade of
rippling auburn. ''How do you deserve to be taken?'' He jerked
her around to face him. ''Like a woman who is loved? Like the
cherished wife of a king?''

Tears spilled from Gelina's eyes. ''You've got me on my
knees, Conn. In all the time I've known you, I have never asked
for your mercy as high king of Erin. I am asking now.''

Conn visibly recoiled. '' 'Tis a cruel jest for you to call on the
king when you have brought him nothing but dishonor and
death. The king has killed for less. It is the man who holds your
fate in his hands this night.''

Gelina bowed her head. ''Then there is no hope for me, is
there?''

Conn loosened his bruising grasp to brush away her tears. She
slipped through his hands and sprinted out the door into the
misty night. He jumped to his feet with a curse. A splash
sounded, followed by a deafening silence.

''Gelina,'' he cried hoarsely.

Conn's dive split the glassy surface of the lake. He swam to
and fro under the water, frantically searching the murky depths
for a glimpse of pale skin or a hint of auburn. He rose for a
panicked breath, then dove again, frustration giving way to
despair. His hands clawed at the rocks, tangling in what could
have been hair but was only weeds. The elusive softness of the
strands he had tugged so mercilessly only minutes ago taunted
him with their memory. The water went black around him, and
he knew consciousness was a second away from deserting him.

He heaved himself onto the muddy shore and lay gasping into his folded arms, his mind a desperate blank. He opened his eyes to find a pair of bare, muddy feet splayed in front of him. His gaze traced those feet to a pair of shapely calves and up to find himself staring at the gleaming point of his own sword held in the hands of a woman with a very cold grin.

"The splash?" he asked.

"Your knapsack." The emerald eyes sparkled like the eyes of a vengeful leprechaun.

"And if I had drowned while searching for you?"

Gelina shrugged, and Conn came as close to hating her as he ever would. He rested his head on his arms with a sigh.

"Do come in," she said flatly. "I fear you'll catch a chill lying in the mud."

"How could I resist such a charming invitation from a lady with a sword?" He sat up with a mocking grin, and she took two steps backward.

"Slowly now. I haven't handled a sword for a long time. I should hate to inadvertently lop your head off."

Conn had to laugh as he moved toward the hut. Gelina followed with the sword pressed to the small of his back.

He ducked through the door. "Little girls should take care when they play with warrior's toys. They just might—"

The flat blade of the sword caught him between the ear and the temple. He sank to the stone floor, knowing before the blackness took him that his mother hadn't lied when she told him he never knew when to stop talking.

Chapter Thirty

❖

Conn opened his eyes to a clangorous ringing in his head and a numbness in his arms that warned him he was bound. He blinked. Sunlight filtered through the shuttered window to caress the charming scene at the hearth with a glow that made him wonder if he was still dreaming. Gelina dipped a rag into a chipped basin of steaming water and ran it over her shoulders and arms with the lazy insolence of someone accustomed to being alone. Her skin gleamed. The water flowed in tiny rivulets down the smooth column of her throat and into the shy valleys hidden beneath the shift.

Conn struggled to a sitting position. Gelina dropped a shapeless dress over her lithe form, and he stifled a groan.

Her startled gaze flew to his hungry eyes, then jerked away. She threw open the shutters, and the sun burst into the hut, kindling her hair to a halo of fire and throwing her face into shadow.

"Why is it that whenever I underestimate you, I awake with a tremendous headache?" he said.

Gelina shrugged and sat on the edge of the hearth, her chin cupped in her hand. After a moment's silence in which they regarded each other warily, she said, "I've never taken a king hostage before."

"You cannot prove it by these knots. I feel like a prize pig trussed up for Large Bob the butcher. Surely you could untie me like a good girl before my arms and legs fall off."

She chewed pensively on her lower lip. "'Tis a pity there is no one to deliver a note to Tara to tell them of your sad predicament."

He flashed his white teeth in a winning smile. "If you'll untie me, I will be more than happy to deliver the missive myself."

She sighed. "If only I could swim."

"Do try. 'Tis never too late to learn."

"I suppose ransom is out of the question if there is no one to deliver a message." She shook her head with a bereft sigh.

Conn's smile was frosty. " 'Tis just the sort of task Nimbus would have delighted in."

Gelina's head flew up. She turned to the hearth and slapped a cold boiled turnip into a bowl with shaking hands. She slammed the pestle into it, grinding and pounding as if it were Conn's heart at the bottom of the bowl instead of a hapless turnip.

"There is no meat," she said between blows. "I ate the last of it a week ago. Sean hasn't brought any more."

"But, my dear, your meat is at the bottom of the lake in my knapsack. Surely you didn't think I came here just to ravish you?"

The pestle came down on the bowl with enough force to shatter it. Gelina sent the broken shards flying off the hearth with a sweep of her hand. She jerked another bowl and turnip toward her.

"Unless you'd fancy eating this turnip whole, I'd suggest you leash that vitriolic tongue of yours until I finish," she said without looking up from her task.

"Do hurry. I've always had a penchant for cold, whole turnips."

She glared at him, and Conn knew he was one word away from having the turnip and possibly the bowl crammed down his throat. He wisely clamped his lips together.

She knelt beside him, wielding a wooden spoon heaped with turnip.

He clamped his lips together and leaned away from her. "How do I know 'tis not laced with hemlock?"

She sank back on her heels with an exasperated sigh. "If I had wanted to kill you, I could have done it last night while you slept."

"There is a hair's difference between sleeping and being rendered unconscious with the flat side of a sword."

"Do stop quibbling. Open wide."

He opened his mouth with a mutinous glare, and Gelina poked the spoon in his mouth. He choked down the cold lump of turnip with a theatrical swallow. Gelina stared into the bowl to hide her smile.

"I cannot eat any more," he announced. "I have to step

outside.'' Gelina's eyes widened at his request. "I have . . . how did you put it so prettily that night at the cavern? Ah, yes . . . needs to attend to.''

She stood and paced the length of the hut. "I cannot untie you. You are not to be trusted.''

Conn nodded. "True. You could untie my feet, but not my hands. I would be more than happy to let you do the honors.''

She blushed furiously, and he laughed out loud. She leaned down and peered into his face. "Why did I ever think you were such a nice man?''

He leaned forward until his nose touched hers. "I was a nice man until I met you.''

She took a step backward, and he fell on his face with a beleaguered sigh. He felt a knife slicing his bonds. The sharp tip pressed to his ribs was unmistakably the point of his sword.

"If you make one suspicious move, I shall run you through,'' she said flatly as he climbed to his feet.

"I would rather run you through,'' he murmured, just loud enough for her to hear.

She twisted her wrist; the tip of the sword pierced his tunic and came to rest against his bare skin. He choked back a laugh.

He stretched as they left the hut for the warm sunshine, hiding a grimace of pain as his muscles throbbed to life. Gelina stood as far from him as her outstretched arm and the blade would allow and studied the distant peaks.

"Your maidenly modesty is touching, love,'' he said, his shoulders shaking with laughter.

"I forget. You have no respect for modesty or maidens. A trait you inherited from your father, no doubt.''

Conn whirled, jerking the drawstrings of his breeches tight. His breathing was audible, and Gelina knew the only thing standing between herself and being throttled was the four feet of steel pressed to his taut belly.

"Back in the hut,'' she growled to hide her sudden trembling.

He did not move for an eternity. Then the suave veneer slid over the icy blue rage in his eyes, and he sauntered to the hut.

He sank to the floor and held out his wrists, raising a mocking eyebrow. Gelina exchanged the sword for a knife and struggled to hold it and bind his hands at the same time.

"Shall I hold the knife for you?'' he offered.

"Not unless you care to hold the blade between your ribs, sire," she snapped, jerking the knot tight.

She sat lost in thought, staring at the callused palms and the crisp, dark hairs on the back of his hands, remembering the tender strength in the hands that had hurt her and cherished her with seemingly equal delight. She stood and paced to the hearth, not knowing that Conn sat staring at the single hot teardrop that had fallen on his hand.

He sneered to hide his sudden bewilderment. "Tell me, dear, if you don't intend to hold me for ransom, what do you intend to hold me for? Your maidenly pleasure? I know the nights on the crannog are cold and lonely unless you've found a prowling merman to satisfy your needs."

When Gelina whirled on him, her eyes were dry. "I've found a whole colony of mermans—scores of them. They come every night, and they're all better than you ever thought about being."

He surveyed her through eyes veiled with dark lashes. "Then your memory is very short, my dear."

Without another word Gelina slammed out of the hut.

Conn measured the passing hours by the lengthening shadows that crept across the floor. Hunger pangs tightened his belly, and he regretted baiting her. He ran his tongue over his parched lips and thought about calling out to see if she could hear him. Pride smothered the words before they could form in his mouth. The hut was dark and the fire had died to glowing embers when Gelina kicked open the door. She set down a bucket with a slosh and laid an armful of wood on the hearth.

Hunger, thirst, and various other unmet needs collided in Conn. He didn't bother to mask the animosity in his clipped words. "I've tried to be gallant about playing your little game, Gelina, but I find it tiring. I command you to untie me."

She turned with a laugh. "Ever the king, Conn. You never could rule the Ó Monaghans. When will you learn that?"

Her eyes sparkled. Conn clenched his jaw tight to keep his mouth from falling open as she reached for the hem of the shapeless dress and drew it over her tousled curls. She tossed it aside and turned to feed the fire with lazy grace. Conn's eyes remained locked on the graceful curves of her slim back and thighs as she leaned over the hearth in the thin shift. The flames leapt higher, throwing into silhouette any curve of her body his imagination and memory could not supply.

He twitched as a trickle of sweat inched down his brow.

Gelina smiled sweetly and held out a plate. "Would you care for some bread?"

"I'm not hungry," he lied.

She shrugged and tucked a piece of bread between her lips, licking each finger as if it were dripping hot butter instead of dried crumbs. The muscles of Conn's arms knotted as he pulled at the bonds behind his back with all of his strength.

"Perhaps you would care for some water, sire?" Gelina asked.

"Perhaps."

She carried the water bucket to where he sat and knelt beside him. "I was never a very good slave, but I will try to please you," she said earnestly.

Conn's whole body went rigid as she straddled his lap and pressed warm, yielding lips to his. His lips parted beneath hers without thought, his tongue seeking the sweet depths of the mouth that had haunted him in every dream since he had banished her. She rubbed her soft breasts against his chest like a purring kitten. He could feel the trembling of her body and thought if he could not wrap his arms around her and draw her into him, he would surely die. His hips strained upward against her warmth, pressing himself to her soft hollows until she gasped against his lips. She pulled away, her eyes as glazed and lost as his.

"Untie me, Gelina," he said hoarsely.

She stood clumsily. With a deliberate movement her hands closed around the handle of the wooden bucket.

"Your water, sire."

Conn gasped as the cold lake water washed over him. His eyes narrowed. Gelina backed away as if believing in some small corner of her mind that he would burst out of his bonds with the sheer force of his anger.

She laughed—an oddly off-key and breathless sound. "I pity you, Conn. You try so hard, but you still don't hate me very well."

"I'm learning," he said, shaking the water from his hair like an enraged lion. "The longer I know you, the more you look like your father to me."

"My father had black hair."

Conn nodded. "I know. But underneath all of that bravado, he was a bitch, too."

Gelina slapped him hard. The angry palm print on his cheek stood out against the pallor of his fury. His eyelids lowered, veiling his eyes to glittering slits.

"When I get out of these bonds," he said, "I am going to take this rope and . . ."

Gelina backed away as he began to describe with great detail and imagination all of the things he was going to do to her when he escaped from his bonds.

"Stop it!" she commanded.

He laughed like a wild man without slowing his tirade. Gelina had never heard some of the words he used, but there were enough words she did understand to make their gist plain.

With a shriek she clapped her hands over her ears, leapt into the feather bed and jerked the coverlet over her head. She fell into a desperate sleep long before Conn's voice died to a hoarse mumble. He slumped wearily into the chill puddle of water.

Conn awoke to the sound of chattering teeth. Through a fog of hunger and cold, he realized it was his own teeth rattling together. His wet garments clung to his shivering skin. He started as his gaze found the slender figure bent over his feet. Gelina worked his bonds loose with both hands, the knife clenched between her teeth. Their eyes met.

Her hands caught beneath his bound arms, and she helped him to his feet, bracing him with her shoulder when his stiff legs tried to fold. She guided him to a pallet laid on the warm stones beside the hearth. She took the knife out of her mouth and laid it aside. Conn sat beside the crackling warmth of the newly stoked fire, everything unthawing but his tongue.

Gelina sat opposite him, a steaming bowl of soup cradled in her lap. She brought the wooden spoon to his lips. The lentil soup warmed a path from his mouth to his stomach. She fed him slowly until the bowl was empty.

Conn did not protest or speak when she wrapped the length of rope around his ankles and knotted it. He lay back on the pallet, feeling his clothes stiffen as they dried. He waited for sleep, his aching eyes still on Gelina.

She opened the shutter and stared into the faint light that

crept over the crannog. She pushed a strand of hair out of her
eyes and laid her forehead against the window frame, her face as
pale and drawn as the dawn, her eyes as dry as the morning air.
Conn closed his eyes in exhaustion, carrying the memory of
those barren eyes into his dreams. He never felt the hands that
tenderly tucked the linen blanket around his shoulders.

Chapter Thirty-one
❖

"Gelina?"

"Hmmmmm?" Gelina threw an arm over her eyes and
mumbled a loving word at the familiar whisper.

"Gelina?" came the whisper, harsher this time.

She opened her eyes reluctantly, knowing by the way the pale
sun slanted through the shutters that the morning was half gone.

"I hate to trouble you, dear, but another trip outside would
benefit me greatly."

At the clipped words she sat up abruptly, throwing the
coverlet aside. Conn sat with his back against the hearth, his
legs drawn up to his chest and the angle of his brows warning her
that the truce of dawn had ended.

She rubbed her eyes and stretched lazily. "My king has a
request?"

"One that you would grant even to a fortress hound, I am
certain."

"Ah, but a fortress hound has loyalty, has it not?" She
pulled the linen dress over her head with a yawn and placed her
feet on the chill floor.

"The word is an abomination on your lovely lips."

She shook her head and clucked her tongue. "So cranky this
morning, sire! Perhaps you did not rest well?"

He did not answer. His steely blue eyes narrowed, and Gelina
laughed to hide the untrammeled pounding of her heart. Conn's

rumpled hair and untrimmed beard gave him the savage look of a barbarous ancestor who had never heard the words *honor* and *gentility*—a man who would have spat upon the oaths of the Fianna. A fear that had no rational link to the strength of his bonds fluttered deep in her belly.

"Perhaps a trip outside will ease your foul mood," she said.

She knelt beside him and bent her head to the task of untying the bonds around his ankles. Her fingers tugged at the knots. She cursed softly as they resisted her pull.

"Allow me," he said smoothly.

With one swift upward motion, he sliced through the rope around his ankles and brought the knife to rest against her throat. Gelina could only stare at his ankles for a long moment. The gentle but steady pressure of the cold blade against her throat guided her head up until she was forced to meet his gaze. His amused smirk brought every threat he had made last night screaming into her head. The fluttering in her belly deepened to nausea.

She returned her gaze to his feet and said the first thing that came into her head. "I was kind to you."

Conn raised an incredulous eyebrow. "Compared to whom? Eoghan Mogh? The Roman slavers?"

"I gave you a blanket. And I fed you."

Even as he spoke, Conn's other hand gathered the ropes scattered behind him. "I shall do more than give you a blanket. I shall give you a bed." The flat blade of the knife tilted her trembling chin upward. His lips curved in a cruel smile. "And I shall feed you well."

Before Gelina could breathe a word of protest, he had thrown her on her stomach and straddled her. He jerked both of her arms behind her and wrapped a length of rope around her wrists with hands that were anything but gentle.

"Conn?" she said very softly. "I suppose this is an inopportune moment for an apology but I was going to free you today, truly I was. I was so angry. 'Twas just a game. I meant no harm. I would not have . . ." Her words sputtered to a stop as the rope sliced into her tender flesh. She felt tears start in her eyes.

His hands moved to her ankles with cool competence, stilling a rebellious kick with an elbow pressed to the back of her knee.

The floor tilted beneath her as she was hefted to his shoulder and tossed to the bed like a sack of meal. She landed on her face and sank into the feather mattress like a stone.

She felt cool air rush over her legs as he threw open the door. Panic tightened her throat. "Conn?"

She knew from the expectant silence behind her that he had paused.

Her words were muffled into the mattress. "Are you going to leave me here to starve . . . or smother."

"You may wish I had when I'm through with you. If you will excuse me, milady, I am going to attend to my horse. He cannot feed on stones and marsh grass forever."

"You never told me Silent Thunder awaited you."

"I may have been stupid enough to swim to you, my dear, but I was not stupid enough to walk to you. Do not fret. I will return. Tonight."

Gelina flinched as the door slammed. She wiggled her nose until she managed to dislodge it from the smothering softness of the mattress. Her arms and legs rocked, driving the bed into a creaking frenzy. Drawing in a deep breath, she flopped over, realizing too late that Conn had thrown her on the edge of the bed, not the center. She rolled into the floor, landing hard on her stomach. A sigh escaped her as she rested her cheek against the stones and wondered why she had bothered to get out of bed at all.

Gelina awoke to the sound of the door slamming and feet moving rapidly across the floor. She smiled, knowing Conn had seen the empty bed. Drops of water spattered on her bare feet. She peered up with the eye not pressed to the stone to find Conn standing over her in the shadows of evening, one fist clutching a skinned rabbit by the ears. Shaking his head, he tossed the rabbit to the hearth. He peeled off his sodden garments until he wore only a soft leather loincloth. Glistening beads of water clung to his unruly curls. Gelina's eyes were drawn against their will to the dark hairs coiling over his muscled thighs.

She suppressed a shiver as he bent and lifted her to the bed, strength warring with tenderness in his hands.

Her mouth moved against the soft, wet fur of his chest. "Did you hope to find me penitent or rebellious this night?"

He rested his chin on top of her head. "I hoped only to find you miserable and hungry. Are you?"

She nodded, and he let her fall back among the feather pillows. She watched him warily. He untied her feet, then crawled behind her to untie her hands. Before she could bring her aching wrists around to rub them, his warm, powerful hands closed on each side of her head and drew it back until she was forced to look up into his smoldering eyes.

"I must warn you, Gelina. There are instincts bred into me that I would be hard put to restrain if you should try to catch me unawares again. I could have kicked your face to a pulp when you had me bound but chose not to." His lips brushed her temple. " 'Tis such a sweet face."

Gelina hated herself for trembling. Conn loosed her and busied himself at the hearth, whistling cheerfully. She drew her knees to her chest and watched him, fighting the urge to scan the room for a weapon. Conn speared the rabbit with a deft motion. His wicked grin started her trembling anew. The aroma of roasting meat filled the hut, and her stomach rumbled.

He carried her plate to the bed and sat opposite her with legs crossed. She stared at the meat, her appetite decreasing in direct proportion to the benevolence of Conn's smile.

"I cannot—" she started.

He whipped the plate out of her hands and set it on the floor. "I dare say you've had enough."

She stared at him. "But I haven't had any. I was going to ask you for a knife."

He shrugged sadly. "No knives and no meat. 'Tis all gone."

Gelina glanced at the half-carved rabbit sitting on the hearth and wondered which one of them was losing their senses. Conn continued to beam at her. He produced a canteen from behind his back and held it out to her.

She reached for it slowly. Her fingers closed around the cracked leather. Cool water wet her lips, and the canteen was snatched out of her grip. Conn tossed it over his shoulder.

"There now. You musn't overindulge."

Gelina stared into her lap, impotent anger tightening her jaw. Conn's smile lost none of its radiance as he said, "Strip."

Gelina's breath caught in her throat. "Pardon me?"

"Strip," he repeated patiently. "Give me your dress."

She shook her head. Conn's fingers traced the delicate curve of her earlobe.

"But why not? You disrobed for me with such abandon when I was bound." His smile vanished, and Gelina stared into blue eyes darkened in hatred and desire.

Before she could gasp, he had locked his hands in the linen of the dress and rent it from shoulder to waist. One strong finger caught in the sheer fabric between her breasts and she knew the shift would follow the dress into her lap. She jerked away. The cotton shredded in his hands. He slammed her into the mattress and jerked her wrists over her head.

His voice was as cold and smooth as she had ever heard it. "Tell me—have the nights been cold on the crannog, Gelina? Have you ever awoken in tears these long months, aching and moist for my touch?" She flinched as his lips brushed her temple, her cheek, her throat. "You may have hated me but you cannot tell me you didn't want me."

He loosed her hands. She lay still and afraid beneath his burning gaze. His bruising fingers captured her chin, and he stared into her brimming eyes. His other hand slid beneath the remnants of the shift and glided upward along her trembling inner thigh. He touched her intimately, and she bit her lip, trying desperately not to cry. Anger and shame welled up in her throat until she knew she must cry or choke to death. Childish sobs broke forth, and tears streamed down her face.

His hands caught her shoulders; he shook her until she tasted blood in her mouth. Her hair streamed around her face in a tangled cascade.

"Stop it, damn you! Can't you understand? I don't believe you anymore. I know you for the blackhearted little bitch you are."

Pride and truth fought a battle to the death in Gelina's soul, but she couldn't halt the words or the tears. "I never thought you would hurt me like this. I thought you regretted—"

Conn caught her to him and held her as if he would crush the breath from her shaking body. "Oh, I do regret. I regret every word of love we spoke, every tender gesture that passed between us."

He rocked back and forth, his words a litany of pain and loss. "Twice you've deceived me. Twice you've torn my heart in two. I sat out there all day on that forsaken, windswept plain trying to find the courage in my heart not to come back to you. Knowing that if I returned, I would be destroyed. That my violence and my desire to drive you to your knees would kill the last vestiges of everything I believed in when I created the Fianna."

He drew away from her. His thumb gently traced the curve of her cheek. "But I came back, didn't I? Even the threat of my own destruction couldn't stop me from holding you one last time."

Gelina stared into his eyes, hardly daring to breathe. She buried her face in his shoulder, throwing herself on the mercy of the high king of Erin. Conn groaned. His lips brushed her soft curls.

"Your tenderness wounds me more than violence, sire," she whispered.

Conn reached down and drew her face upward. "Then you have put in my hands the weapon to maim your very soul."

His lips captured hers with heartrending gentleness. His tongue explored the warmth of her mouth as if for the first time.

Never, even in their happiest days, had his touch been so agonizingly gentle, so hurtfully patient. She closed her eyes and turned her face to the pillow with a whispered plea.

His mouth and hands took her until she quaked and shivered beneath the slow, lingering agony of his touch. Her body arched away from the mattress. A low moan was torn from deep within her throat as a dark and fearful pleasure spread through every tingling nerve of her body in shimmering waves of velvet heat.

His mouth slanted across hers, moist and burning and desperate. His knee spread her legs farther. She felt the heat of him poised above her. His hands cupped her face, his fingers spreading wide to tangle in her gossamer web of hair.

"Look at me, Gelina," he commanded hoarsely. "I want to see the truth in your eyes."

She reluctantly opened her eyes, praying to some unknown god that he would see the truth within them. He entered her inch by inch, the pressure of his broad hands splayed on her face forcing her to keep her eyes open even when she would have begged to close them. A choked sob escaped her. As she stared into the depths of his sapphire eyes, something dark and terrible and wonderful passed between them until Conn was forced to close his eyes or surrender forever to the strength of it. His lips brushed hers. He moved within her, teasing and taking, each stroke driving him deeper until her lips parted in a soundless gasp beneath his.

A shudder traveled the length of Conn's body, shaking Gelina to the core with its unexpected violence. She sank her teeth into his shoulder to stop herself from crying out the words that welled in her throat, unable to tell if the tears that wet her face fell from her eyes or his.

Somewhere in her dreams, he drew her to her knees but she could not remember when. Her hands could only cling to his shoulders, helpless with want. Her hungry mouth could only trace the curve of his beard. His heavy-lidded eyes stared into her soul as he tangled his hand in her hair. He had won as Gelina had always known he would.

Somewhere in her dreams, she opened her eyes to find him kneeling beside the bed, garbed in his leather vest and breeches, his sword strapped at his waist. He wrapped the tattered blanket around her and lifted her in his arms, his lips buried in the softness of her hair. He carried her to the warmth of the hearth, cradling her on his lap like a child. She burrowed into his tunic, pushing it aside and nuzzling her face to the soft fur of his chest with a contented sigh. He brought one upturned wrist to his lips and tenderly kissed the bruises that marred the creamy flesh.

"No more, my love," he whispered.

Her eyelashes brushed his chest like tiny feathers as she closed her eyes in search of a sleep that was dreamless.

Her hand touched the cold emptiness of the bed beside her. Gelina sat up, Conn's name a whisper on her lips. A fire crackled on the hearth in cheerful mockery of the empty hut. She jumped out of bed without sparing a glance for the torn dress on the floor. Her shaking hands jerked her breeches and tunic from a peg on the wall. She pulled them over her nakedness and ran to the door, too afraid of the answering silence to cry out.

The gray sky spit snow in whirling flurries. She ran behind the hut and around the crannog, her gaze searching the horizon for any sign of a man or a horse. The misty mountain peaks held their secrets.

A desolation as cold and biting as the wind swept through

her. With a muted groan she threw up her arms in utter hopelessness.

"Oh, Nimbus," she whispered.

She sat cross-legged on the ground, not bothering to wipe away the snowflakes that caught in her eyelashes. She watched the falling snow slip into the murky lake without a trace.

Sean came with the sunshine two days later to find her in the same position, a cap pulled over her unruly curls and a thin knapsack at her side. He dismounted with a soothing word to the mare tethered to his horse and swam to the crannog as smoothly as a fish.

Gelina stood as he climbed to the shore. He knew by meeting her steady gaze that no explanations were necessary but the awkward silence forced him to say, "I'm to take you to the coast. To a ship."

She nodded. She didn't protest when he guided her arms around his neck with terse instructions and slipped into the cold water. She clung to his shoulders, her eyes clenched shut.

The mare nickered softly as they rose dripping from the lake. Gelina mounted and held out her wrists without a word.

Sean stared at the bruises, then looked away toward the mountains. "He made me swear not to tell him where you were. I broke my oath."

She nodded again. He slipped the rope around her waist and knotted it without meeting her eyes. He mounted.

"You did what you had to do," she said softly as Sean kicked his roan into a gallop.

Gelina locked her hands in the mare's coarse mane. The tightness of despair choked her in the face of the brilliant sunshine. As they flew across the grass, she loosed a tiny corner of hopelessness, feeling it float across the plains like a tangible thing. The wind whipped her hair from underneath the cap. She closed her eyes and for a brief instant felt the pulsating muscles of Silent Thunder between her thighs.

Her eyes flew open to blot out the dream. She must not feel a gentle hand on her hair, a kiss as soft as a whisper at the nape of her neck. Despair wrapped itself around her like a shroud.

Sean slowed his mount to a walk as they entered a sun-dappled forest.

"Watch for the low branches," he called back.

Gelina's horse reared, snorting wildly as the tree above Sean's head spit out its occupant on the unsuspecting soldier. Gelina struggled to steady the mare as Sean tumbled to the ground, rolling through the crackling underbrush with his attacker. The mare pranced in a circle, facing Gelina away from them.

She heard the clash of steel. She was jerked off the mare on her behind as Sean's horse trotted over to a patch of grass and began to feed. She twisted to find Sean lying among the leaves with her brother astride him. Rodney pressed a dagger to Sean's throat. His triumphant laughter rang out.

"Rodney, don't hurt him," she commanded, seeing Sean's furious glare travel between the two of them.

"If I had my way, I would leave him here in the woods like we left his other comrades with perhaps an arm or a leg chopped off." Rodney giggled. Sean's eyes widened. "But this warrior works for us now. He will bear my message to the illustrious Ard-Right."

"What message?" Sean hissed. "That the two of you planned Nimbus's murder. He's probably discovered that already."

"Ah, but that is a lie." Rodney gestured grandly to Gelina who sat up, her hands clenched into fists. "My sister knew nothing of the jester's death. She was innocent, condemned without a trial by the man she thought she loved."

Sean saw the truth in Gelina's averted eyes. The sun shone through the trees, burnishing her bowed head to copper fire. He closed his eyes for an instant, forgetting the cold steel at his throat as remorse flooded him.

Gelina's head flew up. "Then you killed him," she accused her brother.

Rodney shook his head. "Another misconception, dear Princess. I would have killed him. My hands did remove the buckle from his harness." Rodney's black eyes sparkled; his lips turned up at the corners. "But he watched me do it. The midget saw me remove the buckle. He let himself be murdered. He killed himself. The words of farewell he so gallantly spoke before he died were from the heart."

Gelina shook her head.

Rodney stood. "To your feet," he commanded Sean, pressing the sharp tip of the dagger to his back. "I need your clothes. Now that I and my sweet sister are reunited, we shall continue our journey to the ship Conn so thoughtfully provided."

Sean disrobed, cursing under his breath. Rodney hooked Sean's sword to his belt. Gelina sat unmoving as Rodney cut the bond around her waist.

Sean stood shivering in his loincloth. "You don't have to go with him, Gelina," he said softly.

"I've nowhere else to go," she said as she swung herself on the mare's back with both hands. Sean had to turn away from the bitterness in her eyes.

Rodney mounted behind her. "Take this message to your king. He will never be a good ruler until he learns who to mistrust"—he placed a possessive hand on Gelina's shoulder—"and who to trust."

With a battle cry that echoed through the forest, he kicked the horse into a gallop, leaving Sean to stare after them.

"I know the question, Gelina," he whispered. "I know the question we didn't ask."

He mounted his horse and thundered back toward Tara.

Chapter Thirty-two

❖

Gelina jerked on the reins, halting the horse so abruptly that Rodney slid into her. Ignoring his cry of bewilderment, she dismounted and stalked in the direction they were traveling.

"Lina! Where are you going?" Rodney threw his leg over the horse, entangling himself in the rope that hung useless from its back.

She yelled over her shoulder without slowing her determined pace, "I am going to the ship without you. I am leaving this cursed land forever."

Freeing himself from the rope with a muttered curse, he ran after her. "But, Princess, I fixed everything for us. We can be together now."

He stopped in his tracks as she turned and doubled back to him, fists clenched. As soon as he was within her reach, she punched him soundly in the nose. That blow was followed by a swift uppercut that sent him sprawling in the dirt.

He sat rubbing his chin. "You're angry."

She pointed a shaking finger at him, her face contorted with rage. "You ruined everything. You murdered my best friend. You almost got me killed."

He climbed to his feet, brushing off his breeches. "I knew Conn would let you go eventually. I would have come after you sooner, but it was too dangerous. He always sent Sean in the dead of night. I had no way to follow him until today."

"Risky? Risky for whom? You had no guarantee that Conn wouldn't command Sean to break my neck. Or come and do the job himself." She rubbed her wrists without realizing she was doing it.

He shrugged. "It was a chance I had to take." He backed up and put a rowan tree between them as she advanced again.

"You took a chance on my life?"

"I had to show you what kind of man Conn really was. I did it all for you."

"Spare me any more of your favors, brother," she bit off acidly. "I could have lived my whole life happily without learning what you showed me."

"It would have been a lie. Don't you see that?" He risked stepping out from behind the tree.

"You murdered Nimbus. You murdered him as surely as if you had pushed him off that platform. I should have married him." Her voice gained momentum. "He trusted me and he never used me. Those are two traits I've yet to find in any other man. He was my friend!"

Rodney glanced back at the tree, pondering its shelter as her voice rose to a shriek. She threw up her hands in exasperation and walked away.

He crossed his arms. "You cannot board that ship without an escort from the Fianna. As ironic as it may be, I am that escort."

Gelina turned, recognizing the truth of what he said as he stood smirking in the forest green uniform of one of Conn's soldiers.

Her voice was low and determined. "I shall go with you. But when we disembark from that ship, wherever it may be, you are on your own. I am no longer your sister."

He nodded reluctant agreement. She did not see his sly grin as they mounted the roan and continued to the sea.

Mer-Nod leaned against the wall and watched his king weave among the tables in the great hall. He, like all of the others who knew Conn well, was afraid. There was a brightness to Conn's eyes, a lethal flaw in his swagger that chilled Mer-Nod's heart to ice. Even as he watched, Conn stumbled against one of the tables with a hearty laugh.

Chaotic revelry ruled the hall. Conn had ordered that all of the ale that had been hoarded for the wedding be distributed on this night. He was not the only one who was stumbling. Mer-Nod watched as a young soldier danced around with a capon on his head before falling face first into a tray of pastries. A laughing young girl pulled him out, licking the icing from his cheeks with a greedy tongue.

Veils and gloves sailed through the air as the women joined in a reel that led them around the tables, bodies swaying before the rapt eyes of the men. Conn captured a pale brunette in his arms as she passed and planted a long, wet, open-mouthed kiss on her lips to the cheers of the soldiers around him. The pounding beat of a drum drowned out the flutes and lyres.

Mer-Nod watched as Conn pulled the woman toward the stairs, his mouth never leaving hers. Only Mer-Nod saw his eyes open in a moment of utter sobriety and rest on the empty platform high above them. He shoved the woman away, ignoring her protest and stalked into the study, closing the door behind him. Mer-Nod waited a few long moments before following, shooting a warning glance at the woman who had similar thoughts.

He pushed open the door; the dampness of the fireless room settled deep into his bones. The moon glowed dully off the deserted chessmen. Conn stood at the open window, his hand resting on the frame as if to support his weight.

"I am dying, Mer-Nod," he said without turning around.

"I know."

"I've faced many deaths before but never one so final." Conn shook his head as if to clear it of a distasteful thought. "I should have kept her here at Tara."

"If you'd have kept her here, you would have killed her," Mer-Nod said with conviction, feeling far older than his years.

"Then I should have kept her at the crannog and gone to her whenever I pleased." A slur grew in Conn's speech. "I could have had her until I grew sick of her."

"That would have destroyed you both. You had to set her free."

Conn laughed bitterly. "Those were not the right words to say, Mer-Nod. Nimbus would have known the right words." He stumbled as he faced Mer-Nod. "There are words he said. I cannot remember them but they mattered."

Mer-Nod reached out a hand to steady him.

Catching his hand, Conn looked into his eyes and asked with the bewildered candor of a child, "Why did her blood have to be so tainted, Mer-Nod?"

Unable to find words for the first time in his life, the poet shook his head and murmured, "You should go to your chambers. You haven't slept since you returned."

"Sleep does not await me there. Oh, no, Mer-Nod," he gestured grandly to the window, "the wild and windy moors call me. Can you not hear them?"

Mer-Nod had barely formed a protest when Conn strode out the door into the chaos of the hall. He reappeared outside the window, stumbling with determination toward the stable.

Ignoring the stableboy, Conn led Silent Thunder into the courtyard. He threw himself on the horse's back with such force that the momentum nearly carried him off the other side. Gripping the horse's mane, he laughed in drunken abandon and kicked the Arabian into a gallop. He thundered out of the courtyard and across the moors at breakneck speed. The moon was a thin sliver in the sky, its glow casting more shadows than light over the uneven terrain. A crazed exhilaration captured him as the cold night wind whipped the hair from his stinging eyes.

He sent the massive horse flying over dark shapes his blurred gaze could not see. They rode along the forest, the stallion swerving wildly to avoid the low-hanging branches that reached for Conn. A shadow rose up in front of him. He squinted at the oak branch as it swept him cleanly off the horse.

He raised his head off the cold ground to find Silent Thunder grazing nearby, unscathed. His head ached although he wouldn't know it until morning. Wiggling each limb methodically, he decided he was uninjured or too drunk to care. He could see few stars from this angle. He lay there for a long time. He could not think of any reason to get up. He was content to watch the clouds scuttle across the pale moon. Right before he drifted into the arms of sleep, he heard Nimbus's laughing words, "Just remember, Conn . . ."

"Remember what, Nimbus?" he murmured, unable to keep his eyes open long enough to hear the answer.

He slept there until the soldiers Mer-Nod sent found him and carried him back to Tara.

Morning came. The early hours scuttled across Conn's nerves, twisting and pinching his weary heart. The pain in his head paled in comparison to the agony that doubled him over when, without opening his eyes, he touched the empty pillow beside him. Gone were the disheveled curls, the soft curves, the puffy eyelids that added a morning sensuousness to the angular face. Gone were the laughing grumbles as he lowered himself on her and began his day in rapture. Everything was gone but the ache in his groin and the intolerable pain that pounded him.

Cursing, he jumped out of the bed and paced across the room. Running a hand through his unruly curls, he thought of summoning a woman to his chambers. He could at least soothe one discomfort. He strode to the narrow chest that held his belt and stared down at it, its barrenness reminding him of the black void that had opened in his life. Moira hadn't dared to enter the dusty chambers while he was there, but she had come while he was at the crannog and tactfully removed the ivory comb and brush. Only their faint outline in the dust remained.

Cursing furiously, he slammed his hand across the chest, sending a flurry of dust into the air. It hung there, sparkling in the morning sunlight as a vase shoved to the back of the chest tilted before crashing to the floor. Stale water washed over his bare feet. The flowers lay lifeless among the shards of pottery like victims of a gruesome battle. He knelt and took one in his hand only to have it crumble to ash before his eyes. Dead roses. Nimbus. His wedding day.

The roses had appeared in the jester's hand like a gift from the gods. And he had said, ". . . everything is not always what it appears to be."

It was at that moment that the door flew open and Conn looked up with incredulous eyes to find Sean Ó Finn standing in the doorway clothed only in his loincloth.

Chapter Thirty-three
❖

The sea air washed over Gelina in wave after wave, pounding her like the breakers battering the shore below. They had reached the coast in time to see the sun sink into the sea in a fiery flush of orange and violet. Gelina pulled her jacket tight around her and glanced back at Rodney, who was struggling to build a fire on top of the promontory. He gathered dry brush and sticks into a neat pile only to have a chill gust of wind scatter them. She watched as a branch sailed past her ear and flew off the towering cliff to crash on the jagged rocks below. Scattering the remnants of the debris with a violent kick, he climbed up on the flat rock and sat next to her, chin in hands. She drew in a deep breath. The salty, bittersweet air chilled her lungs.

"We could take shelter, but I fear we would miss the ship," Rodney said, ignoring the fact that she hadn't spoken to him for hours.

"How did you know where to find the ship?" she asked without turning her head to look at him.

"I heard Conn give the order to the runner. He was to go north and send a ship down the coast."

"You were like a vulture hovering around the fortress." She suppressed a shiver and hugged her knees.

"I did it all . . ."

". . . for me," she finished. "I know what you believe. You believe your princess was bewitched by the evil king." She laughed wearily. "I was such a fool."

"He made you a fool."

"It didn't take any help from him," she said, brushing a stray curl out of her eyes. "To think I could marry the king of Erin! How ridiculous."

He laid a comforting arm across her shoulder but quickly withdrew it, noting her frosty gaze and the height of their perch. The sea lulled them into silence with its empathetic rhythm.

Rodney got to his feet, turning away from the sea. "Look behind you, Lina. Are you sure you want to leave it?"

The land of Erin unrolled below them in the half light of the moon. Hills sprouted from the landscape, looming like great guardians over the plains.

Gelina didn't turn her head. "I never want to look behind me. I want to shake the dust of this place off my feet forever."

"It could be different now. Eoghan has his own land now. He would offer us protection."

"And what are we to offer him, Rodney? Civil war? For me there is no protection from Conn. I will not escape the chopping block a fourth time. Even you should be able to see that. We wait here for the ship."

Rodney opened his mouth to speak but, noting the determined set of her chin, closed it again. He went to the roan and pulled forth a long object wrapped in cloth. He handed it to Gelina and watched as she loosened the soft muslin. She studied the scabbard musingly before hooking it to her belt, returning Vengeance to its rightful place.

Rodney stretched out on the rock and closed his eyes. Gelina stared out to sea, the emerald depths of her eyes storm swept. Pulling her cap off, she let the wind whip through her hair, clearing her musty brain with its chill ferocity. She did not dare let go of the anger. Without it, there was no guarantee that she would ever rise from this rock, ever put one foot in front of the other again. Without it, she would surely perish.

Deliberately torturing herself, she remembered the bitter blue of eyes over a sword. There had been no hint of a question in those eyes, only condemnation. She fingered her tender wrists, the ache of her touch summoning icy tendrils of hate to wrap around her heart. She stared out to sea and prayed to nameless gods that the ship would come soon.

When Rodney opened his eyes the next morning, she sat in the same position. Rubbing his eyes, he gazed back at the plains to find them shrouded in a low-hanging mist. The sun shone on their promontory, lending a glowing ambience to the cool morning air.

"You should have woken me. I could have watched part of the night. Didn't you sleep?" he asked.

"I thought I would let you sleep. It takes much rest to plot treachery."

He sat up and whistled, fearful of her ire if he retorted. Deciding it would be safer away from the edge of the cliff, he sauntered over to the horse, untied the knapsack, and pulled forth a flask.

"What's this foul stuff?" he asked, wrinkling his nose. He tipped the flask until its yellow-white contents dribbled to the ground in a steady stream.

"Goat's milk. Moira would have packed it. She knows I detest it."

Gelina climbed to her feet and bent at the waist, trying to drive some of the stiffness from her muscles. Rodney offered her some cheese, but she stepped away from his outstretched hand.

"I cannot bear this," he exploded. "I love you and you're treating me like a leper. I would like to know what he did to turn you against me this way."

"He did nothing. You did it all, Rodney."

He grabbed her arm and jerked her around to face him. "I love you."

"Like you loved our mother?" she asked, eyebrow arched.

The confusion that twisted his face was genuine. "Yes, of course. I loved our mother the same way."

Snatching her arm away from his burning touch, she sneered, "Then why did you let her kill herself? Why didn't you cry out before she embedded father's sword in her gut?"

"I don't know what you're talking about. Conn's men killed our mother. You were there." He rubbed his forehead, seeking to smooth away the lines that appeared there.

"No, Rodney. Our father was murdered. Mother thought we

were dead. She roamed the hall for a long time. There was time for one of us to call out and save her.''

''But she had lost her honor. Why should she want to live?'' he asked, his black eyes puzzled and without guile.

Gelina shivered. ''You left me on the crannog deliberately, didn't you? To give me time to think about what I'd done.''

Rodney reached up to capture one of her loose curls between the tips of his fingers in a mocking caress. ''And when Conn came, I'm sure you saw the wisdom of that. He had to punish you one last time for me. You betrayed me, Princess. You betrayed our hopes, our dreams of vengeance. I'm willing to forgive you, though. I'll take you back. Wouldn't you like that?''

Gelina jerked away from him with a guttural growl. She turned to the sea to remove herself from his vacant, questioning gaze. Two seagulls danced above their heads, then soared over the ocean. She traced their flight down the coast as they glided around the masts that appeared there.

''Rodney! 'Tis the ship! It comes!''

When no reply greeted her frenzied words, she turned to find him staring back over the plains, his mouth a thin line of shock, his pale skin drawn tightly over the bones of his face. She followed his gaze, squinting to dim the reflection of the sunlight off the fog.

He thundered out of the mist like a legend. The breath was sucked out of Gelina's lungs as she recognized the giant of a stallion beneath him. Even as they watched, he pulled the mount up short. The Arabian reared, powerful forelegs flashing. The two who watched him stood crippled by the inevitability of his motion as he aimed the horse for the bluff.

''No!'' Gelina's fierce cry rent the air. She started for the narrow path they had followed to their perch.

Rodney jerked her back. ''You cannot go down there. He'll come up that path.''

''I've got to get to the ship.'' She pulled away, her gaze panic-stricken. It darted across the cliff, seeking a way to the shore, then lit with furious determination. ''If I cannot go down the path, I shall go down the cliff.''

She dashed to the cliff's edge. Her stomach rolled as she stared down at the churning water crashing over the keen edges of the rocks below. Rodney stood paralyzed, torn between the hoofbeats that echoed louder each second and his sister who had dropped to her stomach and lowered her feet over the cliff, kicking until she found a shallow impression to cram her toe into.

Conn burst over the side of the promontory, the black chest of his mount obscuring Rodney's vision for a breathless instant as he halted the monstrous steed an inch from his nose.

"Gelina!" Conn bellowed.

Ignoring Rodney, he leapt off the horse and ran for the cliff. Only Gelina's narrow fingers were visible as they clung to the edge of the cliff. There was a short scream and those, too, disappeared from sight.

Conn dropped to his stomach, terrified at the sight that might greet him as he peered over the cliff. Gelina hung just below his outstretched arm. One foot rested on a narrow slate ledge that tapered into nothingness. The other dangled in midair. Her eyes were clenched shut.

"Give me your hand." Conn struggled to keep his own precarious balance and stretched a hand toward her trembling form.

She spoke without opening her eyes. "No, thank you. I'm going down, not up."

"You're damn right you're going down if you don't give me your hand." He gritted his teeth in frustration.

He glanced back at Rodney but could see no help in his glazed eyes.

"I do not want your help," Gelina cried aloud, her foot sliding toward the abyss below, unable to find a foothold.

"Look at me, Gelina," he commanded in the same tone he had used on a stubborn girl long ago. All of the majesty of Erin was in that voice.

Unable to resist, she opened her eyes a tiny bit and raised her gaze to his.

"If you still want to go to that ship," he said softly, "I will take you there myself. You have my word. Just give me your hand."

The slate ledge began to crumble. Kind blue eyes blocked out the sun. She loosened her grip on the rock and raised one hand in the air as the ledge disappeared into the sea. She lost her grip. His muscular arm grasped hers. He heaved with all of his might, lifting her onto solid ground with one arm. Her legs folded. His arm holding her clasped against him was the only thing that stopped her from falling to her knees. The comforting smell of leather assailed her senses.

His lips nuzzled her ear. "Whether you go or stay, I will love you until I die," he whispered.

She buried her face in his tunic.

"Now, Conn. If you can quit fondling my sister, we shall finish this."

Seeing Gelina safe from harm, Rodney sprang into action. He pulled Sean's sword and brandished it in the air.

Conn loosed her and drew his own sword. Deliverance flashed in the sunlight. Gelina stepped back and sank to her knees, her mind numb as she watched her brother drive his sword toward Conn's chest. Metal clashed against metal, the sound ringing in her ears.

"He's been practicing," she murmured dully as Rodney parried Conn's expert thrusts with finesse.

They moved toward the edge of the cliff. Rodney thrust again and again, seeking the opening that would grant him a death blow. Gelina sensed a reserve in Conn's attack. Rodney should have been no match for him, but there they were, swords crossing valiantly as each sought to disarm the other.

The dull sound of metal slicing flesh brought Gelina to her feet. The unfortunate mare bore the brunt of a blow meant for Conn. The searing pain in its haunch sent it careening madly toward Gelina and the steep cliff.

Conn dropped his sword and dived for the mare. His powerful hands caught in the tangled mane. He dragged himself on the horse's back. His weight shifted the horse's thundering path a fraction of an inch. Gelina rolled to the side, feeling a rush of air as the mare plummeted past her and over the cliff's edge with a whistling scream. She lay for a long silent moment with her eyes clenched shut, afraid to open them and find herself alone with Rodney on the promontory.

She opened them to the sound of Rodney's shrill laughter. Conn crouched a few feet away from her, his nostrils flaring and his eyes on Rodney. With a careless motion, Rodney flung Conn's sword over the side of the cliff.

Rodney advanced on him without mercy. Conn scuttled away from Gelina, following the cliff's edge to the other side of the bluff. Rodney stalked him, each step bringing Conn nearer to the yawning abyss of the sea. Conn stretched out his arms; his lips curled in a snarl. His gaze caught Gelina's as she knelt on the other side of the bluff. The farewell she saw within his eyes twisted her heart. Her brother's back was to her, and she thought dryly that it was his back she had seen more often than not as he abandoned her to this fate or that one.

Conn's astonished eyes followed her sweeping movement as she stood and unsheathed Vengeance. He stretched out his arm, hardly daring to believe what his eyes told him.

Rodney turned, following Conn's shocked gaze and watched as Gelina hurled the sword in a high arc.

The sun flashed from the smooth silver as it turned over and over in the air until the hilt came to rest flawlessly in Conn's outstretched hand.

Conn swung the sword. Gelina closed her eyes, unable to watch her only brother's head roll from his shoulders. She heard a dull thunk. Her eyes flew open in time to see Rodney slide to his knees as the large flat side of the blade stunned him to the ground.

Conn dropped the sword and faced her. His hands were shaking. She met his eyes for a long moment, then turned to face the sea and the ship anchored there—the ship waiting for her.

Conn bowed his head in defeat.

Rodney groaned softly. She pointed to him. "I dare say my brother cannot live at Tara with us."

Conn tried to stop it, but a wide grin spread itself over his face. He stretched out his arms in silent apology. Gelina leapt into his arms and threw her legs around him. He swung her in a wide circle and smothered her face in laughing kisses. The waves crashed on the rocks below in giggling rhythm like the laughter of one hysterical midget.

Epilogue

Conn of the Hundred Battles had two daughters and three sons. He was the grandfather of the legendary Cormac MacArt.

In A.D. 280, Oisin led the Clan na Morna Fianna into battle against the Clan na Baoscini Fianna, and, fighting amongst themselves, the Fianna were annihilated.

And Gelina? Women with swords are created, not born. The Irish still speak of a woman who thunders through the windy night on a great black steed, her sword flashing in the moonlight, her eyes alight with the secrets of love and conquest.

*If you enjoyed this book, take advantage
of this special offer. Subscribe now and . . .*

GET A *FREE*
HISTORICAL ROMANCE
— **NO OBLIGATION**(a $3.95 value) —

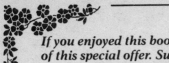

Each month the editors of True Value will select the four best historical romance novels from America's leading publishers. Preview them in your home Free for 10 days. And we'll send you a FREE book as our introductory gift. No obligation. If for any reason you decide not to keep them, just return them and owe nothing. But if you like them you'll pay *just* $3.50 each and save at least $.45 each off the cover price. (Your savings are a minimum of $1.80 a month.) There is no shipping and handling or other hidden charges. There are no minimum number of books to buy and you may cancel at any time.

send in the coupon below